# The Unlikely Occultist

# The Unlikely Occultist

*Isobel Blackthorn*

Copyright (C) 2018 Isobel Blackthorn
Layout design and Copyright (C) 2018 Creativia
Published 2018 by Creativia
Cover art by Cover Mint
This book is a work of fiction. Names, characters, places, and incidents are the product of the author's imagination or are used fictitiously. Any resemblance to actual events, locales, or persons, living or dead, is purely coincidental.
All rights reserved. No part of this book may be reproduced or transmitted in any form or by any means, electronic or mechanical, including photocopying, recording, or by any information storage and retrieval system, without the author's permission.

# Foreword

"Isobel Blackthorn's insightful biographical novel *The Unlikely Occultist* evokes a rich immediacy to the life of Alice A. Bailey and her contemporaries as they forge 'New Age' thinking, in light of perceiving themselves in a new epoch where humans face unprecedented challenges. The novel offers the reader a glimpse into the little known and secretive world of Alice. A. Bailey and fellow contributors to Western Esotericism as they vie for power and influence. In so doing, it provides an important contribution to re-telling received and accepted accounts of historical figures and events. Isobel Blackthorn deftly raises for consideration an alternate historical interpretation of esoteric lineage.

In writing this biographical novel, it is wonderful to see how Isobel has brought the depth of scholarship applied to her doctoral thesis *The Texts of Alice A. Bailey: An Inquiry into the Role of Esotericism in Transforming Consciousness*, to the imaginative creation of this novel."

Lesley Kuhn
   Author of *Adventures in Complexity for Organisations Near the Edge of Chaos*, Adjunct Fellow Western Sydney University.

# Author Note

The Unlikely Occultist is a dramatization of Alice Bailey's life and influence, as it was known to the author via the historical record at the time of writing. Some of the minor characters are inventions. All of the major characters are based on real people, but their personalities, attitudes and opinions have been invented for the purposes of the narrative and may or may not resemble the real persons concerned.

This portrait of Alice A. Bailey is based on a deep and prolonged study of her life and teachings. No fictional character can ever convey the fullness of a real historical figure. The Unlikely Occultist is offered to the reader in good faith.

# Contents

| | |
|---|---:|
| **PART ONE** | 1 |
| New York | 2 |
| The State Library of Victoria | 14 |
| Castramont | 27 |
| Auburn | 32 |
| Ireland and India | 44 |
| An Inheritance | 62 |
| From Cincinnati to Monterey | 71 |
| Discovering Theosophy | 81 |
| Krotona | 94 |
| An Organisational Fracas | 103 |
| State Library of Victoria | 111 |

## PART TWO: 1931-1933    119

Ascona    120

Among Friends    136

Stamford    151

Manhattan    165

A Letter From Olga    178

A Confession    192

A Third Summer School    199

Faversham    207

Some Unpleasant Correspondence    213

Manhattan    231

## PART THREE    242

Akaroa    243

Unfinished Business    256

Conspiracy Theories    266

New York Public Library    290

Epilogue    299

| | |
|---|---:|
| A Selected Bibliography | 303 |
| Acknowledgments | 306 |
| About the Author | 307 |

# PART ONE

# New York

What is it about a death that leaves those remaining at the mercy of time? A single moment, the release of a life, sending ripples through the universe. She hadn't contrived her visit to coincide with the first anniversary of her aunt's passing. Even if she had wanted to, with all of the organising involved—the scheduling of holiday leave, the booking of flights, the itinerary arranged to accommodate the wishes of her companion—such a feat of temporal intersection would have been impossible to pull off. Although another part of her couldn't resist wondering if some entity hadn't orchestrated the entire trip to serve some hidden agenda of its own. It was the part of her that felt connected to her great-grandmother, Katharine, who had died the day she was born.

That it was exactly a year since her aunt Hilary had passed away had only occurred to her as she had entered the building with the others and one of her tour party announced the date to settle some discrepancy of her own. The twenty-fourth, the woman said. And it was June.

They were visiting the United Nations in New York, and she was at last arriving at the key destination of her holiday. She might have come alone. She wished she had. The tour was for Suzanne's benefit.

Heather stood aside a few paces on and let the others file by. Faces rose to the grandeur, the grey concrete of the exterior of the building giving way to sweeping curves and a fluted ceiling high above.

Turning, she beheld tall panels of glass evenly spaced between concrete columns newly painted in yellow ochre, dusky pink and black. A colour scheme reminiscent of Art Deco. The windows allowed in an abundance of natural light. To her left, a flight of stairs led to the upper levels. It was all as splendid as she had anticipated, the building exuding an aura of serious, enlightened humanity. At least, that's how it felt to her.

Her awe was shattered by a commotion nearby as one of her tour party raised his fist and yelled, 'Down with the globalist agenda!' over and again. Heads turned. People shuffled off, shaking their heads. Some ran, scared. The man, large, bearded and middle-aged, made full use of the space around him to pace and rant. 'Don't get sucked in by the power elite! It's a cabal!'

'Oh, shut up,' someone said to his back.

The man swung around and yelled in his face, 'Wake up!' He stabbed the air at others. 'You, you and you. Wake up! The United Nations is a conspiracy. Who funded this place? Rockefeller and the Rothschilds! You,' he said, his wild stare landing on Suzanne. 'You need to wake up.'

'I'm fully awake, thank you.'

Heather cringed inwardly, hoping he wouldn't use her reply to home in on her.

Security descended before he could utter another word, knocking him to the floor and pinning him down and shooing away the onlookers. People muttered and rolled their eyes.

'What a nut job.'

'Yeah, but he has a point.'

'What was that about?'

He was whisked away and the atmosphere soon settled. The rest of the tour party gathered around the guide. Heather hovered behind some stragglers. Suzanne, an inch or two taller than the rest, was huddled in with the pack. Heather caught her gaze.

'I'll be over there,' she mouthed, pointing.

Suzanne glanced in that direction then edged through the pack to say in Heather's ear, 'I thought you were joining the tour.'

'It's the meditation room that interests me. That's all.'

'It's part of the tour.'

'I'm well aware of that.'

Suzanne eyed her appraisingly. 'This has something to do with that woman, doesn't it?'

'That woman, as you call her, is Alice Bailey, and yes, yes it does.'

'You've developed an obsession, Heather, if you don't mind me saying.'

Heather did mind. *She* was not a nut job. She was also well aware that Alice Bailey sat at the helm of the United Nations version of the New World Order conspiracy theory that man had been ranting about. Were they right to put her there? Of course not. But they were not wrong to put her at the helm of the United Nations.

The meditation room represented to Heather the culmination of a mission, a silent memorial of a spiritual activist, a woman who had dedicated her life to righting the wrongs of power, only to be shafted and duly shunted into the margins of history. If Suzanne wanted to label her appreciation 'obsession' then so be it. She left Suzanne and the tour and headed off, divesting her mind of her chagrin with every footfall.

The meditation room was situated past the security desks on the eastern side of the lobby, discretely positioned to the left of The Peace Window. It was this mural of glass that drew the eye, an impressive artwork Marc Chagall had gifted the UN in memory of Dag Hammarskjöld. Heather didn't need to be told any of this by a tour guide. She knew more than she would ever have imagined possible about the second Secretary-General of the United Nations, given her complete lack of interest prior to last year. In the past few months she had come to admire Dag Hammarskjöld, not for his outward achievements, although they were remarkable by any measure, but for his spirituality, his dedication to the study of medieval mystics Meister Eckhart and Jan van Ruysbroeck, and, Heather strongly suspected, his affiliation with, or at least his sympathy for the mysterious occultist, Alice A. Bailey.

It was Donald Keys, a speechwriter for Hammarskjöld's successor U Thant, who had alerted Heather to the Bailey connection. By then she was eight months into dealing with the curious assortment of books, magazines, journals and notes associated with the unpublished manuscript of Professor Samantha Foyle, bequeathed to the State Library of Victoria upon her death. Chair of Religious Studies at a Melbourne university, Professor Foyle specialised in alternative spiritualities and the subject of her latest research was Alice Bailey.

Back at her desk in the manuscript office in the upper reaches of the library, in the thick of unravelling the life of the occult figure, Heather had stumbled on New Age activist Keys' speech – written in the 1970s and later posted online – in which he referred to Bailey's prediction that a leading Swedish disciple would soon be working in the world. Bailey had made her prediction in the 1930s, long before the birth of the UN. In his speech, Keys identified this individual as Dag Hammarskjöld.

Keys was one of the few notable figures who openly admitted to being part of Alice Bailey's coterie. He was almost brazen about it, given the secrecy of most. He even dedicated his book, *Earth At Omega: Passage to Planetization*, to Alice Bailey. When Heather made the discovery, she had succumbed to a frisson of satisfaction. It wasn't easy uncovering the identities of the occultist's notable followers and sympathizers. Unlike the glamorous mystique the charlatans enjoyed, Alice Bailey was the anathema of flamboyance. In true esoteric spirit, she had preferred obscurity, working behind the scenes to achieve her goals.

Which was more or less how Heather had found herself when working on Professor Foyle's collection, the secretive, almost furtive manner in which she had sifted through the contents of all those boxes cluttering her office, reinforced by her colleague Suzanne's dismissive attitude whenever she poked her head in and scanned about, taking in the chaos that was Heather's desk, and Heather's look of startled surprise as she peered at her colleague through her reading glasses.

The foyer felt like a zoo. She had to ease past a throng of tourists who were exiting the Meditation Room and making their way elsewhere, their voices rising behind her. She still wasn't sure what to make of Keys' claim, although it wouldn't have surprised her were it true, and it had added a measure of conviction to her decision to come and see for herself. What she did know was Dag Hammarskjöld had been single-minded in wanting to see the Meditation Room redesigned. He was adamant that the UN needed a place of stillness and silence that would resonate with the whole of humanity. He managed to gain the cooperation of the Laymen's Movement, who were behind the creation of the original room, and had fought a hard battle for its existence. The Laymen were a Christian organisation and they must have been bemused if not outraged by the new and distinctly non-Christian proposal. Heather had no idea how Hammarskjöld had persuaded them, but by the sound of things he would not be deterred. He set up a sort of petition, garnering the support of numerous Christians, Muslims and Jews, his "Friends of the UN Meditation Room". Bolstered, he forged ahead, and once the project was approved he oversaw every detail of the renovation, in there with the painters as they coated the walls. Why such zeal, such imperiousness? Was it his own ego spurring him on, or a higher spiritual purpose as he himself would have it?

Finding herself alone, she stood before Chagall's "Peace Window", taking in the complexity of the artist's vision, his tribute to the United Nations. The work was laden with religious symbolism from the Old and New Testaments, with its tree of knowledge cleaved in two, serpents rising up in the centre, an angel kissing a girl amid a dance of flowers, all rendered in the richest of hues, predominantly blue. The mural was enormous, taking up the height and breadth of an entire wall, there to invite love and harmony and denote the suffering of life without them. She was impressed by the sense of weight of the glass and imagined the effort and care taken during installation. For

Heather, the piece was made all the more significant knowing Chagall was a Hassidic Jew.

She took a step back and expanded her vision to encompass the whole, blurring the details, inhaling as though to breathe in the beauty, to embody it, consume it as it consumed her. Then she blinked, the presence of others gathering behind her oppressive. People were murmuring to each other, sharing what they discovered in the mural. Wanting silence, needing stillness, she entered the meditation room.

Semi-darkness greeted her at the door. The room was small and V-shaped, long walls of off-white culminating at the apex where another artwork hung, a fresco backlit by diffused lighting. More lighting had been threaded along the walls in the place of cornice. The fresco drew the eyes. Centred lengthwise on the tiled floor before it, some four feet in height, was a rectangular block of magnetite, the altar. Heather scanned the small benches lined up in rows on a carpet of deep green for the transient congregation. All were empty. She chose one at the front nearest the wall. Despite the lack of a backrest, she found the bench comfortable enough with its rattan seat.

Hammarskjöld had invited his friend, Bo Beskow, to create the fresco. It was an abstract work, interlocking rectangles forming triangles in muted hues of yellow, blue, grey and brown. She noticed other elements, an arc of moon, and a circle, half black, half white. She thought it might be the sun. A blue rectangle, aligned to the horizontal and centred in the work, receded beneath her gaze. Taking up the foreground was a long and twisted thread that stretched down through the middle at a slight angle.

She let her gaze wander, enjoying the silence of the room. Behind her, those entering remaining for the briefest time.

Her attention drifted to the altar. She hadn't anticipated the enormity of the stone, its weight. For Hammarskjöld, the altar reflected timelessness and strength. She thought few, if any, would understand its significance beyond the magnetic properties of iron ore. If what Heather saw could be described 'significant', and not just an association made by her receptive mind.

For the altar's placement at the head of the V had jolted Heather's memory and suddenly Beskow's fresco became a depiction of a mountain range, and she was no longer in the meditation room of the United Nations building in New York. Instead, she found herself seated in a valley somewhere high in the Himalayas, reimagining a vision Alice Bailey had on two occasions when she was about fifteen years of age, a vision she described in full in her unfinished autobiography.

*She was participating in a ceremony in a large, oval valley. The month was May and the moon full. She formed part of a crowd. She sensed that her position in the crowd indicated her spiritual status. There were high mountains all around and the terrain was rocky. She found she was facing east, where the valley narrowed to a bottleneck. Before the bottleneck stood an immense rock...*

The similarities were striking. Heather half expected the Buddha to appear from behind the fresco and greet the Christ standing before the altar, the heads of a spiritual hierarchy of masters central to Alice Bailey's occult scheme.

In her autobiography, Alice Bailey recalled her vision vividly in every detail. For her, the ceremony represented the unity of all things. Although at the time of its occurrence, she hadn't known what to make of it. All she knew at the age of fifteen was she had had a strange vision that only became significant for her when it reoccurred, as it would have any impressionable child. It would be another twenty years before she found a satisfactory explanation of what she had seen, one that would form the essence of her esoteric worldview. She imbued the vision with meaning retrospectively, deciding it represented the inner spiritual realm that had become her life.

Was it possible the stone, the fresco, the entire shape of the meditation room had been designed to echo, not only Hammarskjöld's but Alice Bailey's vision, orchestrated by him as some sort of secret homage? Or were the room and the dream similar because they both pointed at the same higher truth, one shared by numerous others? If Hammarskjöld had contrived the meditation room in accordance with Alice Bailey's vision, what did that say about a woman no one in mainstream contemporary society had heard of?

Or was she reading too much into the similarity, adding twos and arriving at fives? Ever since those boxes of esoteric paraphernalia had landed on her desk, she had found herself open to seeing correspondences between this and that, connections one part of her latched onto, even as her rational self rejected them as contrivances.

Things just happened.

A speck of black fluff on the thigh of her beige capris caught her eye. She pinched the fluff between her fingers, hesitated, then deposited it in her pocket. Then she took a few photos with her phone and jotted down some notes.

She was small-framed and preferred her clothes close-fitting and plain. She thought the style went with her straight brown hair which she always kept short. She had the sort of face that was neither pretty nor plain, with a pert mouth and a chipmunk inquisitiveness about the eyes. Others might have labelled her nondescript, a mouse of a woman devoid of charm, but even a mouse deserves scrutiny and appreciation. An introvert, she had a tendency to draw the world into herself, a quality that befuddled and infuriated Suzanne.

A tour group wandered into the room. Many stood or sat down quietly, save for the two circling the altar stone. Irritation stirred in Heather's belly. Whatever gave that pair the idea that running their hands along its top and remarking to each other that the stone was cold and hard constituted acceptable behaviour? Besides, what did they expect? Fairy floss? The man's heels clomped on the tiled floor. The woman, garbed in a faux leather jacket, squeaked when she walked. There was no one to tell them to move away. She wondered if the room should even have been a tourist site. There were places, like churches or synagogues or mosques, places that ought to be sacrosanct, the sightseeing restricted.

She waited for the others to move on, which they soon did. Alone again she felt like an interloper, an imposter, a spy almost, even as she knew that was ridiculous. She had become something of an expert in a metaphysical milieu, and she was determined to express her discoveries. Publish. She could only hope others would take an interest beyond the genealogical details. Although the audience would not be found among her colleagues. Especially not Suzanne, who had zero tolerance for the non-rational. Nor at home. Throughout the archiving, Heather's father had only feigned polite interest in whatever new titbit was on her mind, responding with soft grunts. She never broached any of the occult with her mother, who would have swept it all aside with derision. She was forced to leave her new knowledge on the doorstep like soiled shoes whenever she arrived home from work.

Heather had little in common with her mother. The one time she had mused that her great-grandmother, Katharine, had died the day she was born, intimating that she felt bonded to her ancestor as a result, almost as though she contained her spirit, Joan had laughed mockingly. She said Heather had entered the world at two in the morning, and Katharine hadn't passed away until ten that night. She said she would never forget her own mother, Heather's grandmother Agnes, waking her in the middle of the night with the news.

Heather had tried to defend her position, citing her mother's choice of "Katharine" for her middle name, but Joan would hear none of it. Heather was fourteen at the time and she had felt stung. The dismissal of her sensibilities formed a wedge between them, a wedge that had held fast ever since, a wedge that had thickened upon the death of her aunt.

There had never been anyone Heather could talk to about deep and meaningful matters other than Hilary, who was no longer there. In the acknowledging, an all too familiar chasm opened in her. She was so thoroughly alone.

Summoning what fortitude she had she pushed the missing away, steering her mind to the revelation that had ushered her into the building, that she had unwittingly managed to arrange the visit to coincide with the first anniversary of Hilary's death. One whole year, a complete cycle of the sun, it seemed to be reflected in that fresco, although she couldn't work out how.

Despite her best efforts, a wave of sadness rose up to meet the path of her thoughts. Her aunt Hilary would have adored the space. Although "adored" wasn't the right word. Neither was "space". Even the phrase 'Meditation Room' spoke nothing of its potency. That phrase conjured images of incense and yoga mats. Hilary would have known how to describe it. She was an adept when it came to the nuances of language. It troubled Heather that at such a critical moment words eluded her. She hadn't come all this way around the world to dwell on Hilary, but the realisation that it was the first anniversary of her death brought her back with force and she missed Hilary's refined, benevolent face, her wispy hair the colour of straw, the way she would turn towards her as she laughed, as if the amusement were theirs alone. Yet, the memory faded without a tear, and Heather realised she was able, just able to recall Hilary without caving in to that downward pull, that lurching into missing. The ache in her heart gave way to an appreciation of the woman, and their special bond. It was as though she was seated right there beside her, enjoying the atmosphere.

Hilary had never been religious. She called herself spiritual. Heather hadn't known what that meant, not deeply, not until she encountered Alice Bailey. What had begun as one of those dubious manuscript collections shunned by her colleagues as altogether lacking interest and therefore dumped in her office on some pretext or other, had unfolded, box by box, into a quest for understanding that led her first here, then there, as the figure that was Alice Bailey blossomed like a deep red rose.

Difficult, intense and isolating as it had been, looking back, Heather wouldn't have traded her immersion in the worlds of Professor Foyle and Alice Bailey, worlds that had brought her to New York to visit the United Nations, to sit in the meditation room and experience this interlude at once ineffable and grounded in art and stone. She was acutely aware that archiving the manuscript had forced her to question the foundations of her beliefs, catapulting her on a journey she wasn't prepared for, leaving her somewhat and significantly different.

It wasn't until she was dealing with the last of the boxes in Professor Foyle's collection that her interest in the United Nations was aroused. As Alice Bailey had neared the end of her life, in those war-ravaged years when the United Nations came into being, she had invested all her hope in the organisation. The United Nations had become something of a fixation for the ailing occultist, almost as though she had created the organisation herself.

For Alice Bailey, the United Nations was a potential vehicle for the expression of all she believed in and wanted to pass on, a unity of all nations coming together in cooperation to solve the world's problems. There could be no higher purpose for humanity. She had thrown her all at persuading her followers to adopt her point of view. Although Heather wondered if the insistent manner in which Bailey had urged her readers to act was the result of her infirmity. She was gravely ill throughout the 1940s, in enormous discomfort and pain, and emotionally worn out by the war. She had suffered as much as anyone in the face of the dark forces that had scourged the planet. More perhaps, she who had fought so desperately through the 1930s to avert a repetition of the previous world war. It was easy to see how the United Nations had given her hope. Like many at the time, she thought it would be humanity's salvation.

Heather knew that for Alice Bailey the United Nations had the potential to be much more. Through its auspices the externalisation of her Spiritual Hierarchy, something she had become so committed to making manifest, had a real chance of happening. Whacky as that seemed, there were plenty who believed it.

Despite her fondness for a figure she had initially found repellent, she wouldn't commit to believing in the existence of a Spiritual Hierarchy, that cohort of wise men—they were all men—overseeing the spiritual evolution of humanity. Privately, Heather thought the very notion ludicrous and an affront to her feminist sensibilities. Yet their existence was the cornerstone of Alice Bailey's thinking and the whole time she had been sifting through the collection, all she could do was suspend disbelief. She didn't want to dismiss the idea altogether, not in case she was wrong, but because that would have ma[de] and too much like her mother.

Sitting upright in her seat with her knees pressed togethe[r,] hands resting open in her lap, Heather took in the altar and the [room] one last time. Had Alice Bailey been alive to see it, she would h[ave] been delighted.

She was about to leave when another tour entered the room and Suzanne was soon seated beside her.

'Enjoy the tour?'

'It isn't over yet.'

'I'll meet you in the foyer.'

'Better still, there's a memorial of Eleanor Roosevelt in the gardens. See you there.'

Heather needed no persuading. As she headed back through the foyer, she wondered how well Eleanor Roosevelt had known Alice Bailey. Well enough, she imagined. Well enough.

There could be no doubt Alice Bailey was influential in high circles. Eleanor Roosevelt had read out her special prayer, The Great Invocation, in the United Nations building. She read it on the inaugural World Invocation Day in May 1952, not three years after Bailey's death, a day contrived into being by Bailey's followers to call for spiritual leadership of humanity. In her preamble, Eleanor Roosevelt announced that someone had sent her the prayer. Who was that 'someone'? More, what was it about Alice Bailey that garnered the respect and support of such eminent figures? Heather had poured over Alice Bailey's life and works for an entire year and she felt far from fully understanding the attraction, but she sensed it. She more than sensed it. Alice Bailey had managed to touch a centre of benevolence among the world's most powerful women and men. As far as Heather was concerned that just about made her a saint.

## ...rary of Victoria

Heather wouldn't look up from the clutter of manila folders, printed emails, scrap paper and sticky notes on her desk as the man in the shabby work coat wheeled in the last of the boxes.

Her sullen manner made the man awkward. He stacked the boxes on the floor beside the others in forced silence.

'All yours,' he said on his way out.

Only then did she lift her gaze. Sitting tall, craning, stabbing at the air, she counted one hundred boxes. They took up half the floor space in her already crowded office, fanning out in front of her desk, squashed against the wall below the window, and stacked untidily beside the longer wall that supported a low bench along its length.

She wasn't given to rudeness. Her eyes were all puffy and red from last night's tears and they still burned from those she had cried that morning. Her aunt's funeral, a small, family affair held at the Anglican Church in Hawthorn, had been as harrowing as she had anticipated. While her mother had stood at the graveside, her expressionless face matching the grey outfit she wore, Heather was opposite, shuddering with grief, her gaze fixed on that deep chasm of earth between them.

The wake back at her parents' house was equally gruelling. Various cousins huddled round the small buffet, sipping sherry. Heather had chosen to stand by a window overlooking the garden, avoiding contact with the others, riding out the ordeal with the large glass of whisky she had snaffled from the drinks cabinet in the other room.

With all the ceremony behind her, ahead lay only the missing.

She knew her grief would destabilise her but she couldn't have anticipated how all-consuming her feelings would be, how they seemed to change her entire point of view. Staring at those boxes she felt instantly irrational. When Ms Emily Prime, who had taken on the appraisal and acquisition, had asked around to see if anyone was into religious beliefs, she expressed a vague interest in Buddhism. That interest was thanks to her aunt, and she hadn't been religious either. Hilary had taken a lay interest in faiths of all kinds, in much the same way a spectator follows chess, all analysis and no participation.

She wished she had kept her mouth shut, not that it would have made a jot of difference. Resentment snaked around her abdomen as she realised the collection would have fallen to her regardless. She felt put upon, discriminated against in a department filled with assertive extroverts. At least, that was how her colleagues all came across. The dull projects, those doomed to be relegated to the backwaters of the library, always fell to her, the departmental doormat.

Eyeing the collection, she suspected Suzanne had been meddling behind the scenes as well. All week she had been going on about the grieving needing distractions, and there could be no better distraction than work.

Adding to her discontent, when Heather went over and pulled off the lid of the nearest box she was hit with that musty smell of paper left in damp conditions. She all but gasped. Inside, a pile of letters and papers was crammed to the top. It looked as though they had been tipped out of a drawer, shuffled about on some fetid floor and then scooped up in indifferent handfuls and tossed in. So much for the original order. She put back the lid and rummaged through her bag for her inhaler.

She might have opened the window but it was June and a winter wind was blowing off Port Phillip Bay. Facing south, her office received little direct sunshine and tended to be cool yet stuffy. The room was situated in the upper reaches of the State Library of Victoria, in an area not open to the public and lacking the grandiosity of the main reading rooms below, rooms accessed via marble staircases. Still, her office was pleasing enough, with its high ceiling and thick walls. Although once the door closed, the room seemed to seal in its occupant, for better or worse.

Expecting another rush of allergen-laden air, she held her breath as she lifted the lid off the next box. This time, the interior was filled with nothing but books with deep-blue covers. It seemed as good a place as any to make a start. She would easily be done with assessing the entire contents of that particular box by the end of the day. She cleared a cursory space on her desk thinking with luck, she would whip through the other boxes containing nothing but books and be done with the collection altogether by Christmas.

Before she set to work, she lined up the other boxes in neat rows on the bench and under it, and two-deep on the floor under the window, shoving the remainder in rows three-deep in front of her desk. There was little space left to stand but at least she had a direct path from her chair to the door. Surveying the scene, Professor Foyle's collection had the feel of a house removal put in storage.

She inspected the boxes one by one, holding her head away as she opened the lids and noting the contents at a glance. She counted seventy boxes that contained nothing but books, leaving thirty filled with bundles of newsletters and pamphlets, magazines, journals, notebooks and correspondence. Fortunately, none smelled as bad as the first.

She held fast to her initial decision, rounded her desk and delved into the second box she had opened, withdrawing the blue books and piling them on her desk. Then she read the provenance, outlined in a media release Emily had composed, clipped to the front of a buff file that contained nothing but the picking sheet.

The State Library of Victoria has just taken delivery of a sizeable collection of books, serials and archival material relating to the unpublished manuscript of the late Professor Samantha Foyle, a notable Australian historian of religious studies with a special interest in alternative spiritualities. More commonly termed the 'New Age', alternative spirituality encompasses a wide range of belief systems, often with an esoteric religious element. The New Age is informed by Eastern religion and philosophy, and Humanistic and Transpersonal psychology.

Samantha Foyle received her Doctorate in Religious Studies from Deakin University in 1996 for a thesis titled *A Crisis of Belief: New Age Seekers in Australia*. The work encompasses an in-depth study of intentional communities, with special emphasis on the cult surrounding Bhagwan Shree Rajneesh, or Osho as he is known by devotees. Before a series of scandals broke open the cult, 'sex guru' Osho had a sizeable following in Australia, particularly in Byron Bay and Perth, along with smaller communes dotted around the country.

A small quantity of books in this collection relates to the practice of magic and Wicca. Professor Foyle's investigations resulting in her internationally bestselling work *Witches in the Suburbs*, built up an extensive collection of literature in this regard.

At the time of her death in 2013, Professor Foyle was working on a scholarly volume in which she revisited the genesis of the New Age movement, tracing its origins back to breakaway Theosophist Alice A. Bailey. A complete set of books, along with partial sets of newsletters and magazines pertaining to the era of the occult figure form a substantial part of the collection.

In June 2017, library staff visited the Foyle property near Healesville to pack the collection. A total of one hundred boxes were packed and dispatched. By coincidence, the two days spent at the residence fell on the full moon of May, known as Wesak in the Buddhist calendar and acknowledged as a significant date by Alice Bailey's followers.

Heather's heart squeezed in her chest. Professor Foyle's collection was less a chore or a distraction and more a hand clenching the back of her neck, pushing her head forward into her pain. For Hilary would have loved this collection. With her fascination for new religious movements, an interest she enjoyed and shared with her friends but not her family—not even Heather—Hilary would have relished every moment, participating vicariously as Heather gave her little updates at the end of her day.

Heather fought back the tears, removing her glasses and wiping beneath her eyes. She had to summon her will to continue, to not bolt from her room, seek out her line manager, Shona, and beg that the collection be given to someone else. Her reaction soon gave way to resignation, almost defeat.

She scanned through the media release twice more, absorbing the information, gaining a sense of the late Professor Foyle. The mention of Osho repelled her. Hilary had talked about him from time to time. She had had a friend called Aashti who had spent time at his ashram in Pune. A single mother who had complained of the prurient goings on.

Wicca wasn't something Heather took to either. Paganism in all its forms seemed to attract a peculiar type of devotee, one fond of dressing up and enacting weird rituals.

She had never heard of Alice Bailey. With sudden conviction, she decided she would archive the collection for Hilary, for it occurred to her with force that this was the perfect way to understand a part of her aunt she had overlooked when she was alive. She felt guilty in the remembering, the way she would steer the conversation elsewhere, onto topics that ignited her instead. 'I'm sorry,' she said aloud, chastened.

She set the file to one side and drew the piles of blue books closer. They were leather-bound, with titles including, *A Treatise on Cosmic Fire*, *Initiation, Human and Solar* and *The Externalisation of the Hierarchy*. Strange titles and she felt strange even holding them. She leafed through the first, skimming over the language, comprehending nothing. She examined the cover, her eyes drawn to the bottom right corner where a white equilateral triangle was positioned with its base running to the horizontal. Inside the triangle, three straight lines, the tallest reaching the triangle's apex, descended to meet a horizontal line above the triangle's base. That line continued on a little before switching direction and rising to form an X with another diagonal line. It was all most uniform and perfect and she hadn't a clue what it signified. She noted that the author's name only appeared on the spine.

She scanned the front-end pages of the book in her hand. The volumes were published by the Lucis Publishing Company, owned by the Lucis Trust, a tax-exempt, religious and educational organisation based in New York. She set down the book thinking she would arrange the series in publication date order. A simple yet absorbing task and she lost herself to the process.

The first was released in 1922, the last in 1960. The texts appeared to all have been written by Alice Bailey, but when Heather scrutinised further, she noticed many were written by someone else. He called himself The Tibetan. So that was the Buddhist connection, right there. In a statement written in August 1934, and included before the tables of contents of many volumes, the Tibetan referred to Alice Bailey as A.A.B. It was all most peculiar.

Flashing into Heather's mind was an image of a candlelit room, a round table covered in black baize, a crystal ball in the centre, a gathering joining hands. A séance, the stuff of Spiritualism. Hilary had told her once that her great-grandmother, Katharine, had been a Spiritualist. Heather hadn't bothered to ask Hilary what that meant. She knew Spiritualism involved mediums contacting the dearly departed. Hilary said Katharine had been one of those mediums. That was all Heather knew about her great-grandmother, other than that when her husband died she brought up her two daughters and never remarried.

Heather wondered if Spiritualism had anything to do with this Alice Bailey.

Among the volumes was one she knew she could read. It was titled *Unfinished Autobiography*. Contained in the front pages was an image of the woman herself.

Heather was immediately struck by the benign-looking visage. Alice Bailey was seated sideways at the head of a small wooden table. She sat with a slight forward lean as though poised to stand. Soft light shone in through a window behind her. She must have been in her sixties when the photograph was taken. She was garbed in a light coloured, loose-fitting top over a simple dress that had a large rosette of flowers attached to its breast. Her hair, dark and voluminous, was swept back from her face. A face that wore a warm, closed-mouth smile, with eyes the kindest Heather had ever seen. Alice Bailey exuded benevolence and humility. Staring into that face for the first time, Heather trusted her instantly.

She turned the pages and arrived at a moving foreword by a Foster Bailey. A son? A husband? It was composed in the form of a letter dated December 16, 1949, a day after Alice Bailey's death. The man talked of her steadfast dedication, her resolve to press on despite the poor condition of her heart and her blood, and of her utter exhaustion. Right to the last she worked, receiving visitors, writing letters, meeting with executives. The letter seemed addressed to her followers. He spoke of aspirants and disciples and of her esoteric school, the Arcane School. He described the work she did, her chosen path, as that of world salvation. His words were infused with love and yet also with detachment. It was, after all, an official letter. There was a subtle sense of sadness but also of relief.

Heather was struck by the detachment she felt as she read of the woman's passing. Then again, this particular death had occurred decades before and was far removed from her. It wasn't sudden or tragic. It was a release. Heather read on.

In the introduction, Alice Bailey described herself as a rabid orthodox Christian turned occult teacher. Not the most endearing of characters, Heather thought with bitter irony. Likely as not she would repel just about every modern reader who came across her. She could imagine the ladies of Hilary's book club issuing disdainful remarks amongst themselves, aspersing or commenting that the topic wasn't exactly their thing.

Alice Bailey wrote briefly of her unhappy childhood, her life as an evangelist and a social worker, and her role as the wife of a rector. When she mentioned her second husband, the Foster who had written the foreword, it was with much fondness and appreciation. They had been married for over twenty-five years. She went on to state outright that she would not write about their relationship. That to do so would most likely do damage to what they had and sound hollow and pointless.

Heather paused, her curiosity aroused. She had read enough biographies to know when to look between the lines. She pondered over the passage. The author had to be responding to the opinions of others. Unfavourable judgements and criticisms? On the surface, as far as Alice Bailey was concerned, they were not worth contesting. Yet they must have been and she was clearly hurt. Otherwise, why mention it at all? The veiled defence was an approach Hilary would use, indirect and pointed all at once, when she was offended by some remark or action of her sister, Heather's mother Joan. What sort of marriage had Alice and Foster to warrant such a defence?

From the writing style, and the words she chose, Heather decided Alice Bailey was a bright and determined woman, witty at times, with a soft, nurturing centre. She sounded down to earth, sensible and pragmatic and not at all the wafty air-head Heather had anticipated. Curious to discover her background, she permitted herself time to read on, dipping into the early pages.

At first, the author rambled, taking tangents into astrology and esotericism. She seemed too fond of her own opinions and speculations. After seven more pages, Heather felt ready to put the book down, and was about to do just that when she came across a name that caused her to do the opposite.

Alice A. Bailey, born in Manchester, England, on the 16$^{th}$ June 1880, began her life as Alice Ann La Trobe-Bateman.

Heather knew that surname, or at least half of it. How could she not? The very building she worked in had been instigated by Charles La Trobe, the first governor of Victoria. There was a statue of him outside the library building. She skirted by it every day. A statue of a slim, noble-looking man garbed in ceremonial dress, his long, double-breasted jacket buttoned to the neck and held at the waist by a cummerbund replete with tassels. He wore a cocked hat decorated with long gum leaves high on its crown. The sculptor had gone to town, the collar and cuffs of red and gold brocade catching the eye.

It had been Charles La Trobe's idea to build the public library. Designed by Joseph Reed in Roman Revival style and opened in 1856, the library was an impressive stone building, distinctly symmetrical with rounded arched windows. Heather never failed to enjoy the feeling of entering into history when she crossed the grounds and climbed the stone steps, soon to be embraced by the fluted columns of the portico.

Melbourne was proud of this heritage; the La Trobe society had been founded to honour the first governor's memory. They had a website. She had attended some of their events.

Heather placed a bookmark in the autobiography and moved her keyboard to the edge of her desk. In moments, she was staring at the La Trobe family tree. She had come across it before, when Suzanne had linked her to the site to encourage her to attend an exhibition of early Melbourne paintings. Back then, she hadn't given the genealogy a second glance. This time she pored over the names, arriving at Alice Ann La Trobe-Bateman, married first to a Walter Henry Evans, and second to a man called Bailey. It was her. She had one sister, Lydia, married to a Parsons.

Heather confirmed what she saw as she traced the family back through the generations, arriving first at her father, Frederic Foster La Trobe-Bateman, one of seven, and then her grandfather, John Frederic La Trobe-Bateman, Charles La Trobe's cousin. She searched the grandfather and discovered he was an eminent water engineer and consultant to the British government, best known for his development of municipal water-supply systems in cities such as Manchester and Glasgow. John Frederic had married Anne Fairbairn, Alice's grandmother. Anne was the daughter of the eminent Scottish engineer Sir William Fairbairn, 1st Baronet of Ardwick, who was renowned for his pioneering work in bridge building, ship building and railway locomotives. The family luminaries went on and on. Another great-uncle was acclaimed book illuminator and Pre-Raphaelite watercolourist Edward La Trobe-Bateman, who, like Charles La Trobe, had chosen to live in Australia.

Her office felt suddenly claustrophobic, too small to contain the revelations. Succumbing to a need for air, she left the jumble on her desk and went and stood in the corridor. Thinking a glass of water was in order she headed in the direction of the staff kitchen. Then, recalling the excitement expressed by staff at the release of a new biography of Charles La Trobe, she changed direction.

Her line manager Shona's office was down a wide carpeted hall. The door was open but she knocked anyway. Her office was the immaculate, orderly contrast to Heather's. Shona looked up from her computer screen all calm assurance and took in Heather's visage with a single sweep of her eye.

'How are you holding up?' she said. Her face exuded professional warmth.

Heather gave her a thin smile in return. It was all she could manage.

'That book on La Trobe, the one just published, do you still have it?'

'By Professor John Barnes? I do, but you haven't answered my question.'

Heather avoided her gaze. 'The Foyle collection,' she said inanely.

'What about it?'

'It's...' Her lip quivered. Embarrassed, she flushed, cursing the dam of tears, forever fit to burst.

'I'll fetch the book,' Shona said quickly, sweeping past Heather as she left the office, returning moments later.

Heather took the book and mumbled her thanks, hurrying back to the sanctuary of her own office, resisting the urge to lock herself in.

The edition was a hardcover carrying a less than flattering image of La Trobe on the cover. Publishers.

She had no idea what she was looking for, but she found it in the first chapter. Alice Bailey had described herself a rabid Christian. That mindset had its roots in a Christian sect. Whilst the aristocracy of Victorian Britain observed the High Church of England, the La Trobe-Batemans were Moravian. Bailey's grandfather John Frederic La Trobe-Bateman, was the eldest son of John Frederic Bateman and Mary Agnes La Trobe, whose father and Alice Bailey's great, great-grandfather was Reverend Benjamin Boneval La Trobe, a well-known Moravian minister.

Barnes provided a detailed description of the sect. Founded in Moravia, Central Europe, the denomination was thought to be the oldest of all Protestant faiths. Moravians held a deep belief in Jesus Christ, and upheld values of love and respect for others over adherence to doctrine. The faith carried a strong emphasis on leading the life of a missionary, simple, spiritual and pure.

Reverend La Trobe passed on his faith to his children, and them to theirs. Alice Bailey's grandfather was born into a Moravian settlement and attended Moravian schools. Barnes was at pains to show the extent to which the Moravian faith had influenced his cousin Charles La Trobe. Had the faith coloured Alice Bailey's life too, with a religiosity she was later to make manifest in her own peculiar fashion?

Charles La Trobe could not have known of his third cousin. He had died five years before she was born. Yet they were related, and sitting in the library with his statue right outside, Heather felt peculiarly connected to Alice Bailey. It was as though the very walls were taking an interest.

Heather returned to Alice's own account. There was aristocratic pedigree on the mother's side as well. A quick cross reference on genealogy sites and she discovered that Alice's mother was Alice Harriet Holinshed, eldest daughter of a William Holinshed. The socially prominent family were descended from Raphael Holinshed, the English chronicler who inspired Shakespeare.

Alice Bailey had quite a pedigree but she put little store in the achievements of her ancestors and she had little to say that was positive about her childhood. Although as she read on, Heather found that unsurprising. Alice Bailey lost both parents to tuberculosis before she was eight. Her grandfather, John Frederic, passed away a few months later.

She spent much of her formative years at Moor Park, a fine old house in Surrey, once known as Compton Hall, remodelled and renamed in the 1680s by diplomat and essayist Sir William Temple. The property enjoyed five acres of magnificent formal gardens. Alice Bailey's grandfather purchased Moor Park in 1859 and, long before the girls came to stay, he established a highly popular hydrotherapy spa at the residence. Among the regular attendees was Charles Darwin, who had worked on his *The Origin of the Species* there. The hydrotherapy spa was the culmination of a life's work given over to the salvation of humanity through water engineering. Heather could only imagine how Britain's cities would have smelled before sewers, and how tedious things would have been for all concerned without running water.

Unable to restrain her habit of jotting down points of interest, Heather opened a drawer in her desk and extracted the clothbound notebook Hilary had gifted her one Christmas and until then, she had found no suitable use for. Observing the elephant on the cover her heart squeezed, her grief poised on the upsurge. She inhaled, waited, and let the feelings subside before opening to the first page and making some brief notes on her discoveries.

Alice had lived at Moor Park in the 1880s. For a moment, Heather pictured her and Lydia in their pony carriage, travelling down the pretty country lanes, but that image faded as fast as it came. Despite the obvious luxury, life at Moor Park for the little La Trobe-Bateman girls sounded severe. They had been under the strict supervision of a governess, nurse and maid, and had to adhere to a daily routine segmented by the half hour. It was all lessons and more lessons, walks and formal dining. There was certainly no opportunity to be idle. The regimen was echoed in the La Trobe-Bateman's religious observances. Daily prayers involved the entire household from the grandfather, who would sit at the head of the dining room table to lead the prayers, through to the scullery maid.

Alice sounded like an impressionable child. Had all that religion she was exposed to crusted over the hole left by her parents? What other comfort had she?

With the passing of her grandfather, she subsequently endured a lonely and disrupted childhood as she and her younger sister Lydia were shunted between their grandmother's residence in London and various aunts scattered across Scotland and England, with a healthy portion of the winter spent on the French Riviera.

It couldn't have been easy. The poor girl's grief must have been immeasurable. There Heather sat in her mid-forties having just lost an aunt and she was barely coping. She could feel the hurt, the anguish in what Alice Bailey said and what she left out. The only mention of her mother was her golden hair. Alice Bailey unwittingly juxtaposed that poignant image with a portrait of an irascible sounding father who, for the few years remaining of his life, chose to blame his eldest daughter for the loss of his wife. He passed away on a ship off the coast of Tasmania, leaving Alice, a withdrawn child, maudlin, living in the shadows. Her wretched state of mind was exacerbated by her remarkably charismatic and talented younger sister who cast a dazzling light wherever she went.

Odd that through all her summing up of her childhood, she didn't mention her sister by name. Had Lydia forbade it? Surely not. Was it that she couldn't bring herself to name the sibling who had caused her so much unhappiness simply by being who she was? Or was it another hurt? A deep hurt perhaps, one she carried with her into her sixties, the decade she composed her autobiography.

# Castramont

'I told you to leave me alone!'

Aunt Margaret rushed into the drawing room, coming to an abrupt halt on the hearth rug. She surveyed the girls, gave Alice a disapproving look and said, 'There really is no need to shriek.'

'She is taking my light.'

Alice was seated on the settee. Behind her, Lydia lounged on the window seat, warming her back.

'Alice, all you need to do is move aside.'

'Why should I move? What about her? No one ever tells *her* to do a thing; she who can do no wrong.'

'That's enough insolence from you, little madam.'

'But Aunt, you don't know her as well as I do,' Alice whined. 'Wherever we go, she makes herself the centre of everything.'

'Don't be ridiculous.'

'Ask Miss Godby if you don't believe me. She'll tell you.'

Although the moment the words exited her mouth, Alice doubted their veracity. Only last week she had flushed all of Miss Godby's jewellery down the lavatory. She was furious with her governess for refusing to let her leave the schoolroom until she'd finished her maths. She hated maths and was no good at it and she was rapidly developing a headache. Lydia had finished her exercises and was permitted to go down to the kitchen where Cook was baking girdle cakes. Alice could smell the spices wafting upstairs. Hot girdle cakes straight out of the oven were her favourite. By the time she got to eat one, they would be cold. Seeing the others downstairs, she took her chance. Miss Godby's jewellery was no more. Nothing was said and nothing was done about it. Three days later, upon reading Miss Godby's diary, something she had taken to doing with fascination after discovering it in her room, she realised she had been found out. Riven with guilt and not knowing how she would ever repay the loss, Alice confessed, only to be surprised by Miss Godby's consternation, not over the loss of her jewellery, but of the intrusion upon her privacy. Now she doubted Miss Godby would ever take her side in sibling disputes.

'It's all right, Aunt,' Lydia said obligingly as she crossed the room. 'I shall retire to the library.'

Her remark, her manner altogether, incensed Alice even more. Did she have to sound so proper and mature and in command of her feelings? She was only thirteen. Alice was fifteen and she was rarely in command of hers.

Aunt Margaret waited until Lydia had left the room before sitting beside Alice on the settee and remaining silent for a long time. It was her aunt's way of deflecting her wrath. She sat with perfect deportment, radiating from deep inside a serene beauty and Alice was instantly chastened and soothed. She really oughtn't lose her temper so often, not in front of her favourite aunt, but she couldn't seem to help it. Looking out of her own emulous eyes, Lydia had inherited all the intelligence and all the charm there was to be had, winning everyone's affection without effort, leaving her, the elder sister, to languish in her shadow.

They were staying for two months at Castramont House, a charming white building perched on a knoll on the banks of the River Fleet, amid the rolling wooded lowlands of Scotland's southwest. Alice adored the setting. Castramont was her favourite of all the places they were required to reside for short spells. There were fine walks to be had in the bracing Scottish air, and best of all, conversations by the fireside at night. Her aunt would furnish Alice with talk of little incidents at the Young Women's Christian Association, of which she was president, and of the goings on at the cottage hospital, which she had founded and took an active interest in.

Eventually she said, 'What are you reading, my dear?'

Alice showed her aunt her book. It was *Heidi*.

'Ah.'

'Have you read it?'

'I have.'

'Poor Heidi.'

'No, not poor Heidi. She was much loved. And you are much loved, too. By God, especially.'

'I suppose so.'

'I know so.' She paused. 'Whatever are we going to do with you, dear Alice? Now run along to Miss Godby. She wants a word with you.'

Another one, she thought, getting up off the settee and smoothing down her dress, humiliation rising like bile.

The following Sunday, the rest of the house set off for church in the nearby village. She should have gone as well, and not stayed home alone, but she told her aunt she was feeling unwell with an upset tummy and a headache and was excused. Even as the buggy disappeared down the lane she regretted not going with them. It was summer and the day was sunny and warm. There were flowers to enjoy and the chitter chatter of birds. She supposed she could wander outside and sit in a field but she couldn't muster the will, her mind filled with the injustices that dominated her life, not least her sister.

Lydia had managed effortlessly to steal all the attention at last night's dinner, flouncing about all gay and winning in front of the guests. Alice had wanted to stick out her foot and trip her up. So grim was her mood she even contemplated ending her life, but recalling her previous attempts—once when she threw herself down the stairs, another when she tried to bury herself in sand, and a third when she tried to drown herself in the River Fleet—she thought better of it. Bruises, sand-filled orifices and icy water were simply too much. Face it, Alice, you are a coward.

Deciding to escape from her melancholy by taking on that of her literary ally, she took *Heidi* to the drawing room and sat on the settee. She must have dozed for the next thing she knew she was startled by the arrival of a tall man in European clothes who entered the room unexpectedly. He had a turban on his head and to her astonishment he came and sat down right beside her.

Petrified, she remained silent. She couldn't think of what else to do. She could leap up and scream but there was no one else in the house. She was convinced she was about to be attacked, but instead the man talked. He talked and talked, and he seemed to have much to say so she listened.

He told her there was work planned for her, her Master's work, and that this work would see her travelling to many countries, but whether she was given this work was contingent on a radical transformation of her disposition.

'You need to stop being unpleasant and gain some self-control, and you need to do it immediately.' He sounded emphatic so she nodded her ascent.

'I will be in contact with you every few years. In the meantime, see to it that you change your behaviour and your attitude.'

'Yes, sir.'

'I hope that you do.'

And with that, he departed, pausing in the doorway to give her a penetrating look. She knew she would never forget that look. Through it, the man managed to convey disappointment, censure and profound expectation all at once.

Alone in the room, Alice first thought she was losing her mind. She knew she hadn't been asleep and she hadn't dreamt the encounter. It wasn't any sort of vision. It was a real event. A man had walked into the drawing room and spoken to her directly. She had seen him walk in the door, have his say and walk out again.

Confusion soon gave way to smug satisfaction. There was special work ahead of her, hers and hers alone, should she decide to change her manner.

Nothing of the sort had ever happened to Lydia.

The visit had the desired effect. In the certain knowledge that she was special—something that had never occurred to her before—Alice pulled herself up, drew herself out of her malaise, and made a determined effort to change. No more the self-absorbed, grumpy and sullen teenager with a volatile temper. She would be virtuous, virtuous as to be almost saintly. She put on a smile. She was polite. At first it was an act but with time the façade grew real. She couldn't say she felt any happier, but from that moment on, she practised being nice.

Aunt Margaret, indeed the entire household could scarcely believe the change in her. Miss Godby would marvel over how pleasanter she was. Only Lydia remained doubtful.

In the weeks that followed, she took long walks or lay on her back in a nearby field and listened to the silence, trying to connect with an unseen reality that was becoming more real to her than the tangible reality she was surrounded by. She had been raised to believe in God transcendent, a harsh, judgmental, punishing God, who was distant, unknowable and unapproachable. After the strange man with the turban came into her life, something inside of her kept reaching for God immanent, a loving and compassionate God, one that existed inside of her. Sometimes, she thought she could really feel it.

# Auburn

The descent to her platform at Melbourne Central involved the usual dodging past people who found it appropriate to stand still wherever and whenever they felt like it, no matter who was behind them, or how much of a hurry they might be in. Rush hour meant nothing other than an even more chaotic interplay of movement and obstruction. Battling her way through as deftly as she could manage, cursing her apparent invisibility, Heather often wondered who thought of putting a multilevel shopping complex above a busy city train station. She supposed the rationale was expediency, but it had created a conflict of interest. People halted in their tracks to browse the shops or because they had lost their way in the confusion of escalators and poor signage.

That afternoon, Heather found herself more peeved than usual. She had in her satchel something important, something that shouldn't be there, a book that belonged to the collection of Professor Foyle. She knew it was forbidden to take a part, any part of a collection home. If she were caught, she might lose her job. Yet she couldn't leave *The Unfinished Autobiography* there on her desk, not after only managing to get through that one chapter. Curiosity had the better of her, even as she found the prim and proper aristocrat and mystic anathema to all she stood for as a left of centre feminist and atheist, someone who saw truth in the tangible and the empirical and liked to put life in neat boxes. Although she shared Alice Bailey's sense of being an outsider in her own family. Had this simple identification propelled her to break a cardinal rule?

On the platform, she budged past others milling by some seats and found a spot further on, away from the throng. There, she clutched her satchel to her chest. She thought perhaps she looked a little furtive and tried to relax her grip, when a man in a hoodie strode by on his way to the outer reaches of the platform and she gripped her satchel all the tighter.

The train was no better. Stepping onto the 5.08, she was forced to stand, all the way to Glenferrie, where she alighted to catch a second train to Auburn. The whole journey took a total of sixteen minutes, which she couldn't complain about. Although Auburn was a station the express services passed on through, so she had to catch the two trains, which was something she *could* complain about, and sometimes she did.

Leaving the station, she hesitated, curbing a habit. She knew every paving slab of the walk to Hilary's where she would often call in on her way home. She wanted to show her the autobiography, tell her all she had discovered. She had to reign herself in, not wanting to cry in public.

Hilary's death was all too recent, too unexpected. Up until the day she died she never succumbed to any illness, scarcely even a cold.

Hilary had been a St Catherine's girl, like her sister, Heather's mother, Joan. The only children of a professor of English Literature and a novelist, the girls enjoyed the privileges of an elite private school education, replete with blazers and bows in their hair. From that cloistered upbringing in the leafy suburbs of Melbourne's east, Hilary had gone on to read English at the University of Melbourne before undertaking a post-graduate course in library studies. She had been a librarian ever since.

Neither Hilary nor Joan had moved away from Hawthorn. Joan studied History and met her husband-to-be, William, on campus. They had married two years later. She never completed her degree.

Heather's arrival had seen to that. Meanwhile, William Brown, a law student, went on to become a lawyer, then barrister.

Much to the family's consternation, Hilary never married. In a private moment, she told Heather that she had spent her whole life far too busy for a relationship. Then she had drawn in closer and whispered that she had been fulfilled her whole life by books and ideas, and there really had never been any room in amongst all those covers for a man.

The two sisters, Hilary and Joan, had enjoyed filial loyalty and shared history and little else. When Heather had come along, Hilary formed an instant bond with her niece. Heather discovered much later that her mother had been as much relieved as peeved by her sister's intense affection. Every weekend Hilary would visit the Browns to see her favourite, her only niece, and as Heather grew older, there were trips to the park, the beach, the cinema, the theatre. Older still, and they would talk for hours about the mysteries and meaning of life.

Up until the day her aunt suffered heart failure, Heather's life had followed along a single set of tracks. At weekends, they would go out somewhere, and after work, she would take a detour to Hilary's.

There were several alternative routes home. On impulse, she chose a new route that took her past Talana, a beautiful Queen Anne-style mansion on the corner of her street.

With its red brick asymmetry, its corner tower and oriel window, and its high chimneys and mock Tudor strapwork, Heather felt thrust between the covers of a century past as she approached.

She stopped at the gates and took in the manicured lawn, the neatly clipped shrubs, the large windows in the façade. She imagined her great-grandmother Katharine, hosting a séance in a room downstairs. It might have been the sort of residence occupied by Alice in her La Trobe-Bateman years. At least, it was grand enough and she would have been twenty when Talana was built. But it was an idle thought, for she doubted Alice Bailey had ever lived in Australia. Somehow, if she had, Joan—who took an avid interest in local history—would have known about it, given the La Trobe connection.

Even the suburb, Hawthorn, was rumoured to be so named after Alice Bailey's third cousin, Charles La Trobe, remarked that the native shrubs in the area looked like hawthorn bushes. It was another little moment of serendipity, as though Heather was destined to encounter Alice Bailey. Her ponderings released her from her guilt at stealing away Alice's book. She felt more like she was taking her home.

Her parents lived in the house they had inherited from Heather's paternal grandfather. It was a modest affair for Harcourt Street, two-storey and Victorian in style and, like Talana, set well back from the street. Her father William, being an only child, had inherited the house and since so was she, Heather presumed that one day she would do the same. It had always been a given and she had always lived there, but she was forty-five years old and knew it about time she relied on her own resources and found a place of her own. She had been saving her whole working life, and had accumulated a tidy sum, yet she never seemed able to keep abreast of the price rises that in recent years had doubled the value of any property she would have liked to buy.

She made her way down the long garden path that carved a sweeping course through manicured lawn, opened her satchel and fished out her door key.

Inside had the feel of old money, the hall a pleasingly proportioned rectangle with doors leading off left and right. Ahead, the staircase was wide and inviting. Heather removed her shoes and shuffled her feet into slippers, abiding by her mother's rule, instituted to preserve the polish on the oak floorboards.

She found her mother in the sitting room, holding a glass of gin and tonic and reading a book, as was her custom at that time of day. William partook of a single malt to honour his Scottish blood on his mother's side. It was all so staid, and Heather usually joined them. She would quietly take up the chair over by the upright piano that no one ever played, and enjoy a small glass of Chablis.

This time she stood in the doorway to exchange pleasantries before heading up to her room feeling like a schoolgirl running upstairs to write in her diary.

She sat down on her bed and extracted her precious blue book, forgoing wine in favour of the second chapter. She wanted to go over the first chapter again too, and research the details to flesh out the story. Alice was in the habit of skating over important references as if the reader would already be furnished with a wide-reaching knowledge of late-Victorian British aristocracy. Heather was not.

She learned that Alice had come through finishing school and spent her early adulthood living with her sister, Lydia, in a rented house near St Albans. She became a society girl, attending garden parties, teas, dinners and dances. She was well travelled, spoke fluent French, and had a good classical education. In all, a typical Edwardian lady. An attractive young lady at that, who was expected to find herself an attractive young husband.

Yet Alice's assets could not compete with her religious fanaticism. Being raised in a pious family wouldn't have helped. It was as though she were a throwback to her great great-grandfather and Moravian minister, Reverend Boneval La Trobe. Unfortunately, she had ended up with a deep knowledge of the Bible and no knowledge at all when it came to men and relationships. To make matters worse, she was earnest. Heather had once been accused of being earnest. She had been insulted. Although she was nothing like Alice, who had the kind of superior holiness that lent no favours when it came to finding acceptance in her social milieu. It would certainly not have found her a husband.

It became hard to keep reading. There she was in her childhood bedroom, a room she had slept in her whole life, she, a spinster with no wish to ever wed. She was suddenly grateful for modern society, which allowed her freedom to be single, although her parents were disappointed at the lack of grandchildren. Sitting there in a room that, despite the alterations over the years—pink curtains, teddies and dolls, replaced with decor and accoutrements appropriate to her age—remained essentially the same. It had all been tolerable until Hilary's death. Now she was suffocated by her surroundings. She felt imprisoned; her release, her singular distraction from the loneliness she couldn't face, had always been Hilary. A familiar pressure behind her nose and her eyes and she reached for a tissue to stem the flow of tears, tears that she couldn't fight back a second time.

Five sodden tissues later, and she forced her attention back to the autobiography.

Alice wrote little of her sister, except to say that when Lydia came of age, she received a period of special training in preparation to study Medicine at the University of Edinburgh. Heather couldn't help being impressed, although it did seem to account for why Alice felt she lived in her shadow. Lydia must have been exceptionally passionate and gifted to be granted this opportunity, at a time when it was the privilege of boys to attend boarding school, with all the advantages of future university places that entailed, while girls were educated at home by governesses in preparation for life as wife and mother. A university degree in Medicine was a courageous and difficult choice for a woman to make at the turn of the twentieth century. Few women back then were permitted to study Medicine, and matriculated women doctors were restricted from post mortems, surgical procedures and certain wards. In 1900, there were only two hundred women doctors in the whole of Britain.

Had Lydia inherited her paternal grandmother, Anne Fairbairn's strict and formidable manner? She was certainly ambitious. Lydia became one of the first women to win a university distinction. She went on to become a doctor, wrote an elementary biology textbook for children, and took up important research into cancer. She also wrote three books of poetry and was hailed as one of England's greatest living poets. Her poem "*A Vision of Immortality*", originally released in 1917, was republished in 2011, and considered by historians to be of cultural significance. All of which spoke of an accomplished and rounded out sort of life.

What would it have been like for Alice, watching her sister shine like that when she had nothing much other than a good dress sense? How does any sibling cope with her sister's accolades? At least Alice had been in receipt of a small allowance from the family estate, as was her sister, enough to afford a measure of financial independence. Reading between the lines, all of the tragedies that had befallen her, along with the ingrained attitudes of her class, her disjointed upbringing and her over-developed faith, had left her confused and disconnected from her social milieu. It was with a heart filled with sympathy for a sad little girl in a handsome woman's body that Heather turned to the next chapter.

She was making herself comfortable on her bed when her phone beeped three messages in quick succession.

She swiped the screen and tapped on the message icon. They were all from Suzanne. She had composed a three-part invitation. The opening message offered her sympathies, again. The second was a repeat of the advice she had given before, the same advice she had issued the moment she had heard about Hilary's death. Keep busy. She wasn't to know Heather was doing just that. The third message was an invitation to a weekend getaway in Daylesford. To make use of the two-for-one voucher Suzanne had for a massage and dinner at a health spa.

A winter break? Little wonder the spa was offering a deal. It was perishing in Daylesford in winter. The temperature scarcely rose above ten degrees as far as Heather knew.

She wrote back, thanking Suzanne for thinking of her, but saying she couldn't go as she was saving for a house and couldn't afford to dip into her savings.

Suzanne's response was an open-mouth emoji and the word: Rubbish!

I'll see you at work.
It'll do you good.
I know. But like I said.
It won't cost much.
It'll be freezing.
Stop making excuses.
Pick somewhere warm and cheap and I'll think about it.
Fine.
Don't be like that.
Only kidding.

See you at work.

Night.

Heather returned to the chapter. She hadn't been entirely honest about disliking the cold. It was true, she despised it, but she also shunned the idea of any sort of holiday with Suzanne, even as she found her reaction churlish.

Alice was twenty-two when she stood poised to break away from the bonds of her family, shun her society girl lifestyle and set off into the world. If only she could figure out how. She had never been alone before, yet any fears and uncertainties she had were eclipsed by an unwavering resolve. She had in her sights a life spent saving souls and doing good works, something that made Heather groan. Worse, she described herself as a prize snob, seeking to carry out her missionary work in a fashion commensurate with her social standing. It was a choice that must have come as a great disappointment to her family. Through their eyes she would have appeared an extremist and one for which she was doomed to pay a high price. Despite three seasons, she had failed to find a husband. She was incapable of interacting socially with her party-loving contemporaries, her upright temperance and piety too off-putting. No one in the society scene would have been interested in being saved. She would have been a laughing stock.

'She was one of those Bible thumpers you talked about,' Heather said aloud, realising as she spoke that Hilary wasn't there. Not even as a ghost.

Do ghosts exist? She thought not, but she needed her aunt and she felt her presence nevertheless.

Heather didn't need Hilary to help her picture the sort of woman Alice was. With her degree in History, in which for her Honours year she wrote a dissertation on the rise of Feminism in Federation Australia and late Victorian Britain, Heather could easily imagine the situation Alice found herself in. She closed the book, drifting into reverie, picturing the Edwardian dress that she associated with that pivotal moment when history was forced to make way for women.

It was a reverie short-lived. Her mother was calling up the stairs. Heather set the autobiography on her desk and went down to dinner.

William and Joan were already seated at the table before plates of steamed fish and vegetables. Joan was on a diet, which meant the whole house was.

'Not like you to miss an aperitif,' William said jokingly, reaching for his glass. He had moved on to red. He proffered the bottle and Heather held out her glass.

'I'm rather involved in something.'

'So it would appear,' Joan said.

'Do tell.'

Heather doused her food with sesame oil and soy sauce to try to give it some flavour. She explained how Professor Foyle's collection had landed on her desk, and outlined the basic content, watching her mother's face as she said mentioned the New Age and the occult.

'Interesting provenance,' Joan said disinterestedly, cutting into her bok choy.

'The question with something like that is, where to start,' said William.

'With the manuscript, surely.'

'I was drawn to a box of books. I wanted to find out more about Alice Bailey. She was born Alice La Trobe-Bateman.'

'Fascinating. La Trobe-Bateman, did you say?'

'She's a third cousin of Charles La Trobe.'

'Really?'

Her parents both looked at her at once.

'Although he never knew her,' she said, suddenly self-conscious. 'She was born in 1880.'

'Charles died in 1875, in December, if I'm not mistaken.'

She wasn't.

'And what's so special about her?'

Heather didn't know where to start. 'Other than she was an aristocrat, from what I've gleaned so far as a young adult she wanted to do good works. Of the evangelical kind.'

'When was this?' Joan asked.

'1902.'

Joan set down her fork. 'Then she picked a good time to be an evangelist,' she said, raising her eyebrows and puckering her face. 'King Edward VII had taken the throne by then.'

'Philanthropy was thriving too,' Heather said, already regretting she had raised the topic at the dinner table, her mother poised to take the podium. She knew there'd be no stopping her.

'Philanthropy had been seen as an essential attribute among those who could afford it for a long time,' Joan said, putting down her fork and raising herself up in her seat. 'Largely due to the Protestant upper classes, like your La Trobe-Bateman woman, who saw it their duty to help the poor and disadvantaged. Of course, evangelism was expanding too, but that had more to do with the lower classes.'

Heather inhaled to speak, but Joan seemed bent on trumping her daughter's knowledge.

'The times would have made it easier for Alice in other ways,' she said authoritatively. 'The status of women was rising, and participation in social work was seen as an honourable pathway for those of the middle and upper classes.'

'Good works.'

'Yes, good works. They were viewed as a way for women to participate in life outside the home through an extension of their domestic and motherly duties. Ladies played a large role back then in fundraising; putting on dinners, banquets, and charity bazaars, that sort of thing.'

'Thanks, Mum,' Heather said, cutting in while trying to sound deferential. 'The trouble is, none of those roles would have held any appeal for Alice. She admits to having a talent for needlework, but her sensibilities were not stereotypically feminine. Besides, her religious zeal would never have been satisfied through the roles allotted to young ladies of social standing.'

She looked from her mother to her father. Both had turned their attention back to their food. She hesitated, not knowing whether to continue, but the urge to air her thoughts held sway.

'Her aspirations weren't all that revolutionary either. In fact, I find her to be rather conservative in her outlook.' She paused to sip her wine. 'I suppose her attitude is unsurprising given that she had led a sheltered life.'

'She must have known about women's rights though,' Joan said without looking up.

'Wasn't 1902 the year women gained the right to vote in Australia?' William said with his mouth full. Joan shot him a disparaging look.

'And be elected for national parliament,' Heather said, pleased to have a chance to show off her knowledge. 'We were the first country in the world to do so. It was also the year a delegation of women textile workers presented the British parliament with a petition carrying 37,000 signatures demanding suffrage for women.'

'They were heady times,' William said with an ironic ring in his voice.

Her mother made no comment. Heather inserted her fork into her fish and was about to take a mouthful when she changed her mind and continued. 'Alice makes no mention of the movement, other than to describe herself as not a feminist.'

'Fascinating,' her mother said, losing interest.

Making a valiant effort to eat her food, Heather took a mouthful of fish. She privately found Alice Bailey's silence on feminism notable in the light of her strong opinions on other matters that had thus far been peppered through her autobiography. 'She appears to belong to that cohort of women who generally prefer the company of men,' she said, thinking aloud. 'Those who believe any woman can achieve great heights if she puts her mind to it.'

'Conservative, as you say.'

'Very, by the sound of it,' her father added.

'I'm not so sure. Perhaps she found those political activists as distasteful as she did the evangelists with all their yelling and ranting. She didn't seem to like them much either.'

'She sounds far too well-groomed to belong to that set,' Joan said.

She was so unlike any historical figure Heather had ever held sympathy for, she succumbed to an all too familiar resentment at having been saddled with the collection. On reflection, she supposed she was already drawn into the narrative to some degree, and she couldn't go through all those boxes without knowing what the woman was about. Although mild interest was hardly going to carry her through the burden ahead of her.

# Ireland and India

At twenty-two, Alice stood on the threshold of independence, uncertain yet determined, carrying deep in her heart the knowledge that her life held a special purpose, and that someone, a man who wore a turban, would tell her what that purpose was all about. After all, it had been seven years since he walked into her aunt's drawing room at Castramont and scared the life out of her. He had told her to shape up. Which she had. She had done it for him and she was driven too, to prove to herself and the world that she was at least half as good as Lydia.

She'd been living near St Albans with her sister and their chaperone for three seasons. It was all gaiety and garden parties, luncheons and balls and she enjoyed herself to a degree. She didn't have a care or a worry. Everything was taken care of by her aunts, just as it had always been. Yet she harboured a craving for a life direction. Lydia had her life all mapped out. She was off to Edinburgh to study Medicine. Alice had no intention of following her sister into higher education. Nothing appeared to her duller. Besides, she wanted to go out into the world and be of some use. Uppermost, she wanted to save souls. Not the souls of wealthy young men. She had had enough of that sort, for their souls wouldn't be saved. They were as stubborn as donkeys.

One day, while she was packing up the Bibles after a service at her local church, a visiting clergyman, who had taken an interest in her situation, suggested she visit Elise Sandes in Ireland. 'You and she have much in common.'

'How so?'

'She's an evangelist and a philanthropist.'

The mention of evangelism repelled her.

'She sounds fascinating,' she said, trying not to sound disinterested.

'She's a lot more than that. She's set an example for us all. She runs soldiers' homes in garrison towns.'

'Why do the soldiers need homes? Don't they have families of their own?'

The man laughed and went on to explain to his naïve parishioner how things worked in the British Army. He talked of Miss Sandes, of how she established her first soldiers' home in Cork back in 1887, and how in the space of fifteen years, she managed to establish many more. 'Story has it the whole thing came about when Miss Sandes responded to a request to befriend a desperately unhappy soldier. Out of that friendship grew a remarkable life's work. She's an exceptional woman, Alice. There are now twenty-two homes in Ireland and another nine in India.'

'That many?'

'Indeed, there are. What's more, she only employs ladies like yourself. Ladies of good standing.'

'I've never heard of her,' Alice said doubtfully.

'Miss, there are hundreds of thousands of soldiers idle in those garrisons. If you want my opinion, they're a social and moral disaster. Those boys are looking for entertainment and finding it in pubs and houses of ill repute. All that drinking and gambling are sure to lead those men straight to hell.'

Alice absorbed his words, images of debauchery shading quickly into those of eternal damnation. 'How do I apply?' she said, yielding to a change of heart.

She wrote to Miss Sandes the following day, and her inquiry was well received. Once her sister was settled at university, she took whatever talents she had, along with her religious fervour, to the Elise Sandes soldier's home in Belfast.

She had travelled a good deal in her childhood, but other than in her earliest years when her father took his young family to live in Montreal, trips overseas had always been across the English Channel. Her journey over the Irish Sea to Belfast was much further and far less pleasing, and pulling in at the river port, she knew she had arrived at a city not dissimilar to the one she had just left. Liverpool and Belfast were both industrial centres, cities where the working classes went about their business, places filled with factories and slums as far as she could tell, and not a place for a refined young Edwardian lady. Standing on deck that early Monday morning, what she saw terrified her. She covered her mouth and her nose with a handkerchief, the air thick with industrial odours from nearby chimneys. She was confronted by the enormity of the ship building going on, the scaffolding, the gantries, the cranes, the gargantuan scale of operations all around her, and the throng of hardworking men in shabby suits and flat caps. They all looked far too rough to be saved, at least, by someone as refined as she.

As the ship passed by the vastest concatenation of scaffolding of all, she overheard the man next to her announce to his companion, 'There's an ocean liner in there. They're calling her the *Titanic*.'

Her own ship decanted and she was met by a polite young soldier who escorted her to the soldier's home in his gig. He was plain looking and had a thick accent and as he chatted she had to strain to understand him. She wondered where on earth he was taking her as she absorbed the city, the hubbub of people going about hither and thither, the young men on bicycles meandering by or loitering on street corners, the horse-drawn tramcars, the shops with cloth awnings flapping in the breeze.

The home was situated on Clifton Street, near Victoria Barracks, and when they pulled up outside she had to resist an urge to cry. Behind the home, the barracks were visible and comprised an austere three-storey building with rows of horridly small windows facing a vast quadrangle skirted by other buildings, all of them long and plain.

The entire complex resembled a prison. She took some comfort from the buildings on the opposite side of Clifton Street, a grand Methodist church and an equally grand-looking hall.

The soldier, Jimmy, helped her alight and collected her trunk and together they entered the home. There was no one about in the dim and cold interior that smelled faintly antiseptic, so he offered to show her around. He deposited her luggage in the hall and indicated upstairs where a large dormitory served for overnight accommodation.

'Should the men need it,' he said.

Downstairs, he led her into the coffee shop, a cavernous room containing rows of long benches, refectory style. A servery lined half the far wall, behind which were high shelves filled with crockery and pans. The room, functional and devoid of comfort, was empty.

'It's still early,' said Jimmy.

They stood in the doorway of the next room, given over to recreation and filled with smaller tables, each covered in a nice cloth. There were chairs, lots of chairs, some of them occupied by men in army fatigues stealing glances her way.

'The men come in here to write letters, play games, or just to sit and read. Some play pool,' he said, gesturing at a large table covered in green baize.

Another door led to the Gospel room, complete with harmonium, hymn books and Bibles. Rows of seats faced a small platform where someone would expound the Scriptures.

On their way back to the main hall, they encountered a woman who introduced herself as Miss Fry. She was young and petite and had a surprisingly loud voice.

Without further ado, she escorted Alice to their separate and modest ladies' quarters adjoining the home. Her room appeared no larger than a cupboard and the furniture was plain. Miss Fry responded to the look of dismay on Alice's face and, drawing close she said, 'You'll get used to it.'

What had she expected? She knew her childhood days were over, that the society lifestyle was behind her too, but she hadn't anticipated leaving it all would result in quite such a resounding thump. She prayed that night, pleading prayers, seeking God's guidance, His strength.

She needn't have fretted. Miss Fry was right. She fitted in nicely, making friends and acquiring the skills needed for the work. She especially enjoyed circulating tables in the recreation room and the cafeteria. Each would often contain hundreds of soldiers. She befriended the lonely, the fed up, the homesick. She would sit with them, play checkers, and let them know she cared and wanted to help. She did it all with a warm smile and a gentle manner. She was cautioned to retain her reserve and so she did, never once slipping into impropriety, no matter how flirtatious the men were. It was a habit that came easy to her, for she was a snob to her core and she was unreflective about it.

A few weeks into her stay, she faced leading her first Gospel meeting. The night before, she sat up on her single bed—squashed up against the wall of her drab little low-ceilinged room—with her Bible open beside her, drawing on the times she had spoken at prayer meetings and led Bible study. She crafted something she imagined suitable and read it over a few times. Satisfied, she set her speech down on the floor and snuggled into her bed. She slept soundly that night, filled with self-assurance.

It wasn't until she was standing up on the Gospel room platform empty handed in front of a few hundred soldiers—not exactly a sympathetic audience of well-wishers and religious devotees—that she realised how misguided that self-assurance had been. She didn't get far into her speech before her mind went blank. She could recall nothing, not one skerrick of what she had written. She stared into a sea of expectant faces, stricken. Her pulse raced. Her vision blurred. She burst into tears and fled the platform, vowing she would leave the espousing to her colleague, Miss Fry, who had no trouble at all with that big voice of hers. She decided then and there she would never, not ever become accustomed to leading a Gospel meeting.

Yet she was a determined sort, she had inherited that from her grandfather, and after a few weeks, she made a second attempt. In the hope of averting another catastrophe, in the time she had at her disposal in the hours before bed and in the early morning, she assiduously memorised her speech, pacing back and forth, notes in hand, reciting line by line every word. She stood by the little bedroom window, looking out at the Methodist church and the hall, imagining all the espousing going on in both buildings, drawing fortitude from all those arched windows, all that heavy stone. Line by line she practised until she thought she knew the speech backwards.

The following day, she stood on the platform of the Gospel room thinking things were going well. She began to relax. She would get through it. Yes, yes, she would. She reached midway. Now for the poem. The first verse was already in her mind. She recited the words with ease. The second came to her as well, but as she said the words of the first line the rest faded away. She stood, dumbstruck, not daring to catch the expectant gazes of her audience. A soldier at the back, who apparently knew the poem, spoke up, offering to fill in the blanks while she gathered her composure. But she didn't have it in her to let that happen. Panic took hold. She bolted from the stage before the men had a chance to burst into an uproar of laughter.

That night, she lay awake in her bed in a fit of melodramatic despair.
What was the matter with her?
Miss Fry had no problem at all.
Miss Fry wasn't gripped by anxiety.
Miss Fry didn't lie in bed at night agonising over what she had said. What did she have that Alice lacked? She hadn't a clue.

Still, she refused to give up. Week after week, Sunday upon Sunday, she took the platform.

Then one night, as she prepared for her talk, pacing back and forth reading over her notes, fighting back the nauseating anxiety that would hold her in its grasp before and after each and every Gospel meeting she gave, she stopped in her tracks and put down the speech, asking herself why Miss Fry never suffered the same. What was it about Miss Fry that meant she could espouse so eloquently and without fear? Then, she saw it in a flash. Miss Fry didn't feel anxious because Miss Fry didn't care a fig about how she came across. There was not a speck of self-consciousness in her delivery. She lost herself to the moment, gave herself to the audience, read their needs and responded to them.

Whereas she, Miss La Trobe-Bateman, was far too self-conscious, and she was far too self-conscious because she was much too self-centred. If she put others first like Miss Fry then maybe her confidence would grow.

The next day in the Gospel room, she tried focusing on her audience, connecting with them instead of worrying about how she was coming across. It worked, not completely, but she thought with time and practice that it would.

Despite her impediment, word went around that Alice was good at her job. So much so that Miss Sandes invited her to the Artillery Practice Camp in Kildare. Miss Sandes had opened the home a few years before and needed an assistant. And Miss Fry was fond of saying wild horses wouldn't get her anywhere near the place.

Kildare was nothing like Belfast. It was all vast plains of vivid green, with copses and hedgerows and whitewashed houses with grey slate roofs. The day she arrived a wild wind was blowing. Travel weary, she stood down from her carriage to face the most forthright and practical woman she had ever met. Her aunt Margaret hadn't a patch on Miss Sandes. Even a glimpse revealed a powerhouse of commitment. She was tall, big boned, with a robust pallor and shrewd eyes and Alice adored her in an instant.

The home was arranged in much the same fashion and Alice settled into her new accommodation shared with her mentor. In the weeks that followed, under Miss Sandes' watchful eye, she went about her duties as she had in Belfast, baking buns, bookkeeping, arranging flowers, writing letters for the soldiers, taking Gospel meetings and leading prayers.

One cool and blustery summer's day, Miss Sandes summoned Alice to her office. A letter had arrived from Miss Theodora Schofield in India, announcing she was unwell and needed to return home to rest.

'I've been expecting this, Miss La-Trobe-Bateman,' Miss Sandes said, acknowledging her entry with a rustle of the letter. 'Miss Schofield has been in charge of the soldiers' homes in India for some years, having taken over from Miss Ashe. The climate is quite harsh over there, and the workload heavy. Miss Ashe has had to come home to recuperate on many occasions. Now it's Miss Schofield's turn.'

Miss Sandes looked up from the letter. She studied Alice as though she were a specimen in a jar. 'I need to send someone to replace her.' She pressed her lips together and emitted a long sigh. 'Unfortunately, there is no one with sufficient experience.' She set the letter down on her desk and swung round in her seat, putting a hand on each knee. 'But without someone to oversee the homes, there is no telling what chaos they'll fall into.'

'What will you do?' Alice said, fearing Miss Sandes was about to announce she would go herself.

'I have no choice.' Hesitation flickered across her face. 'I must send you.'

'Me?'

'You'll simply have to do, won't you?'

'Thank you, Miss Sandes,' Alice breathed, her chest filled with a mix of terror and delight. 'I won't let you down.'

She hadn't a clue what she was about to step into. She knew nothing of India other than it was far away and some people wore turbans. If she had, she might never have gone. Yet even from the moment she agreed to Miss Sandes' request, providence, fate, or perhaps it was serendipity crept in to propel her forwards. The first in a long line of incidences that spoke of some kind of inner guidance at play was the unexpected arrival of the necessary funds for her dispatch.

Lydia and Aunt Agnes saw Alice off at Tilbury Docks for the three-week voyage to Bombay. Alice stood alone on deck, all proud in her brand-new dress, her voluminous dark hair swept up from her face.

She was an attractive woman, with soft brown eyes beneath self-assured eyebrows, and lips that broke into the warmest of smiles. Yet for all those months working in the homes, she hadn't lost an ounce of her snobbery or her religious piety. As she entered the lounge, she was affronted by what she considered to be the loose morality of her travelling companions.

There were two other women and five men on board. Alice had the choice of remaining all day and night in her cabin, or being social. Finding the cabin cramped, she chose the latter, and was forced to condone the men drinking and playing cards. She listened to their talk of racing cars and gambling. She sat to dinner with them on the first night, aghast that no one, other than she, said grace.

By breakfast the next day, she could endure their company no longer. They had filtered in all chummy camaraderie, and before the other ladies appeared, Alice seized her chance to tell them what she thought. She was quaking, nerves threatening to choke her, but she spoke regardless.

'Gentlemen, since I am not a gambler or a dancer or a drinker or a card player I really ought to be seated somewhere else.'

One of the men stood immediately. Bemused, Alice took the hand he proffered. 'Miss, we will promise to be good in your company and hope we can be friends. Mr Ewan Pargiter, at your service.'

'Miss La Trobe-Bateman. Alice.'

From that moment on, they were gracious and polite and at the end of the passage, Mr Pargiter drew her aside and pressed a first-class rail pass into her gloved hand.

'I really couldn't.'

'You must. You'll need it, by all accounts.'

Alice arrived in Bombay two decades before E.M. Forester wrote *A Passage to India*, and over two decades after founding Theosophists Madame Helena Petrovna Blavatsky and Colonel Henry Steel Olcott had made their spiritual foray into the continent. Unlike her esoteric forebears, who had engaged with society both Indian and British, for the duration of her stay Alice would remain cosseted inside the British

Army. She wasn't to know it then that the current head of the Theosophical Society, Annie Besant, was busy at work in Adyar, Chennai, far away in the southeast.

The port of Bombay was a confusion of colour and majestic buildings and throngs of men in white, many of them wearing small hats and some with turbans. The scene, the strange smells, the noises, the thick heat, it was a wall of vibrant intensity like nothing she had encountered before and she found it hard to take it all in.

As she disembarked she asked Mr Pargiter for directions to the ticket office. He was a dapper man in a linen suit, and he insisted on coming with her. She needed to confirm her board onto another ship bound for Karachi and collect her ticket, but instead, when she made her request she was handed a telegram. The note informed her that she was not to travel to Quetta as planned, but to make her way to Meerut instead.

Meerut?

She hadn't a clue how to get there. Before she left Ireland, Miss Sandes had furnished her with an explanation of the situation in India. She said the homes were run along the same lines as those in Ireland and the main challenge was getting around between them all. They were arranged in the north of India along two axes, the first stretching between Lucknow to Peshawar and up to Khyber, the second from Bombay through Mhow to Quetta. The homes serviced the British Army garrisons that had been relocated to defend the North-West Frontier against a Russian invasion via Afghanistan. She reassured Alice that she would be quite safe, although already, Alice wasn't so sure.

Her bottom lip quivered and she had to fight back the tears. How ever did this Miss Schofield think it was satisfactory to change her plans? Mr Pargiter was also at a loss, and after telling her she could get there by train he said he was terribly sorry to leave her stranded but he had one of his own to catch.

She was on the verge of booking her return passage to London when a refined looking lady entered the office and asked the man behind the counter if he could spare some change. As she handed him a note, she glanced at Alice inquiringly and with much relief the young man explained her situation on her behalf.

'You better come with me,' the woman said. 'We have a YWCA right around the corner. You look like you could do with a cup of tea.'

Relief swept through her.

She arrived in Meerut to the briefest of handovers from a tired and ill Miss Schofield, who explained she hadn't the strength to travel to Quetta as pre-arranged, and apologised for the telegram. The following day she was on her way to Quetta, a journey involving several trains. In daylight, when she wasn't sleeping Alice absorbed the verdant landscapes of the plains and the Himalayan foothills, and when the train pulled in at a station there would be swarms of men, women and children, a clamour of activity and trade. Exotic smells greeted her through open windows. She saw elephants and water buffalo and odd-looking carriages. As the journey wore on the scenery changed to desert. The mountains were rugged and barren. She might have thought she were arriving at the very edge of civilisation when at last the final train made a long ascent, entering a vast elevated valley cradled by mountains that towered in the distance all around.

It was sunset when the train came to a hissing, clunking halt at Quetta station. Eager for stillness and quiet, Alice stepped onto the platform in her Edwardian dress, pure, chaste and God-abiding and filled with optimism.

At Quetta, like all the homes, the running fell to two ladies, along with two managers, usually ex-soldiers, who were in charge of the coffee shop and general maintenance. Only one lady was present at Quetta and Alice saw by her harried manner and breathless gratitude that she had no authority whatsoever over the men.

Later, when Alice walked into the coffee shop to find a gang of soldiers running amok she knew she had to take action and fast. They were hurling the fried eggs and cocoa they'd ordered at the walls which were already streaked in yellow and brown. She raised her hand

and called out but the men took no notice. She stood on a chair and raised her voice and this time the men paused to jeer before carrying on with greater enthusiasm.

Realising her presence made things worse, she left them to it.

How ever would she cope? She hadn't a clue.

Days passed as she considered her options. She could banish the culprits but that went against the principles of the homes. She could visit the barracks and ask a major to intervene but that would do nothing to instil respect and obedience and might serve to alienate the men. The only other action she could think of was to befriend the ringleaders. She had no idea if it would work but she would give it a try. Thinking a change of setting was in order, she decided on a picnic.

She sent out the invitations for the following day and all came along on the promise of cake. They sat around on a rug in a park beneath the canopy of a large tree. As they ate and drank, she asked their names and if they knew any jokes.

'Not ones for your ears, Miss,' Paul said, biting into his cake.

The others sniggered.

'Well, tell me what's the worst thing you ever did as a child.'

They took it in turns to share their naughty tales of childhood.

'I've a better one. I flushed my governess's jewellery down the lavatory.'

'You never did.'

'It's true. Every last scrap. Bracelets, necklaces, rings, the lot.'

'Why? You must have had good reason.'

'Could there ever be?' She laughed. 'The truth is I had an awful temper. I was terrified I'd get found out and be forced to scour the sewers and fish it all out.'

There was an uproar of laughter. By the end of the outing she knew by their friendly manner she'd won the men over but she had no idea to what extent.

The next day she entered the coffee shop to find those ringleaders cleaning and painting the walls.

She was relieved more than triumphant. She'd managed to make a good decision. It would be one of many she faced in the years to follow as she made long and arduous journeys from home to home, dealt with correspondence and laboured over the accounts, talked to the ladies and the managers, sorted out all the problems, visited the dying in hospital and gave Gospel meeting after Gospel meeting. The homes were popular, feeding five or six hundred men each evening in the coffee shops. Making her heavy schedule even more difficult, the decisions she had to make in the course of her responsibilities filled her with uncertainty. She lacked the self-assurance and the experience to sit comfortably in her overseer role and was prone to blaming herself if things went wrong. Yet she executed her responsibilities with diligence and without complaint, even as she was affected by the climate as were her colleagues and the men, especially in the monsoon. She quickly discovered that few acclimatised to the strange and exotic land that was India.

One evening in Chakrata, tired of the millionth game of checkers and wondering if there wasn't a better way to entertain the men, she eyed the piano in the corner of the room. She was a young Edwardian lady who could play the piano and sing. She loved to sing. She had been told she had a good voice too. She knew hymns and the favourite songs of the day. She left the table and crossed the room, opened the lid and played a song. Then another. The room fell into silence as she played. At the end of each song the applause was deafening. She soon found she was a consummate performer. What began as something tentative quickly became a habit. Night after night she would entertain the men with her songs. No one had seen anything like it, at least, not from a Gospel preaching evangelist in a white dress and a pretty blue satin sash.

The soldiers and the officers loved her. She was having a marvellous time. She was well-known and much loved by all of the forty regiments she worked with. The affection was reciprocated. She enjoyed the company of the men and they enjoyed her. Some of the men had a special name for her, too. They called her 'china'. She had no idea what that meant except she knew it was a term of endearment.

The missionary work satisfied her most. Feeding bellies was one thing, feeding souls another.

She had always been devout. She had swallowed with an insatiable hunger all the doctrine she was taught. Her version of Christianity was absolute and unequivocal. There was simply no other way to God.

One day, as they were walking through the grounds, her personal bearer, Bugaloo, a wiry man with large eyes and a broad smile, spoke to her of a religion far more ancient than her own. They were in Ambala opening a soldiers' home. It was evening but still hot and a light wind rustled the nearby trees. As Bugaloo spoke of his own faith with its unique pathway to God, she filtered his words through her own doctrine, dismissing as heathen everything he told her. Then, she stopped in her tracks. Something compelled her to listen to his words, and as she listened she saw through his eyes all the millions and millions of people in India, and indeed the world over who had never heard of Christianity. It suddenly occurred to her that the world had teemed with people before the birth of Christianity. Surely even her vengeful God hadn't damned the whole lot of them to hell?

Doubt crept into her religious edifice like a feather blowing in through a window that had opened just a crack.

It would take a lot more than a feather to shake the foundations of her faith. Dogma still filled her to the brim, taking the place of her mother, her father, her grandfather, stability, security, a hearth. Her faith was all she had to hold on to. It was her fortress. She wasn't about to let it go any time soon.

In the months that followed she travelled again to Quetta. As the train rattled across the desert she decided it was about time she delivered a lecture on hell. She'd never lectured on hell before. It had always seemed to her an abhorrent topic and she had been avoiding coming out with her interpretation of that infernal place, even though she was certain it existed. No more.

In Quetta she read and researched and devised her talk. A fire and brimstone lecture on the nature of hell it would be, filled with warnings of a God poised to smite the heathens. She stood before hundreds of men in the Gospel room and espoused with consuming passion. On and on she raved.

She didn't notice the men leaving. She was so caught up in her own head, so full of her own righteous importance, she failed to see the men stand up one by one and walk out. When she finally did look around, only a handful of the faithful remained. She was devastated. One of them took it upon himself to tell her that the men had left because they didn't want to hear her lies.

Lies?

It was an unconscionable thought. How could the Bible teach lies? At first, she rejected the notion, but that exodus created a cauldron of doubt, doubt that insinuated itself into the foundations of her faith, small cracks at first, cracks that deepened and widened until her religious edifice threatened to tumble.

After her failed hell lecture, she began to question the purpose of converting souls to the faith. The thought nagged at her, day and night, waiting in the wings of her awareness to consume her as she went about her day.

In 1906, after four years in India, Alice found the workload heavier than ever. She seemed to be losing her strength. One morning, she woke with a headache. She ignored it at first but as she opened her Bible to prepare for a Gospel meeting later in the day, her head began to throb as though someone was in there kneading her brain, sending sharp flashes skittering in her skull. She felt dizzy and nauseous. She dragged herself back to her room, drew the curtains and lay down.

She remained on her back, unable to move for four days. When the headache eased, she relinquished her bed to fulfil her duties.

She thought no more of it until a few weeks later when the headache returned with force. Again, she returned to her bed, waited for the pain to subside and the instant it did she was up on her feet.

The third time the headache came she sent for a doctor. After a brief examination, he told her she was exhausted. She knew that. He prescribed bed rest. She ignored the advice and carried on working. She carried on because she wanted to please Miss Sandes. She carried on because wanted to prove her worth in her own eyes, the eyes of her family and in the eyes of God. How could she stop when there were so many souls to save? It never occurred to her that she had martyred herself to the role.

The monsoon, it is said, is intense enough to send any white person mad, never mind a frail, naïve aristocrat, of some twenty-six years, filled to the brim with the Bible she no longer unequivocally trusted.

One hot night in Lucknow, she was unable to sleep. After pacing back and forth in her room, she went out to her veranda only to find it filled with mosquitos. She withdrew. Moments later, she was standing by her dressing table when a broad shaft of light entered the room. Then she heard a voice. A voice that seemed to belong to no one but she instantly took it to belong to the man in the turban who had come to her when she was fifteen. She listened. The voice told her the work he had marked out for her would start, but at first, she would be unable to recognise it.

His visit provided an anchor, reminding her that the task he had planned was still ahead of her. It wasn't running soldiers' homes, that was clear. Hopefully whatever he had in mind wouldn't be anywhere near as onerous as the last few years.

The workload, the doubts, the migraines worsened. She had exhausted her reserves. Her spiritual crisis had rent her open and she was a living breathing wound. All that emotional steam was mirrored in the thick heat of the monsoon. How would she carry on?

After dealing with a pile of correspondence one afternoon, she sat down at a table in the reading room and stared into the eyes of the most handsome man she had ever seen. There was something magnetic in his gaze, in the turn of his lips, in the timbre of his voice, in his being altogether. She couldn't stop the colour rising in her cheeks.

'I haven't seen you in here before,' she said. 'Are you with the Hussars?'

'That I am. Private Walter Evans.' He held out his hand.

'Checkers?' she said.

'If we must.'

They chatted. She discovered he was handsome, educated and clever. He was all charm and gallantry. In the weeks that followed she talked to him of God, of Jesus. She told him if he opened his heart to God he would be saved. He attended her Gospel lectures and hung on her every word, a convert.

If he had any flaws she couldn't see them. His attentiveness to her every need convinced her of his love for her well before he expressed it. Her love for him grew more ardent by the day and with it grew an equally powerful sense of doom. Theirs was a love forbidden and she was terrified of being found out.

Alice had a problem. The ladies working at the soldiers' homes had been carefully selected from aristocratic backgrounds in order that there be many degrees of class separation between them and the soldiers of the British army. A lady could not fall in love with a man in the ranks. Marriage was out of the question. She had taken on that rule as an absolute. She was beside herself. She'd made a commitment to Miss Sandes. The homes were her mission.

At the end of the monsoon, as she was closing a home in the Himalayan foothills, she could bear the strain no longer and called Walter to her office and told him things had to end.

'I'm sorry, Walter, but I am sure you understand.'

'As you wish,' he said politely, but she could see the disappointment in his face.

Watching him walk away she felt as though part of her had gone with him and she was left bereft.

She made it back down to the plains before collapsing. There, she was put on a train to Delhi and another to Bombay and passage back to Britain was arranged. She cried the entire trip home, and was forced to spend many months convalescing back at her aunt Margaret's at Castramont.

Her body recovered but her heart did not. The enchantment grew and grew and her melancholy along with it. She was lovesick. Lovesick and determined. Perhaps her earnest nature, no longer shored up by religion, took over her sanity. All she knew was she needed to find a way of marrying Walter without offending her family. Finding her aunt Margaret of little help, she persuaded Margaret's father-in-law's sister to intervene.

As head of Church of Scotland deaconesses, Aunt Alice had considerable authority and influence. Since Walter Evans was born into a lower-class family with no servants in Brotton, an ironstone mining village in the county of Redcar, the marriage was unsuitable. Yet he was about to be discharged from the army, and seeing an opportunity to ally her niece's distress, Aunt Alice arranged for him to travel to the United States and take a Theology course. He was to become an Episcopal clergyman, rendering him an acceptable match in the eyes of her family. Duly dispatched, the couple would be far enough away from the attention of her social milieu to avert gossip. Reassured, Alice returned to India. As the weeks dragged by, her migraines became so severe two colonels arranged for her passage back to England.

# An Inheritance

Heather had never cared for wearing suits. They made her feel stiff in her skin, as though she were on trial or being assessed in a job interview. She wore one anyway, out of respect. It was the same suit she had worn for the funeral, brightened up with a pale green blouse and matching scarf. She sat, swallowed in one of the heavy, leather-bound chairs in the family lawyer's office. Her mother was sitting squarely beside her. Behind them, seated in a row of wooden chairs that had been brought in from another room, were three of Hilary and Joan's cousins on their mother's side, all women in their sixties whom Heather had scarcely ever met. Heather felt crowded despite the size of the room. Before them, the partners desk of polished mahogany with its weathered top spoke of social prominence, as did the floor to ceiling shelves of law books lining the back wall. Behind the desk, swamped in a swivel chair too large for his frame, Mr Fenston, a doddery man well-past retirement who had been representing the family for decades, observed his audience through rimless glasses.

Heather had taken a day's compassionate leave after Joan insisted all the beneficiaries were present at the reading of the will. Hilary had appointed Mr Fenston as executor, which had upset Joan, who thought the role should have fallen to her. Heather wasn't sure what to think, although judging by her mother's irascible mood that morning, she feared if things were not favourable, Joan would even consider contesting Hilary's wishes. It was a sickening thought.

Mr Fenston read out the bequests in order of significance. Cousin Beverly was to have Hilary's dog, a cocker spaniel who went by the name of Stanton, along with a sum of fifteen thousand dollars to cover his expenses. She had been looking after Stanton since Hilary's death, and the bequest put a seal of approval on the dog's new master.

Maureen inherited all of Hilary's fine china and antique bric-a-brac that she had been bequeathed by her mother, Agnes, who had inherited the collection of antiques from her sister, Maureen's mother Margaret. The shunting of the china in this fashion seemed to complete a circle, and judging by the murmur of satisfaction behind her, Maureen felt the same.

Joan shifted in her seat. She seemed put out by the bequest but remained tight-lipped. Maureen's sister Veronica, was next in line. She was to receive Hilary's car, a brand-new Subaru.

When Joan heard her name, she stared intently at Mr Fenston who didn't look up. She was to receive all of Hilary's jewellery, he said, including the family heirlooms once owned by their grandmother Katharine. It was quite a cache, Heather knew. When she was young and curious she had tried much of it on, dipping into Hilary's jewellery box as though it were treasure. There were vintage gold necklaces, replete with rubies and diamonds, along with earrings and exquisite brooches. It felt strange to her that all the gold she had worn against her skin, gold worn by Hilary and Katharine before her—the two most significant women in her life—would go to her mother. It was with a renewed sense of loss that she realised she had hoped the jewellery would be hers. At least Joan seemed satisfied, but when Mr Fenston paused and cleared his throat, the room began to stir.

He flashed a wary eye over his audience before reading out the last of the will.

'The remaining estate, including the property at 21 Bowler Street and all its chattels, I bequeath to my niece, Heather Katharine Brown.'

There was a long pause. Heather could scarcely take in the meaning of the words. She sensed the jealousy emanating from all four women. It was palpable. It occurred to her they had all been hoping the estate would be divided up between them. 'Thank you very much Mr Fenston,' Beverly said eventually. 'We better get going then. Maureen, Veronica.' She led her sisters out the room.

'At least she didn't leave it to a dog's home,' Maureen muttered, closing the door behind her.

There was a titter of false laughter in the hall. No congratulations. Nothing. Heather was astonished.

'I have no idea how all this works,' she said to Mr Fenston.

'I shouldn't worry,' her mother said. 'Mr Fenston will take care of everything, I'm sure.'

Mr Fenston got up to show them out. 'I will be in touch.' As he opened the door, another opened in Heather's imagination, and she experienced a small thrill as she glimpsed a new life, a proper chance at long last to move out of the family home.

She followed her mother out onto the street and stood to one side, watching her rummage through her handbag.

'You seem upset,' Heather said.

'We'll talk about this at home, I think, Heather.' Her tone was curt, her demeanour uptight. The will had obviously not satisfied her. What had she been expecting? That the house be left to her instead?

Annoyance reared up in her heart and, seeing the sign for the train station on the other side of the street, she told her mother she was heading into work.

'You've a day off.'

'I have things to attend to.'

'Suit yourself, but don't think you can avoid a conversation that has to happen.'

'Don't you want me to have the house?'

'It isn't my decision, obviously.'

'No, it was Hilary's,' Heather said.

'I will not talk further about this in the street,' Joan said between gritted teeth. 'For heaven's sake!'

Heather responded by crossing the road, taking advantage of a gap in the traffic.

At the station, a train pulled up as she reached the platform and she was at her desk in the State Library within the half hour.

Shut in the privacy of her office, the tears she had been fighting back made rivulets down her cheeks. Her heart made a fist in her chest. She shuddered, rummaging in her bag for a tissue to wipe her face. She pulled out a pack of ten, which suddenly seemed woefully insufficient. She sat there for a while, struggling to stem the flow, the tissues forming a mass of crumpled soggy white in her bin.

Suzanne was right. She did need a distraction. She put on her reading glasses thinking she would scroll through real estate sites on her computer. It was a kind of defiance, as though through her will Hilary had effectively booted her out of the family nest and she better get on with it. She got as far as entering Ballarat in the search bar when her glasses fogged. Another tissue, the last in the pack, and she was back, thinking about the reading of the will.

That morning had been worse than the funeral. The relatives were like vultures, circling for carrion scraps. Yet none of them had been kind to Hilary when she was alive. They had regarded her a failure, partly because she was an intellectual with otherworld interests, and partly because she had never married. There was speculation she might have had a secret lover of her own gender. Heather thought that had never been the case, but it would not have mattered to her if it had. She missed her aunt intensely and would always think fondly of her lovely little home. For a fleeting moment, she even thought of keeping it, but she couldn't have borne the energy, the presence of her aunt in every nook and cranny.

Hilary's house in Bowler Street was nothing like the splendid homes of Harcourt Street. Situated on the south side of the railway line, it was a humble, rendered-brick cottage built in the 1930s on a narrow block. The size and location had given Joan the opportunity to treat Hilary like a poor relation, something she had done, subtly, as often as she dared. Yet that Bowler Street house would still be worth at least a million dollars and her aunt had owned it unencumbered by debt.

Hilary was not the sort of woman to incur debt. She had paid off the house loan decades before. She may not have had much by way of superannuation, and had to rely on the state pension for her day-to-day existence, but she had had savings and considered herself comfortable, which she was.

Heather thought of her own savings, which had seemed sufficient to purchase something modest in the outlying towns around the city. She put on her glasses and continued scrolling. Places like Gisborne, where Suzanne lived, or Ballarat. A lot of people were heading out to Ballarat. She was drawn to the country town after discovering the number of heritage-listed buildings there dating back to the mid-1800s. Now she could purchase a property almost anywhere in Melbourne, outside of suburbs with a Toorak price tag. But she didn't want to move east, into that sprawling wasteland of housing estates. Or to the Dandenong Ranges, which was too damp for her asthma. The peninsula was out, the distance tyrannical. Much over an hour on the train she considered beyond the pale. Which left Ballarat, with its rolling green countryside and its relative proximity and affordability.

The office door opened on the knock, and Suzanne poked her head in.

'We weren't expecting to see you today. How did it go?"

'Fine,' she said without taking her eyes off her computer screen.

'Clearly not, then. I have to drop off a bunch of files downstairs. Back in a tick.'

Heather wished she would stay away. Although she needed a distraction other than online house hunting.

She scanned the top shelf beside the door where all those blue, leather-bound books that she had catalogued and should have dispatched into circulation remained. Unlike the volumes on witchcraft, which she had recorded last week as an easy task, dispatching all into the library's main collection. It had been straightforward, there being no attendant magazines, notes or papers, presumably because Professor Foyle was a tidy sort and her book on Wicca had already been published. Having dealt expeditiously with the Wicca portion of the collection, she felt satisfied. She had emptied seven boxes. Barely a dent in the collection, but satisfying to be rid of the hocus pocus nevertheless.

She had no intention of setting to work on her day off and began to wonder why she'd come into work. It had been an impulse, nothing more, the library a sanctuary despite her feelings of being put upon.

She opened the top drawer of her desk. She had tucked *The Unfinished Autobiography* beneath her clothbound notebook, having finished the chapter on Alice Bailey's time as a missionary in India deciding the life of an evangelist was not her thing. Yes, the poor woman suffered a nervous breakdown but she had brought it on herself. In modern parlance, she had burnt out. She sounded like the sort of do-gooding stalwart who opened schools in Africa. Good, without a doubt, but blinkered. It was her way or the highway.

Then again, Alice Bailey had achieved something. Whereas she, Heather Brown, what had she achieved? Little, because she had never thought to achieve anything much. Ambition was not in her nature. Her life had always been circumscribed by her family and her place in it, by Hilary, and by her work at the state library, which she had to admit she acquiesced to, despite the resentment she harboured. She was lumbered with the Foyle collection no one else wanted because she didn't assert herself. She had always been too scared of what might happen if she did. The timid don't get on in life. She felt insipid, underdone, inadequate. She ought to at least think about achieving something in her life instead of forever archiving the achievements of others.

Alice Bailey was undeniably brave, going off to India in her twenties, travelling the vast distances between the homes. It was a mission and she threw herself into it, but it was not *her* mission, it was Miss Sandes'. Life, through mysterious visions, pointed elsewhere. Heather began to wonder what became of her next.

'Coffee!' Heather quickly closed her drawer as Suzanne barged in holding two takeaway cups. She handed one to Heather, set down her own, shunted a box to one side and sat down on the bench in its place. Heather had the only chair.

'Shona has me checking Rosie's collection,' Suzanne said without preface.

She stared at Heather through impassive eyes. She was a tall, fair-haired woman in her fifties. She had a no-nonsense manner and Heather found out long before that when Suzanne had an idea, she was a train pulling out of a station. The listener had no choice but to wait until she arrived at her destination.

'The new girl?' Heather said tentatively.

'I honestly don't know what H and R were thinking. That flibbity jibbit won't last long. Too busy examining her nail polish. She's made a total shemozzle of the Bertram manuscript collection. The original order is lost. I don't know what she was doing when she was training but she certainly wasn't paying attention. She managed the books, and that's about it. Any fool can deal with the books. Shona's furious.' She paused and pointed at the blue books on the shelf by the door. 'Those shouldn't be there by the way. You've already logged them in the system. They should be out on the stacks.'

'I doubt anyone will be interested.'

'You never know.' She took a slurp of coffee. 'I'm putting in a complaint.'

Alarm rippled through her before she realised Suzanne was talking about Rosie.

'Doesn't sound like you need to.'

'Not to Shona. To human resources. That girl should never have been hired. They need to tighten their criteria.'

A siren bellowed in the street below. Suzanne turned to stare out the window. She drank her coffee as she watched. 'Ambulance,' she said after a long pause. 'Idiots not getting out of the way.'

She looked back to the room, taking in the contents as if for the first time, her eyes settling on Heather's face. There was no avoiding the conversation she came in to have.

'She left me her house,' Heather said flatly.

'Her house! Details, please.'
'It's a small cottage in Hawthorn East.'
'There are no small cottages in Hawthorn East.'
'You're mistaken.'
'By my comment I meant cheap. Your phrasing makes your aunt's house sound diminutive, like a shack.'

Suzanne was fishing. Heather knew there was no downplaying the reality of its worth. She took a slow sip of coffee, keeping hold of the cup. She never put food or drink on her desk when there was even one scrap of paper relating to a collection on its surface.

'Mortgage?'
'No.'
'You're a millionaire then. Congratulations.'
'So are you, Suzanne.'
'It's all tied up in real estate. Meaningless, as you know.'
'Do I? My inheritance will end up the same.'
'Doesn't have to. You still planning on moving to Ballarat?'
'I think I'll love it there.'
'Then you can put a fair bit of whatever you end up with into your superannuation. Or invest. I can put you on to a financial planner if you like.'

Heather eyed her friend. She was in one of her fiercely practical moods, abstracted yet engaged, as though Heather's life presented a situation that needed to be fixed, forthwith, in theory at least and regardless of practicalities, contingencies or, indeed, Heather's feelings.

'I'll think about it,' she said, hoping that would be the end of things, even as she realised Suzanne hadn't quite rounded off her thoughts.

'I think putting it all into a house would be stupid in your position. It's not like you need a great big place. You're single, and childless.'

And you are blunt, she thought but didn't say. She drank more of her coffee. Suzanne did the same.

'This solves all your problems. You must be over the moon.'
'It hasn't sunk in yet.'
'I bet the others are jealous. Who was there?'

Heather filled her in. 'Mum wants to talk to me. She's furious.'

'I bet she is. Don't let them manipulate you. That money is yours.' She slid off the bench. 'Right. Back to it, then.' She drained her cup and made to leave, pausing in the doorway on her way out. 'About that holiday.'

'Daylesford's too cold.'

'Not Daylesford, then.'

The door clunked shut. Heather took another a sip of her coffee. It had gone tepid. She put Suzanne's empty cup in the bin and put hers on the floor beside it. Then she glanced up at the bookshelf. Suzanne was right. Those books did belong out on the stacks. But she had no intention of moving them. Instead she slid open her desk drawer and extracted the autobiography, thinking she might as well find out how things went with Walter Evans.

# From Cincinnati to Monterey

In India, Miss La Trobe-Bateman had been adored, looked up to. She remained a snob and she was unapologetic about it. There were degrees of separation between herself and her kind, the aristocracy, and the people beneath her, from lowly servants through various trades and professionals, and she regarded them all indiscriminately. What was she doing marrying beneath her station? Her love-struck state wouldn't let her ponder that. Her love for Walter was all-consuming as was his love for her. Hadn't he written to her almost every day from the seminary in Cincinnati, words of ardent affection?

The wedding was held in a private chapel, not the grand affair of her parents who had married in St Margaret's Church in Westminster, but it all seemed good enough to her, so desperately did she love her beau. No one else shared her view. Not her family, whose discouraging looks only made her more determined, nor her servants, who had no right to warn her that Walter was no good.

After a brief and awkward visit to her in-laws, they headed to America, Alice brimming with excitement and wonder all the way to the boarding house where Walter had a room on the top floor. There, as she unpacked her trunk and placed her things in an empty drawer in the dressing table and hung others in the drab-looking wardrobe, a strange unease took hold of her. Up until she alighted the train, Cincinnati had been a name in an atlas. The reality was altogether not what she had expected. A bustling industrial border city on the banks of the Ohio

River, Cincinnati had as many black people as it did white, as far as she could tell. Even the owner of the boarding house was black. Upon entry, Mrs Snyder had greeted her warmly and made to shake her hand. Taken aback, she had given hers freely along with a warm smile, while Walter offered a brief grunt of acknowledgement and climbed the stairs to their room. Mrs Snyder seemed pleasant enough and Alice had no issue with her race. Her unease had a different source, one she couldn't place.

The boarding house was close to the seminary and affordable on Walter's stipend and the small allowance she received from Britain, so she supposed the room would have to do. With Walter out all day, she soon became bored and listless. She passed the time of day with Mrs Snyder, who had taken a liking to her, but she had nothing whatsoever to fill her time other than needlework. The weeks trundled by. She was wandering through the seminary grounds one warm afternoon, when an open door presented an opportunity. She stole a peek to find students listening to a lecture. Spotting an empty seat at the back, she slid inside and sat down. What began as a moment of brief inquisitiveness grew until she was attending as many lectures as her husband. She justified her attendance by telling him that those lectures gave them both something they could share, feeding the one thing they had in common. For her unease grew on the realisation that they shared no interests and had widely different outlooks on life. All of which may not have been problematic, were it not for the little jibes and dismissive remarks he subjected her to.

Mrs Snyder loathed Walter and made no effort to hide her antipathy. Alice suspected he may have been a little wary of her. What was it people saw in him that she couldn't? In the spring of that year she fell pregnant. As the child grew in her, Alice enjoyed the feelings of self-containment that came with pregnancy. Walter, while happy at the prospect of fatherhood, behaved as though he were jealous. He was more demanding of her physically, something she was growing numb to, and other than the bedroom, he was distant. Mrs Snyder was the opposite. She fussed and fed and cosseted Alice all through her pregnancy. It was Mrs Snyder she turned to for support in every imaginable way.

After the birth, the small family moved to an apartment nearby and Alice lost her only ally. She faced the reality of married life with no servants. At the boarding house, she never had to wash a teacup, now she faced the cooking, the washing, the cleaning, the shopping, every aspect of keeping house with a baby. Her, Alice La Trobe-Bateman, incapable of boiling an egg.

She didn't know who to turn to. She would have liked to turn to her husband, but she soon learned she couldn't trust Walter to do a thing. She sent him out to pay a bill one afternoon and he returned with the unpaid bill in one hand and a gramophone under his other arm.

'What did you buy that for?' she asked, knowing by the expression on his face she would have done better to have said nothing.

'I'll buy what I damn well like!' And with that outburst came a tirade of words. He plonked the gramophone on the table and made full use of his free arms to emphasise his fury. Alice had never seen him so angry. Without Mrs Snyder in earshot, he let loose his recriminations and his condemnations as he backed her into a corner.

She felt the fear rising in her chest, the tension in her body as she braced, shielding. She took a breath as though inhaling courage. She wasn't sure if Walter would hit her, but right then, he was capable of it.

He soon calmed down, but she was shocked and uncertain and her desperate love transformed in an instant into desperate misery.

'I'm sorry,' he said. 'I didn't mean to upset you.' He looked genuinely remorseful. He took her hand and pulled her close and embraced her. Then he kissed her passionately and led her to their bedroom.

His lovemaking was needy, demanding, selfish. Lying on her back afterwards, she wasn't sure she could forgive him and she wasn't sure if he would do it again.

He did.

It was as though, having succeeded in instilling terror in his wife with his words and his menace, he'd unleashed a demon, a demon who from that moment had permission, from him, to unfurl whenever the occasion arose, which it did, frequently. There were times he would storm down the stairs after an outburst and wouldn't return for hours. Always, when he had calmed down, he would seek her favours. She never resisted for fear of triggering yet more wrath.

Her dire situation was brought home to her when Dorothy was a year old and Alice took her to England for her sister, Lydia's wedding. She was marrying their cousin, Laurence Parsons, one of Aunt Agnes's sons. It was all very fine and grand and Alice was thoroughly unhappy throughout the entire ceremony. To see her sister so happy, so radiant, having made a good match was more than she could bear. She tried to put on a front, but everyone knew, or guessed, that things were not right between Walter and she, although no one said a word. Neither did she, for her pride was too strong. She made the journey back to New York feeling unimaginably depressed and homesick, and when she disembarked with Dorothy in her arms she had to resist the urge to book a return passage.

Walter was ordained while she was away and sent to work as a rector under Bishop Sanford of San Joaquin, in the small town of Reedley. Alice had no choice but to make the long train journey across America with a restless Dorothy on her lap. She could scarcely believe what she was heading into as the train rolled through the flat plains of central California. Walter met her at Selma station in a buggy and two hours later they arrived in the main street of Reedley. When she saw the hitching posts and the shops with false fronts, her worst fears were realised. She stepped down from the buggy and sunk lower than her boots. She would have to be the clergyman's wife too, a role she knew she would find intolerably dull, in a location equally so.

Life in Reedley was all Ladies' Aid and Mothers' Meetings and having to sit and listen to all of Walter's sermons. She went through the motions, all smiles and grace, while privately determining she could have nothing whatsoever in common with any of the people who surrounded her. How could she? Reedley was a remote farming town where all the people spoke in broad American accents. Why would she have had anything in common with tradespeople, railroad workers, fruit pickers and schoolteachers? The only real friend she had was the bishop's wife, Ellison, a woman of similar social standing.

One dreary Sunday afternoon in late-autumn, she sat by the fire in the kitchen nursing her gently swelling belly and sipping tea with Dorothy on her knee, when she heard the front door slam. Walter was home from church. She braced herself, almost as a reflex.

'Would you like some tea?' she said when he appeared in the doorway.

'Tea? No, I don't want any of your stinking tea.'

'Walter, whatever is the matter?'

'You think you are so much better than me, don't you?' he said between gritted teeth.

So that was it. He was furious that the Bible class she ran attracted more attendees than his sermons.

'No, Walter, I do not think I am better than you. Really I don't,' she said, holding Dorothy to her chest.

He wasn't listening. He stormed off about the house. A sudden burst then the tinkling of glass falling on the floorboards. She didn't get up. He was smashing more of the framed photographs of her family that decorated the mantels. He'd already ripped to shreds all of her books. Hearing the crash and tinkle of falling glass she feared there would be nothing left of her possessions at all. What next? Would he start shredding her clothes?

She told herself to stay calm. Things would be better if she didn't react. If she remained demur, soft, accommodating. It was no use. Her biddable nature seemed to aggravate him further.

The fists landed on her arms, her legs, her face while Dorothy napped in her cot. He launched into her as she cowered, whimpering, pleading, trying to protect her now swollen belly. *At least he isn't harming Dorothy. Better he hits me than our child.*

His anger spent, he stood back, shocked at himself for the briefest of moments. Then, he flung himself into an armchair and sulked. She spent the rest of the day tiptoeing around him.

Later, when Dorothy was tucked up in bed, he came to her filled with remorse. She wasn't taken in by his fawning. He pulled her to their bedroom where she endured another night of his violent passion. She ached, inside and out.

After that first beating, she was terrified of him. She was equally terrified of the congregation finding out. But there was no hiding what was going on. They all knew. She couldn't mask the bruises on her face, the swollen eye. When she went out for groceries or Bible class the town stared. She wasn't sure which was worse, fielding fists or avoiding the gazes of concerned onlookers. There she was, an aristocratic lady, enduring violence on a scale she could never have imagined possible, in the tiny backwater town of Reedley.

On the day of her second daughter Mildred's birth she revised her view of the town. California was enduring a heat wave and she was ill with a migraine that wouldn't go away and ten days overdue. When she at last went into labour and telephoned the doctor, she was told he would be delayed. She went out onto her front porch, searching for Dorothy who had run off into the garden when Walter disappeared. A contraction took hold and she bent double and cried out. The neighbours heard. Moments later, Mary, the saloon keeper's wife rushed over. Discovering the whereabouts of the doctor, she then called a local nurse. When the nurse arrived, Mary grabbed Dorothy and took her back to the saloon.

The contractions came and went for hours. Alice slipped into delirious exhaustion, drifting in and out of awareness. When lucid, all she knew was a wall of pain. She discovered days later that her baby had been delivered with forceps and she had haemorrhaged twice and almost died.

The women of Reedley rallied. While Alice lay in bed, they took it in turns to cook and clean and wash clothes. Two weeks later, she recovered enough to attend to the household chores, and one fine day, she went out to buy groceries. While she was unpacking her purchases, Walter arrived home unexpectedly. What was it about her manner as she put away the salt that caused him to pick up the pound of cheese on the table and hurl it at her?

The cheese hit her in the face.

The bruise was undisguisable. Two days later, the church warden's wife visited. Seeing the bruise, she alerted the bishop, who visited to see for himself.

'I am appalled, Mrs Evans, that this has come to pass. Your husband's behaviour will not be tolerated by the church.'

'I wonder of the pressures of his current position,' Alice said, making excuses.

'Are you capable of finding forgiveness in your heart?'

'Of course,' she said, thinking the only good thing to be said about her husband was he never harmed the children.

'Then we will offer him a chance to prove himself. There is a position available in Fowler.'

Fowler was a larger town benefitting from the railway, and a little closer to the bishop and his wife. Alice was much happier there and she regained her strength after Mildred's birth. She fell pregnant again in early summer.

It was then that the violence worsened, the attacks more frequent and more intense. Alice would look at her battered body and face in the mirror and wonder how she would get through to the end of each day. She wasn't capable of taking much more. He threw her around as though she were an inanimate object then used her to assuage his remorse. She was terrified of losing the baby.

The congregation, seeing that things were not well at the rectory, rallied. Young Miss Prentice suggested she boarded, hoping a stranger in the house would calm things. Local farmers took it in turns to plough the adjoining field, so that someone was on call through the day. Her friends took it in turns to telephone every afternoon to check she was all right. Her doctor, most concerned of all and convinced Walter would kill her, advised her to keep the axe and sharp knives hidden under her mattress at night.

Walter seemed oblivious to the strategies the community were taking. He attacked Alice in the kitchen, in the hallway, anywhere he chose and then, he attacked her in their bedroom.

Everyone waited with bated breath as the violence worsened. Miss Prentice with terror.

Alice thought a day would come when he would go too far. She was so tired of the beatings she began to wish for that day to come, even if it meant her own death, for she had reached her limit.

That day came when in a savage fit of rage he hurled her down the stairs.

A few weeks later, Ellison was born blue. Alice put her fragile health down to the attack. Walter had harmed their child. She knew then she had to act. As soon as she was able, she telephoned Bishop Sanford with the news.

'I don't know if he is mad or bad.' Neither did anyone else. He was always charming to the parishioners and charismatic in the pulpit. Walter didn't drink, gamble, or even swear, so there didn't seem to be any reason for his violence. The bishop suggested a psychiatric assessment in San Francisco.

Alice thought she had hit the bottom, that her situation could not get any worse, but while Walter was away and she was enjoying the reprieve, life dealt a blow of its own. Ellison contracted infantile cholera and became instantly and desperately ill. She was rushed to hospital in San Francisco. No one expected her to live. Alice remained at home with Dorothy and Mildred. The depth of her anguish was so strong she felt she had been turned inside out.

Miraculously, Ellison survived and arrived home from the hospital at the same time as Walter, who had received his diagnosis. He had an uncontrolled temper. He was bad, not mad.

It was the turning point. By then she'd endured five years of his behaviour. Courage reared and before she lost it, she had a private word with the bishop by telephone, then approached Walter the moment they were alone.

'If you don't stop mistreating me, I'll have plenty of grounds for divorce, and then you will be unemployable within the church.'

Walter was silent.

'I won't apologise for going behind your back, Walter. Bishop Sanford agrees and has suspended your employment. Readmission into the church will only be granted if I tell him you have reformed.'

They moved to a three-room shack in the pine forested hinterland of Pacific Grove. There, Alice faced a new kind of struggle. Walter had no income. The First World War meant her allowance from Britain was reduced and often it didn't come at all. Alice decided to keep hens and sell the eggs. She collected firewood, baked bread, cooked, washed, cleaned and cared for the children. While she did all that, Walter sat and sulked. He refused to help and he refused to speak to her. She supposed that, for him, was reform.

At the end of six months, Bishop Sanford posted Walter to a mining town in Montana. Alice and her daughters never saw him again, and the vicious letters ceased after a time as well.

She moved into a three-roomed cottage in Pacific Grove. She was thirty-five and an impoverished single parent of three young daughters. Ellison was one, Mildred three, and Dorothy five. Her small income from Britain came erratically. None of her friends were in a position to help, and she refused to seek assistance from her relatives. Perhaps she had made her bed and must lie in it, but it was a bed of nails and she was pierced through and through. She had been betrayed by her husband, she lacked faith in a theology that taught ludicrous falsehoods and she felt abandoned by God who was nowhere to be found in her life, despite her prayers and pleas.

She couldn't shake the wretched way she felt. She had gone from being needed by hundreds and thousands of men to the drudgery of housework. No one needed her, other than her three daughters, whom she could scarcely feed. Her self-pity was intense. The needs of her girls were all that kept her going. Buried in those habitual tasks of motherhood lay her strength, one that prevented her from taking the drastic course of action she had experimented with as a child: suicide. Even so, her frustration was all-consuming. She was, after all, an intelligent, passionate woman with a strong sense of purpose. She wouldn't be defeated. Since no one was going to help her, she would have to help herself. She went downtown to the only industry in the district and applied for a job as a factory hand at one of Monterey's sardine canneries.

She found the work hard and the workplace rough and ready. It was piecework. She gave half of whatever she earned to a neighbour who minded her daughters. She went down to the cannery at seven in the morning and returned home at four. They put her to work in the labelling department at first, but she couldn't earn enough to cover her expenses and the childcare, so she took some advice and went down to the packing department to join an even rougher group of workers.

She applied herself to the task of packing sardines with dogged resolve to earn enough to get by, and she proved good at it too, gaining the respect of her co-workers. Yet with her posh British accent and her refined manners, she was out of place and vulnerable. In response, many had looked out for her. Unsolicited acts of kindness—a newspaper on her seat, a clean cloth to wipe her hands—never failed to touch her. At Cincinnati, Reedley, Fowler and Monterey, she learned one simple lesson in humility and loving kindness.

She worked at the cannery for two and a half years. In that time, she filed for divorce but then discovered that Walter had left Montana and entered the war. When she learned he was awarded a Croix de Guerre she was consumed with bitter irony. Women divorcing their husbands while they were at war was frowned upon, so she withdrew proceedings to avoid the stigma. Even though she was fully aware that fighting a war does not automatically make a man good at home, despite any heroic acts on the battlefield.

Meanwhile, she existed in wall-to-wall drudgery and hard labour. She couldn't have known it then how dramatically her circumstances were about to change.

# Discovering Theosophy

'You were clearly her favourite,' Joan said without any preface, her face buried in Luke Slattery's *Mrs M*.

'I was her niece,' Heather said, making her way to the dining table with her bowl.

'Sleep well?'

'Thank you, Dad. I did.'

Heather took up her usual chair facing the window that looked out over the back garden. The weather was squally, the bare branches of the trees swaying stiffly. She made a mental note to put her umbrella in her bag.

'You may just as well have been her daughter,' Joan said, decapitating her boiled egg with a rigorous swipe of her knife.

'That's so unkind,' Heather said, wishing to eat in peace, wishing she could avoid her mother's ire.

Joan inhaled as if to say more, when William threw her a stern look.

'There's no need to be quite so, blunt,' he said.

Joan wouldn't be defeated. Instead, she spoke to her husband as though her daughter was absent.

'My family has always had its favourites, as well you know. My grandmother Katharine favoured my mother Agnes, leaving her sister Margaret, out of her will save for a small sum. Agnes, in her turn, favoured Hilary. Which is why Hilary inherited the family furniture, despite the fact that she's the youngest.' She began stabbing the table with her index finger. 'That dresser in Hilary's bedroom belonged to Katharine's sister Emma, and I believe dates back to the mid 1800s. The armoire was shipped over from England not long after. The dining table, so well suited to our home, William, with its upholstered chairs, was my mother's wedding present from her husband's parents. I have no idea why Hilary insisted on holding onto it, for you could scarcely get around it in her house. The table comfortably seats ten and I've always found ours cramped when we're entertaining. As for the escritoire. Oh, the escritoire! How I coveted that piece as a child, with all of its secret drawers. William, you are an only child. You wouldn't understand. Neither,' she said, turning to her daughter as she thrust her spoon in her egg, 'would you. I think your special relationship with your aunt has blinded you, Heather, I really do…'

'If you want the furniture, have it,' Heather said, talking over her mother. 'Please. I hadn't even thought about what to do with all of Hilary's things.'

Her mother held her egg-laden spoon mid-air. 'You mean that?'

'Take what you want. Have all of it.'

'No, no. Just the pieces I mentioned.'

'The heirlooms,' William said, folding his newspaper.

Heather made an effort to eat her stewed fruit and yogurt. It slipped down her throat along with her chagrin at her mother's callousness. Hilary was still warm in her grave. Not even a month had passed since she had died. That her mother, a woman as staunch and dignified as they come, could behave so petulantly towards her own blood was astonishing. She felt as though she had inherited the crown from some monarch and, despite the rules of succession, she wasn't entitled to it.

Keen to leave the house, she caught an earlier train to work. She was at the library at eight and in her office long before Shona and Suzanne were due to make an appearance. She leaned back against her office door, wishing it could be locked from the inside, wanting to lose herself to the room with its boxes and boxes of Professor Foyle's collection. She was still reeling over her mother's attitude. Where was her sensitivity, her grief? All Joan displayed was anger, gnawing away at her.

She was riddled with a petty sense of entitlement that had burrowed right into her bones. It wasn't becoming in a woman in her seventies.

You can't own people through their possessions. It was their spirit that mattered and you can't own that either.

She opened her inbox and trawled through her emails, deleting the circulars, shifting the research inquiries into her folder marked Pending. What next? She searched Spiritualism again. It was nothing she could relate to.

The dead are dead.

'You are not here, Hilary, not here,' she said aloud, hoping no one had heard her out in the corridor.

Hoping to spend the morning unmolested, she turned to the collection's most comprehensible source, the autobiography. Heather had already read it twice, the second time taking notes in her special, cloth-bound notebook which had a new home in her satchel. She extracted the notebook and read over her points. Notably for her, were the lengths Alice Bailey had taken to demonstrate that she was neither a racist nor anti-Semitic, pages and pages of illustrative vignettes and explanations. Heather was struck by the defensive sub-text, that she had first noticed in relation to Alice Bailey's marriage to Foster. She was clearly well-aware of her critics. Her work must have come under considerable attack. Were the critics justified? Was Alice Bailey's defence sufficient? Heather didn't doubt the author's sincerity or her integrity but what was it about her teachings, her organisations, her life altogether that warranted the accusations? It was impossible to know without gaining some sort of understanding of Theosophy.

Heather had heard of the Theosophical Society and its founder, Madame Helena Blavatsky, but that was the extent of her knowledge. She was hungry for an overview, a few hints to give her an understanding. She rummaged about in the boxes, stopping when she'd located a box of old books with battered covers. They were Theosophical texts, written by, among others, Helena Blavatsky, Annie Besant, Charles Webster Leadbeater and Rudolph Steiner. She removed them carefully, one by one, and spent the rest of the morning making a record for each, taking note of the condition and any defining marks. Usually, the cataloguing of books didn't require the creation of records, but with the preponderance of Professor Foyle's sticky notes, inserted in page upon page, lending the volumes an additional width of yellow, she felt compelled to preserve the details for the sake of provenance. Besides, it was absorbing work, fascinating. She read a paragraph or two, here and there, and found the language strange and strangely compelling. What was the allure, when nothing made much sense? There was much talk of planes and logoi, rays and chakras, devas and elementals, and root races.

Her mother would scoff, her father would call it gobbledygook. Hilary, on the other hand, would have been enthralled to hear all about it, if she hadn't already known of the weird metaphysical nomenclature.

Searching online among academic articles provided her with numerous reliable sources to flesh out her own understanding. Theosophy, she read, had its roots in Spiritualism, a Christian denomination with a firm belief in the spirit world. Spiritualism emerged in the late nineteenth century, a period when interest in all things mystical abounded. A resurgence in Spiritualism occurred after the First World War, when loved ones sought to contact their departed.

Heather paused, intrigued. Her great-grandmother Katharine had been a Spiritualist for that very reason. She had been devastated by the death of her husband, Heather's great grandfather George, who had lost his life in the Somme offensive in 1916, two years after they were married. Katharine was carrying her second child Agnes at the time. Hilary had told her that Katharine attended séances to try to speak to her husband. With moderate success, she had said. She pictured Hilary standing by her mantelpiece in the front room of her house, holding a photograph of Katharine in an ornate silver frame. She then saw Katharine's benign face, the discerning eyes directed at the camera, the implacable mouth. Her hair was piled high and her dress looked starched. Heather's throat constricted and she had to remove her glasses as she fought back the next flood. Hilary said Katharine had drawn comfort from the words of the medium at the

Brunswick Spiritual Lyceum Church, who had told her George was watching over her and he always would.

As far as Heather was concerned, Hilary hadn't left either. She held no belief in the afterlife, but the more she delved into Alice Bailey's world, the closer Hilary felt. She was there, in the room, a subtle presence following her every move.

She dried her eyes, took a deep breath, and returned her glasses to her face hoping they wouldn't fog.

Blavatsky was a Spiritualist too, but the faith hadn't satisfied the adventuresome and enigmatic Russian aristocrat, who seemed to have traded on a dramatic, almost startling visage, judging by the portraits of her online. The charismatic occultist had travelled far and wide, particularly in India, gathering knowledge as she went.

One fateful day, she began writing communications she claimed she was receiving from a spiritual master, Djwhal Khul, otherwise known as "the Tibetan". Heather searched for his image and arrived at a portrait of a sagely old man. His face was thin, his eyes hooded beneath thick, arched eyebrows. He had a prominent nose, a hint of a moustache and full lips arranged in a pout of a smile. He appeared to Heather kind and wise which was, she presumed, how he was meant to look.

He was the same master who had communicated with Alice Bailey. Heather paused for a moment, taking in that small detail, sensing its import without knowing why.

Helena Blavatsky had established the Theosophical Society in 1875, five years before Alice Bailey was born. Bailey belonged to the second generation of Theosophists, along with Annie Besant, Charles Leadbeater and Rudolph Steiner, and unlike the late Victorian period in which Blavatsky pursued her interests, their era was the grim period of the two world wars. Context was everything. Heather knew that. Every archivist and every librarian knew that. The Theosophical outpourings of the previous century satisfied a particular cultural milieu, one hungry for all things exotic and mystical. By the time Alice Bailey was writing, that hunger had transmuted through war and depression into a kind of desperation for a better world.

Channelled communications from spiritual masters sounded like hogwash to Heather. What did Theosophy actually mean? A definition was easy to find.

The doctrine pivots on a few core beliefs: reincarnation; an epochal view of evolution that takes Darwin's idea and amplifies it to include consciousness and the cosmos and eons of time; a belief in an Ageless Wisdom transmitted from master to disciple; the interconnectedness of everything; and the existence of the soul. Theosophy combines all those beliefs with an ethical commitment to humanitarianism, which makes it a social movement as well.

Reincarnation? Evolution of consciousness? Interconnectedness? Heather took off her glasses, sat back in her seat and gazed vacantly at the opposite wall, plain beige with its single square window off-centre. Her mind tried to piece together the fragments of knowledge she had gleaned into some sort of coherent whole. At first nothing fitted. It was like a foreign language and all she could see were separate words with no logic to put them together. She lacked the syntax, that binding force that generated meaning.

Staring at the wall she was transported back to her university days, when she had pored over the lives of Edith Cowan, Jessie Street and Serena Lake, three markedly different women, all campaigning for women's suffrage. Back then it was the intersection of personal histories and radical ideas that had fascinated her. Now it was the obscurity of the ideas themselves. Even the word 'esoteric' carried a charge, a sense of things hidden, mysterious, secret. Theosophy pertained to metaphysics, to the ineffable, the unfathomable, and something in her wanted to reach out to touch the ideas, capture a resonance, experience the illumination.

It wasn't the idea of reincarnation that drew her, or the belief in the soul. Hilary had introduced her to the theory of the evolution of consciousness years before, through her interest in, among others, Carl Jung. What fascinated Heather was the blending of all of the otherworldly beliefs with the notion of humanitarianism and ideas of social justice. Especially when she discovered second generation Theosophist, Annie Besant, had championed worker's rights.

Besant and Leadbeater also wrote of the reappearance of the Christ, the head of their Spiritual Hierarchy of Masters. The notion would have held much appeal for Alice Bailey, who went on to write her own interpretation of his second coming.

In all, Theosophists believed the purpose of individual existence was to grow, branch out, unfurl and blossom and ultimately bear fruit.

Alice Bailey had wanted to take that trajectory one step further. It was a giant step, an ambitious step. Her aim was world service. Her disciples forewent individual campaigns such as those exemplified by Annie Besant, in favour of something universal and overarching. Global ideas and projects that would transcend all the limitations of gender, race, class, colour, creed and national boundary, yet manage to include them all. That, for Alice Bailey, was the essence of the New Age of Aquarius and she had taken it upon herself to make that vision a reality. It appeared she had taken the notions of Christian goodwill and service, and blended them with the Buddhist idea of right relations. She never left her old faith behind; she dressed it up in new clothes.

A sudden awareness rippled through her. Hilary was always going on about the need for right relations in their conversations on other topics. Heather had scarcely paid that term any attention.

'Did you know all this?' she said to the wall. 'You must have. And I must have had wax in my ears.'

As if in response, the door swept open. Heather nearly leapt out of her skin. It was Suzanne.

'You all right?' she said, scanning about, her gaze settling on the used tissues in the bin beside Heather's feet.

'I'm fine.'

'Who were you talking to?'

'No one,' she said quickly.

'I thought I heard voices. I'll be back with coffee in a bit.'

Heather watched the door close.

Had Alice Bailey succeeded? Plainly not. When Heather thought about the New Age, all she saw were star-gazers or people fixated on personal growth. The movement was for the wounded or the self-obsessed. Serving others didn't enter into it. If Alice Bailey was the mother of the New Age, her main point seems to have been missed.

Of course, the New Age movement had emerged in a different context to the one Alice Bailey had grown up in and lived her life. She had had the idea of service drilled into her at Moor Park by her grandfather. She had spent her twenties serving soldiers in Elise Sandes' homes. Those experiences, indeed the zealous evangelist that she was, meant she was fitted to take Theosophy to the next level.

Heather found herself wanting to defend Alice Bailey. Against what or who? Against the naysayers? Those invisible enemies whose accusations Alice Bailey was at pains to address in her book? For her, it seemed a point of honour. Why?

Maybe Heather's impulse had nothing to do with Alice Bailey. Maybe it was because when she was a little girl, Hilary had instilled in her the need to care for others. Not that she had acted on that ethos. Heather had never been the good works type. Looking back, she realised that although Hilary had never said her parents were selfish, she had implied it.

Again, there was that pressure behind the eyes.

Before her grief took hold, she diverted her attention to Professor Foyle's notebook, scanning through the pages, searching for something of interest. She stopped at a page that was dog eared. She made a mental note to record the observation and left the corner bent, her attention arrested by the description of a dream.

I made an appointment to visit George Monbiot at his house. I wanted to talk to him on behalf of my daughter. I thought he could help her. The door was open but out of politeness, I knocked. I heard him call out. I was about to walk in when I looked down and saw, not only that I was dressed in a drab black coat, I was wearing black slippers. Why ever had I failed to put on my shoes? Why hadn't I noticed before? Aghast, I fled the scene.

Later, George Monbiot phoned to complain that I'd not shown up and accused me of wasting his time. I tried to explain I'd arranged the appointment on behalf of my daughter, for whom I was hoping to make an introduction, and that I was very sorry. I wanted to tell him that I had been wearing slippers, but he was too impatient. Most grumpy he was.

On the facing page was her analysis.

Slippers: A slip, an oversight. I'd caused myself shame as a result. Standing there, I felt like a lesser human being. Not good enough. Not worthy of George Monbiot's attention.

I was in too much haste and was therefore ill prepared. I thought it was inappropriate to bring a part of my private sphere into public scrutiny. I felt ridiculous. I either needed to stop doing that or stop caring.

After all, the door was already open. I was free to cross the threshold. It was my slippers that stopped me moving forward and entering that world. My shame.

I was frustrated too, that my attempt to help my daughter failed because of this slip.

Could my daughter represent my work?

George Monbiot??? Why him?

Could it be his initials? GM? Could that be referring to Great Man? A representative, a gatekeeper maybe. Yes, I suspect my dream is being a trickster. I rarely dream like this.

I can see why it's so important.

In the dream, I was overly concerned with how I appeared. In that instant, I appeared to myself a bag lady, someone destitute, and certainly not an adequate representative of my daughter/work.

This dream is no longer about me.

The last line was underscored several times in red ink. Heather read over the dream and the analysis. What was Professor Foyle implying? That the dream was about Alice Bailey?

Heather wasn't in the right state of mind to think it through. She left the notebooks on her desk and poked about among the other boxes, this time pausing to examine the magazines. There were boxes and boxes of them. First, she delved into the last box taking up space by her desk, and extracted a very large bundle of the *American Theosophist*, which became the *Theosophic Messenger* before reverting back to its original title for a period, followed by a spell as *Messenger*, then finally settling on *Theosophic Messenger,* according to a sticky note stuck on the top copy. The name changes spoke of trouble at the top, squabbles or an identity crisis.

In a box on the floor under the bench, she found a few copies of *Theosophical Forum*—with the word 'Judge' and in brackets 'not relevant,' scrawled on a note on the top copy—along with a few copies of *Theosophical Path* and *Universal Brotherhood*. Both had a sticky note with the word 'Tingley' in Professor Foyle's hurried scrawl. Heather reached for her notebook and wrote down Judge and Tingley.

There were numerous copies of various Spiritualist magazines which Heather set aside thinking her great-grandmother, Katharine, would have had an enthralling time wading through all the articles.

There were small bundles of *The Theosophical Review* and the *Canadian Theosophist*. Another box contained a single bundle of the *Theosophist*, which Foyle noted as *the* most important journal of Theosophy. Another contained issues of *Occult Review* and *The O. E. Library Critic*, along with a single issue of a magazine by the name of *The Aquarian New Age*, dated September 1911. A further ten boxes contained old copies of Alice Bailey's magazine, *The Beacon*, dating back to 1925.

How had Professor Foyle accumulated all those original copies? It was quite a cache. She must have known someone, a collector, an esotericist, a devotee, a friend. Or maybe she had found the lot in a charity shop or at the auction of a deceased estate. An inheritance perhaps. Had the collection triggered the monograph? She suspected not.

She stood over the boxes with their open lids, gazing down at all that printed material, each magazine or newsletter carrying its own esoteric symbols on the header, the front pages weighed down thereafter with serious-looking writing. It was a lot to take in.

Much to Heather's disappointment, reading through Foyle's manuscript, it was apparent she had yet to flesh out the chapter on Alice Bailey's entry into Theosophy, which consisted of a few disparate paragraphs with large gaps between. If she carried any hope of understanding Bailey's relationship with the Theosophical Society, there seemed nothing for it but to fill in those gaps, or at least try. She knew she couldn't write the academic's chapter for her, but she wanted to. She wanted to capture the story, sensing it had never been properly told. She'd write a paper for the library journal, submit it to Shona, at least then somewhere the record would be set straight. It would afford her some acknowledgement, too. Help put paid to her lowly status in the archive office. She opened a blank document and started wading through the magazines.

She began with the single copy of *The Aquarian New Age*. The front cover sported a photograph of an enigmatic man looking hypnotically at the camera as though to mesmerise the reader. The image was of Levi H. Dowling, a New Thought lecturer who had penned *The Aquarian Gospel of Jesus Christ*, a book that set out to fill in the missing eighteen years of the life of Jesus. Foyle's note indicated the book had proven influential in the formation of New Age spirituality. The issue contained an extract from a course of lessons given by Levi. Reading through it, Heather was quick to note references to a 'Universal Brotherhood and 'The White Lodge' and 'bands of invisible helpers,' the sorts of ideas found in Alice Bailey's work. Clearly, she was not alone in thinking what she did. In that issue, Dowling had recently died. Reading the eulogy, Heather saw in Levi a man with a mission, the same sort of zeal as Alice Bailey.

Levi claimed he could read the Akashic records, said to be a compendium of all human thought, words, emotions and desires stored on the etheric plane of existence.

Akashic records? Etheric plane? Heather was stumped. Yet a bell tinkled in her head and Hilary was beside her as though summoned, telling her it wasn't real, none of it was real. The lock, stock and barrel of esoteric thought was metaphor, a way of expressing something ineffable, not literal truth existing in some concrete form.

That was all very well, but where was it leading her? She needed a point of entry. She knew Alice Bailey was part of the zeitgeist of the times. The two world wars and the decades between was a period when hope in a bright new future was paramount. A vanguard of thinkers—esoteric, intellectual, artistic—added their weight to the discourse, notably Aldous Huxley and George Orwell. Looking up at the volumes of blue books filling that single shelf, Heather saw straight away that Alice Bailey had taken things much further than her contemporaries in attempting to make that New Age a reality. Besides, Foyle's premise that Alice Bailey was the mother of the New Age had nothing to do with her coining the term since clearly she had not, despite the occasional scholarly attribution to that end. It was that she had taken the concept of an emerging New Age, and made it her mission to see it realised.

Alice Bailey was one of many who had established themselves as some sort of spiritual authority, there to guide a second wave of devotees that emerged in the aftermath of the First World War. Heather fetched the autobiography and opened it to the frontispiece. The benevolent old lady stared back at her. With her aristocratic background and natural sense of leadership, there could be no doubt she had seen herself as a cut above the rest.

She had had a significant role in the Theosophical Society, too, at one time. There'd been a power struggle and things had gone horribly wrong. In her autobiography, she was evasive and vague, making allusions and passing references and it was hard to piece together the story. When Heather originally read her book, she hadn't even tried.

Surrounded by all those magazines and newsletters, it occurred to her she stood a reasonable chance of unravelling what had happened. She returned to the autobiography and located the relevant chapter. The story had its genesis in 1915 when Alice was working at a sardine cannery, so she started taking notes from there.

# Krotona

Tired of her humdrum existence as a young mother and sardine packer, Alice had begun to crave intellectual stimulation and was determined to find some. After all, she was living in an artistic and progressive community. There was bound to be likeminded company around. She knew of two other English women of a similar background who lived a few streets away. She had seen them in the shops and they aroused her curiosity. When she heard they were hosting a lecture in their drawing room, she secured an invitation through a mutual friend.

She wasn't impressed by the lecturer, who bored his audience rigid with a convoluted and dry explanation of evolution from a Theosophical perspective. As he droned on in monotone, her gaze wandered, lingering here and there on soft furnishings, exotic fabrics, ornaments that reminded her of India, including a brass elephant. When at last the lecture was over and the group were enjoying canapes and wine, she approached the hostesses.

'I must thank you for your hospitality and for putting on this most interesting talk.'

'Did you think so?' The taller of the two leaned forward. 'We thought Edward a little dull.' They all laughed at once. 'But if you are being a little more than polite, we'd be happy to lend you some books, wouldn't we Gertrude?'

Alice read those volumes in every spare moment she had. She read while she cooked and she read while she ironed. She read in bed at night after the children were asleep. Those newfound Theosophical ideas landed in a mind hardwired by Christian orthodoxy. She opened *The Secret Doctrine* scarcely knowing how to grasp the language. She might as well have read the book upside down for all the sense it made. Still, determined to understand, she persisted. She joined the local lodge and gained the help of two old ladies who were former personal students of Helena Blavatsky. It wasn't long before she was holding her own classes in Theosophy.

She learned to accept the Theosophical evolutionary scheme, in which all life emanated from and evolved back to the Source. She accepted with ease the idea of a grand design or pattern to all existence. She was pleased and relieved to discover that Theosophists had a positive, esoteric view of Christ. Annie Besant had already published *Initiation: The Perfecting of Man*, a work depicting the life of Christ as Head of the Spiritual Hierarchy, with much talk of the second coming of the World Teacher. For Besant, Christ was the World Saviour, set to reappear under a definite law. The other Masters were his pupils and disciples. It all slotted into and radically transformed Alice's existing religious framework.

She found the ideas of reincarnation and karma that had been borrowed from Hinduism and Buddhism much harder to embrace. At least at first. It was only when she applied the principle to her own life that it took on some significance. It seemed to her in that moment a reasonable proposition that as you sow so shall you reap. She must have done something truly dreadful to have warranted Walter Evans. Although perhaps it was only right that her pride, her righteousness and her snobbery were beaten out of her. Then again, he hadn't achieved that. It was the goodwill of her neighbours that had transformed her.

Theosophy started to make sense. She began to realise that manmade interpretations of truth were so often wrong, that this preacher or that, with all the best intentions, made claims as to the meaning of Biblical tracts with limited authority. That the mass of people simply accepted those claims as absolute, unequivocal truth and looked no further, just as she had.

She quickly found she could cooperate with the Spiritual Hierarchy. It was all there before her in the realm of possibility, making complete sense of the strange visitation she had when she was fifteen, and again when she had heard her master's voice in India. She packed sardines, she cared for her children and she devoured Theosophy. The world of ideas had opened up but she remained dissatisfied.

In 1917, America joined the war. Bishop Sanford wrote telling her Walter had secured work with the Young Men's Christian Association in France, and he had arranged for a portion of his salary to be paid to his wife. Together with her own small income from the family estate, she could at last leave the sardine cannery.

By then she knew Theosophy was her calling, her life's work, that which the man in the turban had mentioned twenty years before. The fastest, most obvious way to bring into being the life she was destined to lead was to be at the centre of operations. Urged on by lodge members, she wasted no time moving to Hollywood, to Krotona, the Theosophical Society's headquarters nestling in the hills of Beachwood Canyon. The day she arrived, she could scarcely believe her luck. It was as though she had reached paradise.

Several hundred devotees were living in a collection of stunning mansions, many Moorish in style. They were beautiful people and they milled about, talking softly or simply being silent, taking advantage of the peaceful, elegantly gardened grounds, secluded and serene and replete with ponds and vines, citrus and olive trees, eucalypts and date palms.

She spent most of her time at the institute's heart, Krotona Inn. A fine building comprising guest rooms, a dining room and kitchen, offices for magazine staff and Krotona officials, a lecture room for public classes and a meditation room, all looking over an interior courtyard. In the centre of the courtyard was a lily pond. Deep pergolas supported by stout columns shaded the rooms. Between the pergola and the pond, palms and yuccas and vines grew in raised beds. It was magnificent.

She couldn't afford to move into the community itself. She rented a cottage nearby, on North Beachwood Drive. Her daughters were old enough for school and kindergarten, leaving her free to attend classes and lectures. She quickly made friends and when the cafeteria needed a new manager, she accepted the role. The menu was vegetarian. She had adopted the diet the day she became a Theosophist, and taught herself to be a good vegetarian cook.

It wasn't long before Krotona fell short of its idyllic pretentions. In the cafeteria Alice would overhear devotees spitting their harsh criticisms and condemnations of others, or exuding their superior status through eyes filled with hauteur. Standing behind the counter, an aristocrat ragged and worn, she observed the same sort of superiority and snobbery she had encountered among Christians, this time overlaid with Theosophy, which somehow made the posturing worse. In the cafeteria, she was regarded with disdain. To them, she was the hired help. She served and cleaned and prepared food fully aware that the hardships she had endured for the previous seven years were a necessary purging of the same tendency.

She joined the Theosophical Society in 1915. Keen as ever for more knowledge, the moment she had served the requisite two years she joined the Esoteric Section, the inner sanctum of the society. Their meetings were held in the Shrine Room. On a cool December afternoon, she attended her first, arriving early and pushing open the door.

The room was empty. The first thing she noticed was the charged atmosphere and a faint smell of incense. Beneath the domed roof, a large circular rug covered the polished floorboards. Centred on the rug was a round table. Her attention was drawn to the portraits evenly spaced around the room. She studied each one in turn. When she came to the portrait hanging opposite the large window that looked down on the courtyard, she almost gasped. There was the man in the turban who had visited her at Castramont. The likeness was unmistakable. Behind her, a man walked in and was shuffling papers in preparation for the lesson. She went over and said, 'Could you please tell me who that is?' She pointed behind her.

'Koot Hoomi.'

'Then he is my Master,' she blurted.

Mr Fisher looked her up and down. 'Is that right?'

'Indeed. He contacted me once long ago.'

The contempt in his eyes was enough to wither her, but he reinforced his condemnation with, 'Do you mean to say that you consider yourself a disciple?'

She discovered later that only advanced members of the Esoteric Section could conceive of being in any sort of communication with the masters. It was every Theosophical seeker's grail and required the seal of approval from the Theosophical head, Annie Besant. Alice had inadvertently claimed discipleship status for which she was not entitled.

After her *faux pas,* Alice was as much disappointed as she was furious with the esoteric section for reinforcing the exclusivity and the inward-looking, selfish aggrandising that was going on at Krotona. Theosophy was being hijacked to serve the needs of the individual. The trouble was, she lacked an outlet for her thoughts and emotions, a confidante, a trusted friend.

At Krotona, Alice was still Mrs Evans, a frail woman in her late thirties run off her feet caring for three daughters and managing the café. One cool January day in 1919, while she was tidying the counter, a dashing young man walked in and asked for a cup of tea and a slice of her favourite cake. She cut him a slice of the apple pie she had baked that morning and they struck up a conversation. He asked for her name. She asked for his.

'Lieutenant Foster Bailey, ma'am, at your service.' And he gave a little bow.

He was friendly and warm and engaging. Unlike the elitists who drifted about Krotona looking down their long noses, Foster came across as humble and sincere. Even in that initial exchange, Alice felt she had found in Foster an ally.

'You have a limp,' she said as he walked over to a nearby seat.

'The result of a plane crash. Really, I was quite lucky. I escaped with my life.'

She blushed without knowing why. He issued a charming smile and asked what time she finished.

'At four, but then I need to collect the children.'

'I can walk with you, if you like.'

Strolling through the grounds that sunny afternoon, Alice discovered that Foster was a lawyer and Freemason who came from a distinguished family in Fitchburg, Massachusetts. She soon discovered they had much in common; Foster's father, William Kimball Bailey, was a civil engineer. Foster counted among family members, attorneys, politicians, Harvard graduates. Hearing his story endeared him to her. What impressed and puzzled her was that he had rejected the benefits of his heritage, including a career in an uncle's law firm, for the sake of his spiritual quest, and chosen to live at Krotona in a tent.

She couldn't imagine what he saw in her. Despite having lived more than a year at Krotona, she hadn't recovered her health. She was thin and weak and her face was drawn. She fought to overcome her frailties by ignoring them, focusing instead on her thirst for understanding. It wasn't knowledge she was after, it was a penetrating awareness, as though all that she already knew was a veil behind which lay deeper truths and she wanted to rip that veil and see, really see into the meaning of things. Above all, she wanted to know what the Masters wanted. When she told Foster her deepest aspiration, his reaction was positive, encouraging. He believed in her. He didn't idolise her like Walter had, he appreciated her mind. There were days she wondered what else he wanted from her. Theirs was not a romantic coming together. It was more along the lines of friendship, companionship, a meeting of minds and souls. After Walter, she was in no condition emotionally or physically for anything else. Foster respected that. It was a matter she found puzzling but for which she was relieved.

Things between them developed quickly. Alice had already instituted divorce proceedings. That year the divorce was granted, and they were engaged.

Filled with optimism for the future, she wrote and told her sister Lydia. The reply was crushing. Lydia told her she wanted nothing more to do with her. Divorce, for Lydia, was unacceptable. The words stung. It was as though in those few lines from Lydia, she was cut adrift from her entire family.

With the end of the war, a new era dawned, one of optimism, hope and booming wealth. Science and technology were advancing at a rapid rate and there was a prevailing sense of transition from the old to the new in the zeitgeist.

At Krotona, Alice continued to run the cafeteria, and at home in Beachwood Drive she attended to her motherly duties. In Foster, she had a new life partner in the making. She attended Esoteric Section meditations and received the teachings. Meanwhile, her frustration with the exclusivity of the Section, and the somewhat dictatorial manner in which it was run remotely by Annie Besant, grew ever stronger. Privately, she had a rich inner life filled with Theosophical ideas. Yet still, she lacked a clear direction.

One August day, after sending the children off to school, she went for a walk on the hill near her house. She sat down, lost in her thoughts. Suddenly she heard music, a single note, coming as though from the sky. She listened, alert. Then she heard a voice. A man's voice. She knew straight away it was the voice of a Master. It had to be. Either that, or she was going insane.

'Who are you?'

'Djwhal Khul.'

But he wasn't her Master. Why was he trying to communicate with her?

The voice was asking her if she would write some books.

She refused. She didn't want anything to do with psychics and mediums and she had an abhorrence of automatic writing and channelling.

The voice persisted.

Still, she refused. Find someone else, she said.

The voice told her he would give her three weeks to think about it.

Alice went home. She didn't tell a soul. If this was the work that was planned for her, she wanted no part in it.

Three weeks later, while she was seated in her sitting room after the girls had gone to bed, she heard the voice again. Once more the request was made and once more she refused. Only this time the speaker begged her to reconsider. She relented. They agreed on a trial period of a few weeks.

On a balmy late-September afternoon, when she was alone in the house, she took down the first letter dictated by the Tibetan. The letter concerned the powers and methods of the Dark Brotherhood, those who persistently exalted the concrete mind and refused entry of the higher. The result, the Tibetan said, was an over-development in one direction, and gulfs and gaps where virtues should be. The Dark Brotherhood respect no one, regard all as prey and will use anyone to get their own way by any means. The Dark Brotherhood would ever masquerade as agents of the light and retard the progress of humanity. Alice couldn't fail to see the importance of those words, but why did the Tibetan choose letters on evil with which to induct her into the collaboration. Was he trying to scare her off? The letter went on to explain that the way to avoid the destructive power of the Dark Brotherhood was to deal with one's weak spots, remain pure and clean on physical, emotional and mental levels, lead a balanced life with relaxation and play, get plenty of sleep and exercise, and tackle personal fear because fear opens the door to evil.

It all made complete sense and she saw the importance, the relevance of the communication. She even pictured one or two members of the Esoteric Section as having fallen foul of this very overdevelopment. The comment on fear appeared to be more pointed. It was as though this part of the communication was directed straight at her, for ever since one awful night in Quetta, when she had been sure a killer was trying to break into her room, she had suffered from gripping fear of being alone in the dark, fear compounded by the violence she had endured at the hands of Walter Evans.

Two weeks later, she took down another communication. This time, the Tibetan tackled the causes and dangers of obsession, and the need to progress meditation in a slow and measured manner to avoid allowing in low grade disincarnate entities, earthbound spirits, elementals and subhuman spirits all of which sought to possess the host.

After taking down those early communications on the Dark Brotherhood and the dangers of obsession and possession, Alice panicked, worried that if she continued, she might go crazy. She couldn't afford to lose her mind. She had three daughters to care for.

She told the Tibetan, and he advised her to discuss the matter with her own Master, Koot Hoomi. This, in meditation, she did. He reassured her that she was in no danger, and that it would be valuable work. In fact, he had suggested it. Persuaded, but still cautious, she agreed to continue.

She went on to take down the early chapters of a work she would later publish as *Initiation, Human and Solar*, a work that presented for the first time a crucial development of Theosophical thought. It was an early extrapolation of the Seven Rays.

The excitement she felt in light of the fresh Theosophical outpouring she was a conduit for began to consume her. She was bursting with a sense of urgency. She wanted to see those words published. She knew some might look upon her writing with derision but she felt it imperative they were aired in public. She pictured one or two especially tall and thin men in the Esoteric Section, including the one who had poured scorn on her recognition of Koot Hoomi, and she shuddered. She had no idea if those chapters meant she was entitled to think of herself a disciple, although she supposed she must have been or she wouldn't have been given such an important task. Not that her ego was puffed up. Already she was feeling the weight of responsibility. In those moments when she scribed for the Tibetan, she was committed with utmost dedication. It was to be taxing work, involving hours and hours of focused concentration. So onerous was the undertaking, every day she wished the Tibetan had chosen someone else.

# An Organisational Fracas

Alice wasn't sure what to do with the chapters. She tucked them away, waiting for guidance.

Around the time that the Tibetan made his first contact with Alice, Foster was appointed as national secretary of the Theosophical Society. A few weeks later, Alice was appointed both editor of the sectional magazine, *The Messenger*, and chair of the committee running Krotona. They both earned ten dollars a week. Their associate, Dr Woodruff Shepherd, was appointed as publicity director. The three appointments meant Foster, Alice and Woodruff were in charge of all the policies, principles and associated administration of the society. They were also friends with Krotona's founder, attorney and banker Albert Powell Warrington. A self-contained and handsome man, Albert was the personal representative of Annie Besant. In all, it appeared they had the capacity to institute change, and change was needed. There was a shortage of organisational funds. A shadow of debt had been hanging over the utopia that was Krotona for some years prior to Alice's arrival. By 1919, the balance of debt was substantial. There was much discussion and many differing views amongst the membership and the leaders as to how to solve the matter.

Foster devised his own solution. He wanted to modernise the society and make it more open and democratic. When he visited Alice in her cottage in Beachwood Drive he would talk of little else. She agreed wholeheartedly with his vision for reform but she began to wonder where her devoted companion had gone. They both saw beyond the debt to a deeper issue, the lack of autonomy of the various lodges spread around the country through the placement of key members in the Esoteric Section, members like Albert with strong affiliations to Annie Besant. In effect, the leaders at Adyar had full organisational control of the Theosophical Society in America. This was contrary to an organisation founded on the notion of universal brotherhood. There was much discussion in the office, too, and Foster called for a meeting to see if a resolution could be found.

One Monday in late November the administration and various members of the Esoteric Section met in the lecture room. When Alice entered the room, the others were already seated. She saw at a glance the division in the room, Albert surrounded by members of the Esoteric Section, including its head, Marie Poutz, and vice-president of the American Section, Louis William Rogers. Alice took up a free chair over by Foster and Woodruff. Foster trawled as fast as he was able through the short agenda. Then he cleared his throat.

'I propose a solution to the administrative crisis.'

Rogers, a thick-set and fair-haired man, eyed him with derision. 'What administrative crisis?'

Foster held his gaze. 'By devolving power to the lodges, who will be given more say in electing officials to run headquarters, and the merging of the administration with the Esoteric Section into one overseeing body answerable to the membership and not exclusively to the Outer Head, Annie Besant.'

'And what will this achieve?' said Marie. A woman in her sixties, she sat up straight in her long white dress, her hair, parted in the middle and pinned back, the picture of spiritual enlightenment.

'I thought we were here to solve the debt crisis,' someone said.

'The debt crisis will be solved by tackling the administrative crisis,' Woodruff explained.

'There is no administrative crisis,' Louis said.

Albert, who had remained silent for much of the meeting, said, 'What Mr Bailey proposes is the divestment of authority from the Esoteric Section.'

A murmur rippled around the room. Marie responded with genuine alarm. 'But the Esoteric Section is comprised of disciples more evolved and therefore wiser and better equipped to make decisions than the membership.'

'The Esoteric Section, Miss Poutz, is merely the organ,' said Foster. 'The grinder is Mrs Besant.'

'That's outrageous. Take that back!'

Louis folded his arms across his chest. 'I propose we raise the dues and let that be an end to it.'

'I second that,' Marie said.

Foster sighed. 'Members do not see why they should finance Krotona's debt. It is a mortgage debt, after all. Perhaps servicing the debt should be the responsibility of Krotona alone, and not the responsibility of the membership.'

He was ignored.

'We should found more lodges, too.' Louis said. 'More members means more money coming in.'

'Founding lodges in order to service a debt seems to me cynical and unconscionable,' Foster said, raising his voice.

Again, he was ignored.

'All those in favour of increasing dues, please raise your hands.'

Foster counted the hands, a look of defeat appearing in his face. Alice could scarcely contain her reaction. How would the Theosophical Society ever free itself from the shackles of elitism and the odious concentration of power with that attitude?

When she joined the Esoteric Section she had to pledge allegiance to Annie Besant. She had no choice. For her Christian heart, that had been an outrage. Worse, no one could consider themselves a disciple unless it had been confirmed by Annie Besant. In that case, she had been overlooked. She kept her view to herself but it rankled inside like indigestion. Besides, she could not understand why the Masters would look for their disciples only among the ranks of the Esoteric Section of the Theosophical Society. It was preposterous.

She was convinced the Theosophical Society was on the trajectory of sectarianism. It was a path contrary to the principle of universal brotherhood. Theosophy should not be for the privileged few and should not be focused inwardly on founding lodges, but oriented outwardly, expounded to the masses, drawing in all who may be receptive to the teachings. She wanted the doors flung wide open. The old guard wanted them kept shut.

After the meeting, tempers ran high. The atmosphere in the office was unbearable. Foster was more determined than ever to democratise the society. Seeing this, Louis waded into him and Woodruff at every opportunity. Marie backed him up and Albert did nothing to intervene. The matter became so serious Foster cabled Mrs Besant to inform her that the Esoteric Section needed to stop dominating the administration. In response, Besant asked her personal assistant, Bahman Pestonji Wadia to assess the situation and intervene.

When Foster read Alice the telegram, she was filled with anticipation. Wadia managed the Theosophical Society's publishing house and was assistant editor of *The Theosophist*, making him the ideal recipient of her new Theosophical outpouring.

Wadia was visiting America as an Indian delegate to the International Industrial Conference, and on a tour of the Theosophical Society lodges. A month later, he cornered the courtyard beneath the pergola, emerging through a thicket of the foliage like a regal apparition. A handsome man, his brown eyes, intense beneath a prominent brow, granted him a serious, erudite visage. The fullness of his hair, black and short and parted at the side, was matched by his full beard. He exuded charm and sincerity and grace. Others flocked around him. She had to wait, bide her time. She exchanged pleasantries with him, testing the waters. She found in him someone she could trust. When he complimented her editing of *The Messenger*, she blushed.

She seized her chance and asked if he would be interested in reading some of her writing. His face lit from within. 'Of course, my dear. Bring it to me after lunch.'

She rushed home as soon as she could and met him in the courtyard as he ambled out of the dining room. He took the manuscript and sat down by the lily pond. She watched the goldfish dart about as he read.

'This is good,' he said after some time. 'Very good. The Tibetan, you say? So Djwhal Khul has chosen another. Most interesting that it should be you.'

'Thank you. I feel a need to do something with it.'

'I'm sure you do. Well, rest assured I will certainly publish this. Indeed, I will publish anything the Tibetan invites you to write.'

Wadia kept his word, although he held onto the copy for over a year, publishing the first two of her chapters in the February of 1921 edition of *The Theosophist*, with the third appearing the following month.

Meanwhile, official meetings were held and the acrimony was worse than ever but at least Wadia was on their side. With his support, Foster and Dr Shepherd formed the Towards Democracy League in an attempt to garner support amongst the membership. They produced pamphlets circulating their beliefs.

Alice grew upset by the discord in the office and, in her role as editor, the angry letters she received from members disgruntled over increased dues needed to help pay for the upkeep of Krotona and settle the debt. Little wonder. It was a case of the rank and file having to prop up the wealthy elite bent on retaining the luxury they had become accustomed to, with all those elegant buildings set in magnificent grounds.

In response, hoping to lend weight to Foster's campaigning, she wrote a piece for *The Messenger*. She strove to be measured and balanced, outlining their vision for a more unified leadership. To solve the financial issue and streamline the organisation, she wrote persuasively of the need to make changes so that the headquarters of the American Section of the society joined forces with the Esoteric Section to form one overarching governing body. The society's headquarters would then effectively maintain control of the American Section of the society.

The magazine went out and the letters flooded in. A month passed and the row intensified. Albert, who had been showing signs of exhaustion, resigned as president, stating that he intended to join Annie Besant in India. Vice-president Louis Rogers stepped into the role. Alice saw defeat on the horizon. Louis was a trade union activist and bulwark and he loathed Foster and his Towards Democracy League with a passion. He was not alone in his view. Alice was fielding letters attacking the league. Many she filed, but some she knew she had to publish; the authors were too prominent. In the April issue of *The Messenger* she included a number of letters attacking the league. One, composed by a lawyer and priest in the Liberal Catholic Church, Robert Kelsey Walton, was especially cutting, accusing the league organisers of spreading misinformation and making a mockery of the very democracy they purportedly wished to institute.

Attempts were made by league supporters and members to defend themselves, but the tirade against them was unrelenting, especially from the new president. Alice was beside herself with worry. Foster was determined as ever but she could see no future for them under Louis' dictatorial rule.

One warm afternoon in May, Alice was seated by the window keeping a watchful eye on her daughters playing outside, when she saw Foster marching up the road towards the house. He was there on her porch before she had got to the front door. He waved a letter at her and said, 'I've been fired.'

'Oh dear. I knew this would happen.'

'The man is a tyrant.'

'He is popular, Foster. We both know that.'

'You'll be next, Alice. I am sure of it. And Woodruff.'

He was right. When she went to her office at Krotona Inn the following morning, her letter of dismissal was waiting for her on her desk. Stunned, she packed up her things and left the office.

Louis had turned venomous. Not content with sacking the trio, he ridiculed their efforts in the June edition of *The Messenger*. When Alice read her copy, she was struck by his sarcastic and hateful tone and wondered why so many supported the man. Worse, he seemed bent on construing the efforts of the democracy league as a form of attack, accusing Foster and his group of flooding the membership with 'circulars of outrageous misrepresentation by would-be martyrs who have a grievance against the administration...'

'We should leave here, Foster,' she said. 'Find some other place to live our lives.'

'I'm not finished with the league yet. There is still a chance we will win. The Chicago convention is coming up and I want to give my presentation as planned.'

'Do you think it's worth it?'

'While the blood still pumps through my veins, yes, it is.'

He wouldn't be dissuaded. Alice stayed at home, fretting over the lack of income and her dwindling reserves. She had the children to clothe and feed and her housekeeper, Augusta, to pay.

When Foster returned downcast, she knew their time at Krotona was over. Days later, Louis tried to get them both evicted from the grounds. Foster was forced to telegram Annie Besant to overturn the eviction. He succeeded, but it didn't lessen Louis' sense of triumph.

After that, the weeks passed slowly and painfully. She did her best to bury herself in her work for the Tibetan, taking down the rest of the letters in what was to become *Letters on Occult Meditation*. The final dig at all they had tried to achieve in the service of the society came when she read the September issue of *The Messenger* to find Louis describing the organisational row that had gone on for almost a year as a teapot tempest.

Teapot tempest? The diminutive phrase rang in her ears. There was nothing trivial about the outcome. She was frantic with worry. She had no appetite and all she could think of was another period of destitution. What next for her? Another job in a factory? With Foster still living in a tent, and her left with no income and three daughters to care for, their situation was dire. That day they assessed their situation, to find their joint finances amounted to less than two dollars. Bills were mounting and the rent was due. Her income from Britain was not forthcoming.

'It's my fault, Alice. I should have seen it was no use trying to transform the organisation.'

'We both saw the need, as did Woodruff. Whatever Louis does, we would do better to leave well alone.'

'I can't. The man drives me crazy. He's a despot.'

'A popular despot.'

'Aren't they always.'

Two days later, an anonymous donor left some cash in an envelope on her doorstep. Finding that envelope and seeing the cash inside she all but wept with relief. It was symbolic of the support she had, they both had, despite the efforts of Mr Rogers.

Then Mr Ernest Suffern, who had been following the row with interest and met Foster at the Chicago conference, wrote offering him a position as secretary in his Theosophical Association of New York, with a salary of $300. Foster accepted the post and prepared to move across America. Alice stayed behind until it was suitable for her to join him.

Two envelopes, two gifts, and between them they set her on a course that would grow into a life's work.

# State Library of Victoria

An unexpected knock on the door and Heather jumped. Suzanne poked her head in and said, 'I thought I saw a light on. You're not working late again? You need to take a break from this stuffy little room of yours. Go and get some air.'

'I don't need any air.'

'Still not listening to reason then.'

'Stage one, am I?'

'Stage one?'

'Of the grieving process.'

'I think what you are manifesting in here has gone far beyond the stages of grief, my friend.'

'Suzanne, I just want to get to the end of what I'm doing.'

'Of course you do. See you in the morning, then.'

Did she have to sound so patronising?

Heather turned back to her computer screen, picking up where she had left off. She'd become engrossed in a Theosophical Society scandal involving Leadbeater, who admitted under oath in 1906 to the sexual abuse of boys in his care in India. By the time Alice Bailey was on the scene, Leadbeater had moved to Sydney, and while he remained a Theosophist, he was also ordained as a bishop of the Liberal Catholic Church, an organisation he co-founded in 1916 along with Theosophist James Ingall Wedgwood, a member of the Wedgwood family famous for their plates.

Heather wasn't in the least surprised to discover that in Sydney both men had come under investigation for sexual activities involving boys. By then, Alice Bailey was at Krotona.

Heather tried to imagine what it would have been like for a woman as pious as Alice Bailey to have found herself in the thick of all that unsavoury fallout. It must have been momentous for her, the very organisation in which she had found a home riven by one man's debased and evil acts, acts condoned by the Theosophical head, Annie Besant, who, despite what he had done, permitted him to remain in the society. Alice Bailey barely mentions the scandal or the man, other than to mock him in one brief paragraph of her autobiography.

Alice Bailey might have left the Theosophical Society like the others, but she didn't. Neither did she shun its doctrine. Instead, she decided to change things from within. She wanted to purify the occult, elevate it from the gutter of impropriety. Considering the prominence and organisational power of those she stood against, her task appeared doomed to failure before it began.

As if that were not enough, another storm was fomenting. Leadbeater had found an Indian boy in the grounds of Adyar, a boy he decided was special, if his clairvoyant abilities could be trusted. So special, in fact, to be almost a saint. For right there, walking about, was none other than the New World Teacher, the second coming of the Christ. He presented the boy to Annie Besant and they named him Jiddu Krishnamurti. They then groomed him for his high future. Despite widespread ridicule and condemnation, Besant used her position to make pronouncements about this Krishnamurti. To Heather, the entire scenario was delusional in the extreme. She failed to comprehend what went on inside the minds of those figures or their devotees. How could anyone suspend common sense and invest in such a grand deception, especially when one of the key players had been accused of child sex abuse?

Krishnamurti later renounced that status, but he did grow up to be a spiritual teacher, nonetheless. Despite all the allegations against him, Leadbeater retained a loyal following, including Krotona's founder Albert Warrington. Leadbeater was a prolific writer and his large output would go on to stand in competition with Alice Bailey's.

That must have rankled.

Outside, it was getting dark. Heather removed her glasses and went over to the bench to eat the stir fry she had bought earlier, shovelling the contents of the container into her mouth with little interest or care, ignoring the lukewarm temperature of the food. Chasing the last bamboo shoot around in the remaining slurry, she emitted a loud burp and succumbed to a sudden thirst. She deposited the empty container in her bin and reached in her shoulder bag for her water bottle. Fresh water from the staff kitchen might have been preferable to the stale contents she had to hand, but nothing would propel her out of her office, not while she was in the midst of uncovering the truth.

In one of her notebooks, Professor Foyle had outlined a controversy between Alice Bailey and Leadbeater. Heather riffled through until she found it.

The controversy concerns the publication of Leadbeater's *The Masters and the Path* and Alice Bailey's *Initiation, Human and Solar*. Leadbeater's book came out three years after Bailey's. The works cover similar ground and allegations of plagiarism soon abounded, but they were not launched at the obvious party, Leadbeater, but at Alice Bailey. Never mind that Leadbeater was known to be purchasing his copy of Alice Bailey's books the moment they were published. Or that he made enthusiastic comments about them in private, although he never publically commended her work. None of that mattered to Theosophical purists, who were poised ready to denounce Alice Bailey, refusing to read her writing and officially criticizing her for falsely claiming to be in communication, as Blavatsky was before her, with the Tibetan. The matter was never resolved because the allegedly plagiarised material in question had been composed by Besant and Leadbeater specifically for the Esoteric Section, and only available to members and no one else. Since that material had never been made public, it was impossible to assess the claim's validity.

It occurred to Heather that even if it was true, at least Alice Bailey had taken the trouble to make the material available to all and not just a select few. Perhaps that had been her motive. Or perhaps she really was in telepathic rapport with the Tibetan, who desired his own fresh outpouring of the same.

In her notes, Professor Foyle voiced her frustration in the form of thick black lines underscoring the way scholars in the field of Western Esotericism had taken Leadbeater's side through omissions or one-sided accounts, and in so doing discrediting Bailey's work as nothing but derivative. Heather shared Foyle's annoyance. She was a historian and a librarian and she had developed sympathy for her subject. Alice Bailey had been through enough, and when all was said and done only wanted acceptance and belonging. She got neither.

Heather glanced up at her row of leather-bound volumes comprising many thousands of pages of text. No one in their right mind would take the trouble to produce such an exhaustive and astonishingly detailed opus if it amounted to intellectual theft. She sensed the competitiveness of the times, too, as though all and sundry were putting pen to paper wanting to be some sort of spiritual authority.

According to Professor Foyle, the negative reactions Bailey received should be understood in the light of the regular content contained in *The Theosophist*.

"Besant wrote polemics on themes such as racism and slavery, and Wadia composed articles concerning organisational matters and the aims and objectives of the society. Other contributors provided pieces on comparative religion and philosophy, world politics, psychology and second-hand discussions and summaries of Blavatsky's teachings. Bailey's pieces leapt out at the reader. They were authoritative, and clearly designed to represent a new outpouring of the Ageless Wisdom. For orthodox members, this new material would have caused immediate offence. For them, the new teaching was composed by an upstart newcomer and troublemaker who clearly didn't know her place within the Theosophical Society hierarchy, and couldn't possibly have been in telepathic rapport with the Tibetan because Besant and Leadbeater had not affirmed it to be true."

Troublemaker?

As far as she could tell, Alice Bailey had never caused trouble in her life, except perhaps through her grumpy teenage years.

Heather typed up Foyle's notes, reshaping and cross-referencing with her resources as she went. Knowing most of the staff had gone home for the day, she forced herself to take a break and stretch her legs before tackling the next phase of the drama, walking to the kitchen to replenish her water bottle. When she returned, she read over her notes and sources.

She worked tirelessly in the days that followed, drafting, editing and polishing her paper, submitting it to Shona for the next issue of the library's journal.

At winter's end, when squalls charged through the city day upon day, interspersed with sudden bursts of sunshine, Heather began to prepare her aunt's house for sale. Her mother had only needed that initial consent to arrange the removal of the family heirlooms to Harcourt Street, once Heather had prepared an inventory of the contents for Mr Fenston. The moment she was able, Joan had her heirlooms all in situ in their new locations. She executed their removal with such alacrity and precision, Heather surmised she had been planning for their arrival for decades.

Hilary's dining table did look much better at Joan's, it had more space around it, and the escritoire enjoyed pride of place in the front room, facing the upright piano on the opposite wall. Joan had put the dresser and armoire in the guest bedroom, and there was no denying they suited the room which already sported a carved wooden bedstead. Yet the pieces were constant reminders of her aunt, especially the dining table which Heather couldn't avoid sitting at. It was as though Hilary herself had somehow been transplanted along with the furniture.

As recompense, over breakfast one day, Joan gave Heather a brooch that had belonged to Katharine. Heather had a photo of her wearing it. A cameo featuring a pair of birds carved in ivory and mounted on black enamel, set in an oval of ornate gold. 'It isn't of any value,' Joan said, watching Heather put it on.

Satisfied with her acquisitions, Joan wanted nothing more to do with her sister's possessions. Heather invited the cousins, Beverly, Maureen and Veronica, to take their pick of what remained, and they arranged to meet one Saturday afternoon in spring.

Heather arrived at the appointed time and was putting the key in the lock when the cousins pulled up in a convoy of station wagons and trailers. She let the women in and stood by and watched as they poked around her aunt's things. Having steeled herself in advance, she was numb at first, but as they rummaged and ferried things out the door her veins filled with indignation. They were vultures. It was all she could do to maintain her composure.

Between them, they removed a small couch and matching arm chairs, the television, two coffee tables, a whole set of crockery, saucepans, paintings, even rugs. They were thorough and obliging of each other's wants—this would go well in your living room; no, no, you have it; I'm one short, do you mind? It was as though they were rummaging through a charity shop. Which was where Heather supposed the rest would end up.

The rest consisted of her aunt's clothes—minus the two coats, a hat, a woollen skirt suit and several pairs of leather shoes that the cousins had taken—the odds and ends in the kitchen, her linen and towels and an assortment of bric-a-brac. Heather decided to keep the only remaining piece of furniture, her aunt's well-worn oak desk, along with a crystal vase and a decorative bowl Hilary had brought back from a trip to Uluru. Most of the food Heather threw away, only keeping an unopened box of organic rice puffs.

Eyeing the state of the garden while she was there, she made a mental note to find a gardener to attend to the lawn and shrubs.

By the end of the following week, the house was empty and ready for its valuation. Following around a smart man in a smart suit, she saw through the agent's eyes the shabby paintwork and out-of-date kitchen. The bathroom, too, needed a makeover. Was it worth investing in renovations? At the end of his assessment, the agent advised her not to bother, and to wait until spring was fully underway before putting the house on the market as it would most likely fetch a better price. He was confident of a round million.

Meanwhile, her parents had taken to scanning the real estate pages in the local paper, her mother cutting out those she thought suitable and leaving them beside Heather's setting at the breakfast table. Most were apartments in the nearby suburbs of Kew, Malvern and Camberwell. The ones in Kew Heather rejected straight away, telling her mother not to bother with Kew because it was too far from a train station. She entertained the others without any intention of viewing any of them. She had already made up her mind to adhere to her original decision of Ballarat.

One morning, seeing the little pile of cuttings, she decided to reveal her plans. Joan was halfway through her boiled egg when she made the announcement.

'Where?' Joan said, sputtering on a mouthful.

'Ballarat,' William said, putting down his newspaper.

'West!' Joan's spoon tumbled onto her plate with a crash. 'Why on earth would you want to go west?'

'It was where I had planned to live before the inheritance.'

'Even so, now you won't need to. You can afford to live practically anywhere.'

'I don't want to live anywhere. I don't want to live in an apartment or a unit. I'd like my own whole house standing in its own block of land.'

'She doesn't want much,' Joan said to her husband with an acerbic laugh.

'It's what you have,' he said mildly.

'That's different.'

'We do understand the challenges your generation faces,' her father said.

'What's wrong with Ballarat? It's on the train line. It's only forty-five minutes to the city.'

'You won't stop her,' William said as Joan inhaled to speak.

'That's correct. You won't.' She stood. 'I'm sorry if this upsets you, mother, but I've made up my mind.'

She left the room, her body trembling. She felt like a teenager needing permission to go to a dance. It was laughable. At her age.

'We'll never see her,' she heard her mother say as she headed down the hall.

At the library, Heather took refuge in her work. She went in early and left late, filling her mind with Professor Foyle and her collection, grateful to the scholar for her manuscript, her notebooks and her sticky notes, which Heather followed like breadcrumbs.

From the scholar, Heather learned that the New Age movement had embraced, almost revered Alice Bailey. Yet the academics in the field of Western Esotericism, a specialism emerging out of the history of religion, didn't hold her in high esteem. Why? Was it due to that very association with the New Age, her the chief theorist, as one academic, Steven Sutcliffe, had claimed? Had she been ostracised over the disdain and snobbery with which some scholars regarded a popular cultural movement known for being out there and whacky? It couldn't be because she was merely a second-generation breakaway Theosophist, if the same scholars acknowledged Rudolph Steiner, Annie Besant and Charles Leadbeater. Heather decided there must be some other reason why Alice Bailey was not taken seriously. A reason compelling enough to have motivated Professor Foyle to write a monograph.

Then there was Foyle's slipper dream, which must be connected in some fashion or she wouldn't have included it in her notebook. What was it about this mysterious Alice Bailey and her blue books that both compelled and repelled? She added the question to her current to-do list and put an asterisk beside it.

# PART TWO
# 1931-1933

# Ascona

Alice felt blessed to have found herself at Casa Gabriella in a room overlooking the water where, from the purview afforded by the window, she could gaze and ponder while the rest of the household slept. She took in the early morning light dancing across the waters of Lake Maggiore, shimmering silver in the glassy black. The mountains on the far side that rose up sharply, cutting a jagged snow-capped line horizon, their wooded flanks deep in shade, a thick curtain enclosing the valley that was all but drowned by the lake. In all it was a splendid sight to behold.

Her host, Olga Fröbe, had installed the girls in a room down the hall, leaving her and Foster to make use of the large and airy room tucked away in a corner of the house. It was simply furnished with twin beds side by side. She preferred her own room, but the arrangement suited her reasonably well. At least she could rise before dawn without disturbing his sleep, and when he awoke, he went downstairs, as he had an hour before, to ensure her peace, leaving her to scribe the words that entered her mind. It had become her custom, her daily ritual, something she had undertaken for more than a decade. Taxing as it was, she enjoyed the work; her mind, at other times a dance of thoughts and impressions, became still, poised, receptive. Although there were times she wondered if she had been wise to accept the request. For it bound her, not only to scribing; she felt compelled to act on all that the words entailed. They expressed, as far as she knew, irrefutable truth, and they were as good as, no, better than Scripture. The message was relevant, contemporary and vital for the survival of the species, perhaps even the planet.

Did she doubt the veracity of the teachings? Of course she did. Sometimes she thought the words she received were gobbledegook, especially the most abstract of the teachings. Yet she always understood the basic meaning, and above all the intention behind the words, as though her mind were pre-configured somehow.

She taught the words, distilled them and lectured and trained others in their ways.

Women of her standing gave up their life to flower arranging and gossip, or to other trivial social pursuits available to those of the leisured classes. It was rare that she envied them any of it. Although, the work had been easier to manage when she was in her forties, as she rose to prominence as an occult leader. At fifty-one she had reached that age when her aches and her immobility seemed to grow by the day. Not that she ever openly complained, but fatigue consumed her all too often and she wondered in her more debilitated moments for how long she could continue. But there was still so much to achieve! She felt as though she were on her knees, chiselling the foundations of an edifice that would rise higher than the Empire State Building under construction back in New York. There were days, days when her head was wracked with pain and her body scarcely functioned, when she wished she hadn't agreed to any of it.

An hour later and the Tibetan was quiet. She let her gaze rest on the slow blue awakening of the lake. Tufts of cloud hung motionless in the late summer sky, their underbellies a bluish grey. Already the nearby trees were turning autumnal, the fringes of their leaves tinged with brown. She could glimpse through the trees the old town of Ascona rising up at the lake's northern edge. The setting was sublime, and she would remain ever grateful to Olga for the invitation to stay in such exquisite surroundings. Yet she couldn't help harbouring misgivings. If only the human element mirrored the physical, all would have been perfection. But it did not. She had experienced the same misgivings, immediate and strong, when they had visited the year before, and the magnanimous, if somewhat overwhelming Olga Fröbe met them at the station at Locarno, and drove through Ascona to her home.

It was an exceptional drive, Ascona a village of cobbled streets opening onto small piazzas. Tall, four-storey buildings with low pitched roofs and painted facades greeted the eye. Ribbons of narrow lanes threaded their way through the steep, wooded slopes. The weather was glorious, if a little on the hot side. Alice would have enjoyed it all the more were she not feeling the aftermath fatigue of the journey from Antwerp via Domodossola. Part of her rued her decision to take the girls on the Centovalli train, although to be so close to the Simplon Pass and miss the breath-taking scenery would have been a travesty. At times, it had felt as though the train were trundling through the air itself, viaducts taking them over the deepest of valleys. She sat rigid while her daughters were all ecstatic exclamations.

On the way to Casa Gabriella, Foster sat in the front, listening to Olga's gay chatter as she furnished them with a potted history of the area. Sitting in the back seat, squashed in alongside her girls, Alice made a conscious effort to enjoy the scenery. It wasn't until they had reached the outskirts of the town, that she was rewarded with a sight that made her recoil.

Olga had chosen to take them on a small detour past Monte Verità, a Bohemian enclave situated on a hill on the edge of Ascona. Olga indicated the locale with a wave of her hand, launching into an explanation as she swung the car through the bends.

The site was originally established as a health institute, comprising numerous small huts, and for decades Monte Verità supported a utopian community. Since 1900, the locale had drawn an array of freethinking types from throughout Europe and beyond, including all manner of writers, artists, dancers and political radicals. 'You would be amazed who has visited,' Olga said in her heavily accented English. 'Monte Verità has seen Lenin, Trotsky, Kropotkin, Paul Klee, Herman Hesse, Mary Wigman, Isadora Duncan, and even Rudolph Steiner.'

Even? Alice was puzzled as to why Olga had singled him out.

'You've visited?' Foster said, taking an interest.

'Often. It's dreadfully, how shall I put it, risqué.'

Foster laughed. It was a curious laugh.

Encouraged, Olga went on to explain that Monte Verità had received a burst of new life five years before, when Baron Eduard von der Heydt, the former banker to the German Kaiser, purchased the main building for use as a hotel. 'Do you know the Baron? He's a renowned *saloniste*. A pompous old effete really, always fluttering about, *in a dress*.'

Her laugh was mocking. This time, Foster didn't respond. Alice censured the giggles from the back seat with a stern look, wishing her daughters were not privy to the account.

'But you know,' Olga said, 'he's had King Leopold of Belgium there, and Thomas Mann. Numerous luminaries, in fact.'

Alice sensed from her airy tone that Olga saw in Heydt a rival. Her intuition was reinforced when Olga said, 'We shall show him what a real salon looks like, won't we Alice?'

Alice demurred inwardly. She might have accepted the challenge, had it been put in a less objectionable fashion. She hadn't brought her family to Switzerland to satisfy Olga's competitive streak. She contrived a bland smile and stopped paying attention to the running commentary. It wasn't until they were driving by a stretch of open garden that the reality of Olga's words was confirmed. To her horror, right there overlooking the road, stood two men who not only appeared naked, they were kissing. In the front of the car, heads turned. Foster's lingered. Alice averted her gaze. She was well aware that others might accuse her of being a prude, that all free-thinking communities allowed for a certain level of permissiveness, but she didn't want her daughters exposed to such impropriety and dearly hoped they hadn't been looking that way.

Evil had evidently infused the locale. She was reminded that the area was at one time the centre of the Black Mass in Central Europe. Debauchery and the black arts were common enough bedfellows and where one was found, so too the other. No matter what influence the decadent-sounding Baron von der Heydt might be exerting, Monte Verità was a community that transparently lacked moral rectitude in its entirety.

Alice vowed privately that she would move heaven and earth to keep her family from contact with its milieu. She made a mental note that as soon as she had the opportunity, she would sit her daughters down and warn them in clear and certain terms to keep their guard and their distance from the degeneracy she had seen.

Would her words of caution be enough to steer her adventuresome girls? Surely so. She had brought them up well, and by all accounts they were good young women, if a little headstrong at times, like their mother.

With Monte Verità behind them, Olga turned down another road and they received pleasing glimpses of Lake Maggiore through the trees. Soon they were driving on the main road, cut into the mountainside above the lake, and, a short while later, Olga pulled up in a small parking bay.

Casa Gabriella was tucked below a steep embankment, only its tiled roof visible from the road. They decanted and, leaving their luggage in the boot, followed Olga through a low gate and down a flight of stone steps that zigzagged past terraces laden with shrubbery. To one side, coming in and out of view, was the lecture hall, to the other the beautiful old farmhouse.

The path opened out on a narrow grassy area beside the lake where a row of ducks sat contemplating the water. The girls rushed over and the ducks flapped and quacked and went on their way. Alice saw with relief that there were opportunities for swimming and boating to keep the children amused during their stay. The house even had its own little jetty.

Yet they were hardly children. Dorothy was twenty, Mildred approaching eighteen and Ellison eighteen months younger. At those ages she often had to reassure herself they would all be married soon enough. She felt sure of it. She loved them dearly, of course she did, but she was looking forward to that moment when she could close the door on all that motherly worry and effort. She had managed to rear three high-spirited girls, too, although she suspected their exuberance had much to do with the times they were growing up in. As far as she was concerned, with all of its licentiousness and latitude, the last decade had done every young woman a disservice. She wouldn't apologise for her Edwardian piety and neither would she countenance changing her observance of the religious values instilled in her as a child.

The girls, in contrast, were all delighted squeals and bubbling enthusiasm. Alice was reminded of their passage across the Atlantic, of the gowns she had made for them, how patriotic-looking they were in red, white and blue. Such beautiful girls with their blonde hair and winning smiles. They had the time of their lives, rushing around hither and thither and dancing with the officers. None of the girls had travelled abroad before, other than that one occasion when Dorothy had visited Hawaii to stay with Foster's brother and his wife and their young family. Keeping an eye on her daughters' whereabouts had proven exhausting. She suspected as she entered Casa Gabriella that the four weeks they would be at Olga's would be more tiring still.

In that moment of bustle and fuss as the Baileys were welcomed into the house, with Olga fielding a barrage of questions from the girls, Alice succumbed to a rush of sentimental gratitude, wishing her darling friend, who was also an Alice, were there with them.

They would never have been able to come and the collaboration with Olga would not have eventuated were it not for Alice Ortiz. Not content with paying for all of her daughters' schooling, Alice had offered to pay for their future travel expenses as well.

Alice Ortiz was a du Pont by birth, and her wealth second only to her generosity. The very dress Alice had on, the necklace that hung so lightly around her neck, it had all been passed on to her by her namesake, her dear Alice. There were times Alice felt she owed all of her material security to her friend. Although that was far from true. She benefited from many a magnanimous gesture when it came to a roof over her family's heads.

It wasn't her friend's generosity that had swept her up in a spell of sentimentality. Besides, she preferred not to dwell on her own good fortune in this regard. It was simply that she missed her friend's soft face, her demure and gentle spirt. She would gladly have traded the vigorous Olga Fröbe for her soothing company.

Then again, it was the Olgas of the world who got things done.

She walked across the room and settled into the chair Olga proffered, unable not to admire the woman's drive as she issued directions to the others.

A woman in her fifties saw into another, and Alice would never forget that evening in the autumn of 1929 when Olga had arrived on their doorstep and put forward her vision. It was while they were living on Caritas Island. Olga had a brother living on nearby Long Island, which made some sense of the journey across the Atlantic, but truth be told, the purpose of her visit was not her family.

The visit wasn't entirely unexpected. Alice knew Olga, although they had never met. She was a student of the teachings, which was why Alice took her proposition seriously. That, and she proved exceedingly persuasive.

Olga had first contacted Alice in 1928, seeking her collaboration in establishing the school of spiritual research at Casa Gabriella. There had been an exchange of letters. Last spring, by way of endorsement, Alice had published in her magazine, *The Beacon*, a short piece composed by Olga, titled "Know Thy Self".

Through their correspondence, Alice discovered the Dutch artist had recently inherited Casa Gabriella from her father. About ten years before, she had married flautist and flyer Iwan Fröbe. He died in a plane crash just prior to the birth of their twin girls, Ingeborg and Bettina, leaving Olga penniless. Olga said she had returned to Zurich and applied her artistic skills to jewellery and embroidery. How does one derive sufficient income as a single mother from those pursuits? Alice had packed sardines in a factory to feed her three daughters. She couldn't imagine Olga doing that. Olga was a society lady and champion skier and in Zurich, she established a salon and surrounded herself with the region's intellectual and artistic elite. She said she yearned to establish another, along different lines, at Ascona.

In all, Olga sounded like an impressive woman, an achiever, if rather wilful, and as Alice welcomed her guest into her living room, and took in at a glance the tall, strong-boned frame, she sensed her determination knew no bounds. She was a handsome woman too, with locks of wavy blonde hair cut short, her dress, calf-length, made of the finest of fabrics in a pleasing Chantilly cream.

'What a charming house,' she said, glancing around. 'It was a challenge to find, I must say.'

'Didn't you bring my directions? I drew you a map.'

'Which I accidentally doused in tea.' She threw back her head with a self-deprecating laugh. There was a brief moment of silence. 'A whole little island all to yourselves. How remarkable!'

Alice wasn't about to tell her the house belonged to Graham Stokes Phelps, who had invited them to stay when he could no longer bear to be in it himself.

She suggested tea. Olga said she would rather wine.

Foster and Alice exchanged glances.

'There's a prohibition,' Foster said.

'I'm well aware. My brother has a wine cellar.'

'I'm afraid we do not.'

It was true, in a fashion, after they had agreed never to touch a drop of what Graham had left down there.

Olga made to speak then changed her mind. Instead, without invitation she claimed the closest chair and pulled off her gloves, a finger at a time. Foster hovered, expectantly. She set the gloves down in her lap and looked up with a pinched smile.

'Then, I'll have nothing.'

Alice folded her hands in her lap. Olga's reaction bordered on petulance. Alice expected better from her own children, let alone a woman who, in every other respect, commanded high esteem.

Foster, as awkward as she, took up the fireside chair, placing both hands on his knees.

Without further ado, Olga proceeded to enthuse over her beautiful house in Switzerland and its exquisite setting. 'I've had a lecture hall built, as I've already mentioned.' She went on to explain it was constructed of stone and cut into the steep hillside, with large windows opening out onto verandas on the north and east sides, overlooking the lake. 'Now I can't leave it sitting there to rot. I need to put people on all those chairs. I need a presence standing at my lectern. Someone compelling.'

The school Olga had in mind would attract esoteric thinkers and students from all quarters, both from the East and the West, and they could mingle and discuss ideas in a relaxed and inspiring setting. Olga would host. She wanted the Baileys to initiate the project, find speakers, lecture and teach. 'Please, won't you say yes.'

Alice looked across at Foster. That Olga had come in person impressed her, but was it a project too many to add to their already busy lives?

'It's a lot to take on,' he said, as though reading her mind.

'We will need to think about it, Olga,' she said, instilling a resolute tone in her voice. 'I am sure you understand.'

'Do think about it. And do say yes. My home will be yours for the duration.'

Foster frowned. 'A month, I think I recall you suggesting.'

'Indeed, a whole four weeks. Just think what might be achieved. Through this project you will extend your reach in Europe. I can introduce you to many a fine mind.'

'Olga, there are the children to consider,' Alice said. 'We can't very well leave them with the maid.'

Olga hesitated, doubtful perhaps, before a magnanimous smile lit her face.

'I shall accommodate them, too.'

'That is most kind of you, Olga, but…'

'I can see that I must leave it with you,' she said, pulling on her gloves. 'I would like to begin plans for the first session before long to allow ample time to devise an itinerary. If, that is, you decide to proceed.'

'Mrs Bailey has said we'll think about it.'

Olga's gaze flitted between them.

'I would appreciate it if you wouldn't leave it too long to make up your minds.'

'I'll write to you after the New Year,' Alice said.

'Then I'll take up no more of your time.'

She stood abruptly, taking her impatience with her to the door. Foster showed her out.

In the weeks that followed, Alice remained reticent. She had her own organisations to manage and didn't relish involvement in another. The Arcane School already had members in America, Britain, the Netherlands, Italy, Switzerland, South America, Turkey, even West Africa. Although Olga's proposal would be a novel way to consolidate her efforts in Europe and they could always do with expanding membership. Yet the reality was they couldn't afford the travel expenses.

It was Alice Ortiz's offer of financial assistance that finally swayed her. Alice hadn't been outside America for twenty years, and she dearly wanted her daughters to see something of the world. She could regard Olga's summer school as a sort of working holiday, make the month a fulcrum of a longer vacation. Cast in that light, the proposal seemed too good an opportunity to ignore.

A bird, a duck perhaps, glided down and as it landed on the waters of the lake, ripples radiated, fracturing the reflection of the early morning light. Had she made an error of judgement collaborating with Olga? It was a niggle, ever so slight, and she banished it by reminding herself that ever since Olga arrived on her doorstep, she had pondered the potential it represented to advance her cause.

With Olga's connections to Europe's intellectual elite, there was every chance the teachings—six volumes already in print, some composed by the Tibetan, others her own, and another scheduled for next year—would gain acceptance by the academic community and be regarded with scholarly respect. How she craved the endorsement, the validation that would afford! She had already gained endorsement from Mr Harry Overstreet, chair of the Department of Philosophy and Psychology at the City College of New York, who wrote the preface to her 1930 release, *The Soul and Its Mechanism*. It was a good start but more was needed. Above all, she sought endorsement from Carl Jung, who had risen to eminence in the milieu. His approval would secure a future for the texts, singling her out from the plethora of mystical writers, whose quackery cluttered the shelves of bookstores. It wasn't the texts themselves that mattered, but the wisdom they contained, wisdom essential for the evolution of consciousness of humanity. Such acknowledgement would set the writing and her organisations apart, permanently, from all those mystical and occult sects and their ill-informed leaders, sects that seemed to be popping up all over, almost all of them given to nonsense and chicanery.

There was every reason to be optimistic. The lectures were proceeding in a most satisfying fashion and attendance was high. Violet Tweedale had come again, as had her most loyal student, pioneering psychiatrist Roberto Assagioli, bringing his associate, Professor Vittorino Vezzani with him for a second year. She was fortunate to have also secured Mizra Ahmad Sohrad, with his fascinating background in the Bahai faith; the marvellous Gerald Reynolds, director of the American Conservatory at Fontainbleau; and Prince Hubertus zu Löewenstein-Wertheim-Freudenberg who was a most enigmatic speaker, despite giving his lectures in German.

With so many notable figures, how could she not look forward to the day ahead? Some of her students had even travelled from America to attend, and one of them seemed to be forming a fondness for Erlo. What a delight to see young Erlo in love. A Dutchman and loyal student, Erlo Van Waveren helped organise her European lecture tours. A grave young man, he deserved happiness and seemed to have found it. In all, the session was a success by any measure. The only scholar of significance missing was Jung, who had declined her invitation for a second year. His absence seemed to have marred the proceedings for Olga, as though he had sent in his stead a dark cloud that hung over her head, colouring her mood. She knew Olga revered Jung. She had been his patient at one time and it was understandable. Alice just wished she would stop mentioning his name. Jung, Jung, Jung. She dropped 'Jung' into every conversation as though he were as essential a flavouring as salt.

That niggle returned, a little borer burrowing into the bedrock of her mind. She had to reign in her thoughts, telling herself to stop worrying over trifles. Part of her wanted to stand up and read over her notes for the morning's lecture, "The Stages in Meditation", but she remained seated, expecting more words from the Tibetan to enter her mind. She was scribing a section for a new treatise on white magic, and he seemed to have stopped, mid-paragraph. It wasn't like him to hesitate.

The technique was simple. She took down, word for word, what was is given, occasionally smoothing out the language, all the while remaining in full conscious control of her faculties. When she had first started, she used clairaudience but over time she found she was able to attune to the Tibetan's thoughts as they appeared in her mind. She never once doubted the integrity of the impressions she received. Of course there were naysayers, many of them, and the process was impossible to prove. She wouldn't even try.

There were those who accused her of contriving to deny responsibility for the words her texts contained, since they were not coming from her own mind. Others accused her of taking down the Tibetan's thoughts incorrectly. How would they know! Still others said she was a complete fraud, claim making to increase her own spiritual status. Why would she bother to defend her position when she had never made any claim of the sort? She had learned the hard way early on never to even hint at any sort of spiritual superiority. Then there were those, and they were by far the larger group, who dismissed the notion that anyone could be in telepathic rapport with another entity altogether.

Alice looked forward to the day she met Carl Jung so that she could set him straight. She had heard that the eminent psychiatrist believed the Tibetan to be a manifestation of her higher self. If he was correct, then he was unwittingly crediting her with an astonishingly knowledgeable, penetrating and far-reaching intellect, able to interpret and extrapolate ideas impenetrable to almost the whole of humanity. She smiled as she pictured pointing that out to his face. Perhaps next year, he would attend the summer school. It was a hope she shared with Olga, although not with the same obsessive zeal.

She turned her gaze back to the room, eyeing Foster's unmade bed beside her own, neatly made one. He hadn't wanted to disturb her. She was reminded of the limited time, of the obligations of the day ahead. She had wasted too long lost in her own thoughts as her mind squirrelled about. She closed her eyes and focused, slowing her breath, allowing her mind to still and directing her inner sight towards an imaginary vanishing point.

Before long words fell into her mind. She anticipated a follow on from his earlier thoughts, but the communication that came through was a direct instruction concerning another matter altogether. She reached for a fresh sheet of paper and picked up her pen.

The Tibetan informed her that he wished to band together his disciples scattered throughout the world to form a new group. They were to be called the New Group of World Servers. It didn't take long for the Tibetan to outline the essence his idea. There would be two divisions. The first would have a close relationship with the Spiritual Hierarchy and work in an international capacity towards salvaging the world. These World Servers would work to promote three core principles: international understanding to offset the rise of nationalism; economic sharing to foster equality and fair distribution of resources; and religious unity, to temper the divisions between the faiths to help prevent the catastrophic consequences of religious war. All of the chosen members would receive training to help them serve humanity, to enable them to think inclusively, to operate selflessly, and be guided by their own spiritual essence. Selected disciples would be involved in a process of revelation and transmission of higher thought. They would be guided in recognising the spiritual energies that lay behind the ideas revealed to them and they would take part in an experiment involving the development of a form of collective awareness. Out of those ideas they would create thought-forms to send out into the world. There would be ten groups in all, each assigned a role in influencing world affairs.

The second division would be known as men and women of goodwill. He would outline more about them later.

Alice set down her pen. Her mind buzzed. It was an impressive proposal, but was she capable of bringing it to fruition? She supposed some of the members of the various sub-groups the Tibetan had in mind could be sourced right then and there at the summer school.

It occurred to her that everything she had written until that juncture concerned pure esotericism and included teachings on meditation, the soul and consciousness, and cosmology; all of it focused inwards, upon the individual and the inner life. She had established a publishing house, a magazine, and an esoteric training school oriented to cultivating a special kind of esoteric thinker. That work would continue, the Tibetan told her, and this new layer was to be added, one that focused outwardly. For his students would be charged with changing the world through inclusive thinking in the service of humanity. Together, his groups would inaugurate a new age of collective consciousness.

As she read over his communication she was quick to see it would involve a doubling of her efforts. She had a new mission. It was a seminal moment, she felt it in her bones. She saw in a flash that this was what the work was really about, not a re-languaging of ancient truths to suit a modern audience, but a complete reorientation of esoteric practice itself, esoteric practice for too long harnessed to serve selfish and evil purposes.

That the vision should have been born at Ascona, for her a potent locus of evil, was of no small import, but she chose to ignore that fact. She could not have foreseen the repercussions.

Her mind galloped on. She was reminded of her old missionary days in India. Oh, what a Bible thumper she had been! The strain had flattened her but then she was young, very young, and that was child's play in comparison to what lay before her. The burden, she knew, would be heavy, and the impact on her health unavoidable. There she sat, at fifty-one years, saddled with heaven knew how much more work. Already there were times, many times she thought the work she had undertaken for the Tibetan was far too much for her. He expected so much. And now this. Yet humanity's need was great. All the signs of another world war were there. After the crash on Wall Street, poverty and unemployment were rife. Everyone was affected by it. She had endured such hardship. She knew what it was like to count the pennies, to go hungry to feed the children. At last, the Tibetan shared her view, and not a moment too soon.

She was far from alone in sensing another world war on the horizon, and she would have found herself deluded if not certifiably insane were she to think that she alone could avert it. Yet she saw with the immediacy of the visionary mind that the New Group of World Servers would need to do all they could regardless. Together they would attempt to roll up their sleeves and tackle the problems of the times in their unique fashion, through concerted, inner, spiritually focused effort.

She paused, checking herself, instilling realism into her thinking. It would be an experiment, she told herself, nothing more, and success could not be predicted.

She tidied up the morning's writing and put her speech in her handbag. As she stood she felt the effects of sitting too long. Her legs were numb and she felt unsteady. She gripped the back of her seat and waited, moving her legs gently one at a time, hoping to remind them of their task ahead, to walk to the lecture hall.

She was about to leave her desk when something outside caught her eye and she saw Foster, wrapped in nothing but a towel, heading down to the lake.

# Among Friends

Alice heard giggles and voices in the hallway outside her room and knew that the girls were keen to start their day. She readied to join them, sitting down at the small dressing table to pass a comb through her hair, still voluminous and black, although a little grey was creeping in about the temples. She put on the necklace Alice had given her, a single string of pearls that rested nicely above the bodice of her dress.

An hour must have passed since she saw Foster heading off in a towel. She had waited, enjoying the late summer sun streaming in the window, heating the room. He hadn't returned from wherever he had taken himself off to. She eyed his swimming trunks, drying on the back of a chair, and presumed he hadn't gone for a swim. Then why wrap himself in only a towel? With a parting glance at the lake, its surface radiant blue in the sunshine, she went to join the others downstairs.

The dining room overlooked the lake as well, as did most of the rooms at Casa Gabriella. She entered to find Dorothy already eating.

'Morning, Mother,' she said, swallowing first, then smiling. Her eyes sparkled. She had more of her father in her features, thicker lips, waves in her hair, and there was an indecisiveness about the eyes. Alice returned the greeting. Centred in the long table, dense breads and cheeses were laid out on platters along with pots of jam and honey. Ellison and Mildred were helping themselves to scrambled eggs.

'There you are! We're going into Ascona this morning. It's all decided,' Ellison said without preface. She had on a light summer dress and her face had that determined set to it. Of the three, she was the most headstrong. Bright and accomplished, she had her mother's brown eyes and high forehead. Plate in hand, she sat down beside her sister, as though to bolster her position.

'How will you get there?' Alice said doubtfully, claiming the empty chair beside Mildred.

'We'll walk, Mama.'

Alice wished Ellison wouldn't call her that. It sounded awfully British, which didn't blend at all well with her East coast accent, and made her appear affected and pretentious, which deep down she was not.

'Pour me some coffee would you, Mildred.'

Mildred set down her fork without hesitation and filled her mother's cup. The middle child, she had always been obliging and considerate. An inner radiance shone through wide, gullible eyes. Alice gave a small nod of thanks. She reached for the handle, steadying the cup with her other hand. The idea of her daughters making off up the road unaccompanied, passing by heaven knew who, didn't sit well with her. The lakeside properties had been purchased by people little better than the bohemians up at Monte Verità, and she wished she could find a way to prevent the girls from going. Yet she could hardly chain them up. She had brought them to Europe for a second year, and planned to do the same again the next and the next, for there was no better way to expand the minds of the young than travel. Only, she wished the locale afforded a better calibre of citizen.

'Stay in the town, please,' she said, hoping to exert some influence.

'Oh, Mother.'

Ellison rolled her eyes. Alice shot her a reproving look and she slumped back in her seat.

'Carlos said he will walk with us,' Mildred said.

Carlos! That was no comfort! No comfort at all. The man in question, Olga's neighbour, was of indeterminate years and his nature seemed slippery. The sort of young man who always appeared as if from nowhere, the epitome of obsequious deference. She supposed he could be relied upon to keep others at bay, for he seemed a possessive type, somewhat like a devoted pup, and the girls would be his charge. Yes, that was the best that could be said about the man.

She trusted her daughters, of course she did, but reputation pivoted not on acts and truths, but on appearances and perceptions. Had her daughters no inkling of the damage they could cause themselves? It was all very well carrying on in a holiday spirit without a care in the world and they were indeed far from home, but the milieu they existed in was small and gossip travelled faster than a swift.

Unfortunately, the girls had formed a united front and there would be no dissuading them. She didn't have the strength to try. She asked Mildred to fetch her a small plate of eggs and let the view out the French windows distract her. The girls, quieter in their mother's company, talked among themselves. Keen to make a start on their day, they ate and drank quickly, and before long Alice was seated alone.

As she buttered her bread and ate her eggs her mind drifted back to her own upbringing, to other breakfasts taken in the dining rooms of her relatives, and to her beloved Aunt Margaret, who seemed to have known exactly how to offer moral guidance to a child. It was always Aunt Margaret she thought of when she assessed her own mothering and she always seemed to fall short in her own eyes no matter how hard she tried to simulate the gentle but firm style of her aunt. All she could do was rely on her daughters' upbringing, the good values she had instilled in them from an early age and her previous warnings concerning the environs and that den of depravity, Monte Verità.

Alice was jolted out of her musings when Olga swept into the room in a calf-length frock of pale green, replete with a thin woven shawl and an abundance of long necklaces cluttering her neckline. She sat, side on, at the head of the table and announced that the other lecturers and participants were already gathering outside the lecture hall and they had better get going.

Alice sipped her coffee. 'Are you not going to eat?'

Olga looked askance at the breakfast table abandoned by Alice's daughters.

'I was up early, arranging the seating and the catering. The others are already drinking coffee out on the lecture hall deck. Come along. We must join them.'

Alice demurred inwardly. Olga made it all sound like a reproach. Then again, she was probably imagining things. Olga seemed preoccupied, a little on edge. It might have something to do with their joint talk on the importance of occult symbols, which they had decided to repeat for a second year to fill a gap in the program the day before. The talk had left Olga somewhat frayed. She had painted large posters of the symbols and they were really very good, but they didn't receive the high praise she had anticipated. It was Nancy, one of Alice's students, who had dared to criticise. She was pointing to what she saw as an imperfection in the arrangement of the symbols in one of the pieces, but Olga had taken it as an attack on her prowess as an artist. Alice couldn't help seeing the personality-centred awareness at the root of her reaction, thinking Olga had a long road to travel to achieve that disengagement from the ego that represented soul-centredness.

Olga stood abruptly. It only occurred to Alice that she might be mistaken about the cause of Olga's mood when they headed off across the narrow strip of garden beside the lake. Not four paces past the house she turned to shoo away a curious bee and as she took in the magnificent setting which never failed to captivate her, she spied Foster ambling up the small jetty below the house. His hair was dripping wet and he was wrapped from the waist down in a towel. She thought back to his swimming trunks, still damp from yesterday, drying on the back of a chair in their bedroom. What on earth had he been wearing in their stead? She turned to find Olga also staring.

'He must have been taking his morning meditation in the sun,' Alice said, thinking that unlikely. He lacked the discipline for daily meditation and, like the girls, he was in holiday mode. The Dionysian environs seemed to be affecting him as well and she was furious and disappointed in him all at once.

There were occasions when she felt old, too old for him. The eight years between them hadn't mattered when they first met and she was thirty-eight and still quite fit and able. Now in her fifties she felt different in her own skin and the gap in their respective ages seemed to have widened. He remained a dutiful and devoted husband, enabling all the work she undertook, there by her side through all of it. He was a perfect companion who held the vision as close to his own heart as she, yet he didn't share her moral propriety. His was a more fluid, liberal morality and she wondered sometimes if his influence on the girls was at the root of their current boldness.

Raising with him the matter of his apparel, or rather the lack thereof was not something she relished. She could hear herself remonstrating him as she would a naughty child. What could those words possibly achieve? But something had to be said. She saw straight away the judgement Olga had made and would continue to make on the habits and behaviour of her family.

She found Olga's stance oppressive. She was too quick to judge, to condemn through censorious eyes even as she smiled at Dorothy or Mildred or Ellison. At the root of the matter was no doubt the difficult situation Olga found herself in with regard to her twins, who were a year younger than Ellison. One of them, Ingeborg, was mentally handicapped due to a birth complication and resided in an institution somewhere in Germany. It was a lot of heartache for any woman to endure, although Olga never mentioned any of it. She had dispatched her other daughter, Bettina, to visit relatives for the duration of the summer school and behaved as though motherhood had never occurred to her.

With her mind cluttered and her composure off-kilter, Alice followed Olga across the garden, taking a small flight of steps to the lecture hall. She saw with some relief that the round table on which Olga had arranged a light breakfast was unoccupied, the others already inside. A few of the chairs had been left pulled out and askew. Olga pushed one in on her way by. Alice paused. Some used napkins remained on the table along with some breadcrumbs, which a shy sparrow was endeavouring to whisk away.

'I'll be inside in a moment,' she said.

'Very well,' Olga said without turning. The sparrow flew away. Alice stood, enjoying the cool in the dappled shade of a large tree and the pine-infused air.

Along with a few others, Nancy and Ann strolled down the zigzag of stone steps from the road above. She greeted them with a closed-mouth smile, indicating with her eyes that she preferred to be left alone. Even from where she stood, she could hear Olga's voice rising above the rest inside.

Despite her officious manner whenever she addressed Alice, Olga seemed to be enjoying every moment of the summer school, holding court with what could only be described a pleasing and eminent collection of intellectuals and interesting people.

Minutes passed. Foster hadn't appeared as she had hoped. She couldn't delay making an entrance.

Inside, the lecture hall was resplendent with bright, morning sunlight streaming in through open French windows. Soft curtains caught on the breeze and billowed lightly. The middle rows were full, many having accessed the hall via a second, sloping path at the rear, suitable for prams and wheelchairs, and where there was some space to park cars beside the road above.

The audience had come from all over Europe and the world, many from Germany and France. They were there to hear not just her, but the other speakers too, including Roberto Assagioli, who would always pull a crowd, and Prince Hubertus of Loewenstein-Wertheim.

Roberto and Violet had taken up two of the chairs positioned along the far wall, chairs reserved for speakers and also to provide sufficient additional seating for the guests. Olga was there with them. Alice caught Roberto's eye and acknowledged him without changing the expression on her face. She felt the energy of the room, tuned in to it, absorbed it, directed it back as she took up her place before the lectern.

The room fell silent as she drew a breath.

She began with a depiction of meditation as an ordered process involving discrete stages that gradually relocate the centre of consciousness from the personality to the soul. *First, the aspirant must learn to concentrate the mind, focusing the attention on a single point. The second stage, which is commonly understood as meditation, involves sustained concentration on this single point, or idea, holding the mind steady in the light. Third, after sustained effort over many years, when the mind has at last acquiesced and rests quietly in the background and consciousness is seated in the soul, the soul is free to contemplate and spiritual awareness is fostered. This leads to illumination, to fresh spiritual insights and a life given over to service.* She went on to outline the purpose of meditation in terms of the alignment of the mind and the various centres of the body, before spending the rest of the lecture dwelling on the dangers of overstimulation.

It was a relatively easy talk to give. She had revised one of her public lectures to accommodate the calibre of intellect in the room, and added more emphasis on the effects of Eastern approaches to meditation on the Western mind. She spoke as she always did, slowly and clearly, measuring her words, watching the audience, gauging their interest, their understanding.

The room applauded at her close and she responded to one or two questions before taking the seat in the side row vacated by Roberto.

Lunchtime, and the day had warmed up considerably. Alice was glad of the shady canopy that overhung the round table. About halfway through Violet's speech Olga had dashed off to oversee the luncheon and when the party of speakers took up their chairs, there were places laid and wine bottles opened and a large basket of sliced bread, a terrine, and platters of meats, cheeses and preserved vegetables ready to share around.

Alice glanced over at Foster—who had arrived during Roberto's speech—already sloshing back a glass of wine. He had seated himself between Olga and the gifted conductor, Gerald Reynolds, who had travelled from the Conservatory at Fontainebleau especially to be there. They were talking amicably in raised voices about the Women's University Glee Club back in New York, which Gerald was directing for another year. The charisma at that end of the table threatened to dominate the group as Foster furnished his companions with a funny tale of his time in his school band.

Alice had taken up a chair on the opposite side of the table. Violet sat down to her left, Roberto to her right. Vittorino took his place beside Roberto, and Violet was joined by her husband, Clarens. Mirza Ahmad Sohrad, the Bahai teacher who had also travelled from New York, had chosen a seat near Olga, as had Prince Hubertus. The other chairs were filled with selected guests, on that occasion Nancy and Ann, who sat beside Erlo. Those two couldn't take their eyes off each other. The rest of the summer school audience had drifted back to their homes, or their hotels. Many had been put up at Monte Verità or at the much cheaper Kurhaus Collinetta.

She felt the absence of the Grand Duke Alexander of Russia, who had attended the year before and given a little talk on spiritual education. Dear old Alexander. The moment he entered her thoughts, she missed him intensely. He was the brother-in-law of Tsar Nicholas II, and she found him delightful company.

What providence it had been the day they had met.

He had come to New York on a promotional tour after the publication of his book, *The Religion of Love* and given a lecture at the Nobility Club. The club had been established to enable Russian nobility to mingle with cultured and serious-minded Americans, and Alice had been invited by a friend. She accepted when she discovered Alexander was a mystical Freemason and Rosicrucian. As he gave his talk, which concerned the subject of the soul, Alice had turned to her friend, who went on to arrange a meeting the following day.

Alexander had become an instant friend. It wasn't only a social connection they had, but something much deeper. Alice sensed a bond that spanned lifetimes, although she had no idea of its true substance. One just knew these things.

Thinking of him, it was as though he were standing right behind her and Alice felt herself relax. She chose not to concern herself with Olga. She chose not to be concerned about her daughters and their escapades, which she was sure were innocent enough. She pushed to the back of her mind Foster's bathing, hoping no one had witnessed him leaving the water and reaching for his towel. She reminded herself that she was surrounded by good company, enveloped in it, seated there between two of her greatest allies.

As she reached for a slice of the terrine, Violet turned to her with one of her gracious smiles and thanked her for a charming talk.

'You are a fine speaker, my dear. Quite the entertainer.'

Alice laughed lightly, returning the praise. A student of her work, she had met Violet for the first time the previous year at the inaugural summer school. Alice pictured that first moment when she had watched her wending her way down the garden steps with her husband. She was tall, large boned, her fine face framed by an abundance of fair curls that she liked to pile high on her head like a crown. Her demeanour was nothing short of stately. The affinity had been instant and strong and they had become firm friends. Ignoring the others at the table, the two women chatted briefly and quietly about the weather, their pets and various members of their respective families, before moving on to books and publishing.

Violet was twenty years Alice's senior, and well established in her literary career. She was prolific too, having published numerous novels and short stories and works of spiritual non-fiction. Alice supposed being the daughter of Robert Chambers of dictionary fame had given her a head start. But what Alice envied was her stamina. She was a Spiritualist and a Theosophist, and had been a close associate of Helena Blavatsky, something else that bonded them. She moved in the best circles, counting among her friends, the poet, Robert Browning. As if that were not enough to impress, she was an accomplished artist and pianist, and an excellent speaker. In all, she was exactly the sort of woman with whom Alice felt most comfortable and with whom Olga should have been satisfied, although she scarcely gave Violet much more than a second glance.

Her attention was diverted when Roberto placed a light hand on her arm. 'Forgive the interruption, but would you pass the cheese?'

'Not at all young man. I do believe we've been monopolising one another,' Violet said with a soft laugh. She reached for the platter and passed it across, then turned to exchange pleasantries with the others.

Alice quickly thanked Roberto for his talk. He thanked her in return and was about to say more when Vittorino, a round-faced man with a balding pate, addressed him in Italian and they struck up a conversation.

She listened, watching, unable to understand, enjoying the opportunity to observe her companion at close quarters. He had one of those faces, hidden behind a full beard, suggestive of the benevolence and good will in his heart. His eyes were alive and intelligent and seemed to absorb the very essence of his friend as he listened. His was an advanced soul, there could be no doubt about it. A superb linguist, he was able to lecture in French, Italian and English. She found him a highlight of the spiritual school. Like Violet, he exuded spiritual power. He had been a secretary of the Arcane School for a number of years, beginning his training shortly after the school was founded, but they had only met for the first time the year before.

For Alice, that Roberto was Jewish made his participation in her work all the more significant. Times were difficult for the Jewish community with so much anti-Semitism in Europe. It was a worrying fact that Theosophy was already tarnished with accusations of anti-Semitism, the result of an unfortunate interpretation of the root races. As far as she was concerned, nothing could be further from the truth, as the presence of Roberto, and many other Jews in the Arcane School attested.

There would always be critics and they were not so easy to dismiss. She reminded herself that it was scarcely worth her energy defending her position even as she was consumed by that very urge to do so.

She took a slice of bread and some of the cheese and vegetables from the platters being passed around and took a small sip of the wine to be polite. Foster was well into his second glass. The others were all talking at once.

Unlike the spiritual topics that usually infused the centre and created a rarefied air, the conversation at the round table that sunny lunchtime drifted to the primary concern of the day, the awful depression that was affecting peoples far and wide, and the rise to prominence of that rabble rouser, Hitler.

Alice finished the food on her plate as she listened. Her head had begun to ache and she felt tired in her bones, too exhausted to contribute even a single sentence when, had she been in good health, she may have taken command of the table.

Everyone agreed Hitler's popularity was of great concern. Yet his talk of strengthening Germany, of unifying the old German empire was gaining popularity among a people riven with poverty and fatigue, and the National Socialists were on a path to power.

'You have to see things on the ground to understand the true force of his campaign,' Erlo was saying, having just returned from a trip to Frankfurt. He was a spry, earnest man with a goatee beard, who garnered the respect of those around him despite his comparative youth.

'His storm troopers wear brown shirts, I heard,' Violet said.

'They are a band of thugs,' Erlo muttered with his head bowed.

Alice wondered if it were prudent to raise the Jewish question uppermost on her mind, but decided not to bring it up in deference to her companion. Yet it was Roberto himself who raised the topic, albeit in a veiled fashion.

'I believe Hitler is making his supremacist aims very clear,' he said grimly. 'If only the people would see it.'

'Would see how wrong it is.' Gerald sounded tentative. His face, a picture of serenity when in repose, had clouded over. 'For surely they can see it.'

'We're talking about the mentality of the mob,' Roberto said.

'The people are desperate,' Erlo said with a frown. 'They are not thinking beyond their pockets and their stomachs. For them, the Jews control the banks and the businesses, and look after their own while good Germans can't find work and go hungry.'

'Which compromises morality and shrinks the vision.'

'Is it any wonder hatred grows and Hitler gains support off the back of it?'

'When one is so desperate...' Violet said.

Summoning strength she didn't have, Alice spoke. 'A collective turning point is required, one that will lift the hearts and minds of an entire people, and turn them against the forces of separatism wherever those forces are to be found.'

The table fell silent for a moment, each lost in thought and concern.

'For the people, Alice, there appears to be no alternative,' Roberto said at last. 'Hitler offers them a solution.'

'How can so many be so blind!' Vittorino who had remained silent throughout the exchange, banged his fist down on the table.

Alice flinched inwardly.

'Indeed, what are the intellectuals doing to stop this?' Clarens said.

'They are too scared to speak,' Roberto answered.

'I feel it coming,' Violet said quietly. 'Another war.'

'Such an ugly word, I find,' Olga said. Her comment jarred. The others ignored it.

Alice waited for the conversation to wane. The importance of the morning's communication from the Tibetan, the timeliness of his project weighed on her. Was it prudent to announce the New Group of World Servers at the round table, just at that moment? Shouldn't she wait until she was back in her office in New York to share with her co-workers, glean their reactions first? Yet she was among friends and allies, and the communication was apposite. She awaited her chance.

Interest in Hitler was diverted to the food as Olga again handed round the platters of cold meats and salads, insisting everyone ate their fill. She replenished glasses and smaller conversations sprung up around the table.

When the last of the wine had been drunk and everyone had become reflective in the warmth of the sun, Alice spoke.

'I received an important message from the Tibetan this morning.'

Gazes fell on her face.

'The real one?' Olga quipped. 'Or that astral version you complained about.'

There was an awkward silence. Olga looked embarrassed.

'The astral version, as you put it, was dispatched last year,' Alice said firmly.

'My apologies, then. I never intended to cause offence.'

Alice was unsure whether to continue. The table waited, all ears. On impulse she said, 'I think what the Tibetan has in mind is most relevant.'

Olga folded her arms. Foster looked on, his expression impassive.

'He wants to start a new project.' She gave a brief outline of the group experiment. An experiment in group awareness aimed at influencing world politics, economics and education. At the end of her description she looked around, studying the faces in turn. No one gave an opinion. Her gaze settled on Foster, who wore an open-mouthed expression, part astonishment, part irritation.

'You were nowhere to be found, Foster.'

'Another project.' His tone was less than encouraging.

'This will take our work in a new direction. There will be more to do; that is unavoidable, but you can see the value in it.'

'The New Group of World Servers?' Olga said. 'The Tibetan is getting ambitious.' She laughed. No one joined her.

'I'm telling you now because students of the Arcane School will be approached with an invitation to participate.'

'What will we be doing?'

Alice was immediately pleased to hear Roberto include himself in the project.

'We'll be working subjectively in groups of nine. By blending our individual awareness, we will intuit fresh ideas, clothe them in language and send them out into the world.'

'Just as the individual occultist has always done.'

'Usually for selfish if not outright evil purposes.'

'Personality-centred.'

'Yes.'

'The New Group of World Servers will be soul-centred.'

'And by working in groups, we offset our natural tendency to be selfish.'

'I can see what he's trying to achieve,' Roberto said slowly. 'The Tibetan seeks to arrest the forces of evil.'

'This is the conclusion I have drawn. It is why I chose to announce it. I realise it will involve more work and commitment for all concerned but I see it as the inevitable culmination of this latest outpouring of the Ageless Wisdom.'

Violet, who had taken out a small piece of embroidery, jogged Alice's arm as though by accident.

'I beg your pardon, my dear,' she said, catching her eye. 'I'm rather fond of this piece.' She lifted it up for Alice to admire, which she did. 'Unhappiness is always born of boredom, I find.' She eyed the others and emitted a soft, self-deprecating laugh. Alice was quick to catch the sub-text.

'It all sounds most intriguing,' Gerard said.

'Indeed, it does,' said Olga without enthusiasm.

Alice eyed her warily. She wasn't sure it had been prudent after all to have informed the others in that fashion. She hadn't anticipated Olga would feel in any way threatened by it. She had underestimated the woman's need to be at the centre of things.

Olga began collecting glasses and stacking plates, and some of the party wandered off to take a walk by the lake, Foster among them. Alice listened with as much attention as she could muster to Violet's description of her garden in Devon and how she and Foster must come and stay with her whenever they came to Britain.

As she sat, watching Violet embroider, her hands directed as though by another will, she couldn't help drifting back to her old missionary days, to the numerous faux pas she had made, and she wondered why, after all these years, she didn't seem to be able to prevent that silly girl who lurked inside her, all excitable and impulsive, taking over her decisions and creating the occasional error of judgement.

She thought of her daughters wandering the streets of Ascona; and their stepfather, Foster, normally a serious man, aligning himself with debauchery. A heavy weight bore down on her, one laden with fear of repercussions.

# Stamford

They arrived home in late September. After two months of travel everyone entered the house with their suitcases poised to return to their normal routines, Alice and Foster to their commute to the office in Manhattan, and the girls to their domestic duties and social lives. The house was soon a hubbub of activity. Alice went and made tea while the others unpacked. She was relieved to find cups and saucers laid out on a tray and the kettle already full on the stove. She made a mental note to thank her maid, Marion, for her thoughtfulness as she lit the gas.

She managed to arrange biscuits on a plate and warm the teapot, but when it came to the kettle she had to use two hands to lift it and didn't trust herself to pour. 'Foster,' she called. Foster entered the room and she stepped back from the stove. 'I can't manage the kettle.'

'I'll call the doctor.'

'For all the good it will do.'

It was when they were seated, cups in hand, that she knew she needed bed rest. The moment she could, she withdrew upstairs to her room at the front of the house. It was large and sunny with windows in three of the walls and its own small balcony facing north. There, in quietude, she lived and worked undisturbed by the comings and goings of the rest of the household. She eyed the bed covetously and once she had closed the door on the rest of the house, she lay down and closed her eyes, too exhausted to move.

She must have slept, for the next thing she knew the room was dim. She emerged from a dream filled with chaotic sequences, one scene transmuting into another and she couldn't make sense of any of it other than she had found herself in a room mingling with a jumble of people. It was an opulent room filled with crystal and mirrors and plush furnishings. Red seemed to be the predominant colour. Those present were mostly garbed in shades of purple. They were all taller than her, even the women. And they were disagreeable too, yelling and gesticulating. She had reasoned, placated, cajoled, even attempted witty remarks. It was all to no avail. She began to feel desperate, eager to leave, but there was no door that she could see, no way out.

She sat up in bed and stared vacantly at the opposite wall. Her head ached and her mouth was dry but it was the dream that troubled her. A salon? Why dream about a salon? She supposed the answer was obvious. There was something about salons that attracted the wrong people. Monte Verità was a case in point. She had to shoo away recollections of the place as fast as they came, rueing the day Olga had driven past. Olga, the saloniste. She was suddenly struck by the irony that Olga had visited with her proposal while they had been living in Graham Phelps-Stokes' house on Caritas Island, for that house, not a mile from where she sat, was where Graham, together with his wife, had hosted a salon, one that caused him untold controversy.

When she had accepted Graham's offer to reside at his country home, and make full use of it as she saw fit, she knew full well why he had suggested it. After the breakup of his all too short marriage, he couldn't bear to be anywhere near the place, and had immediately taken up permanent residence in New York.

Poor Graham. They had become acquainted at one of her public lectures. A socialist from a good family, he had just parted ways with his wife, Rose Pastor Stokes. Graham was a kind man. He devoted his time to helping the poor and disadvantaged, and took a special interest in the deaf and dumb. His endeavours were a striking contrast to his former wife's. He was a man of good works. She was a feminist and ardent communist, the political version of the common evangelist, yelling on street corners, and somewhat like the people in her dream, the people with whom she had been trapped, people garbed in the colour purple, the colour of rage.

Yes, Rose campaigned for the rights of women. Yes, she stood up against violence against women. For those reasons, she deserved respect. But as for her methods, the very act of angry protest was divisive and polarising. Humanity needed unity and peace and goodwill. These would be fostered through economic equality and the sharing of the world's resources; and through those whose desire to do good works arose out of a detached notion of human betterment, those prepared to work in her New Group of World Servers. Not by ranting on the streets. It was undignified and counter-productive. The emotions were too strong. In all, and without wishing to appear patronising even in her thoughts, Rose was a fine example of a fully developed personality yet to walk in the kingdom of the soul.

She was a little like Olga.

Although Alice would never have wished Rose ill will. Especially after Rose was diagnosed with breast cancer the year before. The news hit hard. There was only a year between them, which made it all the more real. Yet Alice's sympathies had always been firmly with Graham, ever since that day they had met for lunch.

She had been living in Ridgefield Park for a few years by then and the Lucis Trust and the Arcane School had entered their third and second year respectively. Graham had invited her to join him at Barbetta, a fine restaurant in Manhattan serving Italian cuisine and known for its opulent interior.

He had booked a small table in the far corner tucked beneath a large, multi-paned window, and over aubergine parmigiana followed by a delicious chocolate and mascarpone cream cake he related in subdued tones the story of his disastrous marriage. He spoke with frankness and clarity and a generous measure of hurt. He told her Rose was born in Russia to an Orthodox Jewish couple and had come to America as a poor Jewish immigrant. Alice was reminded of her own marriage to a man far beneath her social standing, and how it, too, had turned out badly. Although Rose was a different breed altogether. She had spent over a decade working in a cigar factory in Ohio and it was there that she had begun agitating for workers' rights in letters submitted to the *Jewish Daily News*. By 1903 she was employed as a columnist and assigned her first interview. It was with Graham.

'We were married two years later. I don't think I even really knew her.'

'You were in love, Graham. It blinds us all.'

'Doesn't it just. We were both active in the labour movement, but Rose's activism was considerably more intense. She helped lead strikes, and was a big advocate of birth control. Is, I should say.' He paused and took a breath. 'The trouble began, I think, when she became a Communist. It was all too radical for me.'

He went on to describe the salon they had established on Caritas Island, along with an artist's colony. Alice could see how it would have proven all too much for Graham, who was Episcopalian to his core.

He explained how he had inherited the few acres that was Caritas Island and built the lovely cottage residence, replete with its own little beach. Alice couldn't imagine what it would have been like for Graham to have his idyllic little island overrun. Worse, he said Rose was dreadfully flirtatious, and had numerous admirers trailing her about, for she was undoubtedly beautiful and charismatic. Alice's own sensibilities were affronted in the imagining.

At the end of the meal, Alice gazed at her lunch companion and observed a man filled with shame. He picked a crumb off the tablecloth and deposited it on the side of his plate. It was an absentminded act, one that endeared him to her, for he was a man given to caring about the small things in life, the details.

With his head bowed he said his house, the whole island in fact, needed cleansing of its debased energies. 'I can't bear to be anywhere near the place. It's standing empty.'

'That's no good.'

'Look at all this talk of me,' he said with a self-deprecating smile. 'Where are my manners? I don't know what has come over me.'

Alice kept her reaction to herself. People were always sharing with her the intimate details of their lives.

'Tell me about your life, Alice. Where are you living?'

Despite her best efforts, Alice couldn't resist infusing something like frustration in her description of the little house in Ridgefield Park. It was exceedingly generous of Mr Suffern to provide them accommodation to go with Foster's new position as secretary of his Theosophical Society, yet the home was too small for her family's needs and none of the rooms had a view. She censured herself inwardly even as she spoke, cautioning against ingratitude.

Graham didn't share her misgivings. Instead, he looked at her closely.

'You can have my house if you like.'

'I couldn't possibly.'

'You'll be doing me a favour. In fact, I'd call it providence.' He sat back in his seat. 'The whole place is yours for the taking.'

Alice had been very happy in that house. Other than a lingering energy she presumed had been left by Rose, there was nothing about it not to love. It was built of stone with multi-paned windows and a green slate roof. Inside, Herringbone oak floors, ornate wood panelling and open fireplaces greeted the eye. There were Greek columns and chandeliers and twelve bedrooms to choose from. They had only moved out because Graham decided to sell up.

She hadn't been at all surprised. He never could erase the memories of the salon and his wife's behaviour.

Her mind drifted back to her dream. In that salon she had felt trapped, overpowered and desperate to get out, but there'd been no exit. What was the dream trying to tell her? It was as though inside the salon she was cut off from her soul. It was an intellectual hell. Yet salons and artist's colonies were the domain of free thinkers, many of them undeniably interesting men and women. Somewhat strident at times and alternative in their outlook, they stretched human thought.

They were a seed bed of creative group thinking. Yet as Monte Verità had shown, they also provided the soil for moral degeneracy.

Her own husband hadn't escaped their influence. She had no right to dictate to him how he conducted himself, but it pained her to know that he had been seen sunbathing in the nude.

It was Violet who had confirmed the worst. Back at Casa Gabriella, she drew Alice aside as they ascended the zigzag path and asked if she was aware of the rumour. 'Men will be men, my dear. I shouldn't worry too much. It's Olga I'd keep my eye on. She's making rather a song and dance about it, I'm afraid.'

Alice confronted Foster the moment they were alone in their room.

'How could you be so foolish? Anyone could have seen you. Not least, the girls.'

'They'd have needed good eyesight. I was out on the lake on a raft.'

'Well someone certainly did!' Presumably the foolish man hadn't taken account of the upstairs windows. 'There's such a thing as discretion, Foster. What will people think!'

'Alice, I'm a grown man. You are remonstrating me like a child.'

'Your behaviour, Foster, was less than childish. It was sordid. Your actions threaten to bring our work into disrepute.'

'Don't dramatise. Nude sunbathing is commonplace around these parts.'

'That's as maybe, but I do not share those liberal views and I expect you to conduct yourself in accordance with my morals, not theirs. At least in public.'

'I won't do it again if it upsets you so much.'

She had no idea if any of her girls had witnessed the debacle but Olga had. Or if she hadn't, someone had and had told her. Violet was right. The reproving looks she had shot Foster towards the end of their stay had been unmistakable. It appeared to Alice a touch hypocritical, considering the amount of time Olga spent up at Monte Verità.

She told herself it was trivial. That it didn't compare to the immoral acts of homosexuality and wanton debauchery up at Monte Verità. Yet he had set the girls a poor example, lowered the tone of the whole visit and caused unwanted gossip. She wanted to put it behind her and forget it ever happened. She knew she ought to. After all, it wasn't as if he had hit her.

A blade of memory, sharp, sliced through her. She shuddered and let the image fade.

Restless, she sat up on the edge of the bed and eased her feet to the floor, slowly standing. Her head throbbed and as she stood and made to cross the room she had to steady herself. She needed a doctor, not that anyone seemed to know how to fix her condition. They said there was a fault with her blood. Addison's anaemia, one doctor called it, and had advised her to eat raw liver. Raw liver! As a firm vegetarian since the day she found Theosophy, she told him she would be doing no such thing.

'Then you can anticipate needing a blood transfusion soon enough,' he had said without much sympathy. That was before they had gone to Europe. Feeling the way she did now, she knew he was probably right.

She would have liked to have proven him wrong, but the symptoms worsened with every passing year, and now she had reached her fifties, they were fast becoming hard to bear. The travel hadn't helped, but she was not the sort of woman to give in to her frailties. If anything, her condition made her strive all the harder.

She stood by one of the south facing windows, gripping the ledge for balance. The sea breeze had dropped. Winter would soon be upon them but for now, the days were pleasantly warm. The setting sun sent bands of pretty peach across the western sky. Below her, sitting in the garden, she saw her cat, Tom. She opened the window and called out to him. He looked over, nonchalantly. Seeing her there he stared for a few moments, before jumping off the wall and scampering over to the ladder that Foster had placed beneath the window. In moments, he was in her arms. He was a very large cat, and he adored her. Feeling his weight, she thought Marion must have fed him well while they were away.

She sat down in the rocking chair, let him nuzzle and curl up in her lap. Stroking his fur soothed her and she censured her earlier thoughts.

Foster may have shamed himself in one respect, but she mustn't condemn him for it.

Her efforts to reason away his behaviour came to nothing. The larger part of her fretted over his reputation, of the damage it could do to her organisations. She could not afford to have any part of the work tarnished. She stood firm on the side of the utmost purity and high moral values. Every cell of her being was devoted to elevating esotericism, lifting it out of depravity, placing it firmly on a high white shelf. Could Foster have managed to undo all her hard work in one thoughtless act?

Tom purred and she felt the vibrations through her thighs. She sat there, stroking him, until his weight became too much. She set him down, closed the window and all the curtains and took herself back to bed.

Alice could scarcely recall the rest of September. Each day, as was her custom, she awoke at four and spent the pre-dawn hours scribing for the Tibetan and trying not to think about the mounting correspondence at her desk in Manhattan. After that, she would take herself back to bed. The doctor told her she required complete bed rest, but there was enormous work ahead of her and she was falling behind.

It was Mildred who nursed her back to health. She would gently knock and enter with a tray of soup or toast and tea, seeing to it that Alice had every comfort. She would sit by her bed and read aloud and provide little updates of the day, of the efforts Dorothy and Ellison had made helping keep house. She was a charming young woman, instinctively practical and kind, and she never failed to make Alice laugh.

All the girls had done their best, as ever they did when she fell ill. Foster, accustomed to managing the office without her, sat with her each morning, before taking himself off to work, returning with an account of the day.

People stayed away. They all knew not to disturb her when fatigue struck. Her friend Alice Ortiz was the only exception. One cool morning in early October she drove up from Delaware to pay a visit. Alice dressed and took herself downstairs to the drawing room, a downstairs version of her room above. Bookcases and occasional tables, and a radio in its own cabinet were arranged between the windows at the far end of the room. A sofa and two armchairs were arranged around the fireplace. Comfortable in her favoured seat, she waited for her guest.

They had met at one of her lectures. Alice Ortiz asked for a private interview and it was then Alice suggested she join the Arcane School. They grew close and Alice Ortiz became their biggest patron. Four years her senior, she had an enduring interest in Theosophy. Back in 1913, she and her husband, Julien, had founded a Theosophical lodge near their home in Wilmington, and were original members of their local Theosophical library. A poet by nature, her spiritual interests had alienated her from her own, exceptionally wealthy du Ponts. A matter which came as no surprise to Alice, since the du Ponts accrued their wealth out of explosives, and seemed hell bent on being in the business of war.

'May I trouble you, dearest?'

She hadn't heard a knock but when she heard her friend's sweet, cultured voice, Alice leaned forward in her seat.

'Please, don't get up. Mildred is bringing us a tray.'

She planted a soft kiss on her friend's cheek and Alice gestured at the chair opposite.

'You are much improved, I'm relieved to see.'

Alice doubted she meant it. She couldn't fail to see the dark circles under her eyes.

'With so much work to do, this body of mine is an awful encumbrance.'

'You mustn't trouble yourself. Foster will have things ticking along smoothly at the office.'

'And you, my dear. You didn't drive all this way just to ask after my health.'

'It's that time of year when everyone is fussing about with preparations for Thanksgiving.'

'Already?'

'You know what they're like.' She said it with a soft sigh, her gaze drifting.

'Marguerite?'

Alice Ortiz's daughter was three years older than Dorothy, married at nineteen to a man twenty years her senior, lawyer and sportsman, Forrester Holmes Scott.

'I'm a grandmother,' she said. 'They've a baby girl. Eve.' She didn't seem at all pleased. Then again, the marriage was not a happy one. Alice offered her congratulations anyway. 'I suppose Marguerite is fine. They're all fine. Marie is especially fine,' Alice Ortiz said. She was referring to her other daughter, who was the same age as Mildred. She's delighted you've published another of her poems.'

'Tell her she is most welcome. They're very good.'

Mildred entered the room with afternoon tea. The soft chinks of the china, the sight of the orange cake dusted with icing sugar, and Alice welcomed the glow of domestic satisfaction that infused her. Mildred had used the fine porcelain plates Foster's brother and his wife had gifted them one Christmas. She could always be relied upon to arrange things just so.

Her friend seemed distracted. Neither woman spoke while Mildred poured the tea.

'There was no need,' Alice said softly.

'That's quite all right, Mother,' she said, handing Alice her cup.

Alice aligned the spoon and handle before placing it down on the small table by her side.

'I've composed a new poem,' Alice Ortiz said once they were alone.

She handed Alice a leaf of notepaper, her neat script filling its centre. Her poetry wove simplicity, beauty and acute observation in the fewest words.

'Exquisite,' she said, handing it back.

'You like it?' She looked tentative.

'You must never doubt your talent,' she said warmly.

Alice pocketed the poem. Her gaze drifted to the fire.

'How was it at Ascona?' she asked.

Alice took a sip of her tea before offering a reply.

'Roberto and Violet were charming as ever. What fine speakers they both are. Attendance was excellent and there was quite a lot of interest in the Arcane School.'

'The girls enjoyed themselves?'

'Indeed, they did.' Although she privately yearned for the day they would all settle down in some fashion.

'And Olga?'

'The perfect host.'

'What good fortune for you all.'

Alice didn't respond.

'You'll be running the school again next year?'

'She provides an ideal opportunity for us. Cake?'

'I think we must.'

Alice Ortiz moved to the edge of her seat. Alice watched as she levered slices of cake onto plates.

'The Tibetan wants us to embark on a new project,' she said, accepting the proffered plate and napkin. She went on to explain the details of the experiment in group awareness. 'The idea behind it is to create and disseminate thoughtforms to help save humanity.'

'He recognises the spiritual emergency, then.'

'We all do.'

Alice Ortiz frowned. 'With ten groups in total, and nine members in each group, that's rather a lot of people, Alice. How will you find them all?'

'We must be fishers of men.'

They both laughed but Alice was reminded of the magnitude of the task.

'Has he indicated who should participate?'

'To begin with he'll source participants from the school. I have a list for the first two groups. You included.'

She took a small bite of her cake, wishing she were able to enjoy the sweet buttery tang on her palate, but her sense of taste was forever overlaid by another, much less pleasant flavour of metal in her mouth.

'For next year, I thought of planning a much longer trip,' she said. 'To England this time.'

'That will be lovely for you and the girls.' She didn't sound convinced. 'A chance to visit family, perhaps?'

Alice set down her plate. A cold draught swirled around her ankles. Gravestones, she thought. It would be a chance to visit gravestones.

Nothing more needed to be said. Both women felt alienated from their families. Alice had lost her favourite aunt, Margaret Maxwell of Castramont, almost a decade before, and her other aunt, Agnes, and her husband, dear old Uncle Clere, about the same time. That left only her sister, Lydia, from whom she was permanently estranged. She knew they would need to revisit the situation in another lifetime, for forgiveness in this life was not forthcoming. Edwardian values she might have, but her sister's were prehistoric. 'Till death do us part' was all very well, but not when the husband was violent, surely? On the protection of women and children from the horrors of battering, she agreed with Rose Pastor Stokes.

It was perhaps inevitable, if disappointing, that religious beliefs separated good people from their families. She would always be grateful for the day Alice Ortiz had come into her life and filled all her loss with loving kindness.

It was a quality that fitted her for participation in the first of the Tibetan's groups, the telepathic communicators. They would be charged with tuning in to the impressions of the masters and of each other. The group was to carry forth the overarching purpose of all the other groups, adopting a sort of overseeing function.

The other members chosen had already been invited. She told Alice she had written letters of invitation last week and was awaiting confirmation. She was confident Victor Fox and Regina Keller would accept. They were her secretary and office manager respectively, and were among her closest allies. Herbert Adams had a fine mind and would be an asset. Betty Harris too, was loyal. Roberto had already given his agreement, in principle at least, at the summer school. The other member, other than herself and Foster, was John Tassin, a fine occultist and dedicated student.

'Not Olga?'

Alice hid her reaction. 'Her name appears in the list for the second group. The Trained Observers. They've been charged with dispelling illusion on the mental plane.'

'A difficult task.'

'Indeed.'

Alice Ortiz looked thoughtful.

'I'd be honoured to participate,' she said, 'if you think I'd be any good. It sounds to me a worthy project. Anything we can do to offset the dreadful trajectory of the times would be worthwhile. I feel quite helpless.'

It was hardly surprising. News had come through of the unemployed rioting in Glasgow. Fascist youth were on parade under Mussolini in Rome, and the whole of Germany's cabinet had resigned in chaos. There was little on the world stage to feel joyous about. It was as though goodwill had hitched her skirts and moved to another planet. Meanwhile, as America lumbered through the thick of its terrible depression, Hoover was still fiddle-faddling with bank credit.

'A group experiment in soul consciousness,' she said. 'I can't imagine anything more significant.'

'How will you manage the extra workload? Presumably all our instructions will come through you.'

'Worse. The Tibetan tells me he plans to issue each member with personal instructions too. It is all to be conveyed through me.'

'But that's impossible! Ninety individual sets of instructions. There aren't enough hours in the day as it is. I do worry about you, Alice.'

She gave her a rueful smile, hiding from her friend her headache, the weakness in her limbs. She knew Alice had come to her for a reason of her own, an emotional one no doubt. Guessing, she said, 'You haven't told me about Marguerite.' She watched her gentle composure constrict in anguish as she conveyed her sadness over her daughter's unhappiness.

As if in concord, a log shifted in the grate. Flames sparked and flared.

'She married too young, and too impetuously and now she pays dearly. I have to say I find him a despicable and astonishingly self-indulgent man. Always off hunting lions in Africa or India, leaving his wife and child at home to fend for themselves.'

As she listened to the latest account of Forrester's shenanigans, Alice was taken back to the turbulent years of her own marriage. She hadn't married too young. She had been twenty-eight, but the impetuosity that so blinded the inexperienced was the same. She had paid dearly too, as had her daughters.

# Manhattan

Dressed for warmth in a calf-length woollen dress and thick shawl, Alice stood by a south facing window, watching the day struggle to emerge. Below, the lawn and hedge were dusted with snow. The street was empty. In the near distance, the waters of Long Island Sound were a grey ribbon beneath a heavy sky.

She faced a difficult day. The first day back in the office after Christmas and she had decided to break the news she had been holding back, even from Foster, ever since the Tibetan first revealed his plans for the second part of the New Group of World Servers project, plans that would increase the workload considerably.

Feeling the chill through the window, she drew away and returned to the fireside, where her cat, Tom, was curled up on the hearth rug. She had been feeling stronger after the blood transfusion and the fog in her brain had lessened, but her muscles were still stiff and the dark circles seemed to be a fixture under her eyes.

Mentally, it had been a trying few months, although she was satisfied with the first chapter of her new work on the initiations of Christ. The book would contain five chapters, one for each initiation along the spiritual path of discipleship. She enjoyed the conceiving and the crafting, and it had seemed apt to compose those early pages on His birth during the period of its anniversary: Christmas.

Along with a further two chapters on white magic—which she found fascinating—and a series of instructions for his New Group of

World Servers project, the Tibetan had dictated three personal letters to new members of his discipleship groups. The first to opera singer Anne Stevenson Dixon, the second to a promising student and long-standing Theosophist Bernard Morrow, and the third to Ernest Suffern, who had agreed last month to be a part of her second group of Trained Observers. Many others had been invited but the response was slow. She surmised the festive period had much to do with it.

She disliked being the conduit for personal advice that was not of her making. It was disquieting; the Tibetan didn't mince his words. Then again, all disciples needed to accept criticism and observations from those wiser than they. Besides, participants had been chosen on the strength of their spiritual maturity, so she supposed she had no choice but to trust the process and hope for the best.

Although she doubted Ernest would enjoy reading his letter and wondered if he had received it yet. His was especially sensitive because he had been instrumental in the foundation of her organisations, and presupposed some sort of special privilege.

Ernest was born into the wealthy and prestigious Suffern family, and his lineage could be traced back to one of the founding fathers, John Suffern, judge of Rockland County. She was loyal to Ernest after he extended his support and generosity, giving Foster employment as secretary of his Theosophical association, providing them a home at Ridgefield Park. He was a benefactor of considerable import. To be told, even by the Tibetan, that he spent too much of his time focusing on developing and maintaining his business interests—which he somehow managed to keep entirely separate from his deep spiritual aspirations—and that he needed to find ways to unify the two, would be confronting to hear. She hoped Ernest had the capacity to see the wisdom in the letter. Because the Tibetan was right. He did lead two separate lives, and one of them was intensely materialistic.

If the Ernests of the world couldn't change and bend their business interests to a higher spiritual cause, then who could? Group consciousness needed to occur first in those aspirants capable of becoming disciples, those in positions to cooperate with the Plan. If the leaders of the world in business and politics could be taught to forego selfish interests and transition into soul awareness, then humanity would be saved and the real New Age would manifest. A new age in which the White Lodge of Spiritual Masters would be in charge, replacing the Black Lodge who aligned themselves with the purposes of evil. It was all quite obvious to her and it should be obvious to Mr Suffern.

With the cheer of Christmas behind them, Alice stared into the year ahead with resolve. There was much to achieve and times were grimmer than ever. It was all very well for the privileged upper classes, who continued to live off the fat of their wealth, but for the poor, things were dire. She read in the daily news the appalling unemployment figures. People were living on the streets or in their cars. Hoover didn't seem to have the ability to contain the situation. Meanwhile, over in Germany, the political situation was going from bad to worse. If only the forces of materialism could be arrested. If only people were able to see that greed and power would ultimately bring the world to its knees.

In a moment of impatience, she decided more people were needed for the Tibetan's group experiment. The net needed to be cast a little wider. Before she changed her mind. she went and sat at her escritoire and took a clean sheet of writing paper and reached for her pen.

Dear Olga, she wrote, conveying her good wishes, imbuing her words with the utmost politeness. She reiterated the basic outline of the project and went on to list the members of the first group of telepathic communicators, explaining that they were charged with conveying spiritual impressions from the masters and to some degree overseeing, as intermediaries, the other groups. She then listed the current and invited members of the second group, indicating that this next group was of singular importance, and that the task of dispelling the illusions of the mental plane could not be timelier. She signed off, expressing her hope that Olga would accept her invitation to join the second group.

How suited Olga was to that group, so enshrouded was she in her own glamour, driven by powerful and competitive desires. Alice had never encountered ambition quite like it. She was a force of nature, unstoppable, unchallengeable, less like a hurricane and more a stampede of charging bulls. Ambition aside, she still had faith in Olga; she had the capacity to transcend her own limitations. She supposed she saw the soul in Olga struggling for expression, and it was irrefutable that those who struggled most with their own inner difficulties, were best equipped to tackle those same difficulties on a much larger scale. She folded the letter and slipped it into an envelope. She knew the address by heart.

There was a knock on the door and Foster entered the room. He was dressed for the day in a plain grey suit, the paragon of moral rectitude. His face had a careworn, almost gloomy set to it. Gone the carefree Foster of Ascona, and she thought the cold winter must be taking its toll on his spirits. She knew she was about to deepen those worry lines but there was nothing else for it.

'Are you sure you're well enough?'

'As well as I'll ever be.'

He didn't raise a smile at her self-deprecating laugh. 'We'd better get going.'

She collected the letter and put it in her handbag. As she stood, he said, 'I almost forgot. These came for you via the office.' He handed her a letter postmarked Torquay and another from Kent. She recognised the British stamps.

The first was from Violet. On the drive to Manhattan, she levered open the envelope. As the landscape of flat wooded plains slipped by she pored over Violet's words. She had an eloquence, a way with language that could only be admired. Alice read slowly, savouring the phrasing. By the time the greenery had given way to the modern brick buildings of New Rochelle, Alice's face wore a grin.

'Good news?'

'She's reiterated her invitation.'

'Torquay it is then.' His tone was lighter.

'You'll like Torquay.' She described what she remembered of her childhood visits to her aunt, of her half-hearted efforts at swimming in the English Channel.

This time, Foster laughed. 'Reminds me of the time my brother and I nearly died of hypothermia swimming at Old Orchard Beach.'

'Who in their right mind would swim in Maine?'

'I've asked myself the same thing, ever since.'

She tucked the letter away and opened the second. It took her a few moments to assimilate the news, before she put the letter down in her lap. 'My word!'

'More good news?' Foster said, glancing down at her lap.

'Better than good. Remember that request we put out to the school mailing list?'

'About expanding operations in England?'

'The Percy-Griffiths have come forward. Henry and Hilda are giving over Ospringe Place to us. They say Helena Blavatsky and Annie Besant have both stayed there at one time or other. It is only fitting they make the house available to us as well.'

'Where is it?'

Alice scanned the letter. 'Near Faversham in Kent. We can stay there whenever we need to.'

'How serendipitous.'

'Indeed it is.'

Her mind raced ahead. The offer of a house meant she could arrange a semi-permanent residence in England for her girls, where she suspected there might be better marriage opportunities for them. The operations could expand and they could work towards establishing a permanent headquarters there. It would be much easier and less exhausting to travel to Europe and lecture, using their time in New York to attend to the ever-mounting administration. A door had opened, a door that symbolised her return to a country she hadn't visited in twenty years.

Her reverie came to a sudden halt at the hoot of the car horn.

Foster always navigated through the city streets of Manhattan with aplomb, but there was no telling what fool was on the next corner. Things were especially chaotic down Fifth Avenue along the stretch beside Central Park, with drivers pulling out all over the place. Further on, and the traffic thickened, the sidewalks just as congested, men and women heading off in all directions, making a dash in the icy weather wrapped up in trench coats and thick scarves, all of them hurrying about their business. An aerial view would afford a chaotic dance of hats.

They didn't have far to go, but a mile in a car in downtown Manhattan could take just as long as a person on foot.

The office was in Midtown in the brand-new Salmon Tower. They were among the first to move in and they rented the entire top floor with views looking down at Bryant Park; in summer a blanket of green treetops, in winter a confusion of grey twigs. Claiming the park as though it were a back garden was the public library of New York.

At street level, Alice enjoyed the majestic stone and marble of the library building, the edifice reminiscent of the glorious stately buildings of Paris. From high above on the top floor of Salmon Tower, all she got to see was its rooftop. Still, there stood the grandest house of knowledge that New York, if not America had to offer, and right across the street, on the top floor of Salmon Tower, her own house of wisdom towered right over it.

Their floor was smaller than those below; the main office, open in design, contained an arrangement of five desks, one each for Regina, Victor and her, and two others for volunteers. To the left was a room for meetings and private appointments, and then two smaller rooms, the larger of them occupied by Foster, who liked to work in quiet. The second contained office stationery, back copies of *The Beacon*, and a small library of reference materials and their stock of books.

Victor was already at his desk, sitting straight-backed before his typewriter, the epitome of efficiency. He was a humble man reaching forty, slight of build and defined by his high forehead, receding hairline and crooked nose. On the floor beside him was a sack of letters that had the look of a delivery from Father Christmas. Alice was reminded, instantly, of the thousands of letters she had received when she ran the soldiers homes in India. All of those letters had eulogised her and she recalled with an inward smile the day she had burned the lot. The correspondence swamping Victor was different. Mostly, it contained requests for guidance and appointments, book orders, donations, and applications to join the Arcane School.

Victor was attending to the letters he had already freed from their envelopes, letters that formed a paper skyscraper on his desk.

'My goodness,' she said, taking in the scene.

'It's accumulated over Christmas. These are for you.'

He handed her a separate and smaller pile, which she saw at a glance were responses to her request for participation in the New Group of World Servers project. She went over to her desk, positioned in a corner near a pair of south-facing windows overlooking the street. A low winter sun broke out between the clouds, sending its weak milky light onto the desk's largely empty surface, unencumbered by a typewriter.

The room was heated by several large radiators but she always put a woollen rug over her knees to protect her legs from draughts. Not that the warmth had any bearing on the numbness and tingling she endured.

She read through the letters. All of them were declinations. As anticipated, the Grand Duke explained he lacked the time. She was disappointed in Jacob Bonngren, a Swedish doctor who had been a loyal and trusted student for many years, but he said he wasn't finding himself in perfect health and his workload seemed to have grown all the larger. Erlo van Waveren, her secretary and head of operations in Holland, indicated that under normal circumstances he would have happily accepted, but the times were anything but normal. That was understandable. Only last month, Hitler had announced in an interview with the American and British press that he would in fact rise to power. He was probably right given that German inflation was out of control and that fool Hindeberg had slashed wages in an effort to contain it. She hadn't invited Erlo's sweetheart Ann Moyer, or her friend Nancy Wilson Ross; the two students who had attended Ascona lacked the maturity required. She read the next letter with disappointment. Professor Vittorino Vezzani had declined. He was a regular contributor to *The Beacon* and she had thought he would have been an ideal member of the Trained Observers group. Again, he said he was too busy and times were difficult.

Concern impinged on her thoughts. She had to remind herself that it was still early days. She had only two spots left to fill in the first group. She must view that as a good start, but she had only acquired three participants for the second. She wished she could be confident people would eventually find their way into the groups. She refused to give in to defeat, but she couldn't rid herself of a growing apprehension that the Tibetan wanted and expected too much of her.

There was a commotion at the door and Regina burst into the office laden with bags. 'I am terribly sorry to be late,' she said breathlessly. 'There was a traffic jam on Park Avenue. A taxi collided with my bus.'

Victor looked up in alarm.

'No one hurt, thankfully.'

Regina, flushed and flustered and bundled in a heavy coat that strained around her middle, was a small and stocky woman nearing fifty, with thick short hair and deep-set eyes. They engaged in a brief exchange about the perils of the traffic as she unbuttoned her coat.

'Pedestrians really ought to take more care, too,' Foster said. 'They just walk straight out in front of you.'

'They've always had carte blanche to do so,' said Alice.

'Something needs to be done about the intersections,' Regina said. 'We need more traffic lights. They seem to do the trick.'

'The trolley cars don't help,' Victor said without looking up from his desk.

'I'm sure the authorities will come up with something to sort it all out. One day.'

'It comes down to education,' Alice said. 'A system of rules and procedures that we all must obey.' As with traffic, so with humanity, in so many ways.

Regina deposited her bags in the storeroom and sat down at her desk. The rhythm of routine descended, Victor's typewriter soon a clatter, Regina's following suit not long after. The four of them, along with a few volunteers, ran the office and they comprised the perfect team. As secretary, Victor looked after the administrative matters and dealt with the correspondence. Foster was in charge of finance and Regina helped on the publishing side with editing and generally putting things in order. Alice took on an overseer role, ensuring they had good copy for *The Beacon* and enough student materials for the Arcane School. Then there were all of the Tibetan's writings to organise and get into print. They all worked diligently and there was always a backlog of tasks. Which was why, when she called to the others to gather in the meeting room, she was filled with misgivings.

Once they were all seated, she began.

'The Tibetan want us to gather men and women of goodwill, and train them to become Units of Service, little beacons of light in an otherwise dimming world.'

It was a noble idea but even as she spoke she felt the heaviness of the undertaking, as though she already bore the weight of every stone in the library across the street.

Foster's jaw fell open. He was speechless. Regina shot him a cautious look.

'These men and women, will they be Arcane School students?' she asked.

'No. They will be aspirants, not disciples. They will work under the guidance of the seed groups.'

'Then they will be spreading the word and gathering more souls.'

'It's to help birth the New Age with its hallmarks of love, inclusive ethics and an orientation to service.'

Foster shook his head. 'Your health,' he murmured.

'Which is less significant, I think, than the health of the world.' She paused. 'We know the Hierarchy is close, and that the world is in crisis. It is down to us to do all we can to provide an alternative to the path humanity is on.'

'It shouldn't be too onerous,' Victor said. 'We can rely on existing channels. We have the mailing list and we can send out information pamphlets with *The Beacon*.'

'Foster, will you also help? We need to be selective.' She eyed him expectantly. Foster had the role of educating those who could cooperate.

'Alice, I always fulfil my obligations.'

'To the Tibetan,' Regina said, 'I should hope so.'

'Good. Then it's settled. And I will incorporate the program in my lectures and talks.'

'How will we fund the additional printing costs?'

'Times are hard, Foster. That's obvious, but we must ask and hope.' She thought of Alice Ortiz, and of Grace Rainey Rogers. She would have a quiet word with Victor later.

With Victor and Regina amenable, the project felt less burdensome. She was especially pleased Victor was agreeable as she would need his practical efficiency.

'Does this new organisation have a name?' Regina said.

'It does. We will call our new organisation Men of Goodwill.'

'Simple and to the point, I like it,' Regina said slowly. 'Alice, I can see this is the next step for us. It makes perfect sense.'

'The hallmark of the New Age of Aquarius is group consciousness,' Alice said, slipping into her esoteric voice. 'We will be a kingdom of souls. We will say goodbye to the old age of the personality, where nations are ruled by solitary kings or heads of state.'

'Or tyrants,' Victor said.

'Imagine governance on a world scale guided by spiritual impression. Where decisions are made in accordance with the Hierarchy and its plans for humanity.'

As she spoke her entire life's work unfolded before her. She had no idea if she were capable of anchoring the vision, if through her efforts and the efforts of her co-workers, another world war could be averted, or that the descent into the very depths of the destructive forces of materialism could be turned around, but she had to try. She would look forwards, not backwards, and complete all that the Tibetan wanted of her. She only hoped her body would last the distance.

They talked the project through some more, then Foster and Victor took their leave.

'How are you, my dear?' Alice asked Regina once they were alone.

Over the weekend, Alice had read in the newspapers that Regina's homeland, Hungary, was suffering as a result of falling grain prices and had entered a period of political instability. Regina's family were over there.

'I sense a shift to the right,' she said. 'I expect they'll align themselves with Germany.'

She sounded bitter, which was unusual in someone as sweet-natured as she. She said anti-Jewish sentiment was on the rise, especially in the universities. Alice gave her an understanding smile. Both Regina and Victor were Jewish, but as a lawyer, the sense of injustice would have affected Regina deeply.

Alice sympathised with the Jews and what she saw were their difficulties. She knew in her fashion that hers was a perspective born out of her own privilege. She knew, even as it blinded her to seeing the world differently. She also knew that when she was a destitute battered wife in Fowler, California, it was the good grace of her local Jewish grocer who had saved her through his generosity. Her grocery bill had by then escalated to over two-hundred dollars. She had no means of paying it back at that time. Instead of calling in the debt, Mr Weinberg insisted she placed future orders he knew she couldn't pay for, and slipped an extra ten dollars cash in with the delivery. Years later, she paid him back in full and she would never forget the gratitude she felt.

It troubled her that the Jews who, like so many groups, singled themselves out as distinct on cultural and religious grounds, were in turn singled out and attacked. No one deserves to be persecuted. Yet, in her mind, what mattered most was the condition of an individual's soul. To be a Jew was at that level meaningless, just as it was meaningless to be a Christian or a Hindu. The Jewish archetype was especially problematic, had been made especially problematic, by hatred. Regina and Victor knew her view, as did Roberto. Yet as a Theosophist, she inevitably had her critics.

They both stood at once and made to leave the room.

'The proofs of the intuition book are perfect, by the way,' Regina said. 'We can send them to the printers.'

'Excellent. Please tell Foster to raise an account.'

Alice returned to her desk. The intuition book Regina referred to Alice saw as an important work. It was the third she had published in her own right. The first, *Consciousness and the Atom* comprised a series of lectures on evolution which she had given in New York one winter. That book had come out a decade before. *The Soul and its Mechanism* she released not two years ago, and it came with a praising introduction by prominent psychologist, Harry Allen Overstreet, who had described the book as 'not only challenging but singularly illuminating.' High praise indeed, and she would carry it to her grave. Not that she was proud, that trait was long gone, rather she had been at pains to make her case, referencing leading scholars of the day in an effort to establish her own authority and be taken seriously, despite her lack of a college education. She had referred to everyone from Bertrand Russell to Robert Browning, and René Guénon to Arthur Avalon, in the hope of establishing her own credentials.

Western science was beginning to identify the endocrine system and suggest its relationship to the nervous system. In her book, she took that connection a step further, noting the functions of the various glands, and acknowledging that taken as a whole they had some sort of regulatory function, ultimately affecting human behaviour and mood. Meanwhile, the Eastern traditions had long identified the etheric body and its energy centres, the chakras, as having a similar function. What if the seven major chakras corresponded to the seven main endocrine glands? In this fashion, Eastern philosophy provided an energetic overlay informing the physical properties of the glands. Therefore, she argued, behind the scenes of our awareness, the soul worked through the personality via the etheric body and the chakras, and therefore affected the glands, and the whole body in turn.

Had she come up with something truly original? She thought perhaps not, and she was in any case drawing on the teachings of the Tibetan, but Olga's proposition back in 1928 had stimulated her own thinking around the notion of East meeting West and she had felt inspired. Olga saw herself and her centre as the locus of that meeting place of East and West. Alice conceived of a meeting place of an entirely different sort. The meeting place of the personality and the soul.

Her latest work carried the title 'From Intellect to Intuition.' It set out to cement her as an authoritative and sensible writer, distinct from the writers of inspirational works cluttering the shelves of bookstores and filling the minds of the public with hocus pocus and utter nonsense. It was imperative that her work was not lumped in with that lot. It was, therefore, another carefully referenced work that set out to inform in more or less everyday language the importance of meditation, and was aimed at the average intelligent aspirant who had not come across the occult before, or if they had, knew little or nothing about it. In her chapter on the purpose of education she had chosen to refer to Dr C. Lloyd Morgan's Gifford lectures, and in her introduction to Carl Jung, taking the trouble to quote him at length. She made good use of Evelyn Underhill's seminal work, *Mysticism*, and had peppered the entire volume with other luminaries, among them Zen Buddhist proponent D.T. Suzuki and W. Y. Evans-Wentz, who had translated the *Tibetan Book of the Dead*.

Her two recent volumes sat nicely together and helped to form the intellectual foundation for the school at Olga's. She looked forward to holding a copy of her new book in her hands, making a mental note to tell Regina to take a complimentary copy to the library across the street.

It was a busy day. At lunchtime, they remained in the office to dine on a lovely lunch of cheese quiche and pickled vegetables, kindly brought in by Regina, who said she hadn't wanted to go out again in the cold until she had to.

Alice spent the afternoon writing letters of invitation for the third session at Ascona. She thought to try Evans-Wenz again. She had wanted Carl Jung but he had already declined. Albert Einstein too, was on her list.

# A Letter From Olga

The rest of the working week proved arduous. Each day she was up before dawn, stoking the fire to get it going again, wrapping her shoulders in a thick shawl and draping a woollen rug over her knees while she sat at her escritoire over by the radiator.

The Tibetan had reached the last of the fifteen rules that comprised his treatise on white magic. Overall, he was making an important point, that the worker in white magic needed to recognise himself as a spiritual entity, a detached observer, and cultivate a different way of knowing which the Tibetan called the esoteric sense. Namely, to observe reality subjectively, inwardly, knowingly, through specially trained eyes. Eyes that had grown new lenses, at once microscopic, telescopic and wide in scope. Eyes that encompassed the whole and penetrated the depths of meaning in the service of spiritual heights. In all, a mind able to intuit ideas that would help shape the way humanity thought, ideas of inclusiveness, interconnectedness, synthesis.

It would be through cultivating the esoteric sense that the New Group of World Servers would all become Trained Observers.

The Tibetan had been discussing the nature of white magic in the light of the New Group of World Servers since Rule Ten. Up until then, the rules pertained to the Hierarchy and its plans for humanity in the coming New Age in general, and the particulars of thought-form building—that task peculiar to esotericists, involving the clothing of seed ideas in appropriate language, the energising of the entire outfit with spiritual will, and the sending off of the thought-form to do the work for which it was intended.

The new direction arose back in Ascona, and, for the time being, the Tibetan spoke of little else. She had taken down around two hundred pages of his treatise since then, as the rules were highly detailed and complex. It was slow work, painstaking, for she was not an automaton. She thought through everything he told her.

She saw the import. Black magicians deployed the same techniques of manipulation of thought and emotion. Every esotericist knew this, from the alchemists of old to the Freemasons. The propagandists knew it too, as did Hitler, or the powers behind him. Confirmation enough the use of the swastika, the ancient Hindu symbol of good fortune, co-opted to represent racial, or rather Aryan purity. The use ripped a corner of the Ageless Wisdom, that mantle woven out of tiny threads of insight from those who saw beyond the naked eye subtler realities and the vast interconnected web of existence from the atom to a galaxy or a constellation of stars.

The treatise would serve to guide a new breed of esotericist oriented to selfless service. It was important work, although she was glad it was finished, for she yearned to continue with her own composition.

She had the title, "From Bethlehem to Calvary", and the second chapter, the Baptism, mapped out in her mind. The life of Christ portrayed as an initiatory journey along the spiritual path was a shining example, a model for all to follow, yet there weren't enough hours in the day to set pen to paper.

At the office, she had spent Tuesday compiling the content for the next issue of *The Beacon*, with pieces from all of her regulars lined up, including one from Herbert Adams, and a piece each from Roberto and Vittorino, who were always forthcoming with copy. As was her dear friend Dane Rudhyar, the exceedingly intelligent young astrologer fast rising to eminence, whom she had met back in her Krotona days. He had sent her an interesting exposition titled "Integration".

To fill the issue, she had decided to include, "The Use and Development of the Will", an old piece by Franz Hartmann, the German

Theosophist who, together with Swiss parliamentarian Alfredo Pioda and a close friend of Blavatsky, Countess Constance Wachmeister, had established a Theosophical lay-monastery at Locarno near Ascona back in 1889. Her respect for Hartmann stemmed from his interest in the work of German Christian mystic, Jacob Boehme.

She had been including Hartmann's pieces since *The Beacon*'s foundation a decade before. Although this time she was doing so with considerable uncertainty coupled with a good measure of defiance. The last Hartmann piece she published was back in 1929 and she recollected the letters of complaint she had received afterwards, from irate Jewish subscribers who had cited Hartmann's association with prominent Austrian Guido von List as evidence of his, and therefore her, anti-Semitism. It was bad enough that Theosophy elevated the Aryan over the Jewish race, they had said, something she found herself tackling more and more as Hitler rose in prominence, but von List had taken anti-Semitism further with his emphasis on the supremacy of Germanic folklore.

The elevating of the Aryan race was a perversion of the very notion of root races. They were never meant to be associated with actual peoples. They were epochal and conceptual, denoting principles in the evolution of consciousness, that was all. Yet the critics were literal-minded and stubborn and she didn't doubt they would be quick to comment this time.

Responding to students' queries along with the composition of a new lesson plan for the Arcane School took up the whole of Wednesday, and by Thursday she was aching for the weekend. She even had it in mind to forego the office and remain home where it was warmer; the office was comfortable enough but the journey in the car chilled her to the bone.

It was Friday, and hearing one of the girls—probably Mildred who was an early riser—set off for an early walk with the dog, she forced herself to leave her escritoire and throw off rug and shawl, ready and resolved to complete a full week at the office, not wanting the burden of the work to fall on the shoulders of her co-workers, especially on Victor, who was forever swamped by correspondence.

Downstairs, she found Foster waiting by the door in his coat and hat and scarf. She followed him to the car. Neither spoke. Communications between them had been subdued since Monday, when she had announced the Goodwill project. His ego was bruised that she hadn't told him before the others and she knew he was fretting over the additional workload. Not that he would ever be the sort to shirk his duties, just that his enduring concern for her health was clouding his perception and she was irritated by it.

He knew as much as anyone that times were worsening by the day. Things were so bad in Germany that Chancellor Brüning had suspended reparation payments until the nation recovered. There was trouble on the streets in Britain, in Germany, and beyond. Never had world goodwill been more urgent. The global situation was as bleak as the landscape passing by her window, the thick covering of snow and the heavy skies devoid of all the romance they had at the start of the season with its promise of a white Christmas, now more a test of endurance as everyone anticipated spring. The only hope on the horizon lay with Franklin Roosevelt, who looked likely to run for the presidency. Franklin and Foster, himself a descendent of the founding father of his home town of Fitchburg, were acquainted through the Freemasons, and Alice found his wife, Eleanor, charming, dedicated and sympathetic.

They arrived at the office in a timely fashion, entering as Victor slit open the first envelopes of the day's post. Regina was occupied with organising the publicity for *From Intellect to Intuition*. They would take out a small advert in a number of occult and Theosophical periodicals and hopefully attract some favourable reviews.

Foster greeted the others in cordial fashion and went straight to his room and closed the door. Regina and Victor exchanged glances. Alice opened her mouth to speak then changed her mind. She would have a word with him later. It wasn't like him to bear a grudge and she was tiring of his petulance. Although, he was at work on the accounts and it was always better not to disturb him when he was.

They worked quietly through to lunchtime, when he emerged and offered to pop out for sandwiches and hot soup. He took the staff thermos with him. While he was gone, Victor stood up and ceremoniously picked up the mail sack, tipping out the last of the correspondence on his desk in a moment of mock triumph. There was a brief murmur of laughter.

Moments later he came across to Alice's desk and proffered a letter. She saw the postmark and knew it was from Olga. She gripped the bone handle of the small knife she used to open her post and gave the letter a quick slice with the blade. The office had fallen silent, as though in anticipation.

Dear Alice, I trust you and yours had a pleasant festive season. As I have not received word from you since December, I thought I might take it upon myself to put forward a gentleman for our line up in August. Mr Eugen Georg is promoting his new book and I am sure he will be available to speak for us. I understand he is an entertaining speaker and he certainly has some interesting ideas. What say you? We must come up with more variety, Alice. The last two years have been dominated by your people and I am hoping to reach much farther. What a pity Carl Jung is not available! I shall leave it with you and expect to hear from you in due course.

Yours,

Alice put the letter down. There was no mention of the New Group of World Servers. Their letters would have crossed in the post. She realised she must have looked as perturbed as she felt, when Regina said, 'What is it?'

She answered without hesitation. 'Olga has suggested Eugen Georg for the next summer school.'

Victor looked up from his desk. 'Eugen Georg? I'm trying to place him.'

Regina spoke without turning. 'From Germany. He wrote *The Adventure of Mankind.*'

'A pernicious little book,' Alice said. 'I can't think why she would consider him suitable. He's a sordid man with wild theories.'

'I haven't come across it.'

'I shouldn't bother with it, Victor.'

Alice glanced at the proofs of *From Intellect to Intuition* on Regina's desk, and seizing the opportunity to change the subject she said, 'You won't forget to drop a copy of my book across the road.'

Regina furnished her with a wry smile. 'Feed the library? Indeed, I shan't.'

They fell into silence. It wasn't long before Foster came back with their lunch and they all gathered around a spare desk.

The soup was hot and welcoming, the freshly made sandwiches—cheese on rye, and pastrami for the meat lovers—delightful. Altogether the mood lightened and the conversation turned to incidentals, Regina asking after the girls, and Foster relating a funny tale about his old school friend trying to crank start his car, falling on his bottom in the snow and sliding down the driveway and on down the road. It was a funny story, even after hearing it for the hundredth time.

Alice drank the last of her soup and followed Foster into his office.

'Mind if I trouble you?'

'Not at all, Alice. How are you faring?'

He said it matter-of-factly and with little warmth, a marked contrast to the public face he put on for the others. She wished he would dispense with his remote mood. He never raised his voice and was always devoted in his actions, but whenever he thought she ran the risk of working herself to death, he turned as cold as winter.

She chose to ignore it, took up the seat in front of his desk and read him Olga's letter.

'I don't know what to say to her. We'd agreed that we would attend to the lecturers and that Olga would deal with matters pertaining to the venue. That had always been the arrangement.'

He leaned forward in his seat, a shadow passing across his face. 'Sounds to me that she wants more control.'

'Proposing Eugen Georg is an odd way of going about it.'

'Perhaps she's testing you.'

'Testing me?'

'I mean, Eugen Georg, of all people.'

'Perhaps.'

'What will you do?'

Alice considered her answer for the briefest moment, a sudden burst of outrage heating her blood.

'I shall disabuse Frau Fröbe of her pretentions.'

'Tread carefully,' he said, his voice filled with concern.

'I shall not share a stage with Eugen George, Foster. And I see no reason not to tell her straight.'

He studied her face.

'Then do as you see fit.'

Alice would have stood abruptly if she could.

She returned to her desk and spent much of the afternoon drafting her response. She considered various ways of handling the matter but decided the only approach was to explain in full and put Olga in her place. Otherwise, who else would she propose next? She referred to the Black Mass, to a tendency towards the disgraceful in German teachings on spirituality. She pointed out the need to maintain a high standard to attract other speakers of good standing, not least the much-coveted Carl Jung.

It occurred to her as she wrote that Eugen Georg was far more suited to Baron von Heydt's coterie up at Monte Verità. Was that what this was all about? Olga wanted to best Heydt by filching one of his own kind? A ploy to undermine his position as host of his own successful salon? Surely not. Olga wouldn't stoop so low, not even unconsciously, although Alice couldn't fathom an alternative motive, given Olga's demonstrable propriety. That is, if the way she had reacted to Foster's nudity with silent umbrage was anything to go by.

Satisfied with her stance, Alice gave Victor the letter to post that afternoon.

The weeks flew by. It was February before Alice received Olga's reply. By then all of her invitations to potential lecturers had been answered in the negative. She was beginning to wonder if the summer school would go ahead. She would happily cancel but they had already conceived the entire trip, with a fortnight in Giverny in France in July, followed by their first stay at the Percy-Griffith's house in Ospringe after the summer school. Erlo had laid plans for a lecture tour in Holland, Belgium and France, with many dates scheduled. The whole family was looking forward to the trip. The girls had even started picking out dress fabrics.

This time Foster was present in the main office when she slit open the envelope. As she read Olga's words, she was glad of his presence, for she could scarcely believe her eyes.

Olga had reacted badly to the rejection of Eugen Georg. A tirade of reproach leapt from the page. The task of finding satisfactory lecturers was thankless, she wrote, if Alice planned rejecting them all. She had done her best and since her choice was not good enough, one must imagine that she herself fell far short of Alice's lofty expectations.

Alice suspected Olga had received her letter inviting her to participate in the New Group of World Servers. Clearly, the saloniste had taken offence at finding herself in the second group. Yet her very volatility fitted her for the task! For when she *did* learn to transcend the inferno of her passions, she would see clearly into the infernos of others.

Her hand trembled. She set down the letter and caught her husband's gaze.

'What is it?' he said, rushing to her side and reading over her shoulder.

'Olga,' she whispered.

She could say no more. She handed him the letter. A pained expression appeared in his face as he read. When he had absorbed the content, he passed the letter back without comment. He stood, observing her, waiting for a response. When she didn't give it he said, 'What will you do?'

She looked over at Regina and Victor who were busying themselves with other things.

'Everything is planned.' She tried to temper the anguish in her voice. 'But for the lecturers.'

'She clearly wants control. Let her have it.'

She met his gaze, trying to read the intent behind his words.

'I'm sorry, Alice,' he said. 'Ever since you announced the World Servers I've been worried. You know I will always stand by your decisions, but you can't stop me fretting over your health. If Olga wants to take charge, then let her. It will be one less task for you. Now, I, too, have a desk full,' he said, 'and things won't get done if I shilly shally.'

She laughed and he laughed with her.

Once he had returned to his office she took up her pen, wasting no time writing her reply. Prudence restrained her emotion and she smoothed Olga's, too, with measured words. Following Foster's advice, she suggested Olga go right ahead and source lecturers if that was what she wished. Even as she sealed the envelope she sensed the relinquishing of control. Not that she minded. Foster was right. She had enough to contend with. The spiritual summer school had helped expand her reach into Europe; perhaps it was a stepping stone, and while she would never renege on her obligations, she would happily see the back of it, if all it achieved were ructions.

Seated in the drawing room later that evening, the large windows curtained against the cold, she enjoyed the closed in feeling that came with winter, the fire a dance of flame in the grate. She was clutching in both hands a cup of sweet tea, soothing for her tongue which was sore again, and she felt the ache in her head loosen and dissipate. It was the best she could hope for. In the snug warmth, Olga's letter, which had been nagging at the edges of her mind since she opened it, seemed trifling and inconsequential. Indeed, the entire four years of letters back and forth, the grand vision Olga had presented her with, the effort they had all made to see the scheme come to fruition; it no longer carried the weight of importance it once did. The summer schools might, in the larger scheme, be of little import, one centre among many centres of light, and not even an especially bright one. What was needed was something far grander, more all-encompassing, along the lines of the New Group of World Servers, but even that was small. It represented the beginning of something. An experiment.

Reflecting over the last few years, from that moment when Olga had first presented her proposal, Alice saw in a flash that a point of completion had already been reached, an apex, a culmination, and the publishing of her second book, *From Intellect to Intuition*, reflected that pinnacle. She was grateful to Olga for initiating the phase, for providing the impetus for Alice to compose and publish two volumes that pivoted on the theme of East meets West. Without Olga, those works may never have been written. In all, it appeared the devoted student may have served her purpose, although they still had the third summer school to get through.

Alice was a woman and an occultist, one among scores of others of her kind, and it had taken an enormous effort to establish herself as a credible author in her own right, and not merely a conduit for the Tibetan. Nothing had been published solely in his name for seven years. Even *The Light of the Soul* was a collaboration of the Tibetan's delineation of the yoga sutras of Patanjali, along with her own explanations. She knew he had more, much more to say. She felt it like an internal pressure, an urgency. But first, she needed to establish her own standing in the occult milieu and beyond. That was paramount if the Tibetan's objectives were to be realised. She would have liked to be getting on with her latest work on the initiations, but she required a tranquil mind.

She reached into the wicker basket by her chair for her embroidery, taking a leaf out of Violet's book and keeping busy. Embroidery absorbed her mind, drawing her attention to needle and cloth, and as she stitched she let all of the worries of the day fall away.

She had completed a corner of the handkerchief when Mildred entered the room with her usual exuberant flourish, bringing the rich smells of baking with her along with a draught. The rest of the house was heated by the furnace, but on cold days, those radiators had a challenge.

Earlier, Dorothy and Ellison had insisted on preparing dinner unaided. Alice hovered, offering advice, but she was shooed away. Alone in the drawing room she had succumbed to that familiar feeling of loss of control, as though an essential part of her was being wrenched from her, and her mind had kept drifting to the kitchen and what the girls might be doing or doing wrong.

'Where's Father?' Mildred said, sitting down in the chair opposite.

'I believe he's resting upstairs.'

'I wanted to show you both this fascinating book.' She held it up for her mother to see.

'Aldous Huxley.'

'It came out last month.'

'*Brave New World*, yes, I know. Are you enjoying it?'

'Quite a bit. He writes passionately. Yet the story is dreadfully bleak. How can utopia be dystopia all at once?'

'Because utopia for some will be dystopia for many, I should imagine.'

Mildred paused with her mouth ajar and her eyes wide, absorbing the thought, then she opened her book. She was a vibrant young woman who leaped through life as though it offered her boundless joy. She was big-hearted by nature, and somewhat blind to the foibles of others. She always chose to see the good in people. Yet there was a serious side to her too, she was practical, fastidious and prone to worry, which Alice had always thought would serve her well, tempering her natural effervescence. When she bowed her head over her book, Alice observed her, taking in the red, form fitted dress that flared from her knee to mid-calf. The white bow on the bodice. To keep warm, she had chosen her deep burgundy cardigan with the high collar. In all she looked both regal and domesticated with her mane of beautiful soft hair.

Seeing her there reading, all red and picture perfect, Alice was catapulted back to the moment of her birth. Mildred was ten days overdue and the day she chose to make her entry into the world it was well over a hundred degrees on the porch of that horrid little house in Reedley. She recalled how the cesspool had only just collapsed, and how she had worried Dorothy, who was toddling, might fall in.

Dorothy and Ellison burst into the room, bringing in another draught and cooking smells. They stood in the doorway bobbing like a pair of jack-in-the-boxes. Of the three, they got along the best. They had a natural rapport and much in common. They had both taken to wearing those frightfully flared trousers that were all the rage. Gazing at them standing in the doorway, the only thing to choose between them were their different coloured sweaters, Dorothy's blue, Ellison's orange.

'Mildred, go and get Daddy,' Ellison said.

'You do it.' Mildred said, without looking up from her book.

'Very well.' Ellison swept out of the room, with Dorothy on her heels. 'Daddy!'

'Don't call up the stairs,' Alice said, raising her voice. 'Go and fetch him.'

She heard stomping footsteps, a knock, then muffled voices.

Mildred smirked. She had always stood apart from her sisters, not only in apparel, but in manner. There were four years between Dorothy and Ellison, although you wouldn't have known it at times. As the youngest, Ellison took her role as ringleader a little too seriously. Dorothy had always been the sensitive one, and was gentle by nature. Alice suspected she had suffered the most as a result of their natural father. He never harmed her, but she bore witness to the terror and was wont to hold back when courage was called for.

The girls had abundant friends in the neighbourhood and were never short of entertainment, but she was looking forward to taking them to England, to Ospringe, where they were sure to meet more suitable young men. She had nothing against Stamford society, or the cohort of young Italian men who had migrated to the area. Most were unskilled factory workers with whom the girls didn't associate, but there also existed a prominent middle class, and she feared the organised crime that went with it. Above all she feared that like her, her daughters would fall in with the wrong sort. She no longer had the time, energy or impetus for mothering, but even so, she couldn't help watching over her daughters like a bear.

When she heard Foster's footsteps, she gestured to Mildred and they went through to the dining room across the hall. Foster entered behind them, taking up his seat at the head of the table. He was bleary eyed, and she noticed his hair was tousled. Last night, he had attended a meeting at the local Lodge and gone for drinks at a friend's house afterwards. She wasn't sure when he arrived home—his bedroom was in another wing—but it was certainly well after midnight.

The girls took up their usual places, and between them passed around the bowls of roasted vegetables and mock hamburgers, and a jug of mustard sauce, along with fried chicken for the meat eaters.

'I made an apple flummery for pudding, Mummy.'

'Ellison, you are spoiling us.' She had to push aside an image of the mess in the kitchen and felt a sudden sympathy for Marion.

The chink of cutlery and plates, the food warming her belly and any thoughts of the frost hardening the snow outside were gone. It was as though the world beyond the walls didn't exist. It was just the five of them, a family enjoying each other's company, an ordinary event on an ordinary day and Alice resolved to enjoy every moment.

It was Foster who broke the enchantment, by announcing to the table the latest news: Hitler would be granted German citizenship. It was all he needed to sweep to power.

'But, he's Austrian,' Alice said.

Ellison set down her fork. 'What do you mean, Daddy?'

'He did a stint as police commissioner in 1930. Any role as a German official entitles the individual to citizenship.'

'That's absurd.'

'Hitler's downplaying the news, but it's obvious where all this is heading.'

'Not to me, it isn't,' Ellison said.

'If he becomes a citizen, then he can run for government.'

'But the people won't vote for that vile little man, surely?'

'I fear they will,' Foster said. 'He's enormously popular and his party is gaining momentum. The National Socialists are holding rallies across Germany every day.'

'Must we have politics at the table, *all* the time,' said Dorothy.

No one paid her any attention.

'Well, I heard that Mahatma Gandhi's chakra has been seized because he hasn't been paying his taxes,' Mildred said, as though pleased to make a contribution.

Dorothy looked puzzled. 'Chakra?'

'Spinning wheel,' Alice said. 'To spin cotton.'

'Poor man. I quite like him,' Mildred said. 'He's right to seek independence for India. What do you think, Mummy?'

'As I understand it, the British have always done their best for their colonies. But times are changing and nations must be allowed to express their full potential.'

She hesitated on her words, thinking it the wrong trajectory, for nationalism would always obstruct the one-world governance that was fundamental to the new Aquarian age.

'Can't we talk about something else,' Dorothy complained. 'I hear the Olympic games are going down a treat at Lake Placid. My friend, Sybil is there.'

Ellison joined in. 'And Margaret Fairhaven.'

The girls chatted about the games, Foster joining in, interjecting with one of his favourite stories, of the day he had first met Dorothy. She was hanging upside down in a tree.

# A Confession

It was a Friday morning in late February, two days before Dorothy's twenty-second birthday, and the air outside was crisp and fine. The girls had gone for a walk in the park with the dog. Her cat, Tom, was curled in a ball by the fire, and Foster was downstairs with the newspapers. They were having a day off from the office. At last she had a chance to work on the second chapter of her book on the initiations of Christ. She was determined to make good progress but as she reflected on the baptism scene in the Bible, she found herself back in India in the monsoon, reliving her complete physical, emotional and spiritual breakdown.

On reflection, that collapse marked the end of one life and the beginning of another. She didn't know it then, that she was poised to leave India and enter a wilderness, just as Christ had entered his.

For what she had gone through in India was undoubtedly a form of baptism, not that she considered herself equal to Christ, that would be nonsensical. Just that there existed a pattern, a sort of blueprint, and His life exemplified it and hers, up to a point, was a repetition, a distant echo.

She felt that all too familiar sense of urgency, as though her book was part of the Tibetan's plans, the Hierarchy's plans. It might well be her last valiant effort at pulling together her own ideas. Not that she anticipated having nothing further to write about, that she was about to lose her inspiration and become a pond drained dry. No, nothing of that sort. But she wasn't getting any younger and her health compromised her ability, and the Tibetan had already hinted he had another treatise in mind for her to take down, a treatise far larger and more detailed than those on cosmic fire and white magic, something five times as large, encompassing psychology, healing, astrology and the initiations. It would be a comprehensive series of volumes on the Seven Rays.

The Seven Rays. Those vast spheroidal bands of colour that rendered the solar system an iridescent dance of light. A symbolic condensation of consciousness. An understanding of the Seven Rays that would advance humanity's progress on the spiritual path. The treatise, like all his texts, would be written to inform future seekers in the New Age.

He knew her health was poor, that she was declining in strength, that in all likelihood she only had a few more years ahead of her before the blood and heart condition would incapacitate her. He also knew she had the spirit of a king who recognises his duty, and she would continue until it was impossible to do so.

She collected her thoughts and pressed on with her own work. She saw her book as enriching and informing, an exegesis of the unfolding of Christ consciousness within: the soul, that part of the individual that recognises the Kingdom of God as truth and seeks to participate in its plans. Christ, the head of the Spiritual Hierarchy, would be portrayed in all His glory, and esoteric knowledge sanctified in His light.

For the book was to be a blending of Theosophy and Christian thought, relying to a small degree on Annie Besant's *Esoteric Christianity*. She planned on quoting Rudolph Otto, Alfred North Whitehead, Albert Schweitzer and Edward Carpenter, among others. She had their volumes to hand.

She would demonstrate that it was not thinkers and visionaries who bridged the gap between East and West; it was Christ. He had given the East to the West in a form people could understand, underscoring the keynotes of sacrifice and service. He exemplified the Buddhist eightfold path.

Christ was baptised at the age of thirty. She thought to make quite a point of that, shooing away the thought that she, too, had almost been in her thirtieth year when her own baptism experience had occurred.

When Christ entered the stream, he was transformed.

The stream is symbolic of the feeling nature, the world of emotion, the Baptism representing purification by water in a blaze of illumination, after which the initiate is never quite the same. Following the Baptism, Christ had to prove his moral strength. He was tested in the wilderness, thrown back into the world of experience, thrust into a desert, where his thoughts and emotions and his body were strained.

He never forsook God.

Neither had she, even when she was convinced He had forsaken her.

She made good progress as the hours slipped by, composing paragraphs and making notes of references. Later, she heard footsteps coming up the stairs. A soft knock on the door and Foster walked in, bringing with him through the open door the sound of the radio playing downstairs. She thought he might have appeared with a tea tray. Instead, he stabbed the newspaper and said without further ado, 'Goebbels has just announced Hitler as the National Socialists' candidate for president.'

He was silent while she absorbed the information.

'He isn't a citizen,' she said doubtfully.

'It's a formality.' He surveyed her escritoire, her chair and her bed, all littered with books and papers. 'I'm sorry for the interruption,' he said. 'It's just that this situation in Germany…'

'I know. Would you mind asking them to turn that off?'

'They're excited. It's Dorothy's birthday tomorrow.'

'Ask them to turn it down, then, please,' she said.

It took her a full fifteen minutes before she could steer her mind back to her work.

Alice Ortiz had invited the family to visit her in Delaware for a celebration of Dorothy's birthday, then had to cancel when Forrester unexpectedly took off to Africa, leaving a distraught Marguerite at home with a temperamental baby. Eve was teething. The last-minute cancelation left Alice in an organisational frenzy for the whole of Saturday as she pulled together an alternative gathering at home.

She arranged a small party in the afternoon, leaving the girls to invite neighbourhood friends, and it was all gaiety and laughter until the guests left. Dorothy went to spend the evening with a friend, leaving Mildred and Ellison arguing over who should eat the last piece of cake. Ellison was grumpy because they hadn't given her a party the month before. They had planned to, but Alice had been too unwell to manage.

'That's so unfair,' Mildred said, raising her voice as Ellison reached for the cake. 'I only had a tiny piece. You had a big wedge. I saw you.'

'You have to have it all your way, Mildred.'

'I do not!'

Ellison stood back, hands on her hips. 'I was the one who didn't have a birthday party. I was the one who nearly *died*!'

Mildred screwed up her face. 'What *are* you talking about?'

'Ask our mother.'

'Oh, that.' She rolled her eyes.

'I hardly think it trivial!'

Ellison stormed out of the room as Alice, who had watched the whole exchange from the hall, approached to calm things down. 'Sorry, Mummy,' she said as she brushed past, her tantrum already dissipating.

Mildred stood in the centre of the room, surrounded by disarray. Chairs were pushed back against the walls, used glasses, cups and plates were dotted about on every available surface, and the table used to display the cake was covered in crumbs. The remaining slice was untouched. Mildred seemed at a loss whether to take it or let it sit there. With Foster downstairs attending to the furnace and Marion, in the kitchen clearing up, they were alone. Alice could see Mildred was shaken. She went and took her in her arms and smoothed a hand through her hair.

'Trust Ellison to dredge up her own birth on Dorothy's birthday,' Mildred said sulkily.

'She's being melodramatic. It'll pass.'

'Maybe. Or maybe it's because that's all she knows.'

'Mildred, leave it, please.'

Mildred pulled back and eyed her mother quizzically. 'You never talk about the years between. You talk about Castramont and Aunty Margaret. You talk about Moor Park and our great grandparents and how strict they were. You talk about India and I so love those stories. I can picture you at the piano entertaining the troops. You talk about the sardine cannery and Krotona too, which sounds so amazing and I often wish it still existed so I could go and see for myself. But you never talk about the years between.'

'Some things are better left unsaid,' she said slowly. 'Besides, I do talk about that period of my life.'

'You do not. Or rather, you are like an ice skater, doing little circles on the surface. Ellison said she almost died. We all know that story because you told us. But there's more. I know there is. Dorothy says our father was a beast.'

Alice led Mildred to the chairs by the fireside, straightening hers before she sat and indicating to Mildred to do the same. She knew the time had come to speak, not because Mildred had brought it up, but that her daughter's sudden interest coincided with her work in progress, which made the telling apposite. She braced herself and began.

'Your father, Walter Evans, was an exceedingly attractive and intelligent young man, and when we met in India, I fell instantly and deeply in love. It was a desperate sort of love, one I thought doomed, which made it all the more intense.' She paused. 'I was lovesick in the extreme.'

Mildred emitted a coy laugh.

Alice frowned. 'What I'm about to tell you is serious. It should be a warning to all young girls.'

'Yes, Mummy,' she said, chastened.

'You must remember too, that I was ill, Mildred. Physically, emotionally and mentally exhausted. By the time I was in Castramont, convalescing, I was unreachable. No one tried to talk sense into me, but I could tell they were all scared. Everyone but me knew I was making an awful mistake, even the servants.'

'Why? You loved him. They should have respected that.'

'Walter was not of my social standing, Mildred, and that matters. It matters more than you think.'

Alice could see from the faraway look in her eyes that she didn't believe it. Of the three, she was capable of making the same mistake. She was too trusting. All the more reason to tell her the truth while there was still time. She talked Mildred through her time in Cincinnati, of her beloved Mrs Snyder who had protected her so fiercely, of struggling to be a housewife and then a clergyman's wife, of the words and fists in Reedley and Foster, and keeping hens in Pacific Grove while Walter was suspended from the church. Mildred's gaze never left her face. Alice thought any moment she would leap up for a notepad.

Tom, who had been lounging on the hearth rug, spied Alice's lap and sat before her, staring with eyes wide and dark. Then he placed his two front paws on her knees. She patted her lap and he jumped up. She let him circle and settle himself in his favourite position, with head bowed, paws tucked under his chin. She ran a hand down his fur. He purred.

She recalled the desolation she felt, and her self-recriminations. As she fed her children and collected firewood she came to the conclusion that the entire situation was her fault for questioning her faith. That she was paying the price for having doubts. This was her punishment. Back then she had no other way to view it. With hindsight, she could see that it was her inner strength that was being tested, her spiritual resilience. For she had been tested on every level and she had passed.

'How old was I then?' Mildred said.

'You were only two. At the end of Walter's six months of good behaviour I told the bishop that Walter was much improved, and the bishop sent him away to a mining village in Montana.'

'Montana?'

'Montana. And that was the last of him in our lives.'

Other than his abusive letters, she thought but didn't say.

Mildred fiddled with a cuff of her dress. 'It sounds dreadful. I'm sorry all that happened to you. Dorothy is right. Our father was a beast.'

'I was foolish.'

'You fell in love.'

They gazed at each other. Mildred's acceptance that her mother was not at fault was unequivocal. She would have liked to explain further, warn Mildred not to make the same mistake. She inhaled to speak when Ellison flung open the door and stood in front of them, holding a pack of cards.

Mildred looked up. Alice observed their faces, both filled with uncertainty and contrition. The spat was forgotten.

'Mildred, would you like to play rummy?'

Mildred reached out and patted her mother's hand as she stood, and Alice was left alone, shaken.

Confiding to Mildred had aroused intense memories. Yet she could see why composing her book was proving more difficult than she had imagined. Why she had to keep putting down her pen. For she couldn't write about the period between the baptism and transfiguration of Christ without being drawn back into her own past. She didn't much care to revisit those years that saw the birth of her daughters. She still felt the twinges of shame and self-recrimination. She preferred to forget the whole phase ever happened and had managed to do just that, repressing and dismissing the memories bubbling beneath the surface. Then Mildred unexpectedly brought that period of her life into the full light of day, taking a keen interest in the years between, as they had all come to call them.

Mildred carried a fierce pride and protective loyalty towards her mother, qualities that came with the pursuit of self-understanding and an equal and slowly developing respect for the work. Of course, she was still in many ways a child. Alice was consumed by fear that something similar would befall her through a poor choice of suitor.

# A Third Summer School

Apprehension had her in its grasp. She was suffering flashbacks and disturbing dreams and she had awoken unrested, as she had night upon night since they arrived. She could sense echoes of Krotona, as though she had stirred up the ghouls of the past in her very recollecting and she rued the day she had thought to write a book on the initiations of Christ. It was proving, on a personal level, emotionally turbulent, to say the least, and now the demons were stirring, dark forces swirling all around her.

The darkness that Alice had felt on the inner planes the first time they had visited Ascona, one that had taken outward form in the degeneracy she had witnessed at Monte Verità, had seeped into the grounds of Casa Gabriella like a foul mist. Although the magnificent purview from her bedroom window on that bright and sunny day made it difficult for an onlooker to believe.

On this, their third visit, Olga had installed them in a small cottage overhanging the waters of Lake Maggiore, which she had had built in the intervening year, and named Casa Shanti. It was a peaceful location, tucked beneath the steep, richly gardened escarpment with its maze of meandering paths and flights of stone steps. Casa Shanti sat beside Casa Gabriella, with the lecture hall beyond. It was impossible to find fault with either the cottage or the location, yet she couldn't quell her impulse to gather her things and her family and bolt for the train station in Locarno.

She moved away from the window and sat down on the end of her bed, running her hands through her hair.

Olga had taken control of the program after Alice had written informing her that she had fallen ill and couldn't attend to any of it. After composing the third chapter of "From Bethlehem to Calvary", her health had taken a sudden downturn and she had spent a month in bed with the most appalling migraine and chest pains, culminating in a blood transfusion when it was discovered her red blood count was dangerously low again. She had managed to take down a few private letters to the disciples working in the Tibetan's groups and little else. Once she had recovered sufficient strength, she carried through on her other commitments. It was a matter of investment and dissipation of energy. With the administration of World Goodwill in full swing, adding to her workload, she really didn't have time for the summer school.

Perhaps the workload and her poor health were souring her mood. She struggled to keep level-headed when she was ill. Anxieties bubbled up and clouded her mind, wittering voices complaining about little hurts and big fears.

Three weeks into the proceedings and she was becoming concerned for her girls. With Foster and she occupied with the summer school, and Monte Verità close by, her progeny, her pure and chaste progeny, who had always been exceedingly well-behaved, were apt to go wild. After all, they were in the holiday spirit, they were young and full of energy, and they were a whole year older and more confident and adventuresome than they were before. They had lost their original shyness of the first year, when they would make tentative forays beyond the confines of Casa Gabriella, always accompanied. Three years in and they were marching off on their own to wander the streets of Ascona. There were too many undesirables living and staying in the area for comfort. Heaven knew who they were mingling with. She trusted them completely, but she sensed their reputations were suffering. She wanted them married, since none of them seemed inclined to do anything else.

Meanwhile, Olga had taken to holding court like a matriarch, and had developed a hawk-eyed vigilance when it came to the girls' movements. Making the situation even worse, that preposterous and flirtatious Baron Eduard von der Heydt had developed a fondness for her daughters that was little short of sickening. They had taken to wandering up to his hotel practically every day on some pretext or other, having been given an auspicious welcome on the first day of the summer school, when they had been invited to accompany one of the attendees for lunch. Alice wished she hadn't given her permission. Although how could she not, given the conversation they had had?

'He's such a jolly old thing,' Dorothy had said at breakfast that first day.

'He's not that old,' Ellison had cut in. 'He's the same age as our mama.'

'He's awfully good fun. He makes us laugh.'

Mildred's reassurances had done nothing to assuage Alice's misgivings.

'It's harmless,' Dorothy had said resolutely. 'We aren't doing anything. Just chatting in the gardens and playing cards.'

*You are being seen and you are being watched.* Alice couldn't bring herself to say it.

Feeling defeated, she had braced herself and given her consent.

She forced herself from the confines of her room and managed to get through breakfast and the morning lectures—given in German and indecipherable—-but lunch proved a test of endurance.

She was seated at the round table outside the lecture hall, in the shade of the large tree. To one side sat a rotund man with a severe expression fixed on his face and on the other a much smaller man with a hunched back. Olga sat opposite, equally sandwiched between dour-looking men. Foster had lost interest in the lunch party after his second glass of wine and had wandered off to sunbathe. Alice could only hope he had the presence of mind to wear something.

She was left to converse with that most erudite group of men, all of them professors of one sort or another. Some spoke English, others none at all. Their banter, their laughter, their exaggerated attempts to include her in the conversation, in all she felt patronised. Olga, by contrast, was having a marvellous time, quaffing wine and laughing gaily. The luncheon, indeed the entire session had taken on a bacchanalian flavour.

She began to look for a way to excuse herself when Foster unexpectedly reappeared with a newspaper tucked under one arm, taking up his former seat at the table. He'd taken to reading *L'Express* to practise his French.

'I got too hot,' he said with a laugh.

Olga gave him a withering stare.

'What news do you bring us, Mr Bailey?' said an elderly professor. He had a small moustache and round glasses and the table went quiet upon his query.

'Let me see,' Foster said ponderously, opening the paper and pointing at an article. 'Stalin has declared that all property on Soviet collective farms belongs to the State.'

'Unauthorised use punishable by death. I read that. Rather ironic, I think.'

'How so?' Foster asked.

'Street rioting in Germany is being declared political terrorism, also punishable by death.'

Foster nodded, showing interest. 'Meanwhile Hitler has made a bid for chancellor. That about sums up the highlights.'

His comment was pointed. No one spoke.

'There's nothing to choose between Stalin and Hitler in my opinion,' Olga said.

'Except that Stalin is in power.'

'Hitler soon will be,' the professor with the glasses said.

Olga frowned. 'But his party lost the presidential election.'

'Like I said, he soon will be.'

There was universal assent around the table, although it couldn't be ascertained if all stood opposed.

Alice reflected privately on the irony of their little summer school, with its East meets West pretentions, while two vast nations, also East and West, looked poised to turn into totalitarian leviathans. The furore of dictatorship hovered like a cloud of hatred above Europe, the anathema of democracy and universal brotherhood. Seated there at Olga's round table at the epicentre of occult evil, she was overwhelmed by the force of it. She saw the devastation, the destruction that lay ahead if the trajectory were not averted. While there they all sat, drinking wine and communing about philosophy and abstract ideas and theories, from what she could glean. It occurred to her in an instant that Olga's East meets West had descended into a dalliance, a frivolity, an opportunity for clever minds to snatch concepts from other cultures, an intellectual exercise to satisfy the egos of professors.

Whereas her version of East meets West was a chance to transcend differences, to unify, and to foster inclusive thinking, harmony and goodwill among ordinary men and women the world over. Ego didn't enter into it. She couldn't help but be struck by the difference, even as she knew she was being unfair to Olga.

When they began to discuss the Jewish problem, Alice shrank back inwardly. In her mind was the small bundle of acidic letters with European postmarks from irate Jewish subscribers and others who had taken umbrage at her inclusion of German Theosophist Franz Hartmann's piece on the use and development of the will. They continued to voice their concerns, many referring to the reputation of the Arcane School and the Lucis Trust, and Hartmann's association with Guido von List, who had taken to promoting an insidious, racially prejudiced form of Theosophy that was profoundly anti-Semitic. She had dictated a standard reply to Victor, pointing out that *The Beacon* had been including pieces by Hartmann since its foundation, and that what was important was the quality of the ideas, which were of an exceptionally high standard, and not the author's membership of any particular group. She was furious. She wouldn't be dictated to by those who failed in their understanding. The vessel, the man, may have been wanting, and it was common knowledge in occult circles that his standard of personal hygiene was low, but his intellect had been exceptional. In response, in defiance she had arranged with Regina to publish in the October edition another Hartmann piece, this time on thought-form building.

Hearing in snatches of broken English the professors discuss the need for a separate homeland for Jews, the table endorsing the Zionist movement—something she staunchly opposed—Alice made to leave the table, stating that she required a short rest before the summer school resumed its activities. Foster accompanied her and they spent a pleasant hour in the cool of Casa Shanti before feeling obliged to attend the afternoon lecture.

On the penultimate day of the summer school, Olga invited the Bailey family to dine with her in Casa Gabriella. She had put on a lavish array of salads, pate, cheeses and one of her vegetable terrines, along with chilled white wine for those who wished it. Olga's light-hearted banter put everyone at ease. Alice enjoyed the cool breeze wafting in through open windows, and the mellow light of evening.

The discord began over dessert. They were all tucking into strawberries and cream when Olga said, 'In all, I thought our third summer school quite successful. Don't you think?'

Alice and Foster exchanged glances.

'A most engaging line-up of speakers, Olga,' Foster said diplomatically.

'Thank you. Although I have to confess my disappointment at the attendance. Numbers were markedly down on last year.'

She left the table and returned moments later with a copy of Eugen Georg's book, setting it down beside Alice.

'We should have invited him, Alice,' she said, finger stabbing the cover. 'He would have pulled a crowd.'

Alice all but choked on a strawberry.

'Really, Olga. I thought I had made my position quite clear,' she said, recoiling inwardly. 'Eugen Georg is not the sort of calibre we would wish to attract.'

'And what do you say, Foster?' Olga said, shooting him a wry glare.

'I haven't read the work in question,' Foster said, evasive.

'I'm not entirely sure I agree with you, either,' Olga said, twisting Foster's remark to taunt her. 'When I attended Keyserling's School of Wisdom in Darmstadt a few years ago, there were others, like Georg, who held controversial views. But they made for exciting and challenging exchanges. His school is enormously popular.'

Alice was speechless. She admired Count Keyserling enormously. They shared much common ground. Indeed, her own work, and that of the Tibetan, comprised foundational and educational material designed to make manifest the vision they all shared.

'His school won't be allowed to continue for much longer,' Foster said informatively. 'I understand he is already under attack from the National Socialists.'

'Because he has the courage to speak out against them.'

There was a brief period of silence in which Olga finished her dessert. When she set down her spoon she said, 'All I am saying, Alice, is we need variety. The mind cannot expand if everyone agrees with each other. I know for a fact that Carl Jung would see it my way. Indeed, that was the very topic of conversation at the dinner table when we'd met at Darmstadt.' She lifted her gaze to the ceiling. 'Such an erudite and charming man.'

'Indeed, we all agree Jung must be encouraged to attend the next summer school,' Foster said.

'I believe his presence to be essential,' Olga said with gravitas.

It was not difficult to see what Olga was about. Her spiritual summer school was intended to trump not just Heydt's salon, but Keyserling's School of Wisdom as well. She had sought out in Alice a spiritual teacher in order to present to her own intellectual circle a fresh version of the Ageless Wisdom, one they hadn't heard told in that fashion before. Alice had been nothing more than a catch, a prize, no, not a prize, a lure, a small fish on a hook paraded to lure a bigger fish: Carl Jung. Olga had used her and her contacts to put on two, no three summer schools. Alice felt she had been duped all along, tricked into satisfying the ambitions of a woman who wanted nothing less than to stand proud on top of her own mountain.

Olga continued with her Jung reminisces until Alice interrupted by expressing her gratitude for the sumptuous dinner and taking her leave. The rest of the family followed, subdued. When they were alone in their room, she confronted Foster with, 'Promise me you haven't been sunbathing again with nothing on.'

'Alice, what do you take me for?'

'I need you by my side.'

'I am by your side.'

'Then why that look and why evade the Georg issue?'

'For the sake of your daughters, if you must know.'

She was made aware of their unease throughout the meal, the lack of girlish conversation.

# Faversham

They left Casa Shanti the following morning, arriving in Britain in the beginning of September to more distressing news. Every day, grim news to add to the depressing times. Alice had begun to wish Foster would desist from purchasing the newspaper. That day, two hundred thousand cotton workers had gone on strike in Lancashire, and Hermann Göring had been elected President of the Reichstag. The National Socialist's rise to power grew stronger by the minute.

Despite the gloomy news on all fronts, with Ascona behind her, Alice's mood lifted. Hope replaced the heavy, dark feeling she had been unable to shift the whole of the previous month. They took a taxi from Waterloo to Victoria Station and boarded the Canterbury train to Faversham. Everyone was looking forward to arriving at their destination and excited to see the new setting. For Alice, the sights she saw evoked brief reminiscences. She marvelled over how much had changed since she was last in London; the intervening decades had seen something of a revolution, not least in the amount of traffic on the roads. Gone the horses and carriages in abundance when she had left. Now, like New York, there were motor cars everywhere.

Her spirits lifted further when they encountered Henry Percy-Griffith at the station, who had come to drive them to Ospringe in his Rolls Royce. Dressed in a tweed suit and cap, with his broad smile and magnanimous air, he was the perfect English gentleman. As he greeted the family in turn Alice was reminded of her dear old Uncle Clere.

Situated on the outskirts of Faversham, Ospringe Place was everything Alice could have anticipated. It was a white brick building, and in the centre of the main façade was a wide porch flanked by two sets of fluted columns. Large, multi-paned windows were arranged evenly in the walls.

Hilda greeted them at the door, demure in a navy blue worsted suit cut to her figure, her silver hair arranged in neat curls about her face. They made a handsome couple. It was especially refreshing to hear them speak, with the familiar rounded, well-enunciated diction Alice had been accustomed to as a child, and as they shook hands she felt a flood of nostalgia, at once comforting and unwelcome, for it came with memories of a lonely childhood and a single relative, a sister, who had written her off. She had anticipated the mixed feelings she would confront, but she hadn't bargained on their force. Her legs felt they would give way from under her and she reached for the door frame as she stepped inside.

She recovered her composure the moment she found herself in the hall and admired the high ceiling and wide staircase. The interior of Ospringe Place was spacious and airy, and the thought that Helena Blavatsky had been a guest at one time, only added to the feeling of belonging that filled Alice's heart. There was ample room in the house for them all, with numerous bedrooms upstairs and an additional suite in a cottage attached to the end of the main house, which used to accommodate the servants but had been turned over to guests, with three good-sized bedrooms upstairs, and a living room, kitchen and large study at ground level.

They sat down to tea in the drawing room of the main house, and Alice and Foster furnished the Percy-Griffiths with a carefully crafted account of their time in Switzerland while the girls sat primly in their seats, the perfect picture of propriety.

After some time had passed, Hilda gave Dorothy an understanding smile. 'Don't worry, my dear. Betty will see to it you are all adequately entertained.' She turned to Alice. 'She's due to arrive the day before your departure. It's all confirmed.'

Betty Harris was another student, and a member of the Tibetan's special group of telepathic communicators. When she had discovered their plans, she offered to chaperone the girls while Alice and Foster went on the lecture tour Erlo had arranged, and again when they later returned to New York. Betty was well-connected, a society lady with a business in luxury antiques, which scarcely tied her to anything. Alice felt comfortable entrusting her daughters to her care.

She sank back in her seat, confident the whole family would adore Faversham. On the edge of the Kent downs, it was all gently undulating green fields and small woods, in contrast to the alps that rose like shards to enclose the valley at Ascona. It felt more natural to be there in Kent, homier and much, much more convivial.

The following day, before Hilda and Henry set off on their travels, they took the Baileys on a stroll to the nearby village. They passed an assortment of farmers' cottages and grander homes, and an old pub, arriving at a medieval hospital on the corner of a lane.

'It opened as a museum a few years ago,' Hilda said.

They stood in admiration, Henry telling them the building dated back to the 1200s, with bits added on here and there over the centuries. At the corner of the lane, the building retained its original construction of flint walls on the lower portion, topped with heavy timber beams, the upper storey fractionally overhanging the lower as was the style, with diamond paned windows in waney walls.

'How utterly quaint,' Mildred said, drawing close to her mother and taking her arm. 'Just think of all those generations of people who've moved inside those crooked walls.'

'I'm amazed it's still standing,' said Ellison with a giggle.

With its top-heavy construction, Alice had to agree it did look like the building would topple any moment.

They headed up another lane until they arrived at the church of St Peter and St Paul, a stone building dating back to Saxon times, although it was obvious from the structure that little of the original building could be seen. They hovered in the grounds, listening to Henry's potted history.

The girls were accustomed to encountering fine old buildings, but none of them were particularly interested in going inside, although Dorothy remarked that the heritage felt different somehow to that she had encountered in Europe, as though she were connected to it. Alice hoped before long her daughter would make a similar remark about a young man. At least for now, she had fallen in love with her surroundings and that seemed to calm her, for she had been too highly strung at Ascona.

They hadn't walked far but Alice was relieved when they turned back. She hadn't recovered from the long train journeys and the strain of being at Olga's. Foster offered her his elbow.

When they arrived back at the house, Hilda told the girls to make sure they took themselves off for walks to Faversham.

'It's an old market town. The area is positively brimming with fields of hops and oast houses'

'Hops?' Dorothy said.

'Here, beer is made from hops.' Henry said, ushering them indoors.

'Which are dried in hop kilns, or oast houses. You can't miss them. They're distinctive due to their tall round roofs.'

'I would like to try the beer one time,' Ellison said.

'I'm not sure you will like it,' said Mildred. 'You don't like bitter things.'

Dorothy took a surprising interest in local history after that. The girls took long walks on fine days and would report back their discoveries, full of facts about the Benedictine abbey, the gunpowder mill, the alms houses, and the funny way the locals spoke.

Following her usual routine, Alice spent her early mornings taking down the Tibetan's treatise on the Seven Rays. Unlike the detailed presentation of cosmology in *A Treatise on Cosmic Fire*, and the occult rules of *A Treatise on White Magic*, his focus was human psychology, and she found his instructions fascinating and revelatory. She doubled her efforts, taking down pages and pages of delineations and extrapolations. Humanity required a new psychological model, a way of understanding the psyche from a deeply subjective, soul-centred perspective. It was cleansing and centring work and restored her equanimity that had for too long been off-kilter due to her ill health and the summer school.

The week before Alice and Foster were due to leave for the lecture tour, the girls were to attend a ball arranged by the bishop and hosted by Countess Sondes at Lees Court. Invited were the officers at the garrison in nearby Canterbury, and Alice expected it would be the first of many occasions for the girls to mingle with their own kind.

She knew it would be a grand affair and Alice was privately relieved her friend Alice Ortiz had seen fit to arrange the purchase of appropriate gowns for the girls. They both knew fully the need for Dorothy to find a suitable match. She would soon be twenty-three. Alice would never mention it to her friend, but she didn't want her daughters to fall into the situation poor Marguerite found herself in with her lion hunting husband. Worse, the mistake she herself had made marrying Walter.

She was all apprehension on the day. She sat her girls down in the drawing room and gave them a long lecture on manners and the expectations of British aristocracy.

'It doesn't do to be naïve in such matters,' she said to them. 'You must heed my words carefully and follow what I've told you to the letter.'

'We will, Mummy.'

Ellison giggled.

'For heaven's sake take your mother seriously for once,' Foster said, entering the room.

They went quiet. Foster hadn't remonstrated the girls in a long time.

'We will, Father,' Mildred said, staring into her lap.

Alice needn't have worried. Letters from Dorothy, Mildred, Ellison and Betty flew across the Channel at quite a rate, greeting the Baileys at their various destinations as they travelled through Europe. But, it wasn't until they had returned from the tour, and were preparing to farewell the girls and travel back to New York, that a certain Captain Morton came to tea.

He was a dashing young man, six months Dorothy's senior, and they had met at the Lees Court ball.

They all gathered in the drawing room. Ellison had made a sponge cake under Alice's watchful eye. Mildred had prepared sandwiches and Dorothy had prepared herself. She was all blushes and coy smiles, and when Terence asked permission to date Dorothy, Alice took one look at Foster and granted it without hesitation.

She could not have approved of Captain Terence Morton more highly. To find one of her daughters making a suitable match came as more of a relief than she had realised, even as she had spent years worrying. Sensing the spark of love dart back and forth between the pair, her cup trembled in its saucer and she had to set it down in her lap.

# Some Unpleasant Correspondence

It would be a relief to be back at Ospringe with her girls. Christmas in America had been a lonely and empty time without them. Foster and she had driven down to Alice Ortiz' house in Delaware for the festivities. It was always wonderful to be in her company and her husband, Julien, had been charming. It was a delight to spend time with their daughter, Marguerite, too, and her little girl, Eve, who was toddling about all giggles and chirrups. Although the presence of Marguerite had reminded her of Dorothy and Mildred and Ellison. She had tried not to fret and Alice Ortiz had been a great comfort, but she couldn't stop speculating on what they might be getting up to and if they were feeling lonely. The primary distraction in Delaware was provided by Marguerite's husband, Forrester, who was as charismatic and bombastic as ever. He entertained the party from dawn till dusk with tales of his recent trip to Africa, while his wife stared down at her lap and Alice Ortiz looked askance.

Alice's apprehension for her daughters was reinforced when a letter from Switzerland arrived at the office. Victor handed it to her as she came in the door. The return address indicated that the letter was from Baron von Heydt. She went to her desk and opened the letter before she realised it wasn't addressed to her. It had been addressed to the Misses Baileys. Inside, were three identical photographs of the Baron.

One he had signed "to the loveliest", another "to the most charming" and a third "to the most beautiful".

Her mouth fell open. Hoping no one in the office had seen, she hurried the photographs back in the envelope and threw it down on her desk in disgust. She wasn't sure with whom she was angrier, her girls or the Baron. The man was an insufferable flirt and there was no telling what tales, true or false, he was putting about at Monte Verità, tales that would no doubt have reached Olga's ears.

Without another thought she sat down and resealed the envelope, writing on the front "return to sender". Succumbing to a wave of outrage and indignation, she determined that for the duration of the next summer school the girls would remain in England.

A puzzled look appeared in Victor's face when she returned the letter to his desk.

'These came in today's post,' he said, handing her a small pile of opened letters. 'It seems that Hartmann piece in the October issue is causing problems.'

'What people fail to appreciate is a human being is both a personality and a soul.'

Victor gestured at the letters in her hand. 'They're only seeing the personality.'

'Whereas we, Victor, deal in souls.'

She walked back and sat down heavily. The criticism was incendiary, many of the correspondents reiterating their initial protest in letters the office had received in response to the first Hartmann piece that appeared in the March issue. The tone of this second round of complaints was unforgiving. Some threatened to leave the organisation. There was a long rant from one Arcane School member reminding the Lucis Trust of the numbers of Jewish refugees already arriving in New York in anticipation of Hitler's rise to power.

Last year, the National Socialists had lost the parliamentary elections, but the party had campaigned relentlessly ever since and were gaining widespread popularity. She thought back to the grim prediction made by that German professor one lunch at Olga's. The Jews were right to leave. Who in their right mind would stay if there was a way out. People have their limits and despite the hardships those people face as refugees, taking flight was sensible. A woman trapped with a domestic despot was in a similar situation. A battered wife, a battered community. There was never a justification for hatred or the violence that came with it.

Among her followers, the Jewish question had become charged. She needed to handle the situation with the utmost sensitivity. The trouble was, she could see more than one side to the problems facing the Jews. She couldn't escape the understanding that when it came to group consciousness, all forms of separatism, including Zionism, were obstructive. Nationalism of any kind and whatever the justification stood opposed to the inclusive one-world vision the Tibetan and she held dear. Goodwill saw no differences of colour or creed and treated everyone the same. The Jewish problem was fundamentally rooted in the pull of the collective personality in a direction contrary to the requirements of the world soul. The difficulty she faced was enabling others to adopt this higher, abstract view. To do that, people needed to transcend the selfish will of their personalities.

Regina and Victor understood perfectly, as did Roberto. If they didn't question the Tibetan's perspective, why did so many others? But it wasn't righteousness she felt, or indignation. It was self-recrimination that she had been pig-headed or blind or thoughtless or whatever it was that had prompted her to include the second Hartmann piece. It wasn't possible to think through the consequences of her every act. Nothing would ever get done! Had a hidden part of her wanted to provoke, to test? She didn't believe so, but perhaps it was so. No one is perfect, least of all her.

She held the letters in her hand. She wasn't sure how to respond. She decided not to discuss the matter with Regina and Victor. Instead, not wanting to further alienate members, she drafted a brief letter of reassurance, stating she was well aware of the growing difficulties and fears of the Jewish community. She then wrote a short paragraph referring to the Tibetan's World Goodwill program, and that the Lucis Trust was committed to peace and salvation.

Prudence held sway and she decided never again to publish another Hartmann piece in *The Beacon*.

Towards the end of January, Foster and she left for a second lecture tour of Italy, arriving in Rome to news that Hindenburg had appointed Hitler chancellor of Germany. A cold chill swept through her when she heard, and from that point on a grim expression became a fixture on Foster's face. Roberto, who had taken care of all the tour arrangements, had booked them into a hotel near the university and they had arranged to meet in the lobby. It was a cold and dreary day and while they waited for their host, Alice struggled to enjoy the atmosphere, the romance of the streets outside, and the people milling about and chatting in their beautifully lyrical style.

When Roberto appeared, he was flustered and apologetic.

'You've heard?'

Foster held up his newspaper.

She could see that the news of Hitler's appointment had affected Roberto greatly, and at first, he and Foster could talk of nothing else. With Mussolini in charge of Italy, Roberto felt an enduring unease. He, perhaps more than any other student, saw the importance of transforming human consciousness.

As the two men spoke Alice wondered if the lecture she had prepared was relevant. She had taken down a good deal of the treatise on the Seven Rays and had it in mind to present the rays and explain the thinking behind them; that consciousness could be divided into seven distinct energies, an extrapolation of a basic metaphysical truth of emanation. Namely, in manifestation, the One, becomes three, which unfolds into seven (a, b, c, a-b, b-c, a-c, a-b-c); the three major rays of spiritual will, love wisdom and active intelligence, and the four minor rays of harmony through conflict, concrete science, devotion, and ceremonial order. The soul vibrates to a ray, the personality another, and each of the three bodies—physical, emotional and mental—can be found on one or other of the rays. A recognition of the various ray energies enables the aspirant to understand their personal challenges and attune to their soul ray. The rays, in effect, would form a cornerstone of a new psychology and Roberto, for one, would find her words illuminating. It was just that her talk did not address the nature of evil, the dark forces of materialism and separatism, and the polarised attitudes that were gripping the world.

She needn't have fretted. That evening, she gave her lecture to members of his Institute of Psychic Culture and Therapy. Roberto translated her words beautifully. It was a joy to share the lectern with him, and the audience was attentive. He had arranged a second lecture in a small hall and both events were well attended, the applause she received heart-warming. Students approached her afterwards with eyes filled with awe and deferent smiles. She was moved, even as she could scarcely comprehend it. They regarded her as a natural leader. On the inside, she felt anything but.

The following day Roberto whisked them away to Florence, where he had arranged another lecture. Alice found Florence a glorious city and she was able to forget about Hitler and Stalin and Mussolini, at least temporarily. She was able to push away her worries about her daughters, too, after a letter arrived from their chaperone, Betty Harris, full of reassurances. They stayed at Roberto's home, where they were greeted by his charming wife, Nella, who proved the perfect hostess. It was there that Roberto talked about his institute. He said he had decided to re-name it the Institute of Psychosynthesis, which seemed a fitting name. She thought it resonated beautifully with her talk. In all, their time in Italy was a dream, and after the final lecture, they travelled to Torquay, having accepted Violet Tweedale's invitation to visit.

Alice had been looking forward to visiting Violet with much anticipation, but after many hours and days in transit on trains and the ferry across the Channel, upon their arrival at Violet's splendid country house with its sweeping views of the bay, it was as much as she could do not to collapse. Violet welcomed them into her capacious drawing room. And tea had been laid out in anticipation. As Violet poured, Alice couldn't fulfil her social obligations a moment longer and sat forward to make her apologies and asked to retire to her room.

'Violet, my dear,' was all she said.

Violet took one look at her and said, 'You look veritably done in.' She put down the teapot and approached Alice with an extended hand. Alice took her offer, and together they walked upstairs.

'I do apologise,' she said, entering a large and airy room. Seeing the beautifully made bed in its centre she almost swooned.

'Nonsense,' Violet said, drawing the curtains and pulling back the covers and ushering her to lie down.

Alice slept until the following morning.

Over the following days, as she rested and took in the peaceful surroundings from her upstairs window, her strength returned. She was bolstered too, by Violet's upright and robust manner and one afternoon, she indicated she would like to visit her mother's grave.

Alice Harriet La Trobe-Bateman was buried in Torquay and Alice had only the dimmest recollection of the funeral. One crisp afternoon, Violet's husband, Clarens, drove them all to the cemetery and they pulled up in a parking area outside the keeper's lodge. They decanted and headed as a group along a wide path that led out onto manicured lawns. The trees dotted about were all twiggy and bare. Snowdrops and bluebells were making a showing. Alice hung on Violet's arm. When she saw the sea of headstones she said, 'How on earth?'

'There's bound to be an order to it,' Violet said. 'We'll find her.'

'Let's split up,' said Foster.

'Good idea,' Clarens said, and the two men took off in opposite directions, leaving Alice and Violet to stroll through the centre of the grounds.

After about ten minutes Alice stopped walking. She felt breathless. 'No one thought to put in a seat,' she joked.

Violet squeezed her arm. 'Let's wait in the car. The men can find her.'

The path back was on a slight decline and she found the distance shorter. Seated in the comfort of the car, feeling the weak warmth of the low sunlight through the window, she closed her eyes and waited, wishing privately she had had the presence of mind to suggest someone had gone off and located the grave prior to her visit.

After a short while, Foster came bounding up to the car, grinning.

'I've found her,' he said. 'She's not far.'

Alice eased herself out of the car and took his arm and they walked up behind the keeper's lodge and on past another small building. Violet and Clarens followed, a discrete distance behind. They stopped at an untended grave, a tangle of limp weeds growing up hard against the headstone. Observing the grave, Alice succumbed to fleeting memories of the times she had spent in Torquay with her aunt Dora, her father's sister, who had died before Alice had departed for Ireland. Dora had left behind her husband, Admiral Sir Brian Barttelot, and their four children. She wondered where they all were. She strained to recall the funeral, a sad affair that she hadn't comprehended. She was only five and her father had been inconsolable.

Standing before her mother's grave, the depth of emotion she felt surprised her. Her heart ached for memories she had never had, for she was missing someone who for most of her life was never there. The heartache faded as fast as it came and she was left feeling empty, for she could hardly feel stricken after almost fifty years. Even so, a single tear made its way down her cheek as she realised half a century had passed before she finally had a chance to pay her mother her respects as an adult. It was a realisation that came with the knowledge that she would be approaching the end of her own life soon enough, for her blood and heart condition that had dogged her for too long and with ever increasing intensity, was incurable and bound to shorten her time on earth. It wasn't her own death that troubled her, but the incapacity and the exhaustion and the pain she was doomed to endure, in all the suffering that would blight the years she had left and slow down her progress when there was so much to achieve.

They arrived at Ospringe to more snowdrops and bluebells and more loss. Alice had scarcely had a chance to settle in and was yet to confront her daughters about the photographs Heydt had sent when she learned the news of Grand Duke Alexander's death.

Foster read out the obituary in the newspaper at breakfast. But she already knew, or at least, it had come as no surprise. The Duke had entered her room the night before, dressed in his pyjamas. She had woken, opened her eyes and there he was, for a moment at least. Then he faded and was gone. Sadness rippled through her as she buttered her toast. He was only in his mid-sixties and that seemed too young to be taken. She recalled the last time she had seen him, when they were sitting together in the back of the car. Foster was driving the Duke home after a speaking engagement. It was then the Duke had told her he also knew the Tibetan.

Yes, he had been, he was, he always would be an especially attuned soul.

Sitting at the breakfast table, eating her toast and jam, she felt the significance of that comment, knowing they were bound together as spiritual companions, sure to encounter one another in a future incarnation. She drew comfort from that thought.

She drew comfort, too, from life's cycles of life and death, especially when Dorothy entered the room, radiant as a flower in bloom and full of the joys of the season. Her cheeks were flushed and her eyes sparkled. Her young man, Terence, was due to visit for tea.

Mildred and Ellison both appeared at once shortly after Dorothy had taken up her seat beside her father. A new alliance had formed; Dorothy clearly had no time for either of her sisters.

Alice didn't want to spoil their day but the time had come when she felt compelled to raise the matter of von Heydt. She waited until they were all seated and settled before describing the photographs and what a shock it was to discover her daughters regarded in that fashion by a lecherous old man.

'Sorry, Mother, but that's just plain silly,' Dorothy said, cutting into her egg.

'We didn't do a thing wrong, Mummy. I swear it,' Mildred said, clearly the most uncomfortable of the three.

'Mildred's right,' Dorothy said. 'He was kind to us, that's all, and he was immensely entertaining.'

'Indeed, we did have an awful lot of fun.'

Alice caught Ellison flashing Mildred a knowing look. She bristled.

'I would not like to think that any of you had behaved in an unseemly fashion. You are young ladies. You do not run amok. I would not want to learn of anything similar from Betty Harris.'

'We've been paragons of virtue,' Ellison said. 'I promise.'

'Then why look at your sister in that devilish way?'

There was a short pause as she considered her response.

'Whilst we behaved ourselves, others did not.'

All three girls lowered their gazes and smiled.

'I don't think our mother wishes to hear about that,' Mildred said quickly.

Foster emitted a short cough and they were all made aware of him standing in the doorway. No one spoke. He approached the table, put down his newspaper and said, 'Do what your mother tells you and make sure you conduct yourselves appropriately.'

'Yes, Father,' they all said at once.

At Ospringe, life settled into a rhythm. The days slipped by, each a little warmer than the last. Leaving Alice to write and meditate, Foster set about establishing offices in Kent using their local contacts, and conducting meetings and discussions, cultivating a network of co-workers who could take care of operations in Britain while they were away.

Upstairs in her room in the early hours of each day, Alice took down several more chapters of the new treatise on the Seven Rays, and from time to time personal letters to various members of the seed groups, letters filled with observations and advice. She knew even as she wrote that some of the participants, those receiving the Tibetan's more pointed criticisms, would not take kindly to the contents. She thought of modifying or even deleting some of the paragraphs but chose not to.

One morning, she took down a letter for Ernest Suffern. He was already showing signs of irritation after his last letter and she quickly saw the latest would only exacerbate his sensitivities. While at pains to acknowledge the gains Ernest had made, the Tibetan had chosen to reiterate Ernest's need to transcend the dual life he led, to unify his business and spiritual interests. He cautioned Ernest against taking himself too seriously, stating that he was mentally rigid and intense, and apt to serve his own agenda. He went on to urge him to refrain from suggesting aspirants for group work who were plainly not suitable. As she wrote she saw the communication came across a little strong, but she would post that letter, along with the others. She wouldn't disobey the Tibetan.

Spring had come early that year and the trees were coming into leaf, the daffodils along the drive making a grand show. One morning in the middle of March, Foster interrupted her morning routine to announce that just about the whole of America must have tuned into the radio the previous night to listen to a broadcast of Roosevelt's first fireside chat. A newspaper report outlined the gist of the broadcast, in which Roosevelt explained why he had declared a state of national emergency and halted the banks.

'He's wasted no time, then.'

'He said he wouldn't. Decisive action, at last.' His face was alight and it was pleasing to see. Franklin Roosevelt had been inaugurated as President of the United States of America less than two weeks before and since winning the presidency, a glimmer of hope had shone on the nation. Roosevelt was strong and courageous. He would make a visionary leader, just what America needed to lift itself out of the depression. Alice approved of his approach; the fireside chats were a clever way of managing the people and gaining popular opinion. Although while she saw the value of the new technology in broadcasting to the masses, she was at once ambivalent, for an opportunity for good may just as well be used for evil, as Hitler and his men were bent on exemplifying.

Meanwhile, in Britain, poor beleaguered Ramsay MacDonald scarcely seemed able to hold things together. It was worrying that at a time when fortitude was required, the British government showed little other than weakness.

Later that week, a letter arrived from Olga. Dorothy handed it to Alice at breakfast. She had been awaiting the postman in case he had a letter for her from Terence.

Alice hesitated, eyeing the hurried script in which Olga had written the address. Something told her it would not be good news. She put the letter in her pocket and finished her breakfast, refraining from opening it until she was alone.

The girls had arranged to take Foster on a walk around Faversham that day, eager to show him some sites. They would take tea there too before heading back, leaving her in peace to write the final pages of her book on the initiations of Christ.

Alice sat at the escritoire, positioned between two grand windows overlooking the grounds. She seemed to spend much of her life seated at desks positioned by windows, as if it was her lot now she was middle-aged to observe rather than participate in the goings on outside. At least, that was how her life had taken shape, bending as it had to, around the demands of her health. She watched her family as they crunched their way down the drive to the lane, her girls all nicely garbed in smart warm dresses and jackets, matching Foster's quick, purposeful pace. They rounded the corner and were gone.

Only then did she extract the letter. She had been anticipating repercussions ever since those signed photographs from Heydt arrived in New York. She hesitated, the envelope warm in her hand. She examined the hurried scrawl, sloping uphill. Even the stamp was crooked. Bracing herself, she opened the envelope and with much trepidation read the words Olga had composed.

The tone was angry from the first, veering to the hysterical. The content shocking, although not unexpected. As she read, Alice felt winded as though she had been punched in the abdomen. The primary topic concerned her daughters. Olga seemed to take malicious pleasure in informing her that since August, tongues had been wagging and gossip in Ascona concerning their behaviour had not only not gone unnoticed, it was the talk of the town. She went on to state that Foster's nude sunbathing was in flagrant disregard for the tone of her establishment.

Alice paused. Her hand trembled. She had known all along that Foster's behaviour had caused a stir. He had been a fool to imagine he would get away with it, knowing what Olga could be like. But as for Dorothy, Mildred and Ellison, Olga claimed they had flirted outrageously at Monte Verità. They had gone off on escapades, she said.

Escapades?

It was rumoured they had engaged in impure acts.

Impure acts!

Alice was appalled. She could barely contain herself; her mind fit to burst with indignation. Worse, she had to wait for hours before they returned from Faversham and she could give voice to her chagrin.

Was any of it true? How could her own family bring her into disrepute? How dare they!

She felt her entire world unravelling, all she had set up in accordance with the Tibetan, suddenly, potentially, in tatters.

She was overreacting, she knew she was, yet she couldn't help but be consumed by anxiety. She had no idea what to do with herself. All hope of writing was lost. Idle, she waited, trying not to wring her hands.

As the hours ticked by she began to wonder, and a measure of reason smoothed out her tousled mind. Perhaps it was Olga who was overreacting, and stirring up trouble.

The moment the girls arrived back with Foster, she stood up and did something she would never normally do. She yelled down the stairs.

'Dorothy, Mildred, Ellison, come to my room, at once!'

There was the sound of gasps and whispers. Then hurried footsteps on the stairs and three exceedingly meek girls were soon standing side by side just inside the door of her room.

Alice stood by her desk and glared at each of them in turn.

'I had wondered when I opened that letter from the Baron whether what you had been telling me was true. Now it has come to light that rumours have been spread all over Ascona that you have behaved in a highly indecorous fashion. Explain yourselves!'

Dorothy blushed crimson. Mildred looked down at her feet. It was Ellison who spoke for the three of them. She held her mother's gaze and stated plainly that nothing untoward had taken place. 'We were admittedly having fun. But nothing of the nature you imply took place. I promise.'

'You've been accused of dancing and flirting and not just this once but on all three visits. Olga views your behaviour as deplorable.'

'We did dance, but everyone else was, too. It was the Baron's idea. He put a record on the gramophone and invited us to show him how to Charleston. As if he didn't know. The dance has been around for years. Then everyone started joining in. It was all so silly and hilarious.'

'Flirtatious behaviour will ruin your reputations.'

'We did not flirt! We were just having fun. Ask Carlos, he was there. Or the Baron. He'll tell you.'

'I shall do no such thing. I'm asking you and I expect the truth.'

'It is the truth. We would never embarrass ourselves,' Dorothy said.

'Or you, Mother,' said Mildred. 'We would never embarrass you.'

'It's that stupid Baron,' Ellison said.

'It's Olga,' Alice murmured.

'What do you mean?' Dorothy asked.

'Never mind.' Alice sighed. 'I believe you. Why wouldn't I? You've never given me cause to doubt you before. You may go.'

'We're sorry, Mummy.'

'No need.'

She had made up her mind that the source of the drama was Olga. It had to be. All those disapproving looks! She had been looking to cause trouble all along. But why?

Alice replied to Olga's letter the following day. She had wanted to do it sooner, but thought it wise to wait until her equanimity was at least partially restored. In the cool of the morning, while the others were asleep in their beds, she sat at the escritoire and picked up her pen. She wrote slowly, restraining her hand that wanted to race ahead with invectives. After a sentence of politeness, she indicated in the strongest of terms that her daughters, by their own accounts, had not engaged in any impropriety. That she was offended that Olga had chosen to believe the gossip. She explained she was not interested in malicious talk at Ascona and advised Olga to adopt a similar stance and take no notice.

For all the good it would do.

In an effort to appease, she went on to list the invitations she had sent out to potential speakers for the fourth summer school, and informed Olga that she would be back in New York at the beginning of May and would attend to organisational matters regarding the school from there. Part of her wanted to cancel the plans for the fourth summer school after the disappointment of the third, and now Olga's letter, but a commitment was a commitment.

She read over her reply. She thought the tone measured and restrained, considering how she felt. She doubted her reassurances would assuage Olga's chagrin. As she slipped the letter into an envelope, all she could do was hope her words would bring the matter to a close.

At the end of March, they invited Terence Morton to dine with them at home. He arrived promptly on six to an ebullient and coy Dorothy. With Alice's guidance, Mildred and Ellison had baked a vegetable gratin and a peach melba, making use of the last of the bottled peaches in Hilda's pantry. The girls set the table and put on their best dresses. Alice thought the fuss premature, for Dorothy and Terence had only been dating a few months. Still, it was all sweet and charming and she was pleased they shared in their elder sister's joy.

The radio was left on, playing softly in the background.

Terence was undoubtedly a polite and well-mannered young man, perfectly suited to Dorothy. He brought sunshine into the room with his little bouquet of flowers and everyone's spirits lifted. He sat erect, and engaged in conversation without dominating it like Alice Ortiz's lion-hunting son-in-law Forrester had back in Delaware.

The dinner proceeded in a fashion she was accustomed to, the conversation light and gay. Until the peach melba was consumed and Foster uncorked a bottle of brandy. 'To celebrate,' he said, holding up the bottle.

'Celebrate what?'

'Roosevelt's abolished the prohibition.' His face wore a devilish grin.

There were murmurs around the table, the reaction mixed.

Foster had demonstrated restraint for the duration of the meal but she knew he was all but exploding inwardly. The National Socialists had thrown out the government of Bavaria. The morning's headlines had covered the story of the declaration of the third Reich at Potsdam. Hitler, newly appointed as chancellor, had been granted absolute power by the Enabling Act. When he had read the news at breakfast, Foster had been outraged, and his mood had remained sour the whole day. He could think of nothing else and who could blame him. Only, the evening was meant to be for Dorothy.

'Germany now has a dictator in the making,' Foster said grimly, passing Terence a glass of brandy.

Terence leaned forward in his seat. 'Not while Hindenburg's alive, surely.'

'They're unstoppable.'

'Foster, please.'

'No, Alice. You know as well as I that the forces of separatism are gaining strength. The Freemasons and homosexuals are under attack.'

'Foster.'

But he wouldn't be silenced. 'The Jews appear to be the main target, not the only target, but still. There's been in an uproar in New York, with street protests against the persecution of German Jews. They're calling for a boycott of German goods.'

'For all the good it will do.'

'The poor Jews,' Mildred said quietly.

'What would you know?' Ellison said.

Alice shot her a censorious look. They were back to sparring.

'At least Americans will be able to drown their sorrows,' Foster said, knocking back his drink with a short laugh.

No one joined him.

'I don't understand why Hitler is so popular,' Ellison said. 'Don't thousands, if not millions attend those rallies of his?'

'He appears to them to be offering a solution.'

The world was cleaving, rent in two by materialist forces determined to thwart the emergence of a new age of spiritual enlightenment. She was anxious that separatism and hatred would hold sway, and goodwill, that simple expression of the soul, would be crushed by the forces of evil gathering strength on the planet. But it didn't do to turn a happy occasion into something so dismal. She wished Foster would rein himself in, but he was burdened.

'Hitler and his men are fomenting ancient hatred.' Alice made to stand. 'But I'll leave you two to discuss these sobering matters, gentlemen. Girls, come and join me in the drawing room.'

Her daughters obeyed, for which Alice was grateful. She didn't want any of them getting drunk.

A fortnight passed, and another letter arrived from Olga. Mildred handed it to her mother at breakfast. Alice felt drained at the sight of it, uncertain of the contents. She slipped the letter into the pocket of her cardigan and once she had finished her toast she withdrew upstairs to her room to read it.

From the first sentence Alice felt Olga's fury as though it had leapt from the page to strangle her throat. Olga had dispensed with pleasantries and launched straight in, every sentence filled with reproach, Olga expressing her anger and dismay that Alice should choose to believe her daughters' testimonies in the matter of their own propriety, over the reliable sources she herself had consulted. She hurled at Alice the accusation of double standards. She didn't mention Eugen George and his despicable book. She didn't need to. She went on to decry the notion of rising above the gossip, stating that it affected her reputation and the reputation of the school. It was all very well for Alice, tucked away out of sight in Kent, but she had to live amongst the sordid affair and she was trying to establish a centre of integrity. She expressed her utter disgust, reiterating that Alice's daughters' sub-standard behaviour had been going on for the whole three years. She ended her rant on a barb. Not only did she state that she would prefer never to see Alice again, she withdrew Alice's involvement in the next summer school and announced a parting of the ways.

Alice tossed the letter down on her bed. She was shaking. She was consumed with outrage and incredulity. She had been dismissed, sacked, dispensed with. She, an occult leader of good repute, a woman who ran her own internationally recognised organisations, slapped away like an unwanted fly by her own student.

There was a rap on the door and as she looked over, Foster entered. Seeing her obvious distress, he rushed to her side. 'May I?' She nodded as he reached for the letter. She went and sat down by the fire and waited for his response.

'Oh dear.'

She remained silent, staring at the empty grate. A thousand thoughts scurried through her mind but she gave voice to none of them. Instead, she murmured, 'There's nothing to be done.'

'But her remarks are an outrage. How will you respond?'

'I shan't.'

The larger part of her was relieved their collaboration was over, but the acrimonious fashion in which it had occurred left a nasty taste. An organisational dispute she could understand. If Olga had simply taken umbrage over her rejection of Eugen Georg and gone on to assert absolute control of the programme, Alice would have backed away. She was sure of it. But to vilify the behaviour of her daughters was vindictive. To use them, and Alice's apparent double standards, as just cause for ending their friendship displayed not only a volatile temperament, but one laden with hidden motives. Alice knew, instinctively, that she had been set aside as superfluous. That she no longer satisfied whatever it was Olga desired. And what Olga desired was obvious. Not what. Who. Carl Jung.

Foster withdrew without indicating why he had knocked on her door. For a moment, she cursed him. That part of Olga's accusations was true and couldn't be undone. She had little choice but to shove aside his behaviour as thoughtless and foolish. Above all, she was confused, instinctively protective of her daughters, even as doubt crept in and she was left wondering if Walter Evans hadn't insinuated himself into their natures despite her best efforts to set them a good example. It was an unsettling thought. She reminded herself that she had had to deal with animosity and criticism from many quarters ever since she had taken on the role of the Tibetan's scribe and set about putting his words into practice. Putting Olga's letter into that broader perspective, she decided it was no different. It would pass. The animosity would fade away and nothing would come of it. Olga was being petty and insignificant. A teacup tempest, as her old foe Louis Rogers would have put it. She had much bigger things to attend to. Really, Olga had done her a favour.

She picked up the letter again, this time noticing the letterhead. The word "Eranos" was printed at the top of the page in an elegant font.

Eranos?

Was that Olga's own letterhead? Is that what she had chosen to call her property?

Alice wondered what the word meant.

# Manhattan

Alice stood in the storeroom doorway listening to the rhythmic clack of Victor's typewriter behind her. The room was brightly lit and exuded a pleasing atmosphere of order and enterprise. Beneath the window was a small desk where the office staff deposited thermos flasks, beakers and teacups, and beside the door, a stationery cupboard. Tall, grey filing cabinets stood side by side along one wall facing a line of bookcases with deep shelves. The shelves were crammed with back issues of *The Beacon* and copies of each of her titles, along with a small reference library. Several piles of her latest book, *From Intellect to Intuition,* were stacked on a mid-level shelf over by the table. Alice took a copy and returned to her desk.

Stroking the glossy cover of the deepest blue, she wouldn't permit herself feelings of pride or even satisfaction, no matter how private. The title was but one and so very much more was needed.

They had been back in New York two months, leaving the girls behind again at Ospringe in the care of Betty Harris. This time, Alice felt less anxious, Mildred having enrolled in a short secretarial course and Ellison was volunteering with the Women's Institute, thanks to the encouragement of Countess Sondes of Lee Court, who was the president. Betty was proving a blessing. Alice found her a capable and trustworthy sort who wasn't overbearing and neither was she soft. With her girls in appropriate hands, she was able to concentrate on the work to hand.

It was with a measure of reluctance that Alice reached for her pen. A loyal student in California had requested a signed copy. She wasn't one for book signing, but the volume was one of her own and she thought she would make an exception.

Once the ink was dry she closed the cover on her signature and went and gave the book to Victor to post. Returning to her desk she paused to look out the window at the street below and said, 'I wonder what the library has made of my book.' It was an absent remark and she hadn't expected Regina to respond with, 'Oh dear.'

'Is something the matter?' Alice said, glancing over at the volunteers hard at work typing up the Tibetan's latest outpourings.

'I forgot all about it, Alice,' she said, her fingers hovering over the keyboard. 'What with one thing and another.'

'I shouldn't fret. I'll take it down myself.'

'You don't need to do that.'

'But I want to.'

It was true. She hadn't visited the library in a long time and on such a warm and sunny day she thought it would make for a pleasant outing. It was summer, the weather fine, she was reasonably mobile and it was only across the road. What could go wrong?

'I'll accompany you,' Regina said with concern.

'No need.'

Although the progression of her illness was causing her some spasticity and she thought she probably could do with an arm to cross the road, but she disliked giving into the limitations of her body and she had been feeling much better since her last blood transfusion.

She returned to the storeroom for another copy of her book and left the office before Foster, hard at work on the accounts, looked up from his desk and saw through his glass panelled door to find her gone. She was down the elevator and standing on the sidewalk before she had second thoughts.

The traffic and the bustle made her uncertain. She crossed the sidewalk and hovered near the kerb, looking back and forth up West 42$^{nd}$ Street. She must have appeared as anxious as she felt because a young man stopped beside her and asked if she would like his assistance. She accepted without hesitation, taking in the smart suit and hat.

He walked her all the way round to the library entrance on Fifth Avenue, guiding her up the flights of stone steps, not leaving her until she was standing in one of the formidable stone arches. Only then did he bid her a good day. It was another in a very long line of unanticipated acts of human kindness she had received over the years and she was touched. She thanked the man and went inside.

The foyer would make a fitting welcome for a monarch, classically proportioned rounded arches meeting the curve of the vaulted ceiling. She paused for a moment, enjoying the sense of space and civic pride. Ignoring the stairs rising up behind the arches to her left and right, she went through to where she presumed to find some staff.

In the next room, she spotted a man behind a high wooden counter and made her approach. He had the demeanour of someone in charge—elderly with large glasses and a moustache.

'May I help you?'

'May I furnish you with this?' she said, setting down the book on the counter and pushing it towards him without taking her eyes off his face.

'And you are?'

'The author.'

She gave him her warmest smile. He eyed her with suspicion before picking up the book and reading the back cover and the front-end pages. It was a cheeky move, she knew, defiant almost, but it was hard to be taken seriously as a non-academic published by an obscure house, no matter the endorsement she received from high places. It occurred to her that her sister, Lydia, would never have had this trouble.

'I've not come across this publisher,' he said, reinforcing her thoughts. 'The Lucis Trust.'

She was ready with her response. 'We are an educational organisation with offices right across the street in Salmon Tower,' she said. 'In point of fact, my office looks down on the public library. We're dedicated to expanding the mind as, evidently, are you,' she said, maintaining her smile. She could feel the blood pumping through her veins.

'Indeed,' he said, taken aback.

'I shall leave it with you to catalogue, then,' she said, taking her leave before he attempted to hand back the book. 'You should read it. You may find it enlightening.'

On her way outside she had to suppress a girlish giggle. She had no idea if her book would find its way onto the library bookshelves. Once she was out in the street she didn't give it a second thought. Ahead of her was the walk back to Salmon Tower, which had taken on the proportions of a hike across the moors. By the time she reached the corner of Fifth Avenue and West 42$^{nd}$ she was a touch breathless. Thankfully she was standing among others waiting to cross.

A halt in the traffic and they all stepped out onto the road at once. Alice straggled but the traffic waited until she had made it to the other side.

Back in the office, she vowed never to venture off like that again, as much as she would like to. She felt as though she were occupying the body of an eighty-year-old.

She was seated at her desk attending to the correspondence of the day when Foster, ever the workhorse, appeared, bleary eyed from squinting at figures, announcing he needed to get some air around his head and asking what people would like for lunch.

'Sandwiches all right?'

There was a murmur of agreement.

While he was out, the main office door swung open and there stood Ernest Suffern. He must have passed by Foster in the elevator. A large man, he always filled a room with his presence and on this occasion, he was all the more imposing in his dark suit that strained around his midriff. It was clear from his hurried entry and his manner that it wasn't a social call. He managed to greet Regina and Victor and the two volunteers with a measure of cordiality before turning on Alice, the object of his wrath.

She had been anticipating some sort of reaction, but she was alarmed to find he had decided to address the matter in person. He marched over to her desk. He was clutching the last letter the Tibetan had written to him.

'This is an outrage, Mrs Bailey. You have made an error taking down the Tibetan's words.'

'Mr Suffern, I have done no such thing,' she said quietly, struggling to remain calm in the face of his fury and the audience of four.

'You must have. The Tibetan would never say these things. You've no right to judge my efforts.'

'Mr Suffern.'

'I thought you'd be pleased I've been finding suitable candidates for the World Servers project. I've brought many to your door. You should be grateful to have my dedication. Instead, this,' he said, waving the letter in her face.

Regina gasped. Victor stood. Alice shot him a quick glance.

'Mr Suffern,' she said, 'Please sit down.'

'I will remain as I am.'

'Very well. Your candidates were all unsuitable. Every single one of them.'

'You are mistaken.'

'I am afraid that I am not. Besides which, you know as well as I that the Tibetan makes the selection. No one else has a say.'

'You are not the only one close to the Tibetan, Mrs Bailey, despite what you may think.'

At that point Regina stood up as well. 'Mr Suffern! You are behaving outrageously.'

Ernest swung around. 'I'm sorry, Mrs Keller. This needed to be said. I shall take my leave.'

'There are better ways to go about these things,' Alice murmured.

He glared at her before leaving the office in a single sweep, taking his ire with him.

Regina and Victor both looked at her at once.

'I'm all right. Let's just forget about it.'

She was inwardly shaken by his anger and had to remind herself that Ernest had always been hot-headed.

Back when they had moved from California to New York and Foster had taken up Ernest's job offer of secretary of the Theosophical Society of New York, the two men had cooked up a campaign they had called the Committee of 1400. Both were unable to let go of the discord in the administration of the Theosophical Society, which continued to be run like a theocracy with Annie Besant as monarch on her throne in India. Their primary aim was to oust the president, that union heavyweight Louis Rogers, and instil democracy in the organisation, in part by getting themselves elected instead.

They had failed, spectacularly.

All the while, Alice had stayed at home in Ridgefield Park in the house Ernest had provided, caring for her girls. Dorothy was by then eleven and Ellison just seven. Alice had been writing *A Treatise of Cosmic Fire*, a work of abstract cosmology so abstruse she scarcely comprehended any of the many hundreds of pages she took down. The work was otherworldly; she didn't have the time, focus or patience for Foster and Ernest's campaign. Even then, she had found Ernest a railroader when it came to business.

Meanwhile, she had taken matters in hand and begun a Secret Doctrine class in a room she had rented on Madison Avenue. It was well supported. Attendees included Theosophists and other occultists. She would never forget the day Mr Richard Prater, a former pupil of Helena Blavatsky, came one week and handed over his whole class the next. Word went around and soon she was mailing out the lesson plans to seekers all over the country. That same year, Foster and she, along with five close associates, formed a small meditation group and together, the seven envisioned a way forward. By then *Initiation, Human and Solar, Letters on Occult Meditation* and *The Consciousness of the Atom* were all in print. Correspondence from readers of her books and students of her Secret Doctrine class became so overwhelming, in 1923 she founded the Arcane School and directed seekers to it. Tens of thousands of students would go on to join the school. Out of those humble beginnings, the entire organisational edifice grew, and she had been grateful all along to Ernest for his commitment and generosity. Yet in Ernest, Alice was reminded a little of Olga, seeing the similarities of disposition.

Oblivious to the goings on, Foster breezed in with their lunch and the day's newspaper, and she was relieved he hadn't witnessed Ernest's outburst, for he would have been unable to restrain himself and the entire situation might have taken an ugly turn. Victor and Regina took their cue from Alice, who indicated with a slight turn of her head that it was best left unsaid.

Regina went to the storeroom to pour tea, and they drew their chairs round in a circle beside her desk, which she always kept tidy and clear.

'I forgot to mention,' Foster said, addressing Alice. 'I've found another disciple for the seed groups. She's from Australia.'

'Australia?'

'A loyal student of good repute who has been a Spiritualist and Theosophist for many years.'

'My grandfather's cousin went to Australia,' Alice said, oddly wistful. 'Charles La Trobe.'

'What for?'

'To govern one of their states, I believe. There was another one too. Edward.'

Not wanting to dwell further, she bit into her sandwich. The others made small talk, Foster reading the headlines. Together they reflected on the news of the Soviet purges and the failure of the World Economic conference, convened in London to try to reach a solution to the Great Depression. Meanwhile, the National Socialists had just outlawed the political party that had helped Hitler and his men gain power. It was another worrying sign.

'At least here we have Roosevelt,' she said.

'He can't help Europe,' Foster said, setting the paper down on Regina's desk beside his sandwich. He had become so grim it was as though the economic depression had entered his soul and turned it a dour shade of grey.

Regina changed the subject and they all talked of their children and grandchildren and the weather. Losing interest, Alice took the newspaper and browsed the pages. Her attention was drawn to a photograph of Rose Pastor Stokes, the headline announcing that she had died. Hiding her reaction, Alice scanned the article. She had known Rose was unwell but the news of her death came as a shock. True, she found the activist's campaigning distasteful, but Rose was the same age as she and fifty-three was too young to lose a life to cancer. Alice felt sure that Rose would have liked to achieve many things before her passing. She re-read the article then, without a word, she folded the newspaper and set it down. Lunch was soon over and they each returned to their duties.

From the purview of her desk she watched the others, all studious and silent. She had so much work ahead of her. There was the treatise on the Seven Rays, the New Group of World Servers with all that that entailed. Then there were the Arcane School lessons, the personal guidance she offered, and the lectures. On top of that, despite concerns they might be spreading themselves too thinly, only last month they had begun to discuss a project to transform Freemasonry. Foster had been a Freemason all his adulthood and was passionately supportive of the need for change. Perhaps it would give him a much-needed distraction, even lighten his mood if that was not too much to hope for.

Widely criticised for its pledges of secrecy and obedience, Freemasonry had for too long been viewed a sort of exclusive 'old-boys' network, giving advantage to members in the realms of business and politics. To counter these traits, Foster and she, along with some of their Masonic associates, were talking of establishing the Ancient Universal Mysteries. They planned to initiate a re-working of the entire Masonic edifice in line with the Tibetan's teachings, to revitalise the movement and bring Freemasonry in line with the New Age. Gone the closed-door policy. Gone the exclusivity. Men, and notably women of all backgrounds and creeds would be welcome. Even Rose Stokes would have approved of that. The definition of Freemasonry would be re-worked to include the Tibetan's version of esotericism, including the solar Logos, the Seven Rays and various cosmic laws, along with the Plan for universal brotherhood. They would change the Masonic rituals in accordance with her new esoteric overlay. Freemasons would be charged with serving others in the spirit of love and goodwill. It was a fine vision and she was keen to make a start, but they were holding back until the Lucis Trust was better established in England.

How she would manage yet another ambitious project heaven only knew, but she would persist, until the day she was taken from this earth.

It took several months before the Tibetan responded to Ernest's outburst. She was at her desk in the early hours when the message came through. The Tibetan chose to take a critical stance, remonstrating Ernest, noting that the financier was more than happy to bow to authority when what was written conformed to his own ideas, but when it did not, he reacted negatively. He went on to state that Ernest's behaviour had been divisive in the group, setting back the work of dispelling world glamour by six months. He was too much the devotee wanting to be close to his master, and had fallen foul of his own spiritual ambitions.

Even as she wrote, Alice knew Ernest would react badly. Indeed, with such strong language, it was impossible to imagine otherwise. She fully expected him to quit the group.

Yet she would be the first to acknowledge that the spiritual path was tough. There really was no place for petty mindedness or immaturity. Not when the evolution of consciousness of the whole of humanity was at stake. Why ever didn't more people see it? Humanity was forever impeded by the dictates of the individual personality. The core problem was that the more advanced the individual, the stronger the personality becomes, until, at last, they reach a threshold of awareness, a threshold that leads into the realm of the soul. It is there, at that pinnacle of human progress, that a transition into soul consciousness is required. She knew that. All the world's faiths taught it. Yet time and again, even the most dedicated student failed to walk through that door, preferring to bask in their own personal achievements.

Students were held back by their pride or their ambition over and again. They stood in the doorway of consciousness like dark beasts. She reflected on her own struggle with the same, and how hard she had been beaten down before she could rise up purged sufficiently to fulfil her spiritual obligations. Like the rest of humanity, the Ernests and the Olgas of the world had their frailties, and would struggle inside their skins because of them. Yet when they chose to remain blind to themselves, it was troubling. What mattered was the satisfaction of a life well-lived, that sense of having done one's best with what one had been allotted in the service of the whole. Could the Ernests and the Olgas experience that? Or were their personalities so strong they dwelled in perpetual dissatisfaction.

She set down her pen and left the letter open with its envelope, unaddressed, beside it, in favour of her armchair by the fire. She seemed to spend more and more of her time seated in armchairs by open fires. She thought with an inward laugh that she might as well start her own fireside chats. Then again, perhaps not, at least not broadcast on the radio.

She dwelt briefly on her daughters and wondered how each was faring and thought she would write a letter later. First, she anticipated a telephone call from her dear friend, Alice Ortiz, who hadn't been feeling well and had mentioned in a short letter that she wanted to atone for missing Mildred's twenty-first birthday in early August. Alice had missed it too. It wasn't possible to divide her time between New York and Europe and not miss one or other of her daughters' birthdays. She felt a pang of guilt nevertheless.

She looked forward to Alice's visit next weekend—she hoped her friend would be well enough—and they were invited to stay in Delaware for Thanksgiving. They would be visiting Foster's family in Fitchburg in a week or two as well. In all, life could not have been better.

She looked ahead, always ahead, and especially to publishing her book, *From Bethlehem to Calvary,* now the final chapters were being typed and Regina was already editing the first. She pictured her there with Victor at work as ever in the office at the top of Salmon Tower and a wave of immense gratitude washed through her.

# PART THREE

# Akaroa

Heather surveyed the array of paperwork on her desk and again read through the provenance note attached to Professor Foyle's collection file. Then she had a quick rifle through the notebooks on her desk that she had extracted from one of the boxes, along with the draft manuscript that was central to the collection.

It was clear from the outset that Professor Foyle had been working on establishing Alice Bailey as the mother of the New Age. From a draft table of contents Heather could see it was an ambitious project. Fifteen chapters divided into three sections, the first situating Alice Bailey in time and place, the second devoted to her key New Age contributions including who out of the cohort of New Age thinkers and writers relied on her work, the third devoted to controversies and a discussion. There was also an introduction offering definitions of key terms, not least the New Age itself.

How could an entire spiritual movement as eclectic as the New Age be attributed to one woman? Foyle was quick to make it clear that Alice Bailey had harnessed the term "New Age" that was bandied about at the time of her writing, in spiritual circles. Professor Foyle had composed a short introductory paragraph that read:

Alternative, and perhaps utopian, visions of a global, spiritual awakening are advanced by her followers in the hope of fostering a paradigm shift. Bailey's teachings undergird the vision, the aspiration and the hope for a better world. Her legacy is immense yet ever since she first put pen to paper her work has been beset by controversy. Is she worthy of the title "Mother of the New Age"? Or are her detractors right to condemn her?

Among the Bailey books, Heather's gaze settled on two volumes titled *Discipleship in the New Age (Volumes I and II)*, published in conjunction with a third, *Glamour: A World Problem*. Professor Foyle had paid considerable attention to those three books; they looked worn, the spines bent and scuffed. Curious, Heather went and pulled the volumes from the shelf and returned to her desk. She cast an eye over the tables of contents and puzzled over the language.

'I could really do with your help,' she whispered, wishing Hilary could have held on a little longer.

Silence.

She shouldn't think like that. She had to inhale deeply to quell the tide that threatened to rush in.

In the absence of her aunt, she applied herself to the basic details, recalling the piece of notepaper she had found in the first volume, folded in half and serving as a bookmark. The notepaper contained a list of forty-one sets of initials and associated page numbers. She hadn't known what to do with the list so she had put it in her concertina file, labelled "to be decided". She grabbed the file and pulled out the note, along with its record describing where she had found it.

The title read "The New Group of World Servers". Beneath was a short description. The listed initials were the participants in a special project in developing group consciousness. Instructions to that group, collectively and individually, amounted to 1,800 pages of text. Here Professor Foyle had written a string of exclamation marks. The experiment had endured for eighteen years, commencing in November 1931, if the date was reliable. Alice Bailey wrote the last communications to the remaining members in these groups of disciples in the weeks before her death in December 1949.

Heather sat back, thinking it through. What was group consciousness exactly? A group of people all thinking the same? Or awareness of the group, instead of the individual? Both? Some sort of transcendent experience, perhaps. It must be quite something to take up all those pages of text. What was a World Server? Did it literally mean someone who served the world? How? The names of the participants had not been given. Who were those people and why were they prepared to commit to such a long-term project, one with indeterminate outcomes? For if that project, as grand as it was in scope, had been a success, then surely the world would have heard of it? There were religious overtones too, in the very notion of service. Whatever it was, Alice Bailey had given the project her all.

She flicked through the texts, understanding little. She felt as though she was standing on a pavement, staring through a wrought iron fence at an obscure building set in overgrown grounds. Out in the street she couldn't know what was going on inside the walls. She had to get close, walk up to the front door. To do that, she needed a point of entry, a gate.

'You should still be alive,' she said, filled with questions for her aunt.

Someone with a trolley was approaching down the corridor. She held her breath, hoping whoever it was went on by. Yesterday, she was allocated two hours on the information desk to fill in for Emily Prime, and she had spent the entire time itching to return to the Foyle collection. She was so distracted, when a visitor inquired about opening times, she almost snapped a reply as she shoved the leaflet across the counter.

She worked undisturbed. Shortly before lunchtime, she reached into the bottom of the box to extract the last volume. Her eyes went straight to the author. It was composed by Sir John Sinclair and carried the title, *The Alice Bailey Inheritance.*

She sensed the book shouldn't have been buried in the box with all those Theosophical texts and she took offence that someone had dumped it there and piled the others on top. It was a careless act. That book belonged with Alice Bailey's works.

She skimmed the contents. It was a biography. Curious about the author, she searched his name online and discovered he was Sir John Rollo Sinclair, 9th Baronet of Dunbeath. Alice Bailey certainly had friends in high places.

The volume had a black cover framed with a green patterned border. The title was arranged in yellow, and carried a subtitle stating, "The inner plane teachings of Alice Ann Bailey (1880-1949) and their legacy". The cover also featured a headshot of Alice Bailey, taken later in her life.

Heather visited a few key websites and found that the book was out of print and rare. It would form a valuable part of the collection.

She created a new record and scanned through the chapters, Heather could see straight away that much of the content was a rehash of Alice Bailey's autobiography, interlaced with Sinclair's own interpretations of her life in the light of her teachings. Heather was left wondering how far he had ventured beyond what had already been written. It was less a biography and more an homage. Following the trail of sticky notes, she found Foyle's interest lay in the author's references to the New Age, and the emphasis he placed on Alice Bailey's legacy. In the last chapters, the sticky notes were placed where Sinclair mentioned places and names, names Heather thought she might have seen in Professor Foyle's notebook.

She added the names to her list, taking note of one of the places, Broadwater Down, Tunbridge Wells. The names included Ian-Gordon Brown and Barbara Somers. Reading another sticky note, she discovered they were associated with Roberto Assagioli and his formation of transpersonal psychology. Another figure, Vera Stanley Alder was an early and prolific New Age author and personal friend of Alice Bailey. Lily Cornford and Florence Garrigue worked in Alice Bailey's offices along with Regina Keller and Frank Hilton. All of them had furthered Alice Bailey's teachings in some fashion. Not much was noted about these people by either Sinclair or Foyle and a quick internet search yielded little, other than that Garrigue had founded Meditation Mount, a spiritual centre located in Ojai, California.

She checked the time. Her heartbeat quickened. Keeping an eye on the door, she put the record and the book in her top drawer. She was worse than that new girl, Rosie. Holding onto Alice Bailey's books and then ferreting away this other volume—what was she thinking? She could lose her job.

She reached for Professor Foyle's notebook to double check the list of names, when the door swung open and Suzanne marched in.

'Come on, you. I've booked a table at The Moat.'

Heather was surprised. They usually bought sandwiches and ate them in the park, or grabbed something from Queen Vic square.

'What are we celebrating?'

'Nothing.'

Succumbing to a mix of guilt and apprehension over leaving her book stash, she followed Suzanne down to The Moat, an eatery in the basement of the State Library.

Intimate in feel, the café had a pleasing vibrancy, with painted brick walls, plush red carpet and dim lighting, the back wall papered in brightly coloured stripes. Jazz played softly through a hidden sound system. There were piles of books on shelves over by the wine racks. Altogether the café had a European vibe, timeless, and for a moment Heather imagined similar cafés dotted about in basements in the 1930s in New York, Paris, Berlin, a singer in the corner, crooning through a smoke haze. She couldn't imagine Alice Bailey in such a place. Her daughters, certainly.

The restaurant was busy, most of the tables occupied. Suzanne selected a table by the bar and a waitress approached them with menus. Whenever they lunched there, they had a bagel, but Suzanne felt like the chicken and feta meatballs, which came with a tasty slaw. Not wanting to appear meagre, Heather followed suit.

'And two glasses of Chablis,' Suzanne said to the waitress, who had come out from behind the counter to take their order.

'We only serve that by the bottle.'

'Then a bottle it is.'

'Suzanne,' Heather cautioned.

'That's what this is for,' Suzanne whispered, patting her shoulder bag. 'Besides, you need cheering up.'

'I'm okay.'

'Nonsense.' Suzanne waited for a party of four to walk past before going on, lowering her voice. 'Grieving is a process. People go through stages, as you know. Five, or seven, depending on who you believe. Shock and denial, pain and guilt, anger and bargaining, depression and reflection, and acceptance.'

'That's nine.'

'If you break it down. I think you are still in the pain phase. Although you seem to want to retreat back into shock and denial, if you don't mind me saying. Whereas your mother has breezed right on through to anger.'

She was referring to the inheritance. Heather watched her reach into her bag, imagining her extracting a leaflet.

'Hold on. What do you mean, retreat back?'

'You are using that collection like an anaesthetic,' she said, putting her phone on the table beside her. 'You never come out of your office, other than to do your stint on the information desk.'

She knew Suzanne was right but she didn't want to hear it. A waiter came with the wine, distracting them both, and as she took a sip of the cool, crisp liquid, she felt herself letting go a little. Suzanne ruined the moment, pulling her back into the melee of her family life with, 'What's the latest on the will?'

'She wanted the furniture, that's all.'

Heather went on to explain the family heirlooms coveted by her mother.

'How could she be so fixated?' Heather said, cognizant of the brooch on her lapel.

'She feels entitled. We had the same in my family. My grandmother, Emily, left her entire estate to her cat. Just imagine! My mother was incensed. There were no named beneficiaries, and since a pet cannot be a beneficiary, the death was declared intestate and things were divided up amongst the family. I'll never forget how hurt my mother was. She took it as a personal slap in the face. There was the matter of a ring that had been passed down to the eldest daughter for generations, but after the furore over the will, tempers were high and the ring ended up going to her younger sister.'

'It's all so materialistic.'

'Is it? I think it's about memories and personal histories, heritage and deep attachments.'

'She'll be satisfied then, that I gave her the furniture.'

'Good for you. Ever the peacemaker.'

Heather grimaced in reply.

'Be thankful she doesn't want the house.'

'It doesn't compare to what she already has in Harcourt Street. She always saw my aunt as the poor relation.'

'All the better for you.' Her gaze slid from Heather's face to her chest. 'Is that brooch new?'

'It belonged to my great-grandmother.'

'Worth anything?'

'Not according to my mother.'

'Even so, you should get it valued.'

She would do no such thing. Value wasn't always defined in dollar terms.

Two plates of meatballs and slaw drew a line under the conversation. They each attended to their food. About halfway in, Suzanne broke the silence with, 'Any thoughts on Akaroa?'

Heather took a long sip of her wine. She'd forgotten Suzanne had mentioned Akaroa as an alternative to Daylesford.

'I haven't had a chance to look into it.'

'Offer ends tomorrow.' There was a hint of reproach in her voice.

'I'll get to it this afternoon.'

Back in her office she did as promised and jumped online to take a quick look at Akaroa. The area looked charming, so green, with sheltered inlets and rolling hills. The package deal Suzanne had linked her to seemed good too, and not expensive. She lingered, captivated by the images, then she went on to check the climate and shuddered, quickly writing her friend a reply saying the only month she would consider going there was January, hopefully during a heat wave.

Mellow after the food and the wine, she spent much of the afternoon attending to the research inquiries in her inbox. She managed to ignore the book in her drawer.

The following day she was rostered on the information desk, along with Suzanne and the new girl, Rosie, who, despite Suzanne's best efforts, had held onto her job. She wasn't as vague as Suzanne had portrayed her, although easily distracted and her makeup didn't suit the austere setting of the library. Still, she was popular among the young and any inquirer under thirty sought her assistance over her older colleagues.

The main desk was high, with two computer terminals at each end, accompanied by a lower desk set at an angle, for those inquirers who wished to sit. Suzanne claimed the chair behind the lower desk as she always did, leaving Heather to stand with Rosie, and assist her with navigating the search engines when the need arose.

The room was situated beneath the La Trobe reading room—the library's showpiece, a magnificent light-filled atrium. The room beneath had the same octagonal shape and comprised a swathe of desks and comfortable chairs that soon filled with students and readers. Directing tourists and readers to the upper levels formed a large part of operations. Heather always hoped for a serious inquirer, presenting something substantial to while away the time.

Rosie's ineptitude proved to be the biggest consumer of time, as she muddled her way through search engines, leaving Heather puzzled as to how a woman of her generation could be so technologically useless. By the end of the day she considered having a word with Shona about the girl's productivity, but thought better of it.

A staff meeting on Thursday, in which she was saddled with an appointment that same afternoon to assess a manuscript and associated papers donated by a Miss Salford, an ageing widow who claimed a prestigious provenance no one believed, meant it wasn't until Friday that Heather had a chance to return to Foyle's world.

Delving into what had become her treasure trove, she found a box of books on the New Age, and another on Western Esotericism. The titles of the second box enticed her more: *Access to Western Esotericism*, *Western Esotericism: A Guide for the Perplexed*, and *The Hermetic Tradition*. The names of the scholars were just as enticing. Two stood out: Antoine Faivre and Wouter Hanegraaff.

*Theosophy, Imagination, Tradition: Studies in Western Esotericism* by Antoine Faivre piqued her interest and she scanned the end pages. She discovered that Faivre was Professor Emeritus of Religious Studies at the École Pratique des Hautes Études and Chair of the History of Esoteric Currents in Modern and Contemporary Europe at the Sorbonne. Impressive. The eminent scholar had defined the field of Western Esotericism as an academic discipline within the field of religious studies. Yet when she went to the index of his book, she found that he hadn't acknowledged Alice Bailey. Perhaps the occultist was beyond the scope of the work. She read on and noted that breakaway Theosophist Rudolph Steiner was mentioned and discussed several times. She couldn't help wondering if Alice had been snubbed.

Wouter Hanegraaff was Professor of History of Hermetic Philosophy and Faivre's associate. He was also the co-editor of the prestigious esoteric journal *ARIES*. Heather scanned through the index of his book and found that he had similarly passed over Alice Bailey. Puzzled, she scanned the indexes of all the other volumes in the box. Alice Bailey and her work were scarcely granted more than a passing mention. In the introduction to her manuscript, Foyle expressed her bafflement as to why Alice Bailey did not feature in any significant way in any of the primary scholarly texts within the field of Western Esotericism. Throughout the texts, there were a number of annotated sticky notes indicating her fury over the omissions. It didn't make sense to Heather either. Not when Rudolph Steiner's name seemed to pop up everywhere and, like Bailey, he was a second-generation Theosophist who had broken away to form his own organisations. It was as though her work had been dismissed as derivative and inconsequential.

Samantha Foyle, you didn't share their view. And neither, Hilary, would you.

She caught her breath. She was communicating with the dead. She removed her glasses and wiped away a single tear.

She returned the volumes to the box, deciding to make records for them at a later time. She was more than a little curious as she reached inside the box filled with books on the New Age. The small paperback on the top of the pile carried the title *The Aquarian Conspiracy* by Marilyn Ferguson. In a note tucked inside, Professor Foyle had written:

"The New Age began as a utopian counter culture, which rejected mainstream beliefs and values and searched for alternatives. Writing in 1980 from a perspective infused with Bailey's ideas and language, New Age advocate Marilyn Ferguson views the New Age as a benign conspiracy of love and light, an intimate joining and breathing together."

A sticky note stuck to the page said in capital letters, "This title could not be more unfortunate!"

Why? It sounded punchy enough. Heather jotted down the detail in her notebook.

She set the book aside and extracted the volumes, one at a time, examining the back covers and end pages, making records as she went. Three stood out from the rest due to a preponderance of sticky notes indicating the extent to which they drew on Alice Bailey's work. She looked up at the row of blue books, still on the shelf by the door.

At last, some acknowledgement.

Following the trail of Foyle's sticky notes, it appeared that among New Age seekers, Alice Bailey was much admired. One scholar, Steven Sutcliffe, regarded her as the movement's chief theorist. No small claim. His book focused on the alternative community of Findhorn, in Scotland's northeast. Heather searched for their website.

Findhorn—now an NGO at the United Nations—had its genesis in 1962 when cofounders, spiritual seekers and mystics Peter Caddy and his wife Eileen Caddy, along with Dorothy Maclean, moved to a caravan park near Inverness.

The Caddys were typical New Age seekers. Back in London in the 1950s, they had come under the tutelage of charismatic spiritual teacher Sheena Govan. When Govan returned to Scotland, the Caddys followed. They were joined by their friend, Dorothy Maclean, soon after. In 1957 the Caddys took over the management of Cluny Hill Hotel in Forres, a small town east of Inverness. Infused with ideas drawn from Bailey's teachings, they formed a small group that centred around Eileen Caddy's received guidance. Through it, the group believed they were in communication with extra-terrestrials. Bizarre. As a result of their wacky interests, the Caddys were dismissed from the hotel and ended up in a nearby caravan park. Heather was not surprised.

Both Eileen and Dorothy claimed to receive messages from higher sources, and Peter was a longstanding Theosophist. At the Park, they were instructed to plant a garden and so they did. In her meditations, Maclean soon began to hear from nature spirits, or devas, which she ascribed to the plants themselves. The messages were gardening instructions. Whether the garden burgeoned as a result of these messages, or solely as a consequence of Peter's green thumbs, it was impossible to know. Although for Heather, the very prospect of the former was ludicrous and its believers plainly off the planet.

At Findhorn, a myth of manifestation grew along with the vegetables. Events that might appear to others as coincidences, or serendipity, or plain good luck, were construed as evidence of the workings of inner laws. As the garden grew so did the group that surrounded the Caddys. More and more came and many stayed. A community formed.

A community of fruit loops, by the sound of things. Or were they?

Findhorn describes itself as "an experiment in conscious living, a learning centre and an ecovillage". There's accommodation for three hundred residents. The campus at Cluny Hill contains thirty-five resident staff. The foundation has a retreat house on the Isle of Iona and another on Erraid on Scotland's west coast. Over thirty organisations form part of the overarching Findhorn Foundation. Findhorn hosts a range of workshops, residential courses and conferences throughout the year, including massage, ecology and sustainability.

Findhorn might have been founded on what Heather could only regard spiritual insanities, but it was clearly a going concern attracting many thousands.

The Bailey connection became apparent when Heather returned to Sutcliffe, who was at pains to stress that Bailey's influence at Findhorn was far reaching. The foundation held her works in the highest esteem. Possession of at least one Bailey book was de rigueur at Findhorn in the 1970s. All those in high positions at the foundation were expected to have a solid working knowledge of the Bailey texts. After the attacks on the World Trade Centre on September 11, 2001, her prayer, known as the Great Invocation, was used at Findhorn in their memorial service.

Heather sat back in her seat and removed her glasses. It was lunchtime, the day outside was sunny and she had a sudden impulse to take a stroll in Carlton Gardens to clear her head. She shut and locked her office and headed downstairs in the lift, taking the side exit out of the library building into La Trobe Street. From there it was a short walk to the gardens. She strolled up the main avenue to the Royal Exhibition Building and paused at the fountain with its three tiers of splashing water, soothed by the sound. Her mind was cluttered and she felt slightly burnt out by information overload. Yet she couldn't stop. She felt enmeshed in the story of Alice Bailey's legacy that on many levels repelled her, yet this had been one of Hilary's primary interests and she felt bound to pursue the story to its end, for it brought her that much closer to her aunt.

Foyle was clearly single-minded in her quest to prove Alice Bailey had significantly influenced if not founded the New Age movement, and it certainly seemed like there was plenty of evidence to support her thesis. Yet what would it achieve, except to show that this curious and intensely private woman had spawned a cavalcade of spiritual quackery? It seemed to Heather an almost embarrassing achievement, one she would have preferred kept quiet.

Back in her office, she pressed on until she came to the last book in the box. It was by an astrologer, Alan Oken, who drew heavily on Bailey's delineation of the Seven Rays to inform his *Soul Centred Astrology*. In his preface, he acknowledged the assistance and support of a raft of fellow co-workers, including those at Meditation Mount, along with Alice Bailey's biographer, Sir John Rollo Sinclair, Frances Adams Moore, and Michael Robbins of the Seven Ray Institute. The world of Alice Bailey tightened a notch in the reading as it occurred to her those people were not a collection of disparate individuals but a coterie of some kind.

She wrote the new names on her list and researched them in turn. She couldn't find anything on Moore so she turned her attention to Robbins.

By searching both his name and the Seven Ray Institute, she found herself on a website called the "Morya Federation". The home page was all deep blues and cosmic images. A drop-down tab listed the organisation's international sisters. One in New Zealand caught her eye. She clicked on the link and found herself on a website called the Southern Lights Centre. As she read on, clicking through the menu, a tingling sensation spread through her.

Suzanne could have had no idea of any of this when she came up with her latest holiday suggestion. But there was Heather, back in Akaroa.

# Unfinished Business

The trouble with having a million dollars to spend on a house in Ballarat was it cast a wide net and almost all the higher value houses online were too large and too new. Heather scrolled down. She had seen most of the listings before. She wanted one of those nice old houses near the town centre, walking distance from the train station and in a quiet leafy street of established properties. She knew they existed. Last Saturday, taking advantage of the early summer weather, she had taken the train and strolled down the streets to either side of the shopping centre. Nothing was for sale. All she could do was hope someone had an impetus to sell and one of the properties came on the market.

Her aunt's estate had settled in the last days of November. The real estate agent who had done the original evaluation had lined up a number of buyers who had expressed an early interest, and when the house was listed, it sold in five days.

It had been a day of mixed emotions. There was the elation and relief of the sale itself, the feeling that at last all the formalities would soon be over, and signing the acceptance of the highest and best offer had felt like a sort of release. Yet the moment the agent had left her parents' house, Heather had bolted upstairs to her room, her heart bursting with fresh grief.

The following day she had walked to Hilary's, wandering through the rooms as though saying a final goodbye to all her memories, even though she knew she would hold onto that key for another three months; the buyers wanted a long settlement to arrange their affairs. Heather's bank account wouldn't receive the proceeds of sale until early in March. Which left all summer to explore possibilities, all the while resisting the subliminal pressure Joan exerted, with her anxious and disapproving looks whenever Ballarat was mentioned.

Voices in the corridor outside her office grew louder then faded as those conversing passed by her door. She closed the real estate tabs and checked her emails. There was an email from Shona, responding to her submission to the library's journal. A small thrill pulsed through her as she clicked on the message.

Two concise sentences later and Heather succumbed to a bolt of disappointment nailing her to the dungeons of obscurity. Her paper on the Theosophical Society was not quite what the library was looking for, Shona said. She felt demolished. All hope of a bright new future screwed up like scrap paper and tossed in the wastepaper bin.

She stared at the screen, a thousand retorts racing through her mind. Instead, she deleted the email and scanned the others. There was one from Suzanne, this time with links to special offers on a week in Port Douglas. She deleted that as well.

Misery consumed her. It was the fifteenth of December and with ten days to Christmas she wasn't looking forward to celebrating the day without Hilary. She wished she could work right through, skate round the festivities alone in her office with a turkey burger and a mini pudding. Instead, she was to have a week off; the manuscript office was closing for the period.

She felt pent up. Her mind didn't need clearing of Hilary as Suzanne suspected. It was cluttered with Samantha Foyle and Alice Bailey and the one person who could have helped her organise all that thought and knowledge into some sort of coherent order was no longer with her. There was that clenching feeling that had become a reflex, although it wasn't as strong or enduring as before and she managed to push away the tears. She knew Hilary would have wanted her to keep searching and sifting until she had arrived at a satisfactory truth. Yet again she sensed her presence, imagined her voice, and was comforted by it.

Hilary would have understood. It had become almost a mantra. *Hilary would have understood and so must I. I owe it to all the women concerned, including you, dear aunt and even my great-grandmother, Katharine.*

A hand reached for the brooch pinned to the lapel of her blouse as though to confirm her thoughts, and she traced a finger over its surface, the embossed ivory of the birds, the black enamel, cool and smooth. She thought of the twin birds as representations of Katharine and Hilary, absurd as that was to her rational brain.

What began as a distraction had become a compulsion and despite Shona's dashing of her aspirations, she couldn't let it go. There were too many unanswered questions and a nagging sense that history, or at least a bunch of academics, had treated the esotericist unfairly.

She reflected back over what she knew. Alice Bailey was an aristocrat and an evangelical Christian who had done missionary work in soldiers homes in India. She had had three daughters to a violent husband and spent many years almost destitute. For some years—Heather calculated about three—she had packed sardines at a cannery to make ends meet. Then she had discovered Theosophy and undergone a rapid conversion. Her life was transformed. She met her second husband Foster and they were both caught up in organisational politics that led to their ousting from the headquarters of the Theosophical Society. Alice Bailey couldn't be described a breakaway Theosophist because she hadn't done that, she hadn't broken away, she had been evicted, rejected, shunned.

It had been a pivotal moment. In her autobiography, she talked of New York and how she founded and built up her organisations out of a small meditation group she ran. She talked of the workload, the loyalty and the piles and piles of letters she received. She talked of the lectures she gave to rooms packed with hundreds of people. She described the private appointments she would have with seekers asking for advice.

Her own story ended abruptly around the mid-1930s. More chapters were planned but she died before they were written. Her death created a vacuum where knowledge should have been, knowledge of the last fifteen years of her life.

All those blue books and Foyle's manuscript were strong indicators that Alice Bailey was the mother of the New Age. Her mission had been a success. Yet unlike Rudolph Steiner, who was a household name among the progressive middle class, Alice Bailey remained obscure and misunderstood, a shadow figure, revered by some, such as the spiritual seekers at Findhorn, and among astrologers. She had clearly had an impact on prominent thinkers in the field of psychology such as Roberto Assagioli.

Curious to see what she could find out about those last years of Alice Bailey's life, Heather delved back into Professor Foyle's collection. Ignoring all the boxes pertaining to Bhagwan Rajneesh that she still had to deal with, she lifted the lid on a box at the end of the bench near the filing cabinet and lifted out the contents. There wasn't much. Some printouts from websites, an assortment of handwritten notes on scraps of paper held together with a large bulldog clip, along with two books, one by Mary Bailey, who turned out to be Foster's second wife, and Foster Bailey himself.

Heather instinctively reached for the unfinished autobiography to cross reference the materials now to hand with Alice Bailey's own account. She didn't find much to match. Towards the end of the 1930s, the Baileys had established another headquarters in nearby Royal Tunbridge Wells. Heather recalled Sinclair mentioning a house in Broadwater Down. She had made a note of it. She went straight on Google Maps and located the street. It was as she had expected, a quiet street lined with leafy lime trees, with houses the size of small mansions dotted along its length, not dissimilar to Hawthorn East.

Alice Bailey stated their base of operations was commandeered by the British Army for the duration of the Second World War. That meant it must have been requisitioned early on, if her account was to be trusted. The house number wasn't mentioned by Bailey or Sinclair, but Heather soon discovered that the 12$^{th}$ Corps of the British Army, led by General Montgomery, had acquired a number or residences on Broadwater Down during the war. The first was No. 2—the original operational headquarters—and No. 32, the signals headquarters. Both houses were acquired in 1940. General Montgomery took up residence at No. 10 for a period in 1941. The other houses in the street were occupied much later. The area was known most for the establishment of a series of top-secret tunnels leading to an underground war bunker that was created nearby, and only discovered in 1969. Alice Bailey could have known nothing about that.

Heather surmised the Baileys had resided at either No. 2 or No. 32 but she was disappointed not to be able to discover which. Nowhere in Foyle's notes was there an indication of the exact residence. Online real estate sites showed photos of each house. Both were magnificent Victorian buildings that had been converted into flats. She soon discovered that No. 32 had been purchased in 1922 by a George James Lewis, who may have been a baronet. A co-worker? Joan would have been instantly on the case. It was the sort of genealogical note she would have doggedly pursued. Although, how would you discover a deceased person's spiritual affiliations? The chances of finding evidence were slim. Despite the allure, Heather resisted furthering that line of inquiry, reminding herself that it was based on supposition.

Whichever house it was, Alice Bailey had been forced to give it up and reside in New York for the duration of the war. By then, she was almost an invalid. The brief accounts of her decline provided by Mary and Foster Bailey were moving. They said the war period had affected her health greatly. Her efforts to reach and sustain the New Group of World Servers—who were themselves demoralised—proved onerous. The work had taken its toll. Her organisations had suffered financially. Funds to continue the work had been scarce. Yet she refused to be defeated. She had worked and worked hard, just as she had done her whole life, getting up well before dawn, working on her writing, then putting in a full day at the office, and she had done it all without complaint. It appeared she had felt she had no choice. It must have seemed to her that there was every danger all her efforts of world salvation would come to nothing. That her works and her organisations would die with her and the entire edifice she had spent decades building would crumble.

Those around her must have felt the same. Her friends and family had doubled their efforts to support her. In the 1940s, her daughter, Mildred, had prepared the reading sets for World Goodwill.

In the aftermath of the Second World War, when her body barely functioned, Alice and Foster set to task re-establishing their global networks. When the house at Broadwater Down was returned to them in 1947, they made the journey across the Atlantic to hold an annual Arcane School conference. They would make the journey twice more, including 1949, the year of Alice Bailey's death.

Heather returned to the letter Foster had written as a preface to Alice Bailey's autobiography. She had passed away in New York during the afternoon of Thursday the 15th December 1949, with her husband, Foster Bailey, by her bedside. Among her last words spoken to her husband were:

*"I have much to be thankful for. I have had a rich and full life. So many people all over the world have been so kind to me."*

Heather put down the book. She was consumed by sadness. It was different to the loss she had been feeling over Hilary. She was hollow, as though emptied in the face of a loss far greater than her own. Humanity had lost a remarkable woman, someone who had been cherished, respected and admired by many thousands of followers, among them numerous notable figures. Yet sections of the academic community seemed to have shunned her, as had a large portion of the Theosophical Society. Heather succumbed to a double sadness knowing Professor Foyle had died before completing her book. Two women's lives cut short. It was as though a veil would always shroud those last years of Alice Bailey's life.

She read over Foster's letter again and caught her breath. Something in her mind shifted and her insides felt as though they had flipped.

Shocked, she pulled away from her desk and glanced out the window at the bright blue sky. It was ten days to Christmas. It was the fifteenth of December. It was the anniversary of Alice Bailey's death.

She tried to assimilate the revelation, her mind scrambling to dismiss as pure chance something that felt charged with significance. She told herself she had been working on the collection since July. She could have arrived at the contents of that box on any day. It was a random event, and besides, she had already known the date of Alice Bailey's death. She had read it in her autobiography. Could her own unconscious be playing tricks on her, or have an agenda of its own? Insane. She refused to entertain such a notion.

Instead, she steered herself back to the story she was unravelling and marvelled at the stoicism and deep sense of duty Alice Bailey had displayed towards the end of her life. She went through her notes and found her list of the Blue Books, collated by publication date. Many had been published posthumously. All those hours of scribing, teaching, lecturing and guiding others, all the while her health deteriorated. Alice Bailey said she had a blood and heart condition. One of Foyle's notes mentioned that her closest co-worker, Regina Keller, had named it pernicious anaemia. Heather looked up the condition. The list of symptoms was long. Even when treated, it would have felt like straining to move in a crippled body, one that wouldn't follow instructions, one that wobbled and toppled and tingled and cracked and burned.

It made Heather angry to think that a woman so frail, and yet so dedicated, should have been condemned to obscurity. She couldn't help adopting Professor Foyle's stance, wanting some sort of justice for Alice Bailey, a fair hearing at least. She felt suddenly chosen, as though the task had not befallen her by chance, and certainly not because she always got the manuscripts the others didn't want. It was because she was best suited to understanding Alice Bailey's position. As though she had been singled out by a higher power. It was revelatory to her that she should even think like that. Higher power? Hilary once said there were times in a person's life when events and circumstances piled up and things took on a charged feeling and everything seemed significant. She said those phases represented turning points in a life. The ancients called them initiations. She'd been describing a period in her own life, when she had travelled to India. Was that what this was—initiatory?

She found Foyle's manuscript among the piles of papers on her desk and scanned through the table of contents. Then she skimmed through the manuscript, thinking again it an enormous pity Professor Foyle hadn't lived long enough to publish. It was always a pity when something worthy didn't get the chance to see the light of day due to the death of its author. She supposed that was, above all else, what had originally drawn her to work in the manuscript office.

She noticed that towards the end of the manuscript, the chapter page numbers didn't match the table of contents. She wondered why she hadn't spotted that before. She had already filled in one blank in Foyle's work with that paper she had written on the schism that forced Alice Bailey to leave the Theosophical Society's headquarters and set up on her own. That would have amounted to about twenty pages in the manuscript by the time Foyle had justified and clarified all her arguments. She had accounted for that chapter, but running through the manuscript pages she found a second jump of around that length. The chapter listed in the table of contents as "A Point of Principle" was missing.

Heather jumped from her seat and riffled through the remaining boxes lined up on the floor and the bench. Most of them pertained to Professor Foyle's work on Bhagwan Rajneesh. She eyed the one at the end that contained an array of musty papers and hoped she wasn't forced to open it.

She found what she was looking for in a box of manila folders containing photocopies of chapters from scholarly texts, everyone from William James to Martin Heidegger.

Extracting the folders one by one, she came across a manila folder with Foyle's chapter title scrawled on the front in large capitals. Inside was an annotated draft, more a sketch for something much larger. The subject of the chapter revolved around Dutch Theosophist Olga Fröbe

Kapteyn and her spiritual summer school. Bells rang in her head. Alice Bailey had written about the collaboration in one of the last chapters of her autobiography. Heather skimmed over what she had written. She saw warmth in her words, yet there was also much caution. She was guarded and defensive, especially regarding her daughters.

Foyle described Olga Fröbe as a freethinker and spiritual seeker, the sort that was never quite satisfied. She had an enduring interest in comparative religion, mythology, spirituality and Steiner's anthroposophy. In all, the sort of woman suited to Alice Bailey's teachings.

*"Olga Fröbe's desire to found a spiritual centre and not merely an intellectual salon, had been a response to a broader intellectual climate that existed through the 1920s in Europe and particularly Germany, evidenced in the highly popular School of Wisdom founded by Count Hermann Keyserling. There was a prevailing orientation towards Eastern mysticism, Hinduism, Buddhism and Taoism.*

*Fröbe had also been looking for a fulcrum or anchor, a point of focus, a figure who could serve as a vehicle for her vision. She had been influenced by prominent philosopher Martin Buber, whom she met at Monte Verità in 1924 and with whom she had corresponded. She had moved on to become a devotee of poet and eccentric Ludwig Derleth, who had upheld a strict Christian belief in a return to a medieval, male-only hierarchy of leaders, which he had thought should replace democracy, a system for which he held nothing but contempt. Ludwig Derleth, along with André Germain were among a large number of alternative thinkers associated with Monte Verità, an alternative community of freethinkers known for its acceptance of nudity and homosexuality. A hotel at Monte Verità had been purchased by Baron von Heydt, former banker to the Kaiser.*

*Fröbe and Heydt became rivals. She had run her own intellectual salon in the past and she resented the success of Heydt's salon at Monte Verità. In 1928, Fröbe came up with a scheme to outdo Heydt. Apparently without knowing its specific purpose, she had built beside her house a lecture hall."*

Heather knew what was coming. Fröbe had a collaborator in mind and it wasn't anyone associated with Heydt and the milieu at Monte Verità, about whom she seemed to have had little but contempt. Foyle had put an asterisk beside the following sentence. "*Fröbe already knew of Alice Bailey and her teachings and may even have been a student of her Arcane School.*"

For how long Olga had known of Alice Bailey was unclear, but Foyle was convinced she had much more than a passing familiarity with Bailey's work, one that had endured longer than the three short years of their collaboration at Ascona. She wrote:

*On the $3^{rd}$ August 1930, the first summer school commenced. It was to last for three weeks, with an additional week made available for private interviews with leaders. Every day except Sunday three lectures were given, two in the morning and one in the afternoon. There were eighty seats in the lecture hall and over fifteen nationalities were represented.*

*Fröbe gave the opening address: 'Our purpose is to create a meeting point where those of every group and faith may gather for discussion and synthetic work along spiritual lines... We are profoundly conscious that the source and the goal of humanity are one and the same for every unit, and that here lies the fundamental truth of Brotherhood.'*

*Her thinking appears influenced by Bailey's teachings. She refers to people as 'units' and speaks of 'synthetic work along spiritual lines,' language straight out of a Bailey text.*

Heather came to the end of the page. The next was blank. That was all Foyle had managed. Heather felt cheated. She grabbed *The Unfinished Autobiography* off the shelf and pulled forward her keyboard, planning to search online for whatever she could find. She hadn't got far when Suzanne burst into her office, saying, 'Coffee time.'

# Conspiracy Theories

Settlement of her aunt Hilary's house in Bowler Street fell on a kiln hot Saturday in March. Heather had arranged to meet the agent for a final inspection at nine. Already, a hot northerly breathed pollen laden air across Hawthorn East. Standing in the shade of the front porch she reached for her inhaler, thinking she would make an appointment with her doctor to alter her medication which didn't seem to work adequately on bad days.

The agent pulled up in his smart red car on the dot of nine, and alighted feigning cool in an open neck shirt and casual pants. She waited. The garden was the worse for wear. Some of the shrubs looked heat stressed and the lawn was crisp. She hoped the agent would be accommodating. He came up the short path with a clipboard and greeted her with a cheery smile. She opened the front door and they went into the relative cool of the house.

As they walked from room to room, she had to fight back a sudden welling of tears. The rooms were empty, clean as a pin and dust free. She had gone around with her mother's vacuum cleaner and a duster last week. The house was a mausoleum, all that remained of her aunt were faint echoes, a scuff here, a blemish there, evidence of her presence.

At ten she handed the agent her keys and bid him farewell. She turned her back on her aunt's house and headed off on the all too familiar zigzag of side streets to her parents'. The only thing stopping her fainting from the heat was her canvas sunhat. She broke out in a sweat before she had reached the end of the next street. Whenever she was forced to relinquish the shade of the trees to pass by a driveway or cross a road the sun stung the bare skin of her arms.

The funeral, the will, the revelation that a large sum had been bequeathed her, the knowledge that at last, at forty-five, she could finally leave home, the frantic search for somewhere suitable, her mother's nagging insistence that she put down a deposit on a property nearby, and then her resolve to purchase something outright—a decision that had driven her all the way to Ballarat—through it all the parental pressure had been immense. She had stood her ground, repeating over and again that Ballarat was only an hour into the city.

The week before last, she had found a house in Ballarat, an old cottage with high ceilings and hardwood floors, walking distance from the station and the shops. She had been delighted when it came up in her daily search and she had made an appointment to view it on the weekend. She had taken the train and enjoyed the walk to the house, which turned out to be even nicer than the photos.

It was a red brick house with a matching iron roof. The front door was tucked inside a deep porch. The roof was given over to a large and brightly lit bedroom, replete with dormer windows. It was the sort of house Hilary would have loved, the sort of house her great-grandmother, Katharine, would have held séances in. She could picture the two women, seated together around an antique table of polished oak.

She had gone home on the train with butterflies in her belly. She had to force herself to wait until she was back at Harcourt Street before phoning to put in an offer, ten per cent above the asking price. After all, her mind was made up. She didn't want someone else snaffling the one and only house she had been waiting for all those months.

Her offer was accepted later that day. On Wednesday, she had signed the paperwork and used her savings to pay the deposit, after the agent taking care of Bowler Street assured her that the buyers were not about to renege on settlement. They wouldn't dare, considering the penalties.

After all the searching and agonising, she was astonished to find how quick and easy the house buying process was. They had agreed on a two-month settlement date. She had forged on in secret, attending to all the fine details before she broke the news to her parents. It was only when she stared into the future and thought about packing that she worried over the distance, the looming isolation.

Her mother's shocked face and reproachful comments disabused her of her misgivings. She had made the announcement last night, standing in the doorway of the living room while her parents sipped their pre-dinner drinks. It had made for a quick exit. Ten tedious minutes of quizzing and reproving looks later, and she had bounded upstairs to the sanctuary of her bedroom, revelling in the knowledge that she was about to embark on a new and independent life and she already had a companion, Alice Bailey.

Although she knew she would never study the occultist's works. They were too difficult and strange and dated. She might be leaving the words behind her but she would never look at the world in the same way again. A door stood open to an inner realm she never knew existed, but Hilary, yes Hilary had known. Had she walked through that door? She must have done and now Heather stood on the threshold, sensing deeper meanings beneath the surface of things. She thought there might be a higher purpose infusing humanity, one the bulk of us, even those who are religious, deny.

Eager to escape the heat after her walk back from Bowler Street, she rushed into the hall, welcoming the cool air and the empty house. Despite the heat, her mother had gone shopping for new curtains for Heather's bedroom and dragged her father along to help her choose. Heather went to the kitchen for a glass of water to take to her room. The kitchen at her new house was smaller but just as well laid out, with wall cupboards, an island, and granite bench tops. The only point of difference was the shiny red splashbacks lacking in her mother's,

Joan electing to have wall tiles when her kitchen was installed a few years before.

She took her glass upstairs and closed her bedroom door. She wanted to research some details pertaining to a chapter in Professor Foyle's manuscript. It appeared her inquiries into Olga Fröbe had yielded nothing other than that the two women had had an acrimonious falling out over Olga's allegations that Foster had been caught nude sunbathing on a raft and Alice's daughters had been involved in erotic escapades, which Olga used as reasons to end things between them, accusing Alice Bailey of double standards.

Heather struggled to picture a nude Foster. His act brought into question something that had been puzzling Heather in the back of her mind all along. What sort of marriage did they have? One that couldn't be talked about in the autobiography. Why? There was clearly much affection between them. The association of nude sunbathing and the sort of place Monte Verità was had her wondering if Foster had been gay and their marriage, lavender. She supposed she would never know.

She found it hard to believe the girls had got up to anything untoward, given Alice Bailey's moral rectitude. Heather was left wondering why Professor Foyle had chosen to remove the chapter from the manuscript. Perhaps she was still working on it, or she had reached a dead end. As it stood, the chapter led nowhere in terms of her mission to prove Alice Bailey the mother of the New Age. Perhaps that was the reason for its removal.

What next? She had emptied all the boxes and attended to every last detail. All that remained to do was puzzle over the gaps as she digitalised the collection. She was about to begin her own explorations of Olga Fröbe when she heard a commotion downstairs and her name being called.

'Heather! We've the new curtains for your room. I'll be right up to hang them.'

*Now?*

Not much longer, she told herself, not much longer and she would be in Ballarat.

Back in January, Heather had taken a necessary break from Alice Bailey to deal with all the Bhagwan Rajneesh boxes. Thirty boxes of tattered volumes, along with Osho this and Osho that, the entire Osho collection it appeared. Samantha Foyle had taken considerable interest in the cult figure. Heather only knew of him because Hilary had mentioned him on odd occasions in the context of misdemeanours of a sexual nature among his followers. Hilary had been troubled by her friend Aashti's disclosures. Hilary hadn't divulged much, but looking back, Heather guessed that Aashti had. From what she could gather, Osho's style of spirituality was anathema to all Alice Bailey had stood for. His was more akin to the practices found at Monte Verità, or those of Charles Leadbeater.

Once the last of the Osho boxes was empty, all that remained was that one box of musty papers. It was a Friday afternoon, not an ideal time to start recording the contents of another box, but an intense summer heat wave was conducive and she wanted to take full advantage of the hot winds that were whipping round the building and entering through every crack.

She had opened the office window, propped open the door with the waste bin, and taken a blast of her inhaler. Taking no chances, she placed the box in the path of the through draft.

She delved in and grabbed a handful of loose papers and set them down on the bench before reaching for another. She had expected to have to do the same all the way to the bottom of the box, but after a few repeats she arrived at a swatch of notes held together by a large bulldog clip, along with two books, heavily laden with sticky notes. Not wanting the papers to blow around, she inserted each of her loose-paper handfuls into a plastic folder and, retaining the order she had found them in, she put the folders in the bottom drawer of her desk, which was empty. Shut in there that smelly paper wouldn't contaminate her workspace.

The notes and books she took to her desk, examining the books first. One was by Constance Cumbey, released in 1983, and carrying the ominous title, *The Hidden Dangers of the Rainbow: The New Age*

*Movement and the Coming Age of Barbarism.* Even a cursory read of the contents revealed the author to have a strong evangelical mindset. The other, published a few years later by Australian writer, Morag Zwartz, had a similar evangelical flavour. Like its predecessor, *The New Age Gospel: Christ or Counterfeit* responded to what the author considered to be the evil contained in the New Age movement.

Evil in the New Age? It was a fascinating notion. She wouldn't have called Osho evil, not with her understanding of the word, but still.

The collection of notes pertained to another chapter missing in the manuscript, one that appeared in the table of contents under the title, 'Rainbows.' Heather had had no idea what Professor Foyle had been referring to until she saw the title of Cumbey's book.

She took her time scanning through Professor Foyle's notes and reading each volume, guided by the sticky notes. She quickly learned the extent to which Alice Bailey had been accused of racism, anti-Semitism and, unsurprisingly, of being a vehicle for the Antichrist. Foyle noted that while not without substance, the Christian critics offered an unfair assessment of her work.

The trouble for Alice Bailey had its roots back in the 1920s, when she established the Lucifer Publishing Company to publish the books she had composed with the Tibetan. She had quickly changed the name to the Lucis Publishing Company, after she became concerned about public perception of the word 'Lucifer,' especially amongst orthodox Christians. Heather thought she had been wise to make the change, but it came too late to avert the outrage of evangelical Christians who would persist in citing the original name of the publishing company as a basis to their argument that Alice Bailey was possessed by the devil. Foyle had come up with a succinct outline of Cumbey's view.

"*Cumbey had some sympathy for Bailey as a former fellow evangelical. She was at pains to construe the born-again occultist as a vulnerable victim of circumstances, confused, lonely and in despair at the time she encountered Theosophy...* It was an odd character assessment that didn't marry with Heather's view of Alice Bailey as a steadfast convert... *Cumbey thought Bailey was possessed, and as a woman with a deep hatred of orthodoxy. Everything that Bailey wrote was seen by Cumbey through that lens. The Plan of the Spiritual Masters that Bailey and her co-workers spent years meditating on, was for Cumbey, a lot more than simply an unorthodox formulation. It was an attempt to stamp out Christianity altogether."*

Immersed in this new and unexpected territory, Heather felt the full force of the fear and hatred Alice Bailey had attracted from Christian fundamentalists. She was being attacked by the choir. The irony was obvious. Making matters more ludicrous still, Alice Bailey's mission had been about arresting hatred and evil, not perpetuating it.

*"Unfortunately," Professor Foyle wrote, "Cumbey's thesis, while off putting to non-evangelists, fed the fears of a receptive audience of believers. Cumbey's work has been widely discredited by scholars due to its conspiracy theory tone, yet it continues to circulate, aided by Cumbey herself, who maintains a strong online presence."*

She was shocked to discover that the views of Cumbey persisted, almost forty years on. They had become foundational, Foyle referring to the scores of websites and blogs dedicated to attacking Alice Bailey, that were propped up by Cumbey's work.

Heather read on.

*"Cumbey's citing of 'Lucifer' was picked up in 2001 by a leading conspiracy thinker, Jim Marrs, in his book,* Rule by Secrecy, *a comprehensive exploration of 'conspiracy truth,' involving the discovery and interpretation of the various guises of the New World Order plot. Marrs makes just that one reference to Alice Bailey, using it as 'evidence' to support his claim that the core motive of esotericists down the ages is to convert believers to Satanism."*

Heather removed her glasses to rub her eyes, giving the lenses a swift polish on the hem of her blouse before returning them to her face. Marrs, Cumbey, Zwartz, it was all ridiculous. It was mischief making, surely. If Alice Bailey could have known how far reaching the consequences of this single word choice would be, she would have been kicking herself.

As five o'clock drew near she eyed the two books and Professor Foyle's notes and knew she couldn't leave her explorations until the following Monday. She was slipping the materials into her shoulder bag when the door that she had left ajar opened further and Suzanne appeared.

'Phew, it's hot in here! Why is the window open?'

'I needed some air.'

Suzanne gave her a wry look.

'Looks like you're getting to the end of this lot. Bet you can't wait to see the back of it.'

'I'm enjoying it, as a matter of fact.'

'Rather you than me.' She looked back down the corridor then stepped inside. 'I thought you should know that after I spoke with human resources about that Rosie girl, they're having a purge.'

'I don't follow.'

'Don't you read the staff memos? H and R have used Rosie as an excuse to shrink the department. Shona's up in arms. Since staff cutbacks were already on the cards, H and R have decided to target our department.' She paused. 'We're to stick to the guidelines. Let them find someone else to make redundant.'

'What's happened to Rosie?'

'Nothing other than more training. Her salary is low. It's us I'm worried about.'

She took another long hard look around the room.

'Before I forget, I thought you'd be off home soon so I brought you this.'

She took the printout Suzanne proffered.

'What is it?'

'Have a read.'

It was a discounted holiday for two in New York. Enjoy the scintillations of downtown Manhattan, the blurb read. Five-star accommodation and all transfers and taxes included in the price.

'How do you find these things?'

'I'm in a loyalty club. What do you reckon?'

A few months ago, she would never have parted with the cash. Not for a ten-day break in a city halfway round the world.

'When?'

'June.'

Heather grinned. June in New York would be hot. Perhaps that accounted for the discount. 'Leave it with me.'

'I need to know by tomorrow night at the latest.'

'I'll text you.'

With another sweeping scan of her office, Suzanne left the room. Guilt prickled and Heather extracted the materials from her bag. She hesitated, uncertain whether to go home or continue. She didn't want to stop but she hadn't eaten in a while and she couldn't think clearly when she was hungry. She shut the window and removed the waste paper bin still propping open the door. The temperature inside the library was markedly cooler and once she had forced her way through the crowds enjoying the air conditioning and entered the furnace of Melbourne's city streets, she nearly fainted. She battled on. In fifteen minutes, she was back at her desk with a large carton of orange juice and three sushi rolls.

She couldn't help feeling sympathy for Alice Bailey and admiration for Professor Foyle. She needed to do something with the knowledge she was accumulating. Suzanne's warning, along with Shona's rejection of her paper, and she wondered if she should pursue the topic at a tertiary level. She could do a Masters somewhere. It seemed to her a travesty that someone she found to be unequivocally good and sincere, if unusual in her metaphysical beliefs, should be so maligned, and not by one quarter. Purist Theosophists couldn't stand her, fundamentalist Christians thought she was the devil incarnate and conspiracy theorists thought she and her followers were plotting to rule the world. Heather could hear Hilary in her mind, spurring her on, reminding her that there were plenty of intellectuals and academics who subscribed to a metaphysical worldview, many of them eminent, including Carl Jung.

As far as she knew, Carl Jung wasn't the butt of a global conspiracy theory. Surely Alice Bailey didn't deserve such wild accusations, such wrath. She was a victim all over again, subject to the indiscriminate fists of irate zealots determined to beat her into oblivion.

Whacky she might have been, but Alice Bailey had devoted thirty years to the fulfilment of her mission.

Back in the late 1940s as she had neared the end of her life, she couldn't have known there was a nemesis growing up right beside her, one that would culminate in the form of a grand conspiracy theory, one rooted in Cumbey's damning attack on her teachings.

Professor Foyle was at pains to stress that while some of Cumbey's accusations were perhaps not unfounded, others drew on erroneous interpretations of Bailey's central concepts. Conspiracy thinkers had taken those misinterpretations and embellished them, creating an unfortunate veil of disinformation around a body of work intended to foster spiritual enlightenment.

*"That Bailey's work has attracted the attention of such thinking should come as no surprise," Foyle argued. "There is much in her work to arouse the suspicions of conspiracy thinkers, including: The existence of a hierarchy of masters overseeing humanity; the notion of a Plan; a call for one world government; and a belief in the value of the United Nations."*

With those triggers, little wonder Alice Bailey had come under their high beam. A controversy, a disastrous event, a secret organisation, conspiracy theorists seemed compelled to take to task every issue that could be construed by them as evidence of the workings of hidden power. Heather had come across her share of conspiracists at the information desk over the years. She recalled one time when a wizened man in an old anorak had leaned against her desk asking for a title by a David Icke. The book sounded obscure and the library didn't hold a copy. The man started ranting about the importance of the book and how it proved the Royal family were lizard people involved in a plot to impose a one world government. He said it was the duty of the State Library to source a copy to expose the cover up. He had leaned further forward, blasting Heather with his fetid breath, and insisted that she search for the title on bookseller sites and put in a requisition. She caved in to his demands until Suzanne appeared and, overhearing the exchange, gave him a withering stare and told him he was being ridiculous and he better be on his way. Security were there the next instant.

The paranoia that an inner power was at work behind the scenes imposing a new world order was intense in those who shared the view. Heather soon discovered that because of it, the moment Alice Bailey had latched onto the United Nations, history was against her, as was evident in the fuss Cumbey made about it all. Heather vaguely recalled the many references to the United Nations in Alice Bailey's later works. Her memory was hazy and at the time she hadn't taken much notice. Now she wanted to read what Alice Bailey had written.

Wasting no time, she scanned the list of Bailey titles in her notebook, writing down the names of the ones published after the declaration of the United Nations in 1942 on a scrap of paper, and omitting *A Treatise on the Seven Rays* which seemed irrelevant in the context. All the while she wished she hadn't relinquished her row of blue books after Suzanne had issued another friendly word of caution. She had wanted to hold onto the autobiography, but had thought better of it, choosing instead to purchase her own copy. She had been gazing up at her empty shelf by the door for weeks, taking comfort knowing that at least the Sinclair biography remained in her desk drawer.

She located the whereabouts of the volumes on her computer, then headed down through the library to collect the titles she was after in onsite storage. On her way back to her office, she felt like a thief. She hunched over her desk and waded through the references to the United Nations one by one, jotting down whatever seemed pertinent. Riffling through Professor Foyle's notes, she found some typed extracts, the makings of a chapter. It appeared as though the academic was unsure whether to pursue the line of inquiry or dump it as tangential.

*"Bailey's support of the United Nations is unsurprising. The organisation represents a dovetailing of her spiritual ethos with the widespread concerns running through the minds of many during the war's aftermath, concerns centring on finding ways to address the situation that had led to it. Not least among these concerns was the desire to create some form of international law designed to protect individuals and groups from abuses meted out by nation states, challenging the idea that a nation has an inviolable right to treat its citizens or anyone within its borders however it wishes. To that effect, the Universal Declaration of Human Rights was proclaimed by the United Nations General Assembly on 10 December 1948. There was at last hope of a better world, one founded on unity, goodwill and right relations.*

*In 1947, Bailey wrote* Problems of Humanity, *a slim volume composed in her own pen, containing a collection of pamphlets dated from October 1944 to December 1946. As the title suggests, in this work Bailey discusses the pressing problems facing humanity and proposes solutions. In the final chapter, she discusses world unity in a post-war world, a world unity based on goodwill, cooperation and interdependence, noting that since there exists no alternative, the United Nations must be given full support.*

*She knew the task was onerous. In* The Destiny of the Nations, *a volume dedicated to commenting, from her esoteric perspective, on the problems facing the United Nations, she saw that the United Nations faced two fundamental problems: finding a way to distribute the world's resources in order to provide freedom from want; and to bring about authentic equality of opportunity and education for all. Above all, she saw the United Nations as a vehicle for goodwill. It was to her Units of Service that she hailed, those women and men of goodwill, seeking to encourage them to help restore world confidence, and educate the masses in the principles and the practice of goodwill.*

*In the same year, Bailey wrote the later sections of* The Rays and the Initiations, *in which she voices her concerns over the direction human-*

ity is taking in the aftermath of World War II, particularly with regard to the Zionist movement and the formation of Israel. Even as early as April 1942, Bailey saw difficulties emerging in the United Nations, as nations followed their individual desires for victory and peace, and for an end to suffering, cruelty, starvation, death and fear, rather than follow an organised spiritual will. In June 1947, Bailey published a pamphlet entitled 'Preparation for the Reappearance of the Christ' in which her frustrations are evident. After discussing the hindrances to Christ's reappearance—the inertia of the average spiritually minded man and the lack of money and financial support for disciples—she acknowledged that the United Nations was preoccupied with pressing demands from all sides, that various nations were jostling for place and power, and control of natural resources. She then made reference to the behind the scenes activities of the great global powers and of the capitalists they create.

In April 1948, she saw strategic difficulties emerging for the United Nations. Her commentary on the United Nations is given from her esoteric point of view and cannot compare to works of an erudite nature, or comprehensive commentaries of political commentators of the day. Yet the little she had to say in her body of work was sufficient to direct her followers from then on to focus their efforts in the arena of the United Nations. If a new world religion was to emerge, a new world order to manifest, and the Christ to reappear, then the singular hope for humanity was to be found in the United Nations, an organisation capable of holding humanity's highest aspirations.

The United Nations had gifted Bailey a point of focus, and if her following of high achievers working within its auspices is anything to go by, her Arcane School yielded some impressive results. Her co-workers took her at her word and forged links with the organisation, not only through World Goodwill, but via a raft of other initiatives including hosting seminars, conferences, meditation days, and founding magazines, and other organisations. Their aim is not to impose Bailey's texts on the world like dogma, but to gift to humanity their trained ability to think holistically and intuitively, to synthesise disparate perspectives, and to unify. For example, one co-worker and past director of World Goodwill, holistic spiritual counsellor and prominent speaker Ida Urso, went on to found the Aquarian Age Community, an organisation that has as one of its goals the promotion of the United Nations."

Heather was dumbfounded. Alice Bailey's objectives were so noble as to be almost saintly. It was obvious she thought no other global organisation held the key to human and planetary betterment. Setting aside the trigger concepts such as 'unity' and 'synthesis', which were abhorrent to the Christian right, the conspiracy clan didn't seem to have that much to go on to support their argument that the occultist lay behind a global conspiracy. Then Heather turned to the next passage in Foyle's typed notes.

*"On August 9, 1945, in a message titled 'The Release of Atomic Energy,' Bailey claims atomic energy release to be an esoteric symbol of the inauguration of the Kingdom of God on earth, through the liberation of the inner aspect of the atom. She describes atomic energy as liberating. Such liberation would be achieved through the constructive use of atomic energy for the betterment of humanity. All that energy, previously locked in the atom, could be put to good use. Such is its power, atomic energy could ultimately transform the entire world economic structure.*

*Bailey goes on to argue that atomic energy will help to promote globalization, a true synthesis of humanity. She could not have known of atomic energy's toxicity, she couldn't have known the impact of that statement, which served to undermine her body of work and bring into question its credibility. In another message given out a year later, sadly Bailey becomes her own worst enemy. In one paragraph, she manages to reduce her entire body of work in the eyes of her detractors to the senseless rants of a lunatic bent on global annihilation, when she argues that the United Nations could use the atomic bomb as a threat or even as a weapon to keep in check aggressive nations."*

Heather instantly made excuses on Alice Bailey's behalf. She was ill. She was distressed. The war had affected her emotionally which in turn had affected her thinking. Was that why Professor Foyle had been ambivalent about including that chapter in her book? Perhaps she preferred to sweep aside an uncomfortable truth. One paragraph? Could, should an author's entire canon be condemned for one or two ill-conceived sentences? For they were ill-conceived, as far as Heather was concerned. They were ill-conceived and displayed an imprudent mind. Would she have known of the devastation of Hiroshima and Nagasaki? Of the people who had melted? Or was that news supressed? The public didn't understand radioactive fallout until much later. She would have presumed the atomic bomb to be little different to what happened to Dresden, to Coventry. She may well have bought into the idea that those atomic bombs had ended the war.

The trouble was, Alice Bailey had made numerous contentious comments in the same slim volume. The contents of *The Destiny of the Nations* would have been better buried with their writer. Not published posthumously, no matter how loyal to the truth the editors wanted to be.

Setting aside those opinions as emanating from the mind of a woman flawed, a woman writing at a point in time when emotion clouded reason and judgement, it was transparent that Alice Bailey had hoped through the auspices of the United Nations the world would re-orient itself on a better course, and that through her organisations, her works would achieve their intention, to found a new spiritual world order.

Heather was arrested by her own thought process, caught in the irony that conspiracy theorists believed wholeheartedly that Alice Bailey had been successful. Perhaps nothing spoke more loudly of the significance of her achievements than the New World Order conspiracy theory that had grown in her name.

This time, when Heather typed "New World Order conspiracy theory" into her search engine, a photo of Alice Bailey appeared alongside the definition. It was a startling and disturbing juxtaposition. From aristocratic beginnings Bailey, or rather her ghost, had become a conspiracy queen, placed on that odd throne. The search engine had chosen a particularly flattering photograph of her too, replete with a regal red background. Through its own automatic processes of selection and dissemination, the internet, it would appear, stood at the helm of a new era of misinformation. Professor Foyle was thinking along the same lines.

"*All conspiracy theories require a scapegoat or fall guy, a human agent masterminding the plot. Alice Bailey is an easy target. She's a Theosophist, and in conspiracy circles, the Theosophists are thought to be an evil, occult sect aligned with the Nazis. She's dead, so can offer no defence.*"

She was a woman, too, which makes her a soft target, Heather thought, her feminist bones stirring.

"*She moved in high circles, counting among her friends numerous dukes and baronesses and sirs. She was linked to Freemasonry via her husband. As if that were not damning enough, when Bailey made numerous statements in her texts in support of the United Nations, she had effectively handed them the rope for her own execution. Conspiracy thinkers didn't need to delve further than the shallow end of her body of work to come up with such damning finds.*"

That's where Foyle's draft chapter ended and Heather felt cheated. Had Foyle deemed the chapter beyond the scope of her work? Yet surely it was relevant. She must have still been working on it and kept it separate from the rest.

Heather had another scan through Cumbey's book. The author had devoted a series of appendices to Bailey's organisations and ideas, including: World Goodwill, Triangles, the Lucis Trust, the New Group of World Servers and the Unity-in-Diversity Council. A sticky note described the latter as an organisation based on an ancient phrase Bailey utilised to convey an important holistic idea.

In Cumbey's view, New Age conspirators were enacting a plan for a quasi-Nazi new world order that had been set down by Bailey, largely by infiltrating the United Nations. For Cumbey, adherents to the Bailey texts were deluded, naïve, and held by mass hypnosis and mind control. To prove her point, Cumbey had quoted extensively from nine volumes of the Bailey canon, with an emphasis on *The Externalisation of the Hierarchy*. Heather soon had enough of Cumbey's thesis after dipping in here and there and she left her desk in favour of a sushi roll and her orange juice, sitting on the near empty bench while she ate.

Five minutes later and she was back online.

She had never before had recourse to explore conspiracy theory websites. They were fascinating, the detail astonishing. The claims were outlandish but the trouble some of those writers took to prove their points was impressive. Overall, the mindset was as driven and dogmatic as Alice Bailey's.

On one, Heather stumbled on a list of members of the United Nation's Spiritual Caucus, the author claiming that they were all Alice Bailey co-workers.

Could that be true?

It couldn't be true.

What was this Spiritual Caucus anyway?

Heather entered each name into her search engine. One by one there they all were, just as that conspiracist said, card carrying Alice Bailey co-workers; their biographies made it obvious. From what she could gather almost all the members of the Spiritual Caucus had made the Bailey teachings their life. More, their various organisational affiliations were interconnected, forming a web dedicated to peace and goodwill. She had no idea how much power or influence the Spiritual Caucus had over any aspect of United Nations policy and procedure but it felt significant.

As did her discovery in Foyle's notes that the UN's former Assistant-Secretary General Robert Muller, a man who had held the post for forty years and founded the World Core Curriculum for Education, had been, without a doubt, aligned with Alice Bailey, and had applied her teachings in all that he had achieved. According to Foyle, the World Core Curriculum was based on Alice Bailey's *Education in the New Age*, and Muller had attended Arcane School conferences and contributed to her sectional magazine, *The Beacon*. Muller was also instrumental in the formation of the UN Development Programme, the UN Population Fund, the World Food Programme and the World Youth Assembly. As she read, Alice Bailey catapulted through Heather's mind from mystical crank to esteemed thinker. Even as she made the judgement she censured her own thought processes that had elevated a woman and her body of work, because it had been endorsed by a man.

After that, Heather couldn't stop. She went and slurped her juice and ate the second sushi roll, cramming the rice and seaweed into her mouth, annoyed that it all took so long to chew. A slither of avocado fell to the floor. She picked it up, examined it for dust, and popped it in her mouth. She couldn't get back to her desk fast enough.

She forgot about the time and the weather as, fragment by fragment, she pieced together an intriguing story, unearthing new revelations as she searched online to assuage her curiosity. After cross-checking with Foyle's notes and exploring various sites, including Alice Bailey's Lucis Trust, she was certain at least two secretary-generals, U Thant and Dag Hammarskjöld had been associated in some fashion or other, with Alice Bailey's vision. As was United Nations speechwriter, Donald Keys. It had all the appearance of a coterie. How much influence did these various players have over the United Nations? There was no telling who else was involved at administrative and executive levels. Little wonder the conspiracy theorists were wetting their pants.

When she discovered that no less than high-profile political journalist Norman Cousins had written the introduction to speechwriter Donald Key's book, *From Earth to Omega: Passage to Planetization,* a book dedicated to Alice Bailey, Heather's mind became as conspiratorial as the conspiracy theorists who had first alerted her to the array of prominent figures associated with Alice Bailey. Yet these new revelations didn't change all she had learned and understood about the occultist. Beyond the conspiracy theorists and New Age adherents, Alice Bailey remained a woman in every respect languishing in obscurity.

Did it even matter if these various figures had been influenced by Alice Bailey? Surely what mattered more was that a woman, her body of work and her organisations, even as they continued to influence key players at the very locus of global power, remained passed over by the history books. Didn't Alice Bailey deserve widespread recognition for her achievements? A posthumous Nobel Prize? After all, it seemed almost entirely down to her that the United Nations continued to express spiritual values and principles, why it hadn't bowed entirely to partisan shenanigans.

Hilary would have been incensed had she known.

Making a sad situation even sadder, beyond her followers and the Theosophical Society milieu, it seemed the only people taking notice of Alice Bailey were conspiracy thinkers and rabid fundamentalist Christians who labelled Alice Bailey, herself a devout Christian, as a manifestation of the Antichrist. They made such a song and dance about it too, clogging up her search results with their hysterical claims. Heather wouldn't have minded except that she had arrived at the websites of Bailey's detractors, knowing they were pointing at truths and yet were so, so wrong in their interpretations.

Before long, the conspiracy websites led her around in circles of repetition. She left her desk to eat her third and last sushi roll, annoyed at the seaweed splitting down the side as grains of rice spilled out and fell to the floor. Food, she thought, was like a building or an opus. Careful construction was required.

Satisfied with her day's efforts, she switched off the computer and left the office. The private corridors were empty but the public rooms were a hubbub of activity, visitors making use of the air-conditioning. Outside, on the steps, the temperature must have been over a hundred degrees and she broke out in a sweat as she headed down to the station. On the train, on the walk down Hawthorn East's leafy streets, even lying on her bed after a long, cool shower, she kept pondering the same issue: that a leading occultist of her day came to sit at the helm of a grand conspiracy theory. It hadn't taken much of a seed to create that giant tree. Arriving at all those websites had felt like a culmination of all the controversies that had surrounded Alice Bailey during much of her lifetime.

She cast her mind over all she had learned in the past months, trying to locate in time that point when history started to work against Alice Bailey. It wasn't her spectacular exit from the Theosophical Society, although that wouldn't have done her any favours. It wasn't her remarks on Jews, even though they continued to cause outrage and condemnation in some quarters. Neither was it that she had upset many of her own Christian ilk with her reinterpretations of the faith. All those things were damaging, but none of them warranted the way history, in the form of a bunch of stuffy-sounding academics, had turned its back on Alice Bailey and dismissed her altogether as nothing but a second-rate proselytizer with second-hand ideas. That scholarly omission was the impetus behind Professor Samantha Foyle's investigations.

Heather wondered if the key existed in all those unwritten pages of Alice Bailey's autobiography. But that didn't make sense and since she hadn't found any evidence anywhere of a scandal, there remained only one other place she had yet to fully explore: Alice Bailey's collaboration with Olga Fröbe Kapetyn. Perhaps the answer lay there.

She turned over on her side and closed her eyes. The task of archiving a collection of old Theosophical and occult literature that had initiated her inquiry, something she would normally have undertaken with professional indifference and a considerable dollop of resentment, had become all-consuming. She had copious notes and an unpublished paper. She could already imagine writing the missing chapters of Foyle's manuscript and she was toying with undertaking a Masters in the topic. There'd been times, many times over the last months when she had thought she might be succumbing to obsession. If that was what this was, then so be it.

She had no idea how seriously to take Suzanne's warning that they all needed to watch their backs. She felt suddenly sorry for her. Reporting Rosie had drawn the manuscript office to the attention of HR. Shona must be livid with her.

Thinking of her friend reminded her of that holiday in New York. She sat up in a flash and reached for her phone. It would be a chance to visit the United Nations. She fancied looking at the old headquarters too, opposite the public library.

Love to go to NY with you. Please book.

Her phone beeped straight away with a thumbs up.

Her door swung open and her mother barged in with an armful of curtain fabric. Her father trailed behind. Quelling her ire rising in the face of the intrusion, Heather grabbed her bag and went downstairs and slipped on her sandals.

Where to? She didn't feel like heading into the library on her day off. There wasn't anything much to do with the collection other than the digitising. She pictured her office bereft of all those boxes. She thought of the Sinclair biography still in the top drawer of her desk. She supposed it time that book was put out into circulation. That was the last of it.

It wasn't until she was passing the grand old Tarana house that her imagination landed with a sudden thump in the bottom drawer of her desk. She had put away those plastic folders two months ago and forgotten all about them. Despite the heat, her pace quickened.

The journey to the library was an ordeal of sweaty bodies in confined spaces. She enjoyed the heat more than most, but even she had her limits. The only good thing to be said about it, was she could open her office window again and create that through draft that enabled her to trawl through those musty documents.

The first plastic folder ended up containing a bunch of old utility bills. The next a bundle of personal letters she had received from her students over the years. Heather was beginning to think she would find nothing among those smelly papers that pertained to Alice Bailey when she opened the third folder and found she was mistaken.

There was a photocopy of a chapter from an unnamed book, along with a printout of the pages of a website called the School for Esoteric Studies. Heather recognised it as a school founded by Alice Bailey's co-worker, Regina Keller. There were transcripts of speeches Alice Bailey had given in the 1930s and 40s to her students of the Arcane

School. Heather thought they would make interesting reading but she refrained from slipping them in her bag, preferring to leave all those mould spores in her office.

Another plastic sleeve contained more transcripts. It appeared Professor Foyle had printed out the whole lot. Heather went to return them to the plastic sleeve when another printout caught her eye. She extracted it from the others and found it was a list of names, along with some biographical details. The heading stated the New Group of World Servers. She stared, astonished. All the initials she had seen in that list tucked inside one of those volumes on discipleship in the New Age had been given real names. She had no idea if the source was reliable and she knew it couldn't be verified, at least, not by her. It was insider knowledge and that was hard to come by.

She scanned through the first page and immediately recognised the Baileys and Roberto Assagioli and Regina Keller. She skimmed through to the last page and saw that of the ten seed groups the Tibetan had planned, only five had been created: Telepathic Communicators, Trained Observers, Magnetic Healers, Cultural Service (Education) and Political Service. Presumably, they had been unable to attract sufficient numbers for the other groups. The Second World War wouldn't have helped. Heather returned to the start and read through the names one by one, curious to see if she recognised anyone else.

She saw Alice Ortiz and Victor Fox in the first group, and in the second, Ernest Suffern. She recognised no one in the third other than Grace Rainey Rogers, the famous benefactress who Hilary had mentioned in relation to a novel she was reading shortly before she died. The fourth group was headed by Vera Stanley Alder. The name rang a bell and Heather quickly found the mystic's works were a precursor to New Age spirituality. She looked up some other names at random and found Madeleine Z. Doty, the famous lawyer, suffragist and prison reformer. She kept scanning. There was no one else she had heard of and neither had her search engine. She was about to put away the list when her gaze landed on a name she did know.

Her jaw fell open. Her entire being freeze framed.

There could be no mistaking it.

Katharine Mary Prentice-Smythe and her date of birth.

Could there have been two Katharine Mary Prentice-Smythes born on the same day as Katharine? Surely not. Surely that name belonged to only one woman alive in Australia in the 1930s.

Her great-grandmother.

Her world shimmied. She flushed even as goosebumps broke out on the flesh of her arms. There were coincidences, chance moments when events appeared significant, but this was not of that calibre. Hilary had lectured her once on the difference between coincidence and synchronicity. The latter, she had said, was a term used by Jung to refer to two separate chains of events that carry the same meaning intersecting somehow. But this wasn't synchronicity either.

It was more like fate.

The revelation was overwhelming. Her rational mind scrambled to make sense of it, even as a sort of meant-to-be lunacy prevailed. As her heart beat faster, her chest constricted and she scrambled in her bag for her inhaler.

The connection she had felt her whole life, ever since she had discovered she was born on the day of Katharine's death, took on much larger proportions. Part of her recoiled, wanting to dismiss the great-grandmother she had held so dear, as though she had been betrayed, conned somehow. All her life she had felt a sense of special worth by association, and now that mysterious woman she had revered, had been a student of Alice Bailey.

How had Katharine come across the occultist? Heather supposed through her interest in Spiritualism. All along what Heather had assumed was a sense of affiliation born of an anniversary had transmuted into something almost genetic. The only thing she knew for certain was Katharine had kept her spiritual pursuit a secret. No one, not even Hilary, had known about it. Or had she?

Heather would have loved to have told her aunt of this discovery. They could have marvelled over it together.

The revelation sealed her decision to apply to undertake a Masters. She was incapable of thinking about anything else. The sun was setting when she left the library to find a cool change had come through, chilling her bare arms. She spent the journey home on the train eyeing the other passengers, feeling entirely separate, unique, as though she had been chosen.

It was fanciful, delusional, but later, when her mother called her down to dinner, she was still bursting with excitement and incomprehension in equal measure.

She left her room knowing she would say nothing.

# New York Public Library

The Salmon Tower building towered over West 42<sup>nd</sup> Street, its façade a uniform arrangement of office windows, impersonal, imposing, like all the other high rises in Manhattan. Life on the sidewalks felt underground, privy to narrow bands of sky.

Heather had no plans to enter the Salmon Tower building, any more than she had when she had stood outside the United Nations plaza that housed the Lucis Trust's new offices. She was standing with her back to New York's public library, trying to picture Alice Bailey emerging into a 1930s streetscape, mindful that then, as now, the two eras—one modern, functional, austere, the other classical, indulgent, luxurious—melded together in the jarring fashion of all cities.

She preferred the architecture of the Victorian era, with its grandiosity carved in stone, harkening back to the Classical period, all arches and columns, pilasters and pediments.

The library had a block to itself. Bryant Park was attached to its rear like an open garden, replete with large shade trees, paths and paving, and plenty of seating for visitors. Nature had been allowed to express herself, albeit in a contained and orderly fashion. She headed to the front of the library building on Fifth Avenue, where three flights of stone steps, staggered at intervals, led to a triptych of stone arches. The steps were flanked by stone lions and plantings of trees and clipped shrubs. Although larger than the State Library back in Melbourne, the stature was the same. A similar sized thicket of people went back and forth or hovered, chatted, pondered or looked down at their phones.

With Suzanne choosing to visit Ground Zero, something Heather found incomprehensible, Heather had the whole day to herself. They had arranged to meet back at their hotel at five. Enjoying her own company and the freedom of the day, she entered the main foyer, and stood marvelling at the uniformity, the sheer weight of the stone that rose in columns that culminated in rounded arches and thence to a vaulted ceiling. Two flights of stone steps, one at each end, led up to the second level, visible through the apex of the arches in one wall. It occurred to her that Alice Bailey may well have stood in that exact spot, gazing around. Heather wondered what she might have made of the building. Although she was probably indifferent to it. After all, she was an aristocrat used to finding herself in fine buildings.

Heather could have stood there all day examining every detail but she forewent that luxury in favour of her quest. She went through the arches in the back wall and located the information desk, and inquired of a petite middle-aged woman with long blonde hair as to where she might find a section on Western Esotericism. The assistant looked puzzled and turned to her computer. Heather interrupted her search with, 'Jung. Try Carl Jung.'

A light of recognition appeared in the librarian's face.

She was directed upstairs to the Rose Main reading room. Walking through the various halls she drank in the magnificence. Special attention had been applied to the ceilings. The one in the Rose Main room comprised an elaborate series of interconnected frames encasing a mural depicting the sky. Chandelier lighting was evenly spaced throughout the room, although the tables, arranged in rows rather like a school room, had their own desk lamps.

Stacks were arranged around the room's perimeter and upon a mezzanine level. Heather had no trouble locating Carl Jung. She wasn't interested in him, but rather in the works that had been shelved beside his. Although a thick volume, carrying the title *Jung* caught her eye due to its yellow cover, and she pulled it out. It was a biography by Deirdre Bair. She recalled Foyle referring to Bair. Curious, Heather examined the index and turned to the references on Alice Bailey. They took her to a section on Olga Fröbe and the formation of an organisation named "Eranos".

Recollecting some of Professor Foyle's comments, Heather could see the scholar had derived much from Bair's work. Bair depicted Olga Fröbe, a former patient of Jung, as something of a sycophant, yet also as a powerful, influential and ambitious woman, who had set in train the formation of Eranos in the weeks after the third summer school session with Alice Bailey. She had wasted no time. She had even consulted the eminent scholar Rudolph Otto, who had given her new centre its name.

Heather went and sat at the nearest unoccupied desk and read through all the comments Bair had made about Olga. Then she reached in her satchel for her notebook. Those letters Olga wrote accusing Alice Bailey's daughters of sexual impropriety, when were they sent? When did Olga end things with Alice? It had to be after, a long time after she had already come up with Eranos. Heather trawled through her notes, relieved to discover she had made a note of the date of that particular letter. It was dated March 1933, many months after she had met with Otto and named Eranos. So those accusations had been a ruse. Alice Bailey had been ousted. Olga had wanted Jung all along. He would be her drawcard, attracting the world's most eminent intellectuals of the day. She got her wish. Bair stated that in the summer of 1933, a year after her last summer school with Alice Bailey, Jung was in attendance at the inaugural session of Eranos.

Heather was suddenly breathless. She rummaged in her satchel for her inhaler, took a blast and waited for the medication to take effect. Then she returned the Jung biography and browsed the shelves. She found nothing of immediate interest. Still, a niggle lodged in her mind, inchoate, a faint itch telling her she wasn't quite done.

The niggle wouldn't shift but she could see no title that would satisfy it. As a last resort, she scanned through the volumes on a trolley positioned at the end of the stack.

There, to her astonishment, was a book carrying the title *Eranos* by a Hans Thomas Hakl. Leafing through the end pages she found the work had received praise from his friend and founder of Western Esoteric studies himself, Antoine Faivre. Sensing she had discovered a small gem, she went and sat back down.

Following up the references, she was astonished to learn that, for a reason that was unclear, Jung may have held Alice Bailey in low regard. In Hakl's version of events, Fröbe had told philosopher of religion Alfons Rosenberg, who Heather was forced to assume was a reliable witness, that Jung had told her to reject Alice Bailey and her associates. It was a remark that came across like Chinese whispers, one passed on by Rosenberg, a man who had revered Eranos, but if true, it would have been damaging for Bailey. That is, if Fröbe hadn't made it up. She had been Jung's patient, after all. Then again, Jung's opinion may well have been all the justification Olga needed to shun her former associate and teacher. Was Olga that easily swayed? For how long had Jung held those derisive views of Bailey? If he had held them at all. Heather took out her notebook and turned to a blank page.

Scribbling down the details, she paused. How could third-hand testimony be regarded historical evidence? It was unsatisfactory and she could scarcely believe she was giving it credence. But she had become hungry for any information about Alice Bailey, however unreliable.

Hakl went on to cite Rosenberg citing Fröbe's claim that when Jung saw one of the large meditation tableaux of geometrical forms that she had created following Bailey's instructions, he had reacted negatively, telling her the symbols radiated evil. Heather realised Jung may not have said any of this. She knew from Bair's account that Jung remained in loyal admiration of Frau Fröbe. What did seem abundantly clear was that Fröbe had been determined to come away from the situation with Alice Bailey with her own reputation intact.

Hakl's book was published the year after Professor Foyle had died. Heather was glad. She imagined the scholar would have had the same reaction as she. Alice Bailey could certainly have done without the drama.

Heather flicked through the pages, reading the introduction and first chapter. It was plainly evident the author held nothing but contempt for Alice Bailey. Heather had to force herself through his highly selective account of her life. It soon became clear that Jung's endorsement of Eranos opened the gates for Fröbe. In the years that followed, Eranos attracted many academic heavyweights, including: zoologist Adolf Portmann; psychologist, philosopher and student of Jung, Erich Neumann; philosopher, theologian and Professor of Islamic Studies at the Sorbonne, Henry Corbin; and eminent historian of religion, Professor Mircea Eliade. All of those men were said to have held Fröbe in admiration. At Eranos, she was revered as its founder. Dissent came only from Italian philosopher and esotericist Julius Evola, who was said to have described Fröbe as pretentious and detestable. This condemnation resonated with an equally scathing view of Alice Bailey apparently held by Mircea Eliade, who considered her work to be worthless and unreadable. Although as Fröbe's confidant, Eliade's jaundiced view of Bailey was probably biased. Heather thought it curious too, that he could comment on a text's worth if he was unable to read it.

If those remarks could be trusted out of context, the derision meted out by those men was unnecessary and strikingly petty-minded. It was unfortunate that almost all of it fell on Alice Bailey. It appeared the attitudes of those leading scholarly figures had filtered into the hearts and minds of the next generation of academics, not least because, as Heather soon discovered, Antoine Faivre was a close associate of Henry Corbin, and the leading journal of Western Esotericism, *ARIES* originally had on its board Mircea Eliade and other Eranos participants.

To Heather, those men were a cabal. She was furious with Olga Fröbe, too. Then again, a woman like Olga couldn't have singlehandedly damaged the reputation of Alice Bailey in academic circles. It was something much larger that had achieved that. A confluence of taken for granted prejudices that had charged, tried and convicted, en absentia, a woman and her opus, simply because she had come to their attention through the summer schools and they wouldn't tolerate the competition. That's how it appeared. As though from lofty heights, they condemned a woman who through her teachings and the efforts of her co-workers would go on to guide and influence the spiritual future of humanity. Only the day before, Heather had sat in the meditation room at the United Nations, knowing as she did that Alice Bailey's influence behind the scenes of that international organisation was profound and enduring.

Perhaps that was all that mattered.

Her niggle burst into her awareness as she put away Hakl's book. It was Foyle's dream, her slipper dream, a dream in which she had gone to George Monbiot's house in her slippers on the pretext of introducing him to her daughter. Heather riffled through the pages of her notebook and there it was. Only now Heather was certain the George Monbiot figure in the dream, which Foyle had decided alluded to a 'great man', was Carl Jung. It had to be. Foyle had seen all along that Alice Bailey's nemesis was Carl Jung. That's why she wrote it down and that's why she had said the dream was not about her.

Carl Jung and his intellectual coterie were the last piece in a jigsaw of condemnation. The one thing Alice Bailey had wanted all her life was endorsement, ever since she was a little girl living in her younger sister's shadow. Instead she had been abused by a violent husband, and then vilified and ostracised by purist Theosophists, the Jewish community, fundamentalist Christians, conspiracy theorists and leading scholars in the field of Western Esotericism. She had been attacked from every quarter. Even thinking about all that venom was hard to bear.

Heather wandered back to the information desk, no longer taking her time, no longer admiring the building. The woman with the blonde hair was still there, attending to another inquiry. Heather waited. A queue formed behind her. She walked forwards, careful not to lean against the high counter and asked if the library carried any titles by an Alice Bailey.

There was a short pause while the librarian carried out her search.

'No, I'm not seeing anything by that author,' she said, glancing at the queue.

'Nothing?' Heather said, thinking she might ask to scroll down the list herself, wondering what name the librarian had typed in. She was about to walk away when something occurred to her.

'Try including her initial. Alice A. Bailey. Try that.'

The librarian looked at her strangely. 'If you insist.'

In seconds she said, 'Which title?'

'I don't know. Any title.'

The librarian all but rolled her eyes. 'You will find them all in the General Research Room.'

'Thank you,' Heather said, and made to walk out.

'Hey, not that way!'

Heather turned around. 'It's all right, thank you. That's all I wanted to know.'

Heather sat on a train heading into the city from Ballarat, watching the scenery flit by. It was her first day back at work after her trip. A woman sat facing her. She was dressed in mock suede boots with large buckles. Beyond her, a woman in her twenties with dyed grey hair, was talking on her phone. Heather opened her laptop and checked her emails. The first was from the University of Melbourne. Her application had been accepted. A warm glow infused her belly. She read through the email several times, disguising her grin from the other passengers by covering her mouth and gazing out the window.

They were passing through the satellite city of Melton, where hillocks of red earth and tip trucks indicated a new subdivision. Roads had been mapped out but were unmade. Once a horse paddock, soon to become a field of tiled roofs. She was sitting in the quiet carriage, although you'd never know it. Watching the man beside her unwrap a muesli bar, she thought they should ban plastic packaging along with mobile phones, music and loud conversations.

She returned to her emails. She wasn't expecting anything from work, but there was one from Emily Prime, forwarded on by her boss,

Shona. The subject bar said "Apologies". Curious, Heather opened it and read Emily's two sentences. It concerned a note that had slipped out of Professor Foyle's provenance file. She wasn't sure if it was relevant, but please find attached.

Heather opened the attachment. Again, two sentences. Two sentences acknowledging the donor of all those old Theosophical and Spiritualist magazines that Samantha Foyle had received when she was just twenty-eight years old and finally put to use: Katharine Mary Prentice-Smythe.

Her insides made a little squeeze, although she wasn't that surprised. The world of occultism was small. Katharine had been a co-worker and the donation proved it. Heather would never be a co-worker but she would wear her great-grandmother's brooch with pride. She was in the company not of charlatans and fruit loops, but of dedicated individuals with big ideas on how to change the world for the better.

After the long stretch through open and flat country, the suburbs started and the train line was flanked by a designer-rusted corrugated iron fence. There were places where some coloured glass had been inserted, for interest. People of all backgrounds and cultures—many wearing grey beanies and jeans, hoodies, anoraks and trainers—got on and the carriage filled. What would Alice Bailey have made of the diversity? She would have enjoyed it, she would have marvelled over the technology too, everyone with a mobile phone, yet she would have seen the dangers.

They passed through the industrial west. Soon there were silos and old warehouses and as the train neared the city, more warehouses, old wool stores, factories, and little houses, in amongst it all. Graffiti was everywhere, on fences, factory walls, underpasses, all of it ugly and no one troubling to clean it away. The high rises of the city came in and out of view, a visible point of entry into the central business district. Yet out on the western side of the city, travelling past the docklands with its concatenation of cranes and shipping containers, the point of entry into the glitz and the bustle was less than appealing. The train journey put Heather in touch with a reality she had never considered when living out in Hawthorn East. That it took muscle and grit and sweat and decades of determination and planning to build a city.

Alice Bailey had endeavoured to build a city too, a mental city beneath a spiritual sky. Heather had dwelt on the story of Alice Bailey for so long it was as though she had grown new skin. She hadn't even studied the blue books, yet she had gained a new perspective. She was still a feminist, she still looked at the world through rational eyes and she would always like to put things in discrete boxes, but she would not take her awareness for granted again.

The train pulled into the station and she took a metropolitan service to Central Station. She was in the grounds of the State Library of Victoria in minutes and as she passed by the statue of Charles La Trobe, she wanted to stop and tell him about his third cousin, and how the La Trobe-Bateman family might have been impressed by what one of their own had achieved. A family of engineers who had helped progress the industrial revolution in ways that enabled humanity to have clean water, sanitation and transport, had produced a descendent who had sought to enable humanity in a similar fashion on the mental plane, to embody good, clean living as one interconnected spiritual family.

# Epilogue

While this story of Alice Bailey's life has come to a natural end, events continue, not least the marriages of all of her daughters: Dorothy married Terence Morton in Faversham, Kent, in September1934; Ellison married Arthur Gordon Poyntor Leahy in June 1936 and had two children; and around that time, Mildred married and quickly divorced Meredith Pugh and went on to have his baby.

Meanwhile, Alice Ortiz' daughter, Marguerite, had another daughter, Zoe, in 1934. Two years later she filed for divorce, refusing to allow her husband the lion hunter access to his children on the grounds that he was a useless parent. She then married Harry Clark Boden and in 1938, the couple went to Nassau, Bahamas. It was there that Forrester Holmes Scott attempted to kidnap his own daughters. He was arrested and charged and the ensuing custody battle caused a scandal that reached the newspapers.

Following up on some of the titles mentioned in this novel, Alice Bailey published *A Treatise on White Magic* in 1934, *Esoteric Psychology Vol I* in 1936 (the first in her treatise on the Seven Rays), and *From Bethlehem to Calvary* in 1937 (her book on the initiations of Christ).

The tireless occultist commenced working on the transformation of Freemasonry in 1934. Both Mildred and Ellison are said to have helped her with the project. With every passing year her body was riven with pain and incapacity. By 1939, she was almost an invalid.

She went on to compose another fourteen works. Much of her later material concerned the Second World War and her responses to the world situation. Many of her works were published posthumously.

After Alice's death, Foster was helped enormously by the support he received from a part-time worker at their Tunbridge Wells headquarters, Mary Turner (1909-2007).

When the war broke out in 1939, Turner had a seven-year-old daughter and was working as a volunteer in the war effort. She was at that time searching for something more than day-to-day survival, and came across the Bailey books. She joined the Arcane School almost straight away. In 1952, while Foster was staying in Tunbridge Wells, working and resting, the head of the British work, Barbara Amos, became ill with terminal cancer. A replacement was needed and Mary Turner stepped into what she thought would be a temporary role. It was to prove permanent.

When the founder of an organisation dies, a period of chaos will inevitably follow. A schism developed, one that revolved around the purity of the teachings and their intention. This time it was the orthodoxy who broke away, going on to form the School for Esoteric Studies.

The school was founded in New York in 1956 by a number of close associates of Alice Bailey, who had been working by her side for decades. Founders included Regina Keller, Frank Hilton, Florence Garrigue, Helen Hillebrecht and Margaret Schaefer. Roberto Assagioli soon became an active member. This splinter group was determined to honour the deeper aspects of Bailey's esoteric training. They were dedicated to continuing the advanced training that the Arcane School had yet to offer, based on the teachings Bailey had written and not published.

There may also have occurred something of a personality clash between the old guard, with Regina Keller at the helm, and the new, in the form of Mary Turner, who began increasingly to influence the direction the Arcane School.

With his new co-worker at his side, it was left to Foster Bailey to keep the core organisations continuing along the lines Alice Bailey had created. In Mary's view, he proceeded in a manner that was uncompromising, and which may well have been the true source of the schism.

Under the leadership of Foster and Mary Bailey, the organisations flourished. In 1955 a third headquarters was opened in Geneva, Switzerland to serve six European languages. In 1960 the British headquarters were relocated to Whitehall Court, London, where it exists today. In 1965 the New York offices moved to a location close to the United Nations, the right environment for world service. All of Alice Bailey's texts that had yet to be published went to print.

Foster and Mary went on to work together for a decade, finally marrying in 1962. By then Foster's health was deteriorating and Mary began to work alone, travelling, speaking, and meeting students. For the last ten or twelve years of his life Foster was a semi-invalid, confined to their Manhattan apartment. He died on $3^{rd}$ June 1977.

Mary Bailey took on the role of president and head of the Arcane School, and continued in that capacity for about two decades.

All of the organisations Alice Bailey founded exist today. In those years after her death, many followers continued the work in their own fashion. Authors M J Eastcott and Nancy Magor were greatly influenced by Bailey's work. As were, co-founders of transpersonal psychology, Ian Gordon-Brown and Barbara Somers, who took a great interest in the Bailey teachings, Gordon-Brown visiting Mary and Foster Bailey at their house in Tunbridge Wells. Regina Keller and Florence Garrigue, who formed part of the early schism, went on to co-found Meditation Mount at Ojai, California, a centre for meditation groups focused on world betterment, which was completed in 1971 and continues to this day to offer meditation, courses, astrology and study groups.

The New Age movement, or alternative spirituality as it is also known today, is founded in part through works that were a bridge between the Bailey books and popular self-help books. For example, the works of co-worker Vera Stanley Alder (1898-1984), a portrait painter and mystic who popularised Bailey's teachings, particular *Initiation: Human and Solar*, in works such as *The Finding of the Third Eye*. Prior to Alder's works, esoteric healers, including colour therapists, drew inspiration directly from Bailey's *Letters on Occult Meditation*. It is worth reading *Rainbow Body* by Kurt Leland in this regard.

Dotted around the world today are Bailey's Units of Service, comprising small unassuming groups of dedicated followers who continue to hold meditation meetings, the Triangles meditations, and distribute pamphlets produced by the Lucis Trust. Anyone can find their way to Alice Bailey's teachings, and join her Arcane School free of charge.

# A Selected Bibliography

The Alice A. Bailey texts in order of original publication, all published by the Lucis Trust, New York
1922, *Letters on Occult Meditation*
1922, *The Consciousness of the Atom*
1922, *Initiation, Human and Solar*
1925, *A Treatise on Cosmic Fire*
1927, *The Light of the Soul: Its Science and Effect, A Paraphrase of The Yoga Sutras of Patanjali* (with commentary by Alice A. Bailey)
1930, *The Soul and Its Mechanism*
1932, *From Intellect to Intuition*
1934, *A Treatise on White Magic or The Way Of The Disciple*
1936, *A Treatise on the Seven Rays: Esoteric Psychology Vol I*
1937, *From Bethlehem to Calvary: The Initiations of Jesus*
1942, *A Treatise on the Seven Rays: Esoteric Psychology Vol II*
1944, *Discipleship in the New Age Vol I*
1947, *Problems of Humanity*
1948, *The Reappearance of the Christ*
1949, *The Destiny of the Nations*
1950, *Glamour: A World Problem*
1950, *Telepathy and the Etheric Vehicle*
1951, *Esoteric Astrology*
1951, *The Unfinished Autobiography*
1951, *A Treatise on the Seven Rays: Esoteric Astrology*

1953, *A Treatise on the Seven Rays: Esoteric Healing*
1954, *Education in the New Age*
1955, *Discipleship in the New Age, Vol II*
1957, *The Externalisation of the Hierarchy*
1960, *A Treatise on the Seven Rays: The Rays and the Initiations*

## A selection of other works consulted

Bair, Deirdre, 2003, *Jung: A Biography*, Back Bay Books, NY.
Cumbey, C., 1983, *The Hidden Dangers of the Rainbow*, Huntington House, Shreveport, Louisiana.
Faivre, A., 1994, *Access to Western Esotericism*, State University of New York Press, Albany.
Faivre, A., 2000, *Theosophy, Imagination, Tradition: Studies in Western Esotericism*, (translated by Rhone, C.), State University of New York Press, Albany.
Ferguson, Marilyn, 1980, The Aquarian Conspiracy, J.P. Tarcher.
Gulyas, Aaron John, 2016, *Conspiracy Theories: The Roots, Themes and Political Propagation of Paranoid Political and Cultural Narratives*, McFarland & Company, Jefferson.
Hakl, Hans Thomas, 2013, *Eranos: an alternative intellectual history of the twentieth century*, McGill-Queen's University Press, Montreal.
Hammer, Olav, 2000 *Claiming Knowledge: Strategies of Epistemology from Theosophy to the New Age*, Brill, Leiden.
Hanegraaff, W., 1998, *New Age Religion and Western Culture: Esotericism in the Mirror of Secular Thought*, State University of New York Press, Albany.
Keys, D., 1985, *Earth At Omega: Passage to Planetization*, Branden Publishing, Boston, Mass.
Leland, Kurt, 2016, *Rainbow Body: A History of the Western Chakra System from Blavatsky to Brennen*, Ibis Press, Lake Worth.
Oken, Alan, 2008, *Soul Centered Astrology*, Nicolas-Hays.
Marrs, Jim, 2001, *Rule by Secrecy*, William Morrow.

William McGuire, "The Arcane Summer School" in *Spring: An Annual of Archetypal Psychology and Jungian Thought*, 1980: 149.

McLaughlin, C., and Davidson, G., 1994, Spiritual Politics: Changing the World From Inside Out, Findhorn Press, Findhorn, Scotland.

Muller, R., 1982, *New Genesis: Shaping a Global Spirituality*, Doubleday, Garden City, New York.

Sinclair, Sir John R., 1985, *The Alice Bailey Inheritance*, Weiser.

Sutcliffe, Steven J., 2003, *Children of the New Age: A History of Spiritual Practices*, Routledge, Oxon.

Zwartz, M., 1987, *The New Age Gospel: Christ or Counterfeit*, Parenesis, Melbourne.

## Other Sources

A list of Discipleship in the New Age groups can be accessed via http://www.makara.us/04mdr/02comment/dina/dina_toc.htm
Various Theosophical magazines and journals most notably issues of *The Messenger* (between the years 1917-1921), were sourced via http://www.iapsop.com/

The author relied on numerous passenger lists, census records and birth records in the composition of this work, sourced through Ancestry.com and FamilySearch.com.

# Acknowledgments

A small number of exceptionally helpful people have contributed to the completion of this novel. I would like to thank Shona Williams, librarian at the State Library of Victoria, for her insights into the working life of an archivist. I am indebted to Ian Boyle, Elizabeth Jane Corbett and Philip Wallis for their advice and suggestions and comprehensive feedback on early drafts. I am immensely grateful to my daughter, Elizabeth Blackthorn, whose sharp eye helped when I needed it most. A special mention to Mary Cunnane, whose encouragement prompted me to compose this work. I will be forever grateful.

I have relied on numerous scholarly works in the creation of this novel and of course on the Blue Books themselves. I could not have composed this book without first having studied Alice Bailey's texts for my doctoral thesis, awarded in 2006 by the University of Western Sydney.

My warm gratitude to Miika Hannila and the team at Creativia Publishing, for all of their dedication and hard work.

# About the Author

A Londoner originally, Isobel Blackthorn has chalked up over seventy addresses to date, in various locations in England, Australia, Spain and the Canary Islands. Elements of her extraordinary life have a habit of finding their way into her fiction, providing her with a ready supply of inspiration.

Isobel grew up in and around Adelaide, South Australia as a ten-pound Pom. It was in 1973 and she had just turned eleven when she discovered she wanted to dedicate her life to writing fiction. That was the year her parents owned a roadhouse with a pool table, a juke box and a pinball machine. The year she hand-reared a lamb and spent weekends on her best friend's farm. Isobel may have pursued her dream right then, but life had other plans.

Isobel returned with her family to spend her teenage years back in London, where she attended the infamous Eltham Green Comprehensive in the year below Boy George. Her creative passion was crushed in an instant and she endured years of relentless bullying.

When her family returned to Australia once more, Isobel stayed behind. By then she was a rebellious nineteen, and she went on to live wild and free through the 1980s. She first moved to Norwich, where she satisfied her creative impulses writing maudlin song lyrics inspired by Joy Division, and little bits of poetry. Her desire to write novels never went away but she lacked the confidence, the skills and that all too crucial guidance.

She soon moved to Oxford where she became a political activist in the Campaign for Nuclear Disarmament, often protesting at Greenham Common. She lived for a time in Barcelona, teaching English as a Second Language. After another spell in Oxford, she moved to a squat near Brixton in London's south. From there she moved to Lanzarote, where she renovated an old stone ruin, taught English and mingled with the locals.

She never planned leaving the island of her dreams, but she fell wildly in love with a man who swept her away to Bali. When it slowly dawned on her that her life might be at risk, she hightailed it to Australia on a holiday visa and reunited with her family.

During all this time, Isobel was studying for her undergraduate degree with the Open University. She graduated with First Class Honours and not a clue what to do with it.

After that reckless decade, life took a sobering turn. Isobel became the mother of twin girls, and trained and worked as a high school teacher. Deciding teaching was not for her, she then undertook a doctorate. She received her PhD in 2006 for her research on the works of Theosophist Alice A. Bailey. After an interlude as a back-to-earther and a brief spell as personal assistant to a literary agent, Isobel arrived at writing in her forties. By then, her creativity was ready to explode.

Isobel's stories are as diverse as her life has been. She speaks and performs her literary works at events in a range of settings, gives workshops in creative writing, and writes book reviews. Her reviews have appeared in Shiny New Books, Newtown Review of Books and Trip Fiction. She talks frequently about books and writing on radio, in Australia, and in the USA, UK and the Canary Islands.

Isobel now lives with her little white cat not far from Melbourne on Australia's wild southern coast. In her free time, she enjoys gardening, learning Spanish, visiting family and friends and travelling overseas, especially to her beloved Lanzarote, an island that has captured her heart.

*Isobel Blackthorn*

An avid storyteller with much to say, the author's professional ambition is to keep writing suspenseful novels set on the Canary Islands, interspersed with other works of fiction.

## Books by the Author

A Matter of Latitude
Clarissa's Warning
The Unlikely Occultist

Printed in Great Britain
by Amazon